D0862902

SPANISH LAVENDER

Joan Fallon was born in Scotland, but spent most of her formative life in the south of England. After a brief spell working in industry, she became a teacher and later a management consultant specialising in Behavioural Studies. She now lives in the south of Spain, where she has become passionate about both the language and history of her adopted home.

She is the author of:

Daughters of Spain

The House on the Beach

Loving Harry

Santiago Tales

(all are available in paperback and as ebooks)

www.joanfallon.co.uk

@joan_fallon

JOAN FALLON

Spanish Lavender

Scott Publishing

ISBN 978-0-9576891-0-7
Published in 2013 by Scott Publishing
Windsor, England

First published in 2011 by Vanguard Press
under the title Between the Sierra and the Sea

To María Matilde Ramírez, whose accounts of the events which took place in Málaga during the Spanish Civil War inspired me to write this novel.

FOREWORD

War is always a confusing event and none more so than the Spanish Civil War. This short foreword attempts to give the reader a brief description of the main protagonists in a civil war that divided the nation in two.

On July 17th 1936 a *coup de'état* was attempted against the democratically elected Republican government of Spain; this led to a war between the Nationalists on the one hand and the Republicans on the other. The Nationalists, sometimes referred to as insurgents, rebels or fascists, had a well organised, highly disciplined army, including the majority of the Spanish army's officers, trained *Requete* militiamen, African troops and the Spanish Foreign Legion. They also had the support of the Falange party, which played an important role in policing and indoctrination. The Republican Government had troops, very few officers and many untrained volunteers that joined themselves into politically inspired militias: anarchists, communists, socialists, women's rights groups, separatist groups and trade unionists. The Republicans, also known as the Reds, received foreign support from the International Brigades, Mexico and the International Socialist Movement. They bought weapons from Russia, the only country that would sell to them because of the Non-Intervention agreement drawn up in 1936 by

France and Great Britain and signed by the European powers. Germany and Italy also disregarded the agreement and supplied the Nationalists with troops, ammunition, tanks, planes and ships.

The police force was made up of the *Guardia de Asalto* who were loyal to the government and the *Guardia Civil*, many of whom defected to the Nationalist side.

The Nationalists drew their supporters mainly from the conservative, right-wing, wealthier part of society; this included the Catholic Church, landowners, monarchists, fascists and also centrists. They claimed to be fighting for the reinstatement of traditional values and against a Communist threat. The Republicans were drawn mainly from the working classes, the educated middle-class and intellectuals; their supporters ranged from centrists who wanted democracy to anarchists and communists who wanted revolution.

SPANISH LAVENDER

PART ONE

SPAIN
JANUARY 1937

CHAPTER 1

The wind was blowing from the sea, a light breeze that carried the smell of rosemary and thyme in its arms as it passed over the mountain slopes on her right. She breathed in deeply, enjoying the stillness of the morning; the air was clean and fresh after four days of continuous rain, with just a touch of sweetness to it. She felt strangely detached; there was a dream-like quality about everything. Moored just off shore she could see two large ships, motionless, black outlines against the glistening Mediterranean; from this distance she could make out few details but she was sure they were cruisers. She knew she should be frightened at the sight but from here they reminded her only of the toy ships her young brother, Peter, sank nightly in his bath-tub. That was how she knew they were cruisers; he had educated her well in the shape of funnels and gun turrets and even flags of convenience. She could not make out the colours of the flags; they remained anonymous black silhouettes but she already knew their nationality. Conception had been talking about them the night before. One was called 'El Baleares'; it was still a very new addition to the Spanish fleet and the other, slightly older was 'El Almirante Cervera'. They had come to protect them from the Red Terror, Conception said.

The ships had been there for two days now, waiting, it seemed, for someone to give them orders. Still she did not feel any apprehension; the sky was too blue and the sun too bright for fear. A movement caused her to turn around; the dog had startled a partridge and the frightened bird flapped frantically to get away, barely leaving the ground in its haste. As it flew low and fast across the scrubland, she caught a glimpse of the reddish stripes on its flanks. Its fear was infectious and as it flew, other scared birds took to the air, unsure of the exact nature of the danger but fleeing nonetheless in headlong panic.

She called the dog to her side and continued walking along the path. When she reached the corner she saw the wide expanse of the Guadalhorce Valley spread out below her, a patchwork quilt of green fields and orange groves, with its broad river meandering between tall swathes of sugarcane. Beyond it she could see the military airfield, dotted with tiny planes and beyond that the city of Málaga itself. A blue-grey haze was forming over the city, floating gently towards the mountains, delicate wisps of smoke that curled upwards, then broke and went their separate ways, becoming lighter and airier until they gradually blended into the mountain air. Her eyes turned as usual towards the cathedral, with its unfinished tower, a casualty of funds sent to aid a long forgotten cause but today it was hidden from sight inside a cloud of dense, black smoke. A fire was raging in the streets; this much she knew from the chatter of the servants. There would be heat and smoke and the crashing of falling timbers; people would be running, trying to escape the flames; the air would be full of the smell of blistering paint and burning wood. She tried to imagine it but the sun shone too brightly and the singing of the larks distracted her. She stood a while longer watching the destruction below, yet not really taking it in. Then a sound woke her from her reverie; the nearest of the gunboats was firing on the city. She watched as the ship's canon pulled back then juddered, sending up a brief, flash of fire and a delicate curl of smoke, with a crack of sound like distant fireworks exploding. She saw the shell land somewhere near the docks, its position pinpointed by an explosion of earth and debris. Mesmerised she watched as shell after shell was fired at the same spot and the earth continued to heave and turn, changing its form before her eyes. At last, as though waking from a spell, she turned and calling for the dog to follow her, ran down the path towards the village. She felt suddenly very vulnerable and longed for the safety of her home.

As she approached the outskirts of the village she slowed her pace to a walk. Her heart was still beating wildly and she could feel the perspiration trickling down her cheeks. She slipped the lead around Willow's neck and forced herself to walk calmly along the narrow streets. There was nobody about; the main square, where the old men usually gathered to sit and gossip, was empty and the doors to the bread shop and the butcher's were tightly closed. A small boy leading a donkey by a rope halter passed her without speaking; he stopped when he reached the stone water trough, waited while the animal drank, then continued on his way out of the village and up the hill. She could hear the donkey's hooves clattering on the cobbles, sharp, hard sounds reverberating through the silent streets. As she passed Paco's bar, she saw his customers, sitting in silence behind the swaying strands of coloured beads that hung across the door to keep out the flies. She felt the need to speak to someone, anyone, to ask if they had seen the war ships in the harbour, to verify that what she had just seen had actually happened and was not a figment of her imagination. Instead she kept on walking, taking the cobbled path down the hill and out of the village towards her home.

She lived in a rambling, stone built *cortijo,* with peeling white-washed walls; her parents rented it from the local landowner, Don Franscisco. It was a house built to withstand the ravages of time and weather; it looked as if it had been cut into the lee side of the mountain, using the sheer granite face as a defensive wall. Facing south and sheltered from the north and west winds by the mountain itself, the thick, solid walls of the house held an internal patio at its heart, where her mother, always a romantic gardener, had planted pots of bougainvillea, hibiscus, jasmine and sweet smelling *dama de la noche.* Their stems leaned against the walls, feeling their way along the stone surfaces, pulling themselves ever upwards on whatever they could find, reaching for the sun, splashes of brilliant colours: deep vibrant reds, purples, scarlet tipped stamens and golden petals. Long ago someone had planted a lemon tree near the well and built a few ram-shackled pens to keep the animals in; more recently her mother had created a small kitchen garden, where the twisting vines of green tomatoes curled their way along cut sugar canes and rosemary, thyme and parsley sat in terracotta pots by the kitchen door. The windows of the house were narrow and dingy, protected by heavy, green shutters and ornate iron *rejas,* and the only means of entry from the outside world was through a solid wooden door, studded with iron nails.

Today someone had left the front door unlocked and as she pushed her way in, she felt the wood, worn smooth by a myriad of hands, warm and solid beneath her own. She closed the door firmly behind her, turning the heavy iron key in the lock and dropping the wooden bar in place. As she

15

rested in that silent hall, leaning against the door frame, waiting for her heart to stop racing, she could feel the house's durability seeping into her, calming her with the knowledge that it had stood there for many years and would still be there in years to come. At last she felt calm enough to take in the familiar surroundings: the uneven flags of stone that covered the floor, the multi-coloured chandelier that hung above her head, the blues and greens of its Moroccan glass flickering in the weak sunlight that had managed to creep through the shuttered windows, the rag rug that her mother had made from scraps of old clothes one winter. On such a fine, sunny morning it suddenly seemed a little dramatic to be bolting the door.

'Elizabeth is that you?'

A man's voice penetrated the stillness; he sounded concerned.

'Yes Father. It's me.'

She relinquished her resting place and moved towards the sound. She knew her father would be in his study at this hour.

'Thank goodness. We've been getting worried about you. Where have you been? It's almost eleven.'

Her father was sitting at his desk, papers and books spread out before him. Willow was already lying at his feet. He stretched his long arms and leaned back in his chair, looking at her.

'Yes, I suppose I have been a long time but it was such a lovely morning that we walked up to *La Puerta del Diablo* and then came back through the village.'

She bent down and kissed her father's cheek. The lines on his usual placid face seemed to be etched more deeply today and a frown had pulled his bushy, grey eyebrows into a straight line, giving him a worried, yet almost comic expression.

'I'd prefer it if you stayed a bit closer to home at the moment, Darling. There's a lot of unrest in the village. People are frightened. I don't want you getting caught up in anything,' he said, taking her hand.

She pulled away from him.

'Nothing's going to happen to us; they know we're English. We're their friends after all.'

'I know that's how it seems but people can be unpredictable, especially when they're frightened. You never know who they will blame.'

'Well I'm not surprised they're frightened. I could see the fires in Málaga from the top of the mountain; they've been raging for days now. And those gunboats offshore, they've started firing at the port now. Didn't you hear them?'

'Yes. I'm afraid it seems to be escalating. I don't think it's a good idea for us to get caught up in this, you know. Timothy telephoned this morning; he thinks we should leave.'

He looked at his daughter to gauge her reaction.

'Leave? That's a bit extreme isn't it?'

Elizabeth tried to look unconcerned but her heart began to beat faster at this news. She moved across to the window and sat down on the settle, picking up one of its cushions as she did so and unconsciously hugging it to her breast. When she saw her father watching her, she put it down; they both knew that this childhood habit signalled some deeper concerns.

'Well he says that the official line from the British Consul is that all civilian ex-pats should pull out while they can. There's a British destroyer coming up from Gib in the next few days to evacuate us.'

17

Elizabeth did not reply; a dozen different emotions were struggling within her.   She had to admit that she was frightened but she was also excited; something momentous was about to happen and she wanted to be here to witness it. She stood up.

'I think I'll go and freshen up. Where's Mother?'

Her father had returned to his books; he looked up, absentmindedly.

'I think your mother is in the kitchen, trying to calm Conception.   She's in such a state I don't think we will be getting any lunch today,' he said, the shadow of a frown passing across his face once again.

She decided to go to her own room before looking for her mother.   She touched her father's hair affectionately as she passed his chair, receiving a muffled grunt in acknowledgement.   Willow stretched lazily then got up to follow her.

Her bedroom, like all the rooms in the house, looked out over the courtyard.   Besides the kitchen garden, directly below her, where each spring her mother and Pepe planted a range of vegetables and herbs, she could also see over the terracotta rooftops to the bare outcrop of the mountain behind. Very little grew there save some scrubby bushes of Spanish lavender and the occasional rock rose; sometimes she would hear the goat bells and look out in time to see the scrawny creatures scavenging for shoots but, for most of the time, the mountain was bare.   Her room was not very spacious; there was a single bed, a narrow wardrobe built into the wall opposite and a dressing table with a mirror above to it.   When she was a child her father had fixed some rudimentary bookshelves to one of the end walls and here she kept her books and a few remnants of that childhood: a favourite doll, now much battered and worn, a cuckoo clock her grandmother had sent her from Switzerland, a snowman encased in a glass globe that became a snow-scene when you shook it and a wooden musical box where she kept her few items of jewellery. The dressing table was bare except for her camera, a lined notepad and some pencils; she had cleared it of all the girlish frippery that had still cluttered it when she returned this time from England. Underneath the bed was her suitcase.

She lay on her back, looking at the ceiling and clutching her pillow in her arms. It was all so familiar, yet strange. Three years at university in England had changed her; she saw things differently now. Her parents had always protected her from the world but now she had seen for herself how things were changing. There was so much uncertainty; people were frightened by what was happening in Europe. Fascism was on the rise and every day there was talk of Hitler and the Nazis and unspeakable rumours of what was happening to the Jews. Josef Stalin ruled Russia with an iron hand and Mussolini had declared an Italian Empire. The world seemed to be going mad. But she could not ignore it; she knew now that she was part of a larger community, one of many who would fight against the insanity. There were things she had to do with her life if she wanted to make a difference; she was not sure how or where but something inside her was telling her that this was her time. When she had finished her studies she had been reluctant to leave her friends and return to Spain; only Christmas and her parents' insistence had drawn her back but now that she was here she did not want to leave again so soon.

*

The kitchen door stood ajar and the smell of cooking wafted towards her. Her mother was standing at the table arranging wild flowers in an old blue jug, painted with yellow sunflowers. She had strategically placed sprigs of wild lavender, with their fragrant deep blue rods and woody stems, as supports for the more delicate blooms of a second variety that leaned precariously and defied Margaret's attempts to regiment them. Next she trimmed some yellow and white margaritas and inserted them deftly into the water. At the other end of the kitchen table Conception was kneading dough for the day's bread, lifting and dropping it in turn before once again thrusting her hands into the soggy mass. Her sleeves were rolled up exposing strong, brown arms dusted with flour and her apron, which was inadequate to cover the voluminous folds of her black skirt, was tied around her plump waist with a bow. Her straight hair was pulled back into a bun that rested on the nape of her neck; it shone with a fine film of oil that she had applied that morning, the reflection disguising within its blackness the grey hairs that Elizabeth knew were increasing year upon year. Satisfied that she had thumped and bumped the dough enough, Conception deftly shaped it into a cylindrical loaf, covered it with a damp cloth and put it to one side. Then she began to scrub the surface of the table with wide, circular motions. The heat from the cooking range in the fireplace was radiating throughout the room and causing the housekeeper to sweat. She paused for a moment to wipe her wide, round face with her apron then continued with her work, talking all the while to Elizabeth's mother in her gravelly Andalusian voice. The news of their departure had upset her and all the unhappiness that she now felt was being channelled into these routine household tasks.

Conception had worked for the Marshall family ever since they had moved to Spain when Elizabeth was only eleven and before Peter had been born. To Elizabeth she was part of their family; her motherly form and kindly face as familiar to her as her own mother's. Elizabeth's parents were artists; that was what her mother said, and artists could not live in cold, damp England; they needed the sun to warm them and bring their creations to life. So, while still in their thirties, they had moved to southern Spain, where Margaret could paint her rather unremarkable watercolours and Elizabeth's father could divide his time between his research on the life of John of Gaunt and writing rather melancholy poetry. The tiresome business of earning a living was resolved by the occasional literary reviews he wrote for the Times newspaper and amply supplemented after a few years by an inheritance he received on the death of his father, a successful industrialist. Elizabeth had been sent to school in England because her parents considered the local international school only suitable for the education of children up to the age of ten. She had returned at Christmas, Easter and for two months in the summer. Now at last, her education complete, with an English Honours degree in her pocket and a diploma from the Young Ladies' School of Typing and Shorthand, she was free to stay or leave as she pleased. Or so she had thought. Now they were leaving, going back to England, to the damp and the fog and they expected her to go with them.

As she opened the door wider she became aware that there were other people in the kitchen; a young man, with a rather dirty face, was sitting with his back to the wall, watching the doorway attentively and two old women were sitting on a bench by the stove. Hearing her enter Conception turned her tear streaked face towards her and gave her a watery smile.

'Elizabeth. There you are. We've all had breakfast but I can get you something. What about some fresh bread? There's some in the oven; it will be ready in just a minute or two,' the housekeeper said, pointing to the oven. 'Or a piece of *empanada*? Or maybe an egg? Pepe has just brought in some fresh eggs. What would you like, my lovely?'

'Nothing thank you, Conception. I'm not hungry.'

'But you must eat my beauty. You're looking very thin. You'll never get a husband if you get too thin.'

Elizabeth laughed; they always had this conversation. If it had been anyone else urging her to eat and put on weight she would have been irritated but Conception's exhortations only contained the warmth of a familiar ritual which spoke more of their mutual affection than any future outcome.

'I don't want a husband, thank you, at least not yet. And anyway, thin is fashionable.'

'But not here in Spain, my lovely. Spanish men like women with something they can get hold of. Like me,' she said, placing her hands on her ample hips and laughing at her favourite member of the Marshall household.

'Conception do stop spoiling her. If she is hungry she can get herself something,' Elizabeth's mother said.

Her usual placid nature seemed ruffled and there was a hint of irritation in her voice at their frivolity. At last she was satisfied with her flower arrangement and, before she placed it on a small table by the door, took a long, deep breath of its scent. She stood looking at it appreciatively for a few seconds then turned to her daughter.

'Have you spoken to your father?'

'Yes, just now. He seems a bit worried.'

'Well, the situation is not good. We've been advised to leave, you know. The Vice Consul will ring us and tell us when the ship arrives.'

Elizabeth could hear Conception begin to cry again; it was a blubbery sound, interspersed with large sniffs and muffled cries of 'Aaaigh'. The two old women by the door began to join in.

'Are you going to go, then?' she asked her mother.

'I don't think we have a choice Darling, if only for Peter's sake. We need to take him to safety.'

'But you love it here, Mother. You won't be happy in England, you know. Anyway, where will you go?'

'We've already thought about that; we'll go to your Uncle Brian's place in Dorset. It's very pretty there you know and the climate is quite nice, I believe. We can get Peter into prep school a few months early. I'm sure we won't have any problems on that score; Brian is on the Board of Governors, you know. I think it will all work out for the best.'

Margaret's face was pale; she was trying to be positive and keep calm for everyone's sake but Elizabeth could see that she was beginning to feel the strain. She was not by nature a very organised woman; she liked to let the day take her where it might. Now she was being asked to make momentous decisions about evacuating herself and her family and her sad, blue eyes were telling the world she could not do it.

'Who are those women?' Elizabeth whispered in English.

Her mother turned and looked at the two women as though she had only just become aware of them. They were seated side by side, sniffling quietly to themselves. Both were dressed entirely in black: long black dresses that had seen better days and had faded with many washes to a shade

23

more akin to brown than black, black shawls that covered their heads and obscured their faces and black shoes with heels so worn that it must have been impossible to walk without a limp.

'They are the Fernandez sisters, from the village.'

'Why are they here?'

'They feel safer here they say. They say that the soldiers won't attack this house because the Englishman lives here,' her mother replied.

'But what about their families? Where are their families?'

Her mother looked bewildered; she had not thought to ask them. Elizabeth turned to Conception, who had stopped crying now and was busy chopping up some vegetables into small pieces to make a soup.

'Conception, what has happened to the ladies' families?' she asked, nodding her head in the direction of the two women, who continued to keen and moan, rocking all the while gently from side to side in unison.

'Rosario and Mercedes are from the village,' she said. 'I've known them a long time. They heard that some rebel soldiers tortured the women in Artipena to make them tell them where their men were and they're frightened they'll do the same to them. They want us to protect them.'

The two women looked up when they heard Conception say their names. Elizabeth could see that they were probably not as old as she had thought but poor nutrition and a life of heavy, physical work had taken its toll. The younger of the two women smiled at her, a toothless smile that asked her for her pity.

'But what about their families?' she repeated. 'Don't they have any husbands or children to care for them?'

'Mercedes is a widow. She has two sons but they have both gone off to fight for the Republic. She has no-one left except her sister.'

She lowered her voice and continued:

'Mercedes has always had to look after her sister; she's what you might call *loca*, a little mad. She cannot look after herself and she says silly things all the time. Mercedes is frightened that she'll tell the soldiers about her sons and then they'll kill them.'

Elizabeth looked a bit more carefully at the younger sister; there was a certain wildness about her eyes and something strange in the way she kept rolling her head from side to side.

'Well, Conception, have you told them that we're leaving and the house will be shut up?'

'Yes but they want to stay here for now.'

Elizabeth turned to her mother.

'Well I suppose that's all right, isn't it Mother? They're not doing any harm, after all.'

Her mother nodded; she seemed to have left any decision making on the future of her two house guests to Elizabeth. She was now opening all the cupboards in the kitchen and removing certain items.

'Mother, what are you doing?'

There seemed a kind of madness in her mother's actions; it made her nervous.

'We must hide all our good things before we leave. We can't take them with us; they will only allow us one suitcase each. We must only take essentials. I've already told Peter; he's packing his case now.'

'Can't Adela help you?'

Adela was a girl from the village that came in twice a week to help Conception with the laundry.

25

'No, Adela isn't coming any more. She has to look after her mother and her brothers and sisters. They are all frightened to leave their house.'

Elizabeth realised she had not seen her little brother yet that morning. She wondered how he would be choosing between all his model ships; which could go and which would have to stay.

'So you plan to come back then, Mother?'

'Yes, of course. This won't last long; Timothy says it'll blow over in a few months. Then we'll be able to return. The problem is what will happen to the house in the meantime. The Reds are burning all the big *cortijos*; anything that belongs to the aristocracy is targeted. Pepe was telling us this morning that one of the Larios estates was burnt down last week; the family got away but the house was destroyed.'

'So what will you do?'

'Well,' her mother dropped her voice and resumed talking to her daughter in English. 'Pepe has found this secret passage that leads from the cellar into the mountain. There's a small room, a bit like the priest's holes that you find in Jacobean houses in Scotland. It was probably constructed for a similar purpose: to hide someone or something in times of trouble. Well we thought it would be a good place to store our valuables until the fighting is over and we can come back and reclaim them.'

Her mother appeared very pleased with this solution. Elizabeth thought, not for the first time, how her mother never lost the knack of surprising her. She would float about the house, adjusting a cushion or two, arranging her flowers or tending the tomatoes, apparently totally unaware of what was happening around her, then suddenly would surprise everyone with a flash of intuition or downright common sense.

Whatever problem had arisen would be resolved and then she would return to the serenity of her private thoughts.

She heard a man's voice ask for some water and turned around; she had forgotten about the man sitting by the wall. His clothes were dirty and torn and he was barefoot; she wondered if he was a shepherd or a goatherd. As he took the mug of water from Conception she noticed that his hand shook and he had to lift his other hand to steady it before he could drink. When he saw her looking at him he put the mug on the floor beside him and stood up, removing his cap from his head.

'*Buenos días, señora,*' he said. 'My name is Alberto, I am the brother-in-law of your gardener, Pepe.'

'*Buenos días,* Alberto,' she replied politely. 'Have you come far?'

The man sat down and stared at the ground; he found it hard to answer her question.

'He's from La Puerta de Miel,' whispered Conception. 'He's walked all the way across the mountains to be with his sister and her family. It's taken him three days. He had to walk at night across country, avoiding the roads because he was frightened the soldiers would catch him.'

'His sister? Inmaculada? Pepe's wife?'

Conception nodded and a tear rolled down her broad nose and landed on her apron. Pepe's wife had died the previous summer, giving birth to their fifth child. She had been a strong, young woman, full of life and energy but that had not helped when the baby decided to enter the world feet first and with the umbilical cord tied tightly around his neck. Elizabeth had liked the young woman; she remembered seeing her trudging up the hill towards the house, bringing Pepe his lunch of bread and goat's cheese, with the youngest

27

child swaddled across her back and three more trailing behind her. She wondered who was looking after the children now. People barely had enough food for themselves; it was hard to imagine anyone taking in four extra mouths to feed.

'Didn't he know about Inmaculada?' she asked, feeling sorry for this poor, young man who had walked so far for nothing.

'No. There was no way of letting them know. Pepe had hoped that the old man who travels from village to village sharpening knives would take the news but times are so uncertain now.'

She stopped and looked at the man.

'I wondered if he could stay here for a few days, just until he decides what to do?' she asked.

Elizabeth wondered why she was asking her and not her mother; she looked across at her mother but she did not seem to have heard. She had laid their best dinner service out on the kitchen table and was busy sorting through it to find any chipped or cracked pieces to put on one side.

'I'm sure that will be all right, Conception. I'll just check with my father but I know he won't mind,' she replied.

She wondered if the man was a Communist.

'So what is happening in Puerta de la Miel?' she asked him. 'Have ...'

He looked at her with eyes so full of horror that she could not continue. At last he spoke.

'The African soldiers arrived one night, just before it got light. We were all still in bed. They looked like devils, on their big black horses, with bandoleers across their chests and green turbans wound round their heads. They rode down the main street firing their rifles into the air and, when we ran outside to see what was happening, they started shooting at us. People were falling down at the entrances to their homes; some of the soldiers dismounted and went to make sure they were dead. If they were only wounded, they bayoneted them; it didn't matter if they were young men or old. My father was seventy-three and they pulled him out of his house and shot him in the yard like a dog. Some of us got away and hid in the hills but we could hear the screams of the women and we had to go back to see what was happening. The Moors had left but we could see half a dozen lorries parked in the centre of the village; other rebel soldiers were going from house to house questioning people, mostly women or young children because, by then, the men had either all gone or were dead. They even shot boys as young as eight-years-old. We didn't know what to do; we had no guns, nothing to fight them with. We hid until it was dark then we crept down to see if we could help but we were too late. There was not a house left untouched; I've never seen such destruction: doors kicked in, tables overturned and everywhere the stain and smell of blood. But the crying of the women was the worst; I still can't get it out of my head.'

The young man stopped and held his head in his hands, pressing his fingers against his eyes as though he could blot out the awful memories that her question had unleashed. Then he continued in a monotonous, relentless manner, as if he were scared that, if he waited too long, he would never be able to finish his gruesome tale.

'They threw dead bodies down the well to poison it and they took whatever food they could find. They left us nothing. They had no respect for anyone or anything; I saw two soldiers grab hold of a woman; she was old enough to be my mother, and they poured castor oil down her throat until she vomited on the road. "Tell us where your men are

29

hiding," they shouted at her and when she could tell them nothing they shot her too.

That afternoon they left. We waited until we were sure they had all gone then we did what we could. We buried all the bodies we could find in shallow graves on the hillside and marked them with wooden crosses. The village priest said a few words for each of the dead and made the sign of the cross over their graves. Personally I have no special love for the church but I have to admit that our priest is a good man; he was born in our village. Maybe he should have tried to reason with the soldiers but I don't think it would have made any difference; they were out for our blood and nobody was going to stop them. They didn't even try to find out if we were Republican or Nationalist; they didn't really care. Of course they didn't hurt the priest; they just pushed him inside his own church and locked the door. I suppose his cross protected him.'

He paused then said:

'So when we had done what we could, we left the women to grieve and made our way here.'

'We? Are you not alone?' she asked.

'I am now. My companions have gone down into Málaga to join the Militia but I wanted to see my sister first. She and my mother were the only family I had left; they killed my father, my two brothers and my brother-in-law.'

At this point he could not continue and leaning his head back against the wall began to sob silently. The tears streamed down his face, washing away the grime and blood that covered it. Elizabeth realised he was only a child himself, probably not more than seventeen. She did not know what to do; she looked at Conception.

'Best to just leave him for a bit,' she said. 'He's in a state of shock. I'll make him a brew of herbs to settle his nerves.'

Elizabeth said nothing. Her mother was packing the china into a wooden crate and padding it with straw.

'Mother, what will happen to Willow if you go back to England?' she asked.

'She's coming with us of course, silly,' a child's high pitched voice interjected.

Her brother had come into the kitchen, closely followed by the dog.

'Mummy, I've packed my case but I can't get all my models in. What shall I do?'

His mother looked at him vaguely.

'What's that, Darling?'

'My models, Mummy, they won't all fit in the case. I can't leave them behind. What am I going to do?'

'Look pack your very special ones in your case and bring the rest down here and we'll pack them with the china. Then they'll be safe until we get back,' she promised.

Once again Elizabeth had this feeling of unreality; she seemed to be at the intersection of two worlds. What had her mother's Spode china and Peter's model ships to do with Alberto's tale of death and destruction? She looked at the two old women; they had resumed their keening lament and were clinging to each other in desperation.

CHAPTER 2

When Elizabeth went down for breakfast the next morning the kitchen was already crowded with people that she did not know. The two women were still sitting on the bench by the fireplace; they looked calmer than the day before and were eating some of Conception's homemade bread, spread with olive oil and a purée of cooked tomatoes. Another woman, with a young boy on her lap, sat by the door and appeared to be telling Conception about the latest developments in the village. Pepe was there too, talking to an old man, so wizened and bent that she doubted if he was capable of moving from the chair in which he had been sat. There was no sign of her mother.

'More people from the village?' she asked Conception.

'Yes, they just thought they would call in and see how we were,' she replied. 'Everyone is very worried. The soldiers have taken Marbella and people are running for their lives. They're frightened that they will come to our village too. Nobody knows what to do. They've come to see if we're all right.'

Elizabeth now noticed that there were more people standing outside on the patio. She recognised Pablo, the butcher, a tall, broad man with thick, curly hair and a ruddy face. He was listening intently to Alberto, who had washed away the previous day's dirt and was looking quite presentable in an old shirt and trousers belonging to her father. Someone else had given him a pair of brown boots and now, dressed in clean clothes, he no longer looked as vulnerable as the day before.

'What is this, the village meeting place?' she said, opening the back door and stepping out into the wintery sunshine.

'*Buenos días, señorita*,' the butcher said, coming over to her. 'We wanted to speak to your father. Is he here?'

'*Buenos días*, Pablo. Yes, he's about somewhere. I'll go and look for him. But why are you all here? Who are these people?'

'Oh they are just neighbours, poor village people. They want to know if you have any news about what is happening. We hear such awful stories about killings and bombings. Everyone is terrified to go out. They're frightened that the *Moros* will come and burn the village. We don't know what to do.'

He looked distressed and kept running his fingers through his thick hair as he talked.

'Where is the mayor? Doesn't he know what's happening?'

'No, the mayor has gone. Nobody has seen him or his family since Saturday. We don't know if he left of his own accord, or was taken away. It's all very mysterious.'

He shook his head in bewilderment.

'Look, don't worry. I'll go and get my father. He may have heard something on the radio,' she said.

Her father was, as always, in his study. For once his desk was completely clear. The piles of books with dog-eared pages and numerous annotations had been closed and carefully placed in a wooden crate; his notebooks and folios lay on top, with his collection of fountain pens, pencils and a number of ink bottles. Everything was ready to be placed in her mother's hiding place. He was sitting in the armchair by the window, his ear close to the radio and fiddling with the dials.

'Father, Pablo the butcher is here with some of the other villagers. They want to speak to you.'

Her father continued with his task.

'I'm just trying to get some news from Gibraltar but the reception is pretty poor. I've managed to get some information though.'

He looked up at her.

'It looks like all the foreign consulates in Málaga are closing up and leaving. It's just like Timothy said, we will have to go soon or it will be too late.'

There was a loud hissing sound and a whistle; it was obvious that the radio was not going to give out any more news just then, so he switched it off and stood up. He stood with his back to her, looking out of the window. Elizabeth put her hand on his shoulder.

'So, what was it you wanted, Elizabeth?' he asked at last, turning to face her.

'It's Pablo, the butcher. He wants to talk to you; he's got some of the other villagers with him. Can you come down?'

'Of course. I need some breakfast anyway. I hope there's some coffee left and Conception hasn't given it away to every Tom, Dick and Juan from the village.'

He picked up his tweed jacket from the back of the chair and slipping it on, followed her down the passage to the kitchen.

The men stood by the well, looking serious and talking quietly amongst themselves. They fell silent when Elizabeth's father walked into the courtyard and approached them.

'*Buenos días, amigos. Buenos días* Pablo,' he said to them, a warm smile lighting up his face.

'Don Ricardo, *cómo estás?*'

The butcher came forward holding out his hand to Elizabeth's father.

'Very well, thank you Pablo. What can I do for you?'

'Don Ricardo we want to know if you have any news. Have you heard anything on the radio? The villagers are frightened that the *Moros* will come. Some of them won't even leave their houses.'

Elizabeth wondered if her father would tell them about the broadcast he had been listening to. She watched as her father led the butcher over to a stone bench in the shade of the lemon tree and invited him to sit down. Some of the other men moved closer so that they could hear but most seemed reluctant to take any part in the discussion.

'Elizabeth, my love, would you mind asking Conception to bring us out some coffee.'

He returned to his conversation with the butcher.

'I don't know that I can tell you very much Pablo. The Consul has advised us to leave Spain; he says that the insurgents have taken Estepona and Marbella and are heading this way. They expect them to reach Málaga very soon.'

'Don Ricardo, that young man there,' the butcher pointed to where Alberto was sitting, then continued. 'He has come through the mountains of Ronda. He says the fascist soldiers are moving towards Ronda and unless they are stopped they will soon be here. What are we to do?'

'Pablo, I'm sorry. I don't know what to say. I am only a poor writer; I know nothing about these events. I can only suggest that you stay in your village and pray that the troops do not come. They may not need to pass this way. If they come along the coast road, you will be safe here in the mountains.'

'But Don Ricardo, we are not Communists; we do not want a revolution. We are simple people who love God and obey the law. We do not care what happens in the big cities. We just want to get on with our lives in the village. But will they believe us when we tell them this?'

Her father put his arm around the big man's shoulders and repeated:

'I'm sorry Pablo. Who knows what will happen; these are unhappy times.'

'Excuse me, Don Ricardo.'

One of the other men spoke. He held a wide brimmed hat in his hands which he twisted and turned incessantly.

'Ernesto. How are you? Is your leg better yet?' Elizabeth's father asked, looking down at the twisted leg of the goatherd.

'Much better, thank you, Don Ricardo,' he replied. 'Although it gives me some pain on these cold mornings.'

He paused for a moment, frowning at the hat in his hands as though it was not his own, then continued:

'Don Ricardo. The mayor has left; the priest has locked himself in his house and won't talk to anyone and the schoolteacher has gone to Málaga to join the Reds. We have no-one to speak for us now. What will we do when the soldiers come, Don Ricardo?'

'Have you considered joining up with the people of Aznate? Their village is very close to yours. Maybe their mayor will help you.'

Pablo let out a snort of disgust.

'*Aquel pueblo tiene agua mala*, Don Ricardo. You know that.'

To say that it had bad water was the biggest insult Pablo could give to the small village that was perched on a hillside, some five or six kilometres away. Elizabeth's father was reminded of the animosity that had existed between the two villages for years; nobody could remember how it had started, whether it had been a dispute over land or animals or if some bride-to-be had been jilted but, whatever the cause, the hatred burned with an intensity that did not diminish with the years.

'I'm sorry. In that case I don't know what to advise you. Perhaps you could persuade the priest to come out. Maybe he will speak to the soldiers for you.'

'He won't answer us, Don Ricardo. He has bolted his door and pulled his shutters tight,' Pablo replied.

'Won't you come and speak to him Don Ricardo? He will listen to you. You are an Englishman,' Ernesto asked, almost pleading with him.

Elizabeth's father sighed; he looked across at his daughter then addressed the small group of men.

'I'm sorry. There's nothing I can do. I will not be here for very much longer; we have to leave very soon. I'm sure that when the priest realises that you're not going to harm him he will come out and help you. But, as I said, the soldiers probably won't come to your village anyway. You are just as safe here as you would be anywhere.'

He looked away, his discomfort at letting down these men, who had shown him so much friendship over the years, clearly marked on his face.

The butcher stood up.

'Thank you for your time Don Ricardo. I hope your ship comes for you and your family and that you get back to England safely.'

Elizabeth thought she noted a touch of sarcasm in his voice, despite the formality but her father appeared not to notice.

'Wait and have some coffee. Look here it is now,' he said as Conception approached with the coffee pot and two small cups on a bamboo tray.

'No, thank you, Don Ricardo, I must get back to the village. My family are waiting for me.'

Elizabeth watched him leave, accompanied by his silent followers. As he walked away, his head slightly bent and his shoulders down, he seemed crushed beneath the responsibility that fate had forced on him.

Her father had placed the tray on the bench beside him and was pouring out the thick, black coffee.

'Alberto, would you like some coffee? It's hot and strong,' he called to the young man.

Conception brushed past her, carrying another tray, this one loaded with slices of bread, a flask of olive oil and a dish of garlic.

'Thank you Conception. Can you bring another plate for this young man, and some sugar please.'

Elizabeth thought she heard her snort something about "having to wait on everyone in the village now" as she hurried back into the kitchen to do as she was asked. Elizabeth took an orange from the bowl on the table and went to look for her mother. She found her in her bedroom; she was twisting some sprigs of lavender into two buttonholes. Her bed was strewn with her clothes.

'Oh Elizabeth, good, you can help me choose what to pack. It's so difficult. I don't know how they expect me to manage with only one suitcase.'

She tied off the lavender and handed one to Elizabeth.

'Something to remind us of home,' she said with a sad smile. 'A touch of Spanish lavender.'

Elizabeth slipped the lavender into her pocket. Of course, this was her mother's home; she would be a stranger in England after all these years. No wonder she was so sad.

'Well just put in something warm. It will be cold in Dorset at this time of year,' she said.

'Yes Darling but we aren't going straight to Dorset, are we. The ship will take us to Gibraltar first then we will have to wait until we can get a passage to England. I have to have something to wear in Gib. Everyone is so smart there.'

'Well it still won't be that warm, Mother. Look, why not wear this blue coat for the journey and then you won't have to pack it. Then take a few jumpers and a skirt or two.'

'Yes, well I suppose I could take this one.'

She held a white wool jumper with a Peter Pan collar up against her and looked at her reflection in the mirror. Elizabeth thought how young she looked; her light brown hair had only the slightest touch of grey and her rather square face was almost completely devoid of wrinkles. Despite having lived in the sun for ten years, her face and arms were as creamy white as if she were still under the grey skies of England. Elizabeth looked at her own serious reflection towering above that of her mother. The two women were very similar, despite the fact that Elizabeth was taller and much blonder, and had, compared to her mother, received a lot more exposure to the sun's rays, which in return had covered her fresh, healthy complexion with light dusting of freckles. They had the same pale blue eyes and a slightly dreamy look which was offset by the strength of their jaw lines. Both were slim, with small breasts and both had tiny waists that they pinched into even tinier belts.

Elizabeth felt irritated with her mother.

'Does it really matter Mother? Like you said, you'll be home in a few months.'

Margaret's eyes glistened with unshed tears. She pulled out a handkerchief and blew her nose, noisily.

'Of course we will, dear. You're quite right. I'll just pack a few essentials and that will do. Now why don't you go and get your own bag packed.'

Her mother took her sprig of lavender and pinned it on her jacket.

Elizabeth dutifully wandered back in the direction of her bedroom. She could hear the telephone ringing, then her father's deep voice answering it in English. She waited for a moment at the top of the stairs but he didn't call her, so she continued to her room. She pulled the case out from under her bed and began to put a few items of clothing in it.

'Elizabeth, Elizabeth.'

It was her mother.

'The Consulate has just telephoned; the ship will be arriving tomorrow morning at dawn. We have to get down there today.'

Her mother sat down on the edge of her bed, unleashing the tears that had been waiting all morning for this moment.

Elizabeth put her arm around her and patted her back, ineffectually. What could she say?

'We must leave after lunch. It will take us at least two hours to walk down there, maybe more with Peter; you know what a slow-coach he can be.'

'All right Mother, I'll be ready. Don't worry. Have you spoken to Conception yet?'

'No, not yet. Darling would you mind speaking to her? I'm not sure I can do it without breaking down. I wish we could take her with us; I'm not sure how I will manage without her. Your father actually asked the Vice Consul if she could come with us but he said, most emphatically, not. He said he was making a big exception allowing us to take Willow but a Spanish national was out of the question. Anyway I doubt if she has a passport.'

She had stopped crying now and was moving towards the door.

'I had better see if Peter has packed yet. I'm sure I saw him outside playing with Pepe's eldest boy. Oh and I must get Pepe to take those boxes down to the cellar so we can hide them before we leave.'

She disappeared through the doorway, leaving Elizabeth looking at her half-packed case. She threw a few more items into the case and shut it, securing it tightly with a heavy leather belt, before placing it in the entrance to her room. Then she lay down on the bed. She needed a few moments to herself to think about what was going on; it was all happening too fast. This was her chance; she could not just run away and leave it because her parents told her to. Since finishing at university she had spent the last few months wondering what to do with all the education she had acquired. She did not want to teach, her mother's suggestion, nor did she want to become a secretary, her father's idea. She was not academic but she did like to write: not poetry, like her father, nor even fiction; she wanted to be a newspaper reporter but not just any kind of reporter. She wanted to be a newspaper photographer. Her parents had bought her a Kodak a few months before, as a 'well done' present when she graduated. She loved it. She had come out to Spain this time with the specific intention of chronicling Spanish life and had brought dozens of rolls of film with her. What was the point in taking it all back to England unexposed? Here was her opportunity to take some interesting photographs and maybe make a name for herself. Her only concern was how to tell her parents of her plans.

Conception was busily gutting a rabbit that Pepe had brought in that morning; the warm innards lay on the wooden table, alongside the animal's fur, emitting a smell that was both acrid and sweet at the same time.

'God, what a stink, Conception. Why don't you do that outside, by the well?' Elizabeth complained, her anxiety making her speak more sharply than usual.

'Don't make such a fuss, my lovely. I'm almost finished and then I'll put them out for the dog. I'm going to make a nice stew for tonight's supper. I've got carrots and onions and some of your mother's lovely herbs.'

'There's no need Conception. We won't be here. Father has received a telephone call from the Consulate; we have to leave this afternoon or we will not get a place on the boat.'

'What boat?'

'You know what boat. Mother told you that we have been told to go back to England. It is too dangerous for foreigners here at the moment.'

42

Her own distress made her speak plainly. She could see the tears running down Conception's cheeks as she continued to dissect the rabbit.

'Well you still have to eat,' she said.

'Yes but what I'm trying to say, Conception, is that we must go right away. We cannot wait for the rabbit stew. We must go straight after lunch.'

She tried to keep the tremor from her voice. This was the worst part of all, having to leave Conception behind. Their housekeeper had never married and had no family apart from them; her parents had died when she was very young and she had no brothers and sisters. What would she do when they left? Where would she live?

'But I only have *tortilla de patata* for your lunch; it is very little.'

'It will be fine, honestly. Don't worry Conception; it will be all right.'

She moved closer and put her arms around the woman's shoulders.

'Please don't worry, Conception. We'll be all right, you see. In a few months we'll be back and then we'll all laugh about this. Please don't cry, Conception. I can't bear it if you cry.'

The woman's broad back was shaking with her sobs, a succession of racking, tearing sounds that told Elizabeth that no matter what she said, no matter what she promised, despite all her platitudes, Conception knew she was never coming back.

'Do we have any bread? Perhaps you could make us up some *bocadillos* for the journey.'

She knew that the best thing for Conception right now was to keep busy; in that way they could all ignore, at least for a short while, the danger that was lurking just outside the door.

'Of course, you'll need something for the journey. How stupid of me not to think of it. I'll make you some nice fresh *bocadillos* and I'll put in some oranges, in case you get thirsty. It's a long way down to the coast.'

She began to clean down the table, putting the rabbit meat to one side and clearing the detritus into a bowl to throw out. Then she lifted the bucket of water off the floor and began to scrub the blood off the table, once more converting her anguish into hard physical labour.

Lunch was a sombre meal; nobody spoke and Conception kept up a constant clatter of pots and pans, defying anyone to say anything to her. Elizabeth realised that the two women were no longer at their station by the hearth; all the villagers had left, even Alberto was nowhere to be seen. The house was unusually quiet. Peter was the only one who seemed unaffected by events; he ate his tortilla then asked Elizabeth to give him the remains of hers.

'Yes, take it. I'm not very hungry,' she said.

Conception began to clear away the remnants of the meagre meal.

'I've told Pepe to fetch Eusabio's donkey,' she said. 'He'll go with you to Torre Molinos. It's too far to walk carrying those heavy suitcases. He'll be here soon.'

No sooner had she spoken than there was a knock on the door. Elizabeth's father went to unbolt it. It was Pepe. He held a scrawny, brown donkey by a length of rope.

'Don Ricardo, I will accompany you to the beach. If you bring out the suitcases I'll tie them onto the *burro's* back,' he said, his long melancholy face looking even sadder than usual.

The sight of them trudging down the stairs carrying their cases was too much for Conception and she began her long, wailing cry again. She hugged them each in turn, holding them close to her bosom and covering them with her tears. When it was Elizabeth's turn she held her at arm's length looking at her long and hard before finally enveloping her in her enormous embrace. By now they were all crying, even Elizabeth's father had to wipe his eyes with the freshly washed handkerchief that Conception had just slipped into his pocket.

'Here, take this for the journey: it's smoked ham and bread, and a little goat's cheese, and there's some wine in the flask.'

She thrust the provisions into their hands and pushed them gently towards the door.

'Go on now. You don't want to be walking in the dark. Don't worry about the house, Pepe and I will lock everything up and keep an eye on it. Go on now.'

'Goodbye Conception. Thank you for everything. I hope this war doesn't last very long, then we can come back to see you,' Elizabeth's father said, kissing his housekeeper on both cheeks.

'Bye Conception. I'll send you a postcard from Dorset,' Peter said.

He had Willow attached to a length of rope and was already running down the path towards the road, the dog bounding behind him.

CHAPTER 3

As they headed towards the coast the sun was already beginning its descent. They trudged in silence for a while; the only one who was in high spirits was Peter. He skipped along in front of them, keeping up a constant stream of chatter; when no-one else would listen to him he talked to the dog, telling her how much she would enjoy living in England, how there were hundreds of rabbits for her to chase, how he would take her for long walks every day, how she would sleep in his room when he was not away at school.

'Peter can you try to keep quiet for a bit. We've still got a long way to go; save your energy,' his mother said but with little effect.

The truth was that his childish prattle was a welcome distraction from the thoughts that were crowding into their heads. While he laughed and sang his silly songs, they could pretend that there was nothing unusual about this walk to Torre Molinos; it was just an occasion, like any other, when they could meet old friends and catch up with the news. They would arrive at the International Club, a little warm from the walk and Margaret would order a gin and tonic and Richard would have a whisky and then they would wander about looking for acquaintances with whom they could exchange some social chit-chat. This time no-one knew what to expect, so they walked, heads down, not thinking about what awaited them, letting themselves drift towards their destinies.

Elizabeth was glad that Pepe had brought the donkey; her legs were already aching from walking on the uneven road and her camera, slung casually around her neck seemed to weigh more with every step. She felt sure she would not have been able to manage her case as well. She dropped back to walk beside him.

'Are you tired *señorita*?' Pepe asked, solicitously.

'Just a bit, Pepe. I'm glad it's mostly downhill.'

'Yes. It would be easier if we went by the main road but that would lead us through Alhaurin and Churriana. I don't think it is a good idea to go near any of the villages; you just don't know what could be happening there.'

'I'm sure you're right. It's better to keep to the mountain roads but it's very hard on my feet.'

Elizabeth grimaced; despite wearing her oldest, most comfortable shoes she could already feel a blister forming on her heel. She looked around her; the sea still seemed a long way off. They were not even half way there yet.

'Well we will stop soon and have a rest,' he promised her.

She thought of Conception and the others in the village. What would they be doing now? She knew how frightened everyone was; they had all believed Alberto when he had told them what had happened in his village but was it really as bad as he had said? Nobody had really questioned him. Now, walking in the afternoon sunshine towards that glittering sea, she did not know what to believe. The grey haze still hung in the sky over Málaga but there was no sound of guns today; the war ships still lay in the harbour but they were silent, unmoving, once again tiny replicas of Peter's toys.

47

'Pepe, did you talk to Alberto before you left?'

'Yes, *señorita.*'

'Did he tell you what he's planning to do?'

'Yes, he says he's going to go to Málaga to try to join up with his friends. He says there's nothing here for him now, so he wants to fight; he wants to kill the people who murdered his family. I suppose he wants revenge.'

'And what will you do?'

'Me? I will stay in the village; that is where I belong. Besides I have four children to care for and no wife to help me. I can't go off fighting other people's wars.'

'But it's not someone else's war, Pepe. It's your war; it's Spain's war.'

'No, *señorita*, you do not understand. In our village we do not want war. We do not want revolution. We want to work and feed our families; we want to live in peace. If the war comes to us I suppose we will have to fight but I am not going to Málaga to fight it.'

Elizabeth could understand how he felt; he had to put his family first. But there was more to it than that: he had been one of the lucky ones who worked for foreigners. Instead of earning two pesetas a day in the fields he earned fifty pesetas a week working as a gardener and odd-job man for her father. By village standards it was a fortune; her father thought it very cheap. These last ten years, while others worked only six or seven months of the year, Pepe had had regular work and plenty of food. What would he do now she wondered. There was no work to be had; he would have to live off his wits, growing what food he could in this harsh terrain or hunting for rabbits and wild partridge. If he was lucky he might find work at harvest time but in this area the crops were mostly olives and almonds, both harvests already in. There were a few citrus fruits to be picked in the valley but plenty of men to do it. No-one wanted to journey to other villages looking for work; they did not want to try their luck with the large estates that usually hired seasonal gangs of labourers. Everyone was too frightened to leave their own village, unsure of what they would find. It was going to be hard for him now that they were going back to England.

They were almost there. Pepe had promised them that the coast road was just over the next ridge. He led the way now; they followed, hot, tired, and dusty. Nobody complained. Elizabeth had tied a scarf around her head like a bandana to keep her hair from sticking to her face with perspiration. They had all removed their coats and piled them on top of the already over-laden donkey. Even Willow was dragging behind, her tail down and her tongue almost touching the floor. Elizabeth had Peter by the hand and was playing a game with him to encourage him to walk further; for the last half hour he had been asking them to stop and rest.

'We're almost there Peter. Come on chap, you've done really well. Not much further now,' Richard tried to encourage his son but Peter's enthusiasm for the journey had waned.

'Look only another few yards and we'll be able to see Torre Molinos,' promised Elizabeth, pulling him gently forward. 'Come on, I'll race you to the top of the ridge.'

The boy pulled away from her and ran, as well as his tired legs would let him, to where the track turned a corner at the foot of the mountain and offered them a view of the coast. Richard saw his son stop in surprise.

'What is it Peter?' he heard Elizabeth ask.

'Look at all those people,' Peter said. 'Where are they going?'

Elizabeth and Richard hurried to where he was standing, looking in amazement at the scene below.

The road from Torre Molinos to Málaga was filled with people: a winding procession of men, women and children, walking slowly, silently, tired refugees with their heads down, heading towards the capital. Some pushed carts laden with belongings, some led donkeys like their own but most carried their meagre belongings wrapped in blankets and slung across their shoulders.

Richard was reminded of another procession of disheartened men, in France in 1918, when he had stood in a clearing in the woods and watched the remnants of his battalion retreat in silence. Once bright, fresh faced young men that had marched with heads held high to fight for King and Country, now they slunk back from enemy lines, defeated and demoralised, their crisp uniforms and shiny buckles torn and tarnished, hungry, tired, dragging their rifles, the limping, bandaged casualties of war. That time the rain had been falling in leaden sheets, soaking everything and turning the road on which they marched into slippery, black mud. Today the sun beat down, relentlessly, on the heads and shoulders of these weary travellers and their feet kicked up clouds of dust that billowed behind them like a banner. But these people had the same air of fatalism, of being exhausted to their very depths and yet still managing to find the strength to put one foot in front of the other.

'Who are they, Father?'

'I don't know Peter but I expect they're people trying to get away from the soldiers.'

He turned to Elizabeth.

'Timothy told me that Estepona and Marbella had been overrun by the fascists. He said hundreds of people had fled, terrified of what would happen to them. This must be them.'

'What shall we do?'

'We'll do as we planned. We can't go back now. If anything it shows that we're right to be leaving. It will be very dangerous with so many people on the move.'

He looked back to where his wife was walking along the path with Pepe and the donkey; she looked very tired. Her face was flushed from the exertion of walking and he could see a gleam of perspiration along her upper lip. She was talking sadly to Pepe. He knew she was sorry to be leaving, sorry to be deserting these kind friends but he could do nothing about it. His main priority was his family; he had to get them to safety.

Unlike many of his friends he had survived the Great War, invalided out after barely six months. The war to end all wars they called it and yet here they were, less than twenty years later, on the verge of another one. He had come to Spain to get away from it all, the politics and power mongering but it was impossible to escape. He was glad to be getting his family out of Spain but he did not know how he would protect them in the future. Dictators dominated the news: Mussolini, Hitler, now Franco. How long would the democratic nations stand by and watch? He looked again at the procession of people trudging towards Málaga and despite the sunshine felt a shiver run along his spine. These helpless people were seeking sanctuary from the invading forces: the green turbaned Moors, the ruthless mercenaries of the Foreign Legion, the well drilled Requetes. What hope did this ill-fed, ill-equipped rabble below him have against them? He could make out the black caps of a few militiamen but most of the evacuees were women, children and old men. What would they find when they got there? Timothy had told him that people were starving in Málaga; there was no bread to be had anywhere. The bridge at Motril had been down for a few days now and the road was flooded; all links between the Republic and Málaga had been severed and nothing could get through. The city was cut off. He felt a wave of pity for these poor folk, driven by despair to a new home that was not ready to receive them. Once again he thanked God that he could get his own family out. He scanned the harbour with his binoculars looking for a British vessel but there were only the Spanish cruisers with their guns trained on the city and a few small warships. He was not sure but he thought he could make out the colours of the German flag.

'Don Ricardo.'

It was Pepe; he was unloading the cases from the donkey.

'Don Ricardo, I can't go any further. I'm sorry. I must get back to my children. I am sorry.'

He looked very distressed.

'Of course Pepe, we understand. It's not much further now anyway; we'll be at the Club before dark quite easily. You get back to your family.'

They each took up their coats and put them on for ease of carrying, then picked up their cases. How incongruously neat and middle-class they looked; how English they were standing on a Spanish hillside carrying their Burberry suitcases and wearing overcoats. His wife's sunhat sat awry her brown curls; she looked more sad than tired.

'Pepe, thank you so much for coming with us. We would never have got here so quickly without you and your lovely donkey,' she said, taking his hands in her own. 'I do hope everything goes well for you and the children.'

'Thank you *señora*. I hope you have a safe journey.'

Pepe looked very grave. They all shook hands with him in turn, thanking him.

'Pepe, I hope this fighting will be over soon and we'll be able to come back and live here again. In the meantime, here is something to help you until you can find some more work.'

Richard pressed a wad of pesetas into the man's calloused hand. His gardener looked at it in amazement.

'Thank you Don Ricardo. Thank you. A thousand blessings on you. May God watch over you and your family.'

They took their last farewells of Pepe and his donkey and began to make the descent to the coast road below them.

They slipped unnoticed into the procession; nobody looked their way, nobody seemed to care that they were there. Maybe they were so obviously English as to offer no threat to these travellers. Richard held on to Elizabeth's arm and instructed his wife to keep a tight hold on their son. There was no levity now; even Peter was subdued by his new travelling companions. They trudged along in silence until they reached the edge of the small town of Torre Molinos. Richard guided his family down a side street towards the beach and the International Club. They could see the grey stone building in the distance, its flag poles flying the Union Jack and a number of other nations' flags, including the Stars and Stripes.

The International Club was packed with ex-patriots; some were standing outside, smoking and talking, others sat on their luggage, looking lost. One group were arguing with the club's steward about the lack of tables to sit at. Elizabeth had not realised before that so many foreigners lived in the area; some faces she recognised but many were total strangers.

The Marshall family pushed its way through the crowd and into the entrance hall.

'You can't bring that dog in here, sir,' a uniformed man informed her father. 'We do not allow dogs in the Club.'

'Well I think you're going to have to make an exception today,' Richard said firmly, pushing past the doorman and ushering his family into the lounge.

He could see Teddy and Rosalind Harcourt-Smith standing by the window and headed towards them.

'Richard, Margaret. Thank goodness. We were beginning to worry that you wouldn't arrive in time.'

'Hello Rosie. We set off straight after lunch but it's quite a walk, you know,' Margaret replied, kissing her old friend on the cheek. 'Hello Teddy.'

'Walk? Oh of course, darling, I'd forgotten you don't have a car. What a bore. Couldn't you find anyone to bring you down?'

Elizabeth was not surprised that Rosalind looked horrified at the idea of walking; she herself would have found it hard to walk very far in the fashionable crocodile skin shoes that this rather unlikely friend of her mother was wearing. From the top of her gently waved grey hair to the tips of those elegant shoes, Rosalind was immaculate; she wore a pink cashmere twinset with a single strand of pearls at her slender, if somewhat wrinkled, throat and a pencil slim skirt that reached to her calves. She looked as if she were about to join the other well-turned out ladies at the Club for afternoon tea rather than flee the country on a British destroyer. Elizabeth listened to her mother explain about Pepe's kindness and the donkey and tried not to show her irritation when she heard Rosalind mutter something about how quaint it must have been. She had never understood the bond between the

54

Harcourt-Smiths and her parents; they seemed to have so little in common. Teddy Harcourt-Smith was originally something important in the City and according to her father had made some pretty shrewd investments. So well had he invested his money that he was able to retire at a fairly young age and for the last thirty years had lived in the hills above Torre Molinos, making annual trips back home, as they liked to call England, for those important events in the social calendar, such as Ascot, Henley and Wimbledon. Teddy was an ex-guardsman and was much taller than his wife but did not cut such an imposing figure. He had bushy eyebrows and an equally bushy, handlebar moustache; his nose was red and slightly bulbous and his skin had an unhealthy pallor; his once lean figure was now reshaped by the padded cushion of his stomach, which even his buttoned waistcoat could not restrain. Elizabeth saw that the two men were deep in conversation and realised she had not seen her father so animated for quite a while. She walked over to join them.

'Oh it'll blow over very soon, you see. The army will be here any day now then those Commie bastards will be made to hop,' Harcourt-Smith was saying, punching the air to add emphasis to his words. 'Oh, beg your pardon, Elizabeth. Didn't see you there.'

'We saw lots of people walking towards Málaga,' Elizabeth said, ignoring his apology. 'They seemed very frightened.'

'So they should be. Those are crack African troops they're running from, you know. No messing about with them,' he replied. 'They have had plenty of experience dealing with rebellions in Morocco. They don't pussy-foot about, no sir.'

'But aren't they the rebels?' Elizabeth asked.

55

Harcourt-Smith gave no reply but his look was withering.

'I've heard of some awful atrocities being committed,' Elizabeth's father added. 'Women and children being killed and their homes burned.'

'Well the sooner it's all under control the better then we will all be able to get on with our lives. What the Spanish peasants need is a firm hand and, from what I hear, this Franco chap is just the man to give it.'

'Well I for one will be glad when we're all safely in Gibraltar,' said Rosalind, moving over to join them.

'They said they would let us know as soon as a British destroyer arrives to take us off,' Richard explained. 'Probably very early tomorrow morning.'

'It's such a nuisance,' Rosalind complained. 'Teddy insisted we come over right away and now we will have to spend the entire night here and there's nowhere to sleep. I've already asked the steward and he says there's not a single room available.'

She looked around the room; it was gradually filling with people. Soon there would not even be anywhere to sit. A young man wearing a check jacket and a mustard coloured tie joined them.

'I say Teddy, do you think this business is going to affect the Calpe Hounds?' he asked.

'Oh, I doubt it Charles. Nothing's ever interfered with the meet before. I can't see this little disturbance making any difference.'

'Margaret. Rosalind. One of you fancy a rubber of bridge? We need a fourth.'

A rotund woman in a Harris tweed suit and brown brogues pointed across the room to where two elderly women had managed to set up a card table and were busy shuffling two decks of cards.

'Yes, what fun. You don't mind, do you Margaret? I know you're not much of a bridge player and it will help to keep my mind off this dreadful situation.'

'No, not at all Rosalind, I prefer to stay here with my children anyway.'

Elizabeth realised her mother was still holding Peter's hand, reluctant to let it go. The room was beginning to feel crowded; she recognised a few faces: a German family that ran a small shop in Alhaurin were sitting apart, eating a makeshift meal of sausage and bread, a French painter, who had visited her mother once last summer, was there with his consumptive looking wife and their three scrawny sons, and some young men, that she vaguely knew from the tennis club, were wandering about looking for somewhere to sit. At the far end of the room a small group of Danes were conversing noisily in their own language. She felt a hand on her arm; it was her father.

'Elizabeth, I've been talking to the steward. Rosalind was right, there are no free rooms; it looks as though we will have to sleep on the floor tonight. I think it would be a good idea to find ourselves a spot now before any more people arrive. It's going to be a long night; we might as well try to make ourselves as comfortable as we can.'

He led them over to a corner opposite the window and away from the door. There were, by now, no available seats so they placed their coats on the marble floor and propped their suitcases behind them as backrests.

'Stay here with your mother while I go and see if I can buy any food or something to drink,' he instructed her.

Elizabeth sat down next to her mother; Peter had fallen asleep, exhausted from the walk and general excitement of the day. His head rested on Margaret's lap and his breath came evenly, punctuated by barely perceptible snores. How nice it would be to sleep, she thought, to be as trusting as a child so that you could surrender yourself to oblivion with the knowledge that when you woke everything would be as before. Only children could do that; only children could let go of the day so easily and slip into dreamland. She looked around the room; everyone wore that strained smile that said that people of good breeding did not give in to minor catastrophes like civil war, especially when it was someone else's war. But despite the smiles and bright chatter, there was a brittleness about everything, as though the slightest puff of wind would break their world into a thousand pieces. She saw her father making his way through the crowd towards her, carrying a bottle of water and a plate of cucumber sandwiches.

'It's all they have I'm afraid, unless you want something stronger? The bar seems to be well stocked with gin and whisky.'

'No thanks, water's fine.'

'What's going on over there?' Margaret asked, pointing to a group of people standing in the hallway.

'They're listening to the radio. It's Queipo de Llano's nightly report,' replied her father, shaking his head. 'I've never heard such downright rubbish in my life. He's trying to scare us all to death.'

'Who is he?' Elizabeth asked.

'General Queipo de Llano? He's one of the army generals that went over to the side of the rebels. He led the attack on Seville.'

58

Elizabeth looked blank.

'You remember, Timothy told us last week that Seville had fallen to the fascists.'

'Oh yes. Didn't he say that their leader was an awful man: cruel and bloodthirsty?'

'Yes, there are some dreadful stories about what he did in Seville. He hates the Communists. For him, this is a fight of good against evil, a fight for the country's soul. He will never give up until he sees them all dead.'

'Wasn't it him who had the prisoners shot?'

'That's right; they were transported to one of the poorest *barrios* in Seville, where the working class lived, and shot in the streets. Then he gave the order not to move the bodies; he wanted them left lying where they had fallen as a warning to others.'

Elizabeth had never seen her father so disturbed. He was not a political man; to him it did not really matter who ruled the country as long as he could live his scholarly life undisturbed but something about this conflict had touched a raw nerve and she now saw a different man before her.

'But he's a clever man,' he added, reluctantly. 'He knows how to sow the seeds of fear amongst these people. He's a master of propaganda; his speeches are broadcast nightly and according to Timothy he also organises the air-force to drop anti-Republican leaflets over the cities. He wants to break the people's morale with misinformation and malicious threats.'

'I want to hear him,' she said getting up.

'Oh Elizabeth, whatever for? Your father has just told you he's an evil man,' her mother protested.

But Elizabeth was already picking her way through the makeshift barricades of chairs and luggage and heading for

59

the hallway. As she approached the group she could hear a thin, reedy voice speaking in Spanish:

'Our brave Legionaries and Regulares have shown the Red cowards what it means to be a man. And incidentally the wives of the Reds too. These Communist and Anarchist women, after all, have made themselves fair game by their doctrine of free love. And now they have at least made the acquaintance of real men, and not milksops of militiamen. Kicking their legs about and struggling won't save them.'

Elizabeth's Spanish was not perfect and she struggled to understand what the general was saying, finding it difficult to believe that the leader of the rebel forces would make such a salacious statement. The horrified look on the Vice Consul's face told her she had interpreted his words correctly.

'Elizabeth, you don't want to listen to this,' Timothy said, when he noticed her standing next to him. 'It's all propaganda.'

'Sound more like a psychopath to me,' she said. 'How on earth does someone like him get to be in charge of the army?'

'They say he's an excellent general, with a brilliant military mind but he does have a reputation for encouraging his men to be brutal.'

'Brutal? Evil more like.'

Elizabeth moved closer to the radio so she could hear better:

'Malagueños!' it went on. *'Let me direct myself first of all to the cheating Militia. Your luck has run out and you have lost. A circle of iron will soon surround you. We will shoot your men and rape your women.'*

It continued in the same vein for another ten minutes and then she heard the general clear his throat and sign off with his usual "*Buenos noches.*" The radio crackled for a moment then cut out.

'Well, I can't believe what I've just heard from an official spokesman of the Nationalist forces,' said a man, standing next to her.

'Well sounds to me as though he's got them licked,' commented a second man.

'Bit extreme though, don't you think?' the first man added.

The second man, who sported a handle-bar moustache and looked as though he came from a military background, spoke again:

'This propaganda game is an important strategy in modern warfare, you know old boy.   Terrorising the civilian population can have a very demoralising effect on the fighting man, especially when the lines of communication are down.'

'Yes but how do we know if it's true or not?   How do we actually know what is happening here?'

'That's just it.   We don't.   The government will only talk to foreign journalists from left-wing papers and the insurgents will only speak to right-wing ones.   So each side puts forward their official story but it's not necessarily the true one.   I don't think anyone really knows exactly what is going on.'

Elizabeth thought the last speaker was probably a journalist, or maybe someone from an embassy.   He spoke English with a French accent and his knowledge of Spanish seemed to be fluent.

'You're right.   He just said that Madrid was in Nationalist hands, yet I read the other day that the government were still in control and the Nationalists were miles away.'

'So who do you believe?' asked the man with the handle-bar moustache.

'Well I wouldn't believe a lot of Commie bastards,' interjected a rather stout man holding a glass of gin and tonic at a rather precarious angle.

'Shouldn't we give some credence to the elected government?' Elizabeth asked, being drawn into the argument despite herself.

The men stopped and looked at her as though they had only just become aware of her presence, then continued without replying.

'Well I'm pretty damned glad we're off. It'll be nice to have a few days in Gib.'

'Yes, isn't it February when they run the Hounds?'

'That's right. Old Bertie Hyde-White is Master this year,' the handle-bar moustache man replied.

'Come along Elizabeth, I think you've heard enough now,' Richard said, taking his daughter by the elbow and steering her away from the group of men, who were beginning to argue loudly.

The night passed very slowly; the floor was hard and despite her thick coat, cold. At one point some aeroplanes flew very low across the sea, causing the tension to ripple like waves around the room. There were the sounds of explosions but they seemed a long way off and gradually the exhausted guests at this improvised hotel fell asleep.

When Elizabeth awoke it was still dark; she saw her father sitting upright beside her, his eyes wide open. Her mother slept, leaning against him, Peter in her arms. Every so often she muttered something incoherently but, even when Elizabeth stood up, stretching her legs and working her ankles in an attempt to improve her circulation, she did not wake.

'Are you all right?' her father whispered.

'Yes fine, it's my feet, they've gone to sleep. What about you? Have you been awake all night?'

'Yes, most of the time. I did doze off for a bit earlier.'

'Daddy,' Elizabeth began.

Richard looked at his daughter; she had not called him Daddy since she was a little girl. His face was drawn and tired from lack of sleep.

'Daddy, I'm sorry but I'm not going with you.'

'What do you mean, not going with us?' Richard croaked, his agitation accentuated by the need to whisper and not disturb his wife and son.

'I'm going to go into Málaga. No, let me finish. Please Daddy. I want to see for myself what is happening. I want to photograph it, to make a record of what's going on. It has to be done and I need to do it.'

'But Elizabeth it's far too dangerous. You have to get out now, with us. It's impossible for you to stay.'

'I'll leave in a few days; I won't stay long, I promise you but I have to see for myself,' she repeated. 'This is important and I may not have another chance.'

'Elizabeth there will be lots of other chances but not here, I beg of you. You heard that madman on the radio. They have no respect for women or children. It's too dangerous. Look I know you're eager to get your career started but there'll be lots of opportunities for photographers in England. You don't need to stay here.'

Elizabeth did not reply, so Richard put his arm around her and squeezed her to him.

'I'm sorry Elizabeth, I just cannot allow it. You're coming to Gibraltar with us. Maybe when we're there we can find someone who can explain to you exactly what is going on here.'

'No, that's not how it works Daddy. I want to do this. I can't just run away now, the first minute there's a bit of fighting. I want to see what it is that's worth fighting for, what it is that's worth dying for. I want to understand why all those people have left their homes and are running away.'

'Your mother will be distraught; surely you don't want to cause her more grief,' he said, changing tack.

He hugged her tighter against him.

'I know Daddy but you can handle her; you can explain how I have to do this.'

'Why don't you two shut up. People are trying to sleep here,' a harsh whisper broke in.

'Look, if you must go, let me speak to Timothy first. Maybe he can arrange a lift for you into Málaga, and he can tell you if there are going to be any more ships.'

'All right but I want to leave as soon as it's light.'

Their whispers were becoming urgent now and the urgency was transferring itself to Margaret who began to moan quietly and turned restlessly away from her husband.

'I'll go and look for him now. Stay here until I get back. Look after them.'

He nodded towards Margaret and Peter and very slowly and gently disentangled himself from the sleeping figures and went in search of the Vice Consul. Elizabeth watched his retreating back in the half light of the room; dawn was approaching and already a silver line was forming along the horizon, tingeing the sky with the promise of a new day. She knew what Timothy would say; he would strengthen her father's belief that it was too dangerous for her to stay. Her father would return with reinforcements, his energy renewed to stop her from doing what she wanted. If forbidding her to leave failed to work, he would blackmail her into staying.

She could hear his arguments: think of your mother; it will break her heart if anything happens to you; she needs you to help her with Peter; she's not a strong woman; she's never been the same since Peter was born; you can't abandon her now when she needs you most. Then mother and Peter would wake up and her mother would cry and Peter would cling to her and say silly things in her ear and eventually Elizabeth would capitulate as she always did. They would take the ship to Gibraltar with these pretentious people, pass a few days in Gibraltar with them while they sipped their gins and tonics and discussed the progress of the war, offering ill-informed opinions on the routing of the Reds or the advance of the fascists. Then they would go back to England and forget all about it. No, she could not let that happen. It was not that she was not scared; she was. She was not by nature a very brave person but she was tenacious and she knew that she was about to witness something very important. She could not shut her eyes and pretend that it was not happening.

She pulled out a scrap of paper from her bag and scribbled a note to her father. If she was going to go, she had to leave now before he returned. She looked at the sleeping figures of her mother and brother; she would have liked to kiss them and hug them to her but that would risk waking them. She kissed her forefinger and placed it very lightly on Peter's head then, as quietly as she could, she dislodged her suitcase from the wall and hanging her camera around her neck, crept out of the room.

Dawn arrived suddenly in the south of Spain; one moment the sky was a swathe of black velvet, studded with stars then, within minutes, it had all changed. First the palest pink came creeping over the horizon and began to flood the sky, the colour deepening and becoming more intense until, at last, the great orange orb of the sun rose into sight. Then almost as quickly, the spectaculars over, it was day. By then she had left the International Club behind her and was walking along the coast road to Málaga. She would have liked Timothy to have organised some transport for her but she knew it would never have happened. Despite a night on the Club's hard floor she felt rested and strangely elated. She tried not to examine her feelings too closely; she knew that by now her parents would have realised that she had gone and she could imagine the scene. She did not want to dwell on it, better to press on ahead and decide on a plan of action.

CHAPTER 4

The cold morning light identified her travelling companions as two women of her own age, an elderly woman with straggly white hair and two small boys, twins that she guessed were about seven or eight-years old, although it was hard to be sure because they looked so thin and undernourished. Their clothes were little more than rags and she could see their skinny ribs quite easily through the numerous holes and tears in their shirts. One boy wore a pair of boots that were too large for him and the other boy was barefoot. She soon learnt that these were shared boots because at regular intervals the boys would stop and the one with the boots would remove them and give them to his brother to wear. They never spoke but their grave, brown eyes regarded Elizabeth with the same interest that people normally gave to rare and exotic creatures in a zoo. The women were dressed uniformly in black and walked, clutching their shawls around them to ward off the chill air that drifted in from the sea, a fine, grey mist that covered this silent procession in an ethereal blanket. The old woman struggled to keep up; she relied on a staff of polished olive wood to propel herself forward, each twisted step a Herculean labour.

'Have you come far?' Elizabeth asked them in Spanish.

'San Pedro,' the younger of the two women replied. 'We've been walking all night.'

Elizabeth would have liked to question them further about the journey and whether they had seen any troops but nobody seemed interested in talking. They needed all their energy to get them just those few kilometres further to Málaga where they could at last rest. She wondered why they had no possessions; other people carried bundles of clothing on their backs or pulled makeshift trolleys piled high with old pieces of furniture and cooking utensils; one or two people led donkeys, their panniers over-spilling with their own and their neighbours' belongings. Her companions seemed to have nothing more than the clothes they were wearing. She felt she ought to explain why she was there, walking beside them but the words she rehearsed in her head seemed empty and a little patronising. In the end she said nothing. The light was stronger now and she began to take some photographs. She thought this might provoke some reaction from her companions but only the two boys were interested and for the first time she saw them smile. They posed politely as she took their photograph then insisted she take a second one as soon as they had changed the boots over. They did not question her nor ask why she wanted their photographs, instead they walked one on each side of her, still not talking but including her in their companionable silence. Now each time they stopped for a boot change, she had to stop also.

The road drew them away from the sea which disappeared behind a forest of sugar cane. They were approaching the sugar factory; she could see that the red brick building had received a number of direct hits and most of it now lay under a heap of rubble. The air was sweet with the cloying smell of burning sugar; it made her empty stomach heave. They were close to the river; she hoped the bridge was still intact otherwise they would have to make a detour to the beach and wade through the muddy water of the estuary. She breathed a sigh of relief; the people ahead were crossing. The Guadalhorce river was wide and shallow at this point and its meandering course was a favourite breeding ground for many wildfowl; she spotted a heron, motionless on the bank, its gaze on the rippling water below. It was impervious to the rhythmic tramp of feet on the wooden bridge. They were approaching the city now; she could see the spires of the cathedral in the distance and the reddish stone of the Moorish fortress on the hill behind it. Not much further to the centre.

'We're almost there,' she told the women but they did not reply.

She had made a plan of action: she would head for the British Consulate first and find out the latest news; maybe they could advise her where to start. Then she would go to the Regina Hotel and book a room. She had been there on many occasions before but not to stay; usually she had gone there for lunch with her parents after a morning's shopping or sometimes on her own to meet up with friends. She knew that the hotel was popular with both Spanish businessmen and foreign visitors; if there were still any foreign correspondents in Málaga they would surely be based there.

The sight that greeted her eyes when she entered the city shocked and amazed her. All that she had seen from the hillside by her home, all that she had heard from Conception and the people at the International Club had not prepared her for the reality of the destruction that lay before her. The streets were piled high with rubble; the Customs House lay in ruins; there were huge craters in the road that caused the refugees to deviate from their route, breaking off and disappearing into the alleyways and back streets, each one seeking their own salvation. She watched the two little boys grab hold of their mother's skirt; they drifted away from her, eventually being swallowed up in the shadows of the city. What would become of them? She realised in that moment that she did not even know their names and felt a strong impulse to run after them but it was too late. They had gone. The column of refugees that had kept moving forward, relentlessly heading east looking for safety had instead reached another war zone. Now it spread out, dispersed, evaporated, absorbed itself into the streets of Málaga, a díaspora of new souls for the city. Elizabeth stopped, trying to orientate herself in this swirling mass of people; they were no longer orderly and quiet, moving as one towards their goal. Their disappointment was manifest in the shrieks and cries that followed. Instead of reaching safety they had stumbled into yet another scenario of the war; they were strangers in a strange city, not knowing where to turn, panic stricken. She must keep to her plan, she thought, fighting her way against the crowd and heading for Duquesa de Parcent and the British Consulate.

His Majesty's official representative in Málaga was no longer in residence. Mortar fire from the gunboats had breached diplomatic immunity and made an enormous hole in the front of the building. The offending shell had not exploded, so little damage had been done. She wondered if the consular staff had been inside when the shell hit. There was no sign of anyone about. Now she realised why the Vice Consul had been so insistent about them leaving as soon as possible. Did her father know about this? Would Timothy have told him? If she had waited for her father to come back with Timothy would they have told her? Would it have made any difference? She was not sure but it was true that she now felt a little less secure without the safety net of that government office beneath her. One thing was certain, if her father had known about it, it would have made convincing him even more difficult. She pulled out her camera and began to photograph the scene. The flagpole still stuck out from the front of the building, swaying gently and defying gravity but the flag had gone. Removed by a loyal British subject, she wondered, or blown to smithereens in the impact? Who was to know? Somehow seeing this bastion of the British ex-patriot community deserted did not upset her as much as she would have expected. After all, she thought, it would give them something else to talk about in Gibraltar.

She picked up her suitcase and set off in the direction of the Regina Hotel. Not for the first time that day she regretted bringing her suitcase with her; it was heavy and awkward and whenever she wanted to photograph something she had to stop and put it on the ground. Yet she could not throw it away; this was all she had, all her worldly possessions were now in this case. She clung to it as though it were her personal survival kit.

To reach the hotel Elizabeth had to navigate a maze of narrow passageways and back streets. Everywhere she looked there were signs of a heavy bombardment: rubble and broken glass littered the streets; barely extinguished fires continued to smoke, filling the air with the smell of burning and scattering their black ash over the city. It caught in her throat and settled on her hair. She walked past rows of shops, their windows smashed and empty. The streets were deserted but every so often she would see a heap of rags huddled in a doorway and a cough or a moan would tell her

71

that it contained life, or she would come across a couple of stray dogs scrabbling about in the rubble, looking for food. She crossed *Calle Cordoba* and turned into another side street which took her directly to the top of *Calle Larios*. She was in the red-light district now, close to the port but the street corners and doorways were empty; no scantily dressed women displayed their wares this morning. She was still heading east and would soon arrive at the hotel. The street was little more than an alley, narrow and cobbled. Despite the silence, or maybe because of it, Elizabeth felt nervous and quickened her pace; her footsteps bounced off the walls and echoed in the chill air as she hurried towards the pool of sunlight at the end of the alleyway. A sudden movement startled her; a skinny, black cat had jumped onto the pavement in front of her and stood, regarding her quizzically through its one green eye. Then, just as suddenly, it leapt up onto the window ledge of a nearby house and disappeared. Did that constitute good luck, she asked herself but with no real conviction. Elizabeth did not believe in lucky black cats, the number three, four-leaf clovers or anything else in the superstition line. She walked under ladders, lost no sleep if a mirror got broken and did not care if someone spilled the salt; she left her shoes on the table and stepped on cracks in the pavement. What happened next made her reconsider her scepticism.

She had almost reached the end of this interminable alleyway when she heard a faint cry. At first she thought it was another cat but the cry sounded so weak and pitiful that she paused and looked to see where it was coming from. She had stopped outside a shop; it was hard to see what kind of shop it was through the boarded-up windows and its entrance was hidden deep inside a dark porch. The sounds seemed to be coming from within this dark recess.   Cautiously she approached, peering into the gloom. She could just make out a pile of rubbish stacked against the barricaded door.   Once again she heard the cry; it sounded like an abandoned kitten and was coming from somewhere near her feet. She looked down, narrowly avoiding stepping on a tiny bundle of rags. She bent down to examine it, carefully dragging it out into the light and pulling back the covers. Lying inside a filthy, black shawl was, not a kitten but a baby. It was tightly wrapped in a white cloth and its eyes were open. At her touch it began to wail with renewed vigour. Elizabeth put down her suitcase and picked it up. The baby was very thin; it weighed almost nothing.   Its eyes protruded strangely from its head and its face was brown and wizened, like a tiny monkey. She held it in her hands and looked about her; she could see nobody that looked responsible for the child. In fact there was nobody to be seen at all. She touched its face gently with her forefinger; the baby's skin was soft and silky but very cold. She noticed how blue its lips were.   She stroked it gently for a few moments, automatically talking to it in the way countless women spoke to their babies, hushing it and reassuring it that all would be well, while her mind raced ahead wondering what to do next. The most important thing was to get the baby warm. She opened her case and took out the shawl that Conception had given her the previous day. How long ago it seemed now. She removed her coat and wrapped the shawl around her body, looping it over her right shoulder and under her left arm then she placed the baby on her breast and tied it securely in place. Next she replaced her coat and picked up her suitcase. The most logical step was to take the baby to the hotel; someone there would be able to look after it, she felt sure.   She set off, with a renewed purpose; she was responsible for this tiny life now and the sooner she could find it some help the better.

The area around the port seemed to have suffered some direct hits, whether from the ships she had seen firing the day before or from bombs she did not know but whatever it was it had left the area flattened and barely recognisable. She made her way across the square and into *Calle Larios*. Normally at this time of day this busy street would be humming with activity; it was the place the elegant men and women of Málaga came to do their shopping or drink coffee and eat sweet pastries in the pavement cafés; it was also the place where people liked to congregate, to walk up and down, chatting to their companions, greeting friends and generally passing a pleasant hour or so in the shade of its palm trees. Today it was a changed place. The devastation she had seen elsewhere seemed worse here; evidence of bonfires littered the main street and amongst the rubble she could see dead bodies. She walked carefully around them, trying not to look at the staring eyes and the blackened faces. But she had come here to record events so she forced herself to stop and photograph the scene. Some shops were boarded up, others, whose owners' had delayed safeguarding their property, had windows and doors smashed in. Unlike the indiscriminate destruction by mortars and bombs, here the attacks seemed to have been more selective. Some buildings had hardly received a scratch, whilst others were gutted and burned. She photographed it all.

Suddenly she heard the noise of a single engine aeroplane and dodged into an open doorway to shelter, clutching her new charge to her chest. She waited, trembling, expecting to hear an explosion and the splintering of glass but there was nothing. Instead, when she emerged from her refuge in the doorway and looked up at the sky she was momentarily confused; it seemed to be snowing. She looked again; they were too large for snowflakes, more like dying leaves wafting from side to side on their slow descent to earth. One landed by her feet; it was neither a snowflake nor a dead leaf but its contents were as cold as ice:

"MALGUEÑOS! You are surrounded. Your resistance is useless. It is only making things worse. Give up your leaders who have been deceiving you and surrender your arms. Come out with your hands up to meet my troops. This will be the only way to save the lives of all those who are not responsible for the heinous crimes that have been committed in Málaga.

You know my system: for every one of my men that falls, I will kill at least ten of yours, and those that run away, don't let them think that they will be free of me; I will pull them out from under the earth if needs be and if they are dead I will kill them again."

Bloody Queipo de Llano again, she thought; she could recognise his style. She placed one hand protectively on the child and with the other screwed the pamphlet into a ball and threw it angrily into the street. The fluttering leaflets had stopped falling and lay like a covering of giant snowflakes on top of the rubble. She looked around her nervously; there was no-one about so she continued on her way. Up until now she had seen no Republican soldiers, no *Guardia de Asalto* and only a handful of militiamen; all the civilians she had encountered scurried through the streets, heads down, eyes averted, clinging to the walls of the buildings for safety, darting from doorway to doorway like hunted animals. Málaga did not seem like a city about to defend itself; there seemed to be no organisation, no leadership. No-one was cleaning away the rubble that blocked the streets, nor burying the bodies that she had stepped over, nor helping the refugees that continued to arrive with their bundles of raggedy possessions. It was every man for himself.

She crossed the street and entered the small square where she knew the Regina Hotel should be. By now her only hope, the one thought that kept repeating itself in her head, was that the hotel was still standing. It was. Apart from the wooden planks nailed across the downstairs windows it did not look any different from when she had last visited it two years before. It was a tall narrow building, with elaborate wrought iron balconies on the second, third and fourth floors and the glass-plated front door was flanked by two orange trees in pots. She pushed the door open and went in; there was a strong smell of fried fish and stale cigarette smoke. No-one was behind the reception desk so she rang the bell on the counter and waited. A large notice on the wall informed her that she was "Requested not to talk politics." She waited for a few more minutes then, as it was obvious that no-one was going to appear, she went in search of the bar. Two men were stretched out on the floor of the passageway, sleeping. She stepped over them carefully and opened the door to the bar. Here at least things seemed normal: the air was thick with cigarette smoke and a cacophony of sound assailed her ears, loud brassy voices all speaking at once. She looked around the room, hoping to see someone she knew, or if not that, at least an English face. They had become aware of her now and all conversation stopped while face after face turned to look at the newcomer. Elizabeth felt the blood rush to her face.

'*Buenos días*,' she began. 'Can anybody help me?'

'Señorita Elizabeth, what are you doing here?'

It was Alberto; she could not believe her luck. Never had a face been so welcome. She felt as though he were an old friend.

'Alberto, oh it's so good to see you.'

'But why are you here? I thought you were leaving on the ship with your parents. What's happened?'

'I need your help. Look.'

She unbuttoned her coat and showed him the baby.

'I found this child abandoned in a doorway. The poor mite is starving. Is there any milk we could give it?'

Alberto laughed a hard, brittle laugh.

'No, *señorita*, there's no milk; there's no bread, no potatoes, no meat, nothing except fish and there's not much of that. Can the baby eat fried *boquerones*?'

'Nothing at all?'

A woman appeared at her side.

'We could give the poor little thing some warm water with sugar. I have a little sugar still. It's not very nourishing but it may stop it crying.'

She disappeared behind a bead curtain that hung across the doorway and a few minutes later reappeared with a jug of sugared water and a small spoon.

'Here, let me see the baby,' she said.

Elizabeth untied her shawl and un-wrapped the baby. The child was warm from her body heat but otherwise it looked as wizened and sad as before.

'Oh *el pobre niño*,' the woman said as she deftly took the child from Elizabeth and placed it in the crook of her arm.

Elizabeth watched as she began to spoon the sugar water into the child's mouth. Being so young the baby had not yet learnt to swallow and more liquid ran down onto its swaddling cloth than entered its mouth but nonetheless the child took on a more contented air and its feeble cries stopped.

'That's enough for now,' the woman declared. 'Now let's see if this child is in need of changing.'

She unwrapped the roll of cloth that had pinned the child's arms to its side and revealed the puny little body of a baby boy.

'This is soaking,' she said, holding up the cloth. 'Here hold him for a minute while I find something else.'

Elizabeth took the baby, holding him by his shoulders. He began to cry again.

'No, not like that,' Alberto said. 'Here hold him in your arms.'

Elizabeth held the child against her chest and began to croon the only lullaby she knew; it was one she remembered her mother singing to Peter. The child was so tiny; she could feel his heart beating against her chest, a small, regular pulse that told her he was alive and he wanted to survive. She had come to Málaga as an observer, a voyeur, an impartial recorder of history but finding the child had changed all that. Now she was part of it; she was responsible for this small life and she would do all she could to save it. She had never before felt such emotion well up within her, such a need to protect and defend this helpless infant. She stroked his head and gently rocked him in her arms until the woman returned.

'Oh give him to me. I'll sort him out,' she said, in a voice that spoke of years of experience with such a situation as this.

Reluctantly Elizabeth handed over her little charge.

'Don't worry,' Alberto whispered in her ear. 'Ana has had seven children. She knows what to do.'

'But what will become of him?' Elizabeth asked.

Alberto shrugged his shoulders but did not reply.

'What will become of him?' she repeated, this time addressing Ana.

'Who knows. It depends if he has the will to live or not. There are so many children wandering around this city, some abandoned, some lost; some will live and some will die. We can only do so much, the rest is in the hands of God.'

'God? What has God ever done for us?'

A strident female voice cut across the room. Elizabeth looked up to see a young woman come into the bar; she was strikingly beautiful and would have looked quite extraordinary in any situation but here it was because of the clothes she was wearing: blue workmen's overalls and a black cap perched on top of a mass of short, red hair. Her face was heart shaped, with high cheekbones that accentuated her large, brown eyes and her mouth, despite being devoid of lipstick was a perfect cupid's bow. She held up a clenched fist in greeting to the people in the room.

'Maria, thank God you're safe,' a young man who had been sitting with Alberto exclaimed, rushing over and putting his arms around her.

She shrugged him off.

'Don't thank God, Juanito, thank the *Guardia Civil* for being so bloody stupid.'

'How did you escape?' another man ventured to ask this Amazon.

'Well they had us surrounded. I thought we had had it, I can tell you, then their own stupid ship fired on the port and in the confusion we managed to get away.'

'Are the Nationalists in Málaga already?' Elizabeth asked in surprise.

'No, we're still in control but there are some *Guardia Civil* who have gone over to the other side,' answered the man Maria had referred to as Juanito.

He and Maria were looking at Elizabeth with interest.

'I'm sorry, how rude of me. Let me introduce you,' interrupted Alberto. 'May I present the Señorita Elizabeth. My brother-in-law worked for her family. *Señorita* this is my good friend Juan Francisco Gomez and this is Maria Gonzales.'

'Pleased to meet you Maria and you Juan,' Elizabeth replied, extending her hand.

Maria gave her a curt nod and a not unfriendly smile. Juan took her hand in his and raised it to just short of his lips.

'*Encantado*,' he replied.

Elizabeth was instantly charmed. She had never seen such a beautiful smile before; it lit up his whole face and seemed to say that he had been waiting all his life for this moment. His eyes were a deep brown, almost black and his long patrician's nose spoke of noble ancestry. His dark hair was long and untidy; she watched, fascinated as he repeatedly pushed it back from his forehead. He was the most handsome man she had ever seen. She felt a shiver of excitement and slowly, reluctantly dragged her attention away from him and back to the baby.

Ana had dressed the baby in an off-white dress made of coarse cotton and was re-wrapping him in Elizabeth's shawl.

'Here, you hold him until he goes to sleep,' she said, handing the baby to Elizabeth. 'I've got work to do.'

Elizabeth took the baby from her and, as though she had done it hundreds of times before, tucked him into the crook of her left arm. Only then did she remember that she had nowhere to stay that night.

'Ana, wait a minute.'

The woman stopped and turned towards her.

'Do you have any spare rooms? I need a room for a couple of nights.'

'A room? We've half of Málaga staying here. The only rooms we have are taken I'm afraid but you're welcome to stay here and sleep on the floor.'

She indicated, with a sweep of her arm, the people already making themselves comfortable on the floor amongst their bags and belongings.

'Oh, thank you. It's just that I was hoping for a bath and a good night's rest.'

The woman hooted with laughter.

'A bath? For goodness sake child, where do you think you are? We've barely got enough water to drink, never mind to bath in. And how do you think we could heat the water?'

The woman was glaring at her and saying something else but Elizabeth could not hear her; she felt strange, as though she had no strength in her legs, and her head felt hot. The room began to revolve slowly and she put out her hand to steady herself.

'I think I'm going to faint,' she said quietly. 'Someone take the baby, please.'

Strong hands gripped her shoulders and someone took the baby from her arms. She slid to the floor and sat there for a few moments until the room stopped spinning.

'Here drink this.'

It was Juan; he held a glass of water to her lips. She slipped it slowly, waiting for the blood to return to her brain.

'How do you feel now?'

'I'm fine really. It's probably just hunger.'

She realised she had eaten nothing since the cucumber sandwiches with her father. She dragged her suitcase closer and opened it; there was a bar of chocolate in there somewhere she knew. As she pulled it out and began to unwrap the silver foil, she became aware that she was being watched.

'Would you like some?' she asked Juan.

'No, no really. You eat it,' he said.

She took the bar and broke it into a number of small pieces.

'Please have a piece and you too Alberto,' she said offering them the chocolate.

The men made a polite show of not really wanting to eat her chocolate but when she pressed them for the third time, they readily gave in and accepted some. She watched them eat it: Alberto's went into his mouth and disappeared in record time but Juan nibbled his, savouring each tiny mouthful. The chocolate tasted good but did little to fill Elizabeth's empty stomach; she ate two small pieces and rewrapped the rest for later.

'Señorita Elizabeth, you've not explained what you're doing here. Where's your family? I hope nothing has happened to them.'

As Elizabeth related the events of the previous day and how she had decided to stay behind, she was aware of Juan watching her.

'So what did you expect to find?' he asked her.

'I don't know. I didn't expect to find such devastation, I know. I hadn't realised that Málaga had suffered so much.'

'Well you're a very brave lady but maybe a little foolish too,' Juan said. 'After all, this is not your war.'

'Not my war? No I suppose it isn't but then again there are lots of people out there who say it's not their war either but it doesn't stop people dropping bombs on them. What about this poor child?'

She held the child up in front of his face.

'Is it his war? What has he done to deserve to be abandoned in a shop doorway? Did he have a say in whether it was his war or not? Not everyone chooses to be caught up in a war but it doesn't stop it happening.'

'But what do you hope to achieve by being here?' he insisted.

Elizabeth did not want to admit that she did not know, that she had stayed behind on a whim, looking for adventure and the chance to take some interesting photographs. Until now she had not really thought about what was going on.

'I suppose I want the truth; I want to photograph the truth so that the world can see what is happening here.'

'The world?'

Maria had joined them, a glass of anise in her hand.

'What does the world care? Their idea of caring about Spain is to join hands and say we are staying out of it, them and their one-sided non-intervention pact.'

'What does she mean, non-intervention pact?' Elizabeth asked Juan.

'All the countries in Europe have formed a non-intervention committee.'

'So what does that mean exactly?'

'What does it mean?' Maria almost screamed at her. 'It means that they refuse to sell armaments to the legitimate government of this country so that it can defend itself. It means that Germany and Italy can break the agreement and send tanks, guns, aeroplanes, ships and even men to help the rebels but Britain and France sit by and do nothing.'

'But that's terrible,' Elizabeth said, thinking of the German flag she had seen on one of the ships lying off the coast and the rumours about Italian soldiers advancing from the north.

'Well luckily for us the Russians are not so scrupulous. They at least have sold us some guns,' Maria continued.

'Yes but for gold,' interrupted a young man in ragged trousers, who had been listening intently to their conversation.

'Maybe they have but we haven't seen any of them yet. There're none here,' Alberto complained. 'We've got no guns and no ammunition. How are we supposed to fight? With pitchforks?'

'Yes,' agreed the young man with the torn trousers. 'We came here to join the Militia and fight but we're still waiting for our orders.'

Elizabeth realised that Maria had a gun sticking out of the belt of her overalls.

'Is that a gun?' she asked her.

Maria pulled it out and began to wave it around the room.

'Yes but it's no bloody use without any bullets.'

'Maria's an anarchist. She's hoping for revolution but we keep telling her that we must win the war first then we can think about revolution.'

'It's the same thing. We need to free ourselves from the capitalist oppressors, take back our land, free the slaves.'

Maria was still waving the gun about, using it as a prop to emphasise her words. Elizabeth hoped that she had been telling the truth when she said it was unloaded. Maria seemed to be a little drunk; her words resounded around the room, hollow and false, as though she was reciting from a revolutionary pamphlet.

'The anarchists are animals,' Alberto whispered. 'They're as bad as the fascists. They've been using the conflict to get back at people they've grudges against, burning their shops and homes. When the bombing started they rounded up six hundred hostages and locked them in the prison ship in the harbour; every time there was an air raid they took some out and shot them in retaliation.'

'Yes,' agreed the young man. 'At first it was awful. People were frightened to go out in the streets, there were so many murders. In the end the Civil Governor said he would surrender the city if the killings did not stop. So now it has calmed down a lot.'

'Thank God. We can't be fighting amongst ourselves when we have an enemy to fight,' agreed Alberto.

'Pablo, *cariño*. What a welcome sight. Come in, come in. Let me get you a drop of anise.'

Ana's voice rang out across the bar. The object of her delight was an old man, as brown and gnarled as a piece of olive wood; he carried in his arms a pannier full of fish.

'*Buenas tardes* Ana. I thought you might like a few fresh fish. We were lucky last night, not a bad catch, mostly *boquerones but* there are also a few *calamari* and a couple of small *dorada*.'

Ana poured him a large measure of anise and then took the fish from him and disappeared into the kitchen. A few minutes later she came back with the empty pannier.

'Here you are Pablo.'

She gave the fisherman some money.

'At least now we've something to eat tonight.'

She picked up the bottle of anise.

'*Un trago mas*?'

'Just a drop, thanks.'

The fisherman pulled up a stool and sat down, sipping his glass of sweet, white anise. Elizabeth saw him searching for something in his pocket; eventually he pulled out the dog-end of a cigarette and lit it.

'So you managed to get out last night then?' Ana asked, smiling at him.

The arrival of the fish had put her in a good mood.

'Yes we just took out the small row-boat and kept close to the shore. Not such a good catch as in deeper water but safer. We rowed up towards Torre del Mar to get out of the range of the cruisers. They didn't see us.'

He seemed very pleased with himself for having outsmarted the gunboats.

The baby was beginning to feel heavy. Elizabeth looked around; she needed somewhere to sit down and rest.

'Excuse me. I must sit down for a bit,' she told Alberto.

'Here let me help you.'

Juan picked up her case and taking her by the arm, guided her to a table in the corner. She liked the touch of his hand and the closeness of his body. She turned her head towards him; his clothes smelled of the countryside, a mixture of dark earth and wild herbs. He saw her looking at him and smiled.

'Why don't you put the baby down?' he suggested.

She looked at the sleeping child.

'No, I don't want to wake him. It's all right now I'm sitting down.'

What was she going to do with this baby? If only she could find some food for him. He was not going to survive long on sugar water; he needed milk.

'*Señorita*, look what I've found. I'd forgotten it was there. It must have been from when my little Kiko was born.'

Ana came across, smiling broadly and carrying a glass feeding bottle with a rubber teat.

'I've put some more sugar water in it and it's slightly warm. Here see if he knows what to do with it.'

She thrust the bottle into Elizabeth's hand and waited expectantly. Elizabeth gently prised the baby's mouth open a little and pushed in the teat. At first the baby did nothing then gradually he pursed his lips around the teat and began to suck.

'See, it's the most natural thing in the world for him. Well now he's drinking. *Bravo pequeño.* Maybe you will survive after all,' Ana said, delightedly.

'If only we could find some milk for him,' Elizabeth said. 'Then he would have a better chance.'

'The only place that might have milk is the Caleta Palace,' suggested Juan.

'The hotel where all the pilots stay?' Ana asked.

'Yes. It's a long-shot but we could try. We could go tomorrow morning.'

'Tomorrow? Why can't we go now?'

'No, Señorita Isabel, it's too dangerous. It will be dark soon. You must stay here tonight with your friends.'

He pointed to Alberto and himself.

'Tomorrow I will take you there, I promise.'

She looked at the baby. The teat had fallen from his mouth; he was sleeping again.

'All right, tomorrow then.'

She stood the bottle on the table and wiped a tiny dribble of water from the baby's chin.

'Juan. Why do you call me Isabel?'

'Because it is the Spanish name for Elizabeth and it is a very beautiful name. And because it suits you,' he added.

He was smiling at her and so she smiled back. A smell of frying fish floated into the room and her stomach began to rumble in anticipation.

'Ana has started cooking the fish,' Alberto informed them. 'That means that tonight we will eat.'

Elizabeth leaned back on the chair and closed her eyes. Why was she here? She had chosen this; now she would have to live with it. She must have dozed off because the next thing she knew Juan was shaking her gently and there was a plate of fried fish on the table before her. The smell was delicious. She realised how very hungry she was.

'Here, eat it while it's still hot.'

'There's nothing quite so good as fish straight from the sea,' Alberto said, holding an anchovy by its tail and slowly lowering it into his mouth.

They ate in silence, savouring the salty, fresh taste of the fish; she had never enjoyed a meal so much. She realised she had not really known what it was to feel hungry before; food tasted so good when your stomach was completely empty. Afterwards she remained where she was, nursing the baby and watching Juan move around the room, talking to people. He seemed to know a lot of people, which she thought was strange if he had only just arrived from Puerta de la Miel with Alberto.

'Alberto,' she called him over to her.

'Yes, *señorita*.'

'Alberto, is Juan one of your friends from Puerta de la Miel?'

'No, I couldn't find my friends. I've asked for them everywhere. I think they may have already made their way to Almería, to the Republican headquarters.'

'And Juan? How do you know Juan?'

Alberto pulled his chair closer and leant towards her, conspiratorially.

'I met Juan some years ago when I came to Málaga with my father. My father was involved in a dispute over some land and he needed a solicitor. Juan was the solicitor's son; he was just a student then, helping his father with routine bits of paperwork. He was very kind and explained a lot of things to us before we went in to see his father. I don't think we would have understood what was happening, otherwise; his father used such big words and talked very quickly but because of Juan we were able to follow it quite well. Juan is a very nice man but...'

He lowered his voice even further so that Elizabeth had to strain to hear what he said next.

'But he doesn't want people to know.'

'To know what?'

'That he's from a very old family.'

'Gomez? I thought Gomez was a very common name.'

'Yes, it is. But Gomez is not his only name. His real name is Juan Francisco Gomez de la Luz de Montevideo Rodriguez.'

'So he's not a Republican?'

She wondered if he were a spy. It seemed unlikely but she needed to know.

'Yes of course he's a Republican. That's why he's with us now. But his family support the Nationalists; they have left Málaga and gone to stay in Seville, which, as you will have heard, is now under the control of the enemy. They think they will be safer there. They wanted Juan to go with them but he refused. Please do not say anything to anyone, Señorita Elizabeth; there're lots of crazy people here, they would take him out and shoot him.'

He looked nervously about him, frightened that someone might have overheard them.

'No, I won't say anything Alberto. Thank you for telling me.'

'Look, he's coming over now. Don't tell him I've told you.'

'No, don't worry.'

'Ah, still here. How do you feel now?'

'Much better now that my stomach's full,' she replied, rewarding his attention with a big smile.

'Ana is just brewing up some coffee. Would you like some?'

'Please.'

She was unsure why she merited so much attention from this extraordinary man but she was not about to complain. Her arm was stiff from holding the baby so she gently moved him to her other side. Her wristwatch said it was half past six. She could not see outside but she was sure it must be dark by now and it was beginning to feel colder. She carefully removed her shawl from the baby and strapped him against her body as before. It was a relief to have her arms free again. She stood up, stretching her legs and looked around the room. The fisherman still sat at the bar talking to some men; Alberto was arguing with the man with holes in his trousers and there was no sign of Maria. She saw Juan coming towards her with two cups of steaming, black coffee.

'Are you leaving?' he asked, a slight frown creasing his handsome brow.

'No, just stretching my legs. My, that coffee looks good.'

She took the cup from him; the smell, strong and pungent filled her nose and mouth before she could taste it.

'Careful. It's hot.'

It was hot, hot and strong and bitter but it was wonderful.

'I persuaded Ana to part with a little of her precious sugar,' he said, producing a small screw of paper.

'I'll keep that for the baby if you don't mind,' she said pocketing the precious parcel.

He smiled and sat down beside her.

The night passed all too quickly; he stayed by her side and they talked and talked. She told him about her family, their life in Spain, about their flight to Torre Molinos and the International Club. Then she talked about England and her time at university; she told him her dreams and ambitions, she bared her soul to him and told him things she had told no-one before. He listened and then he too told her about his family, how he loved his parents but could not understand them, how much it hurt him to be separated from them but how frustrated he felt when he was with them. He held her hand and stroked it gently; she leaned her head against his shoulder and for a short while they slept. By the time the pale dawn was creeping over the horizon and Ana was rattling the coffee cups Elizabeth was in love.

CHAPTER 5

They stood on the deck of the destroyer, a pathetic threesome, clinging together and looking back at the receding coast. Richard's emotions kept swinging from relief to despair. He should have stayed to look for her; he could read it in his wife's eyes each time she raised them from the rapidly disappearing mountains to his rain soaked face. He had suggested they go below and see if they could find somewhere to sit but she would not move from the rail. She clung to it as though, by letting go of this cold, bar of metal, she would be truly abandoning her daughter. The rain flattened his hair to his head and ran down his neck, soaking his shirt. Gently he adjusted the collar of his wife's coat, pulling it up under her wet hair and buttoning it around her neck. She did not move. She seemed transfixed by the calamity that had befallen them. Even Peter was quiet, subdued by his parents' grief. The boy moved closer to her, trying to shelter from the spray. She put her arm around him, protectively, automatically but her eyes never left the shore. The destroyer steamed onward, parallel to the coast but with each minute it took them farther and farther from Elizabeth; they would be in Gibraltar in less than an hour, he calculated.

'Darling, let's get out of this rain. Peter is getting soaked. He'll catch cold,' he added, hoping to distract her with this concern for their youngest child.

She turned and looked at him with vacant eyes. He put his hand on her arm and tried to steer her away from the rail. Still she clung there. Gently he prised her fingers from the rail and, at last, she let herself be led away. She did not look back.

He pushed a way through a group of bewildered people, who preferred to huddle together on the deck, wet and bedraggled, than enter into the bowels of the ship. A British sailor stood by the hatchway and when he saw them, opened the hatch so that they could enter. Richard climbed down first and stood waiting at the bottom for his family to descend. Peter had livened up at the prospect of seeing the inside of the destroyer and followed his father nimbly down the ladder. They waited for Margaret who, still in a trance, placed her foot on the top rung.

'It's all right Darling,' Richard said. 'I'm right behind you. Come on down.'

Gingerly she moved down into the dark space, one rung at a time. He took her hand and led her gently towards the mess hall, which was now packed with hapless refugees, wet and dishevelled, sitting amongst the few possessions they had been allowed to bring on board. Instantly he could hear the whining tones of Rosalind Harcourt-Smith, rising above the clamour like an angry mosquito.

'I think this is just disgraceful. We've been herded down here just like cattle. And nowhere to sit, I ask you; it's just frightful. Did you speak to the captain, Teddy? Did you tell him who we were?'

'Would you sooner be on deck in the rain?' her husband asked.

'I shall speak to the Governor about this, just as soon as we are in Gibraltar,' she continued. 'Have no doubt about that. After all we are British.'

She tried, unsuccessfully, to smooth the wrinkles out of her skirt before continuing.

'And no restaurant car. What are we supposed to eat, for God's sake?'

'Rosalind, it's a destroyer, not a cruise ship.'

'We still have to eat.'

'We'll be in Gibraltar soon, then you can eat. Just be grateful that we've got out of that God forsaken place.'

Richard thought she looked more dishevelled than when he had last seen her, at the International Club in Torre Molinos; the rain had caused her once immaculately waved hair to frizz and stray bits straggled, wet and lank down her face; a tear in one of her nylon stockings had sent an ugly ladder spiralling down her shapely calf but otherwise she was the same elegant Rosalind. Teddy appeared to have been drinking heavily; he sat with his chin on his chest and his large, red hands resting on his corpulent stomach. The only movement he made was when he lifted his head from time to time to answer his wife. Richard decided not to go across to greet them. It would have meant climbing over prostrate bodies, piles of suitcases and the extended legs of those people stretched out on the floor, trying to rest. Anyway he was not ready to listen to their platitudes about his misguided daughter. Instead he guided Margaret and Peter into a corner and they squeezed in beside the talkative Danes. The Danes, two men and a woman, nodded politely and moved their luggage to one side, then resumed talking to each other in their hard, guttural way.

'Dad do you think Willow is all right?' Peter asked anxiously.

'Oh I'm sure she is. She'll be much happier down there in the hold than she would up here with all these people.'

'What if she needs some water?'

'I'm sure they know how to look after a dog, Peter. Don't fuss.'

Margaret had settled herself on the floor with their knapsack behind her head and closed her eyes. He knew she was no more likely to sleep than he was; this was her way of signalling that she did not want to talk to him.

It had been dreadful that morning when she awoke to find Elizabeth gone; he had given her Elizabeth's note and recounted his conversation with his daughter, as calmly as he could, despite the turmoil that was racing through his own mind. At first she had said nothing, just looked from him to the note and back again, the tears running silently down her face then she had berated him for not stopping Elizabeth, for leaving their daughter alone while he went to talk to Timothy, for not waking her up, for not caring what happened to their daughter, for not staying put in their lovely home in the hills. She ranted on and on at him, all the while in a low, angry whisper so that she did not wake her neighbours. He had put his arms around her and muttered reassuring half-truths and eventually she had calmed down but then she had refused to speak. She locked herself inside her grief. If she could not scream and cry openly she would hold it back until the opportunity presented itself. And so she had remained.

'Dad.'

'Yes, Peter.'

'You know this is a "B" class destroyer, don't you?'

'No, old chap. What's that exactly?'

'Well they're pretty new; built in 1930. They have four 4.7 inch guns, two 2 pounder pompoms and eight 21 inch torpedoes. They're awesome. Do you think they'd let me have a look at the guns?'

'I doubt it very much, son. This is a war. They're not going to let young chaps like you crawl all over their guns. Anyway how do you know so much about this particular ship?'

'All the "B" class destroyers have the same specification. This one is called *HMS Bulldog* and I've got one just like it, *HMS Keith*. Don't you remember? You gave it to me last Christmas. It's terrific.'

'Oh yes. No, I'm sorry son, I don't actually remember but I'm pleased that you know so much about it. Maybe, when we dock in Gibraltar, we can ask the captain about the guns.'

'That would be jolly good, Dad.'

At least the excitement of being aboard a real destroyer had taken his mind off his sister. For not the first time that day Richard thought about his daughter and wondered what was happening to her. He realised that he did not really know her very well after all. It was hard to imagine that his sweet, even tempered little girl could be this reckless. What had happened to her at university? Where had she found the courage, because yes, he acknowledged that however foolhardy, it had required courage to do what she had done? What ideas had she formed? What was it that impelled her to risk her life in this way? She was so innocent. She did not know the horrors of war, like he did. In the last war too, people went eagerly into battle, seduced by the romance of fighting for one's country; they were soon disillusioned. He had tried to dissuade her but had he tried hard enough? The problem was that he had not realised how important it all was to her. He had not really listened to her, he knew that now; he had been too immersed in his own world, a world of medieval romance, a world divorced from reality. He felt a pang of despondency when he thought of his research, the books, wrapped in old newspapers and stored in the passage that Margaret had found, his endless notes and draft papers packed neatly in the wooden crate. Would he be able to continue his work in England? Did he want to? Somehow it no longer seemed relevant. They would not be returning to Spain any day soon, despite the reassurances that he had made to his wife.

When Elizabeth had tried to talk to him about her future he had silently labelled it a fad; his instincts said that it would soon pass and she would take up a real job, secretary or teacher, something more suitable for a woman than a newspaper photographer. How could she think that wandering about a war zone, alone and unprotected, was suitable work for a woman, for his daughter. If only he had taken the trouble to talk to her about it, then maybe, maybe this would not have happened. There might have been a way for her to fulfil her dreams without putting herself in so much danger. The thoughts continued to whirl around his head, each one a lash with which to whip himself. At last, exhausted from this mental self-flagellation, he dozed off.

'Dad, Dad, wake up.'

Peter was shaking him. He looked around; people were standing, stretching, gathering their belongings together and moving towards to door.

'We're coming into Gibraltar. I heard someone say we'll be docking any minute. Come on Dad.'

'All right son. All right.'

He turned towards Margaret. She was awake and already getting to her feet.

'Are you all right Darling? Here, let me take that bag.'

He took the knapsack from her and swung it over his shoulder, then he picked up the suitcase with one hand and took Peter by the other.

The queues outside the Governor's official residence stretched back down Main Street as far as Casemates Square and the soldiers of the Royal Gibraltar Regiment, who regularly guarded the entrance to this converted friary, were hard pressed to control the crowd of agitated ex-patriots. Richard led his wife and son to a rundown cafe in the square.

'Stay here and look after Peter, while I see what is happening,' he instructed Margaret. 'Order some tea or something. I won't be long. Here's some sterling.'

He handed her a pound note and some change.

'Stay with your mum, Peter, and keep an eye on the cases.'

'All right, Dad.'

Richard started to push his way through the crowd but soon realised that it was hopeless. Everyone was going the same way, wanting the same thing; there was nothing he could do but wait his turn with everyone else. He turned back to look at his wife; she was sitting calmly, drinking a cup of tea. Peter had a cream cake and was feeding crumbs to Willow, who appeared no worse for her hours of captivity in the hold. They were both tired. He turned back and looked up the street; the queue had not moved. It would take hours to reach the Governor's Office and by then there might be no available accommodation.   He abandoned the queue and walked back to his family.

'Well?' Margaret asked.

'It's going to take hours.   I've had another idea.   Why don't we look for somewhere to stay tonight and see what the situation is like tomorrow?'

'But everything will be full.'

'Not if we go now.   Come on, drink up that tea and let's go.'

'Do have some, Darling. You've had nothing since we left home,' Margaret said, swilling out the dregs from her cup and refilling it from the pot. 'It's a bit stewed but at least it's wet and warm.'

He took the cup, grateful, not so much for the tea but for the fact that his wife was behaving more like her old self. It was strong and acrid but he drank it down in one go. The caffeine revived him slightly and he picked up their luggage and together they set off back towards the border.

'Where are we going Dad?'

'I saw some guest houses on our way here, down by the harbour. Maybe one of them will have some vacancies.'

He took his wife's arm.

'Are you all right Margaret?'

She turned, a shadow of a smile on her strained face.

'I'm fine. Don't worry about me.'

It took no more than ten or fifteen minutes to reach the parade of Victorian town houses that he had noticed earlier. The first, newly painted and with chintz curtains at the window, was full, according to the large notice in the living room window. When they knocked at the second there was no reply.   It was not until they tried the last house in the terrace, with flaky paint on the door and neglected flower pots on the window sill, that they received an answer.

'Yes?'

A woman in her thirties, with a small boy clinging to her skirt and a baby in her arms, opened the door and peered at them.

'We're looking for a room for the night. There's just the three of us, and the dog.'

'You from Spain?'

She had a Liverpool accent.

'Yes. We've just arrived on HMS Bulldog.'

'I don't know. This is my mother-in-law's house. I'll have to ask her. How long is it for?'

'I don't know, a night, maybe two. It depends when we can get a ship to England.'

She peered at them again; the baby began to whimper.

'Wait there.'

She closed the door. Richard looked at his wife.

'Doesn't look very clean,' she said in a low voice.

'I know but it's only for a couple of nights. Has to be better than sleeping on the floor of the International Club, doesn't it?'

She smiled.

A few minutes passed, then the door opened again. This time it was a rotund woman, with grey, curly hair and rosy cheeks.

'How many nights is it then?' she asked.

'Well, like I said to your daughter-in-law, we're not sure, probably two or three.'

'You'll have to pay for a minimum of three,' she said. 'Cash up front.'

'That's fine,' Richard replied, taking out his wallet.

'It'll be three pounds.'

She stared, daring him to challenge her.

'Fine. May we see the room, please.'

She opened the door fully and they followed her into the hall and up a narrow staircase. Their room was at the front of the house, overlooking the street. It was sparsely furnished but surprisingly clean; there was a double bed, a wash stand with a Victorian style bowl and jug, a large mirror and a chest of drawers. An oil lamp stood on the chest of drawers.

'We have trouble with the electric sometimes,' she said, seeing Richard look at the lamp. 'I can put a cot in here for the boy. The dog will have to sleep in the shed.'

'That's all right; she won't mind.'

'The toilet's down the hall. There's no bathroom, I'm afraid but there's plenty of hot water. Just let me know and I'll bring it up to you.'

'It's fine.'

Richard took three notes from his wallet and gave them to the woman. It was extortion he knew but what else could he do. He did not want his family sleeping on the street.

'I'll go and get you some clean towels,' she said, tucking the money into her apron pocket. 'You just make yourselves at home.'

She stopped in the doorway.

'Would you be wanting your meals?'

'Yes please,' Peter said, before his parents had a chance to refuse.

Margaret smiled at him.

'Yes please,' she said.

'Lunch is at one, and supper at six o'clock.'

As soon as she was gone, Margaret threw herself on the bed and kicked off her shoes.

'Oh, this is heaven.'

'Well not quite heaven. Is the bed comfortable?'

'Sort of, a bit lumpy but not bad. Come and try it.'

He sat on the edge of the bed, beside his wife and held her hand. She seemed so fragile; losing Elizabeth had affected her deeply, he could see. Well, it was up to him to make sure they got home safely and then he would have to see what he could do about finding his daughter. But first his main priority was Margaret and Peter.

'Look Dad, I told you I had a model of a "B" class destroyer. It's this one.'

He had taken out a pack of cigarette cards and was spreading them out on the threadbare carpet.

'See, there are the twin funnels and that's the gun turret,' he said, holding out the card.

'I suppose we were standing about there, weren't we?' Richard said pointing to a place that approximated to their recent position.

His son gathered up the rest of the cigarette cards, shuffled them and started dealing them out like a pack of playing cards.

'We could play snap. I've got lots of doubles.'

'No son, not now. I'm going to head back to the Governor's Office to see what's happening.'

He looked at the cigarette cards.

'God, I could do with a fag, right now.'

'Have you none left?'

'No, I smoked the last one on the ship. You haven't got any, have you?'

She shook her head.

'Come on Peter, I'll play with you. Come and sit up here on the bed with me,' she said.

102

There was a knock at the door. It was the young woman with the baby, only this time she carried a pile of white towels in her arms.

'Here's yer towels. I'll bring the boy's bed up later, as soon as me husband gets back to help me.'

'Thank you.'

Richard took the towels and shut the door again. Then he poured some cold water into the bowl and splashed his face and neck, rubbing himself dry with one of the new towels.

'Right I'm off. If I'm not back by one o'clock, you go ahead and eat without me. All right?'

'All right, Darling. Take care now.'

Back outside he felt rejuvenated; there was no rain today, only low, grey cloud that sat atop the Rock like a coronet, and the air was fresh and clean. There was no smell of cordite, no dust clouds hanging in the sky, no threat of attack, just cool, fresh, sweet air. They were safe. All they had to do now was find a ship to take them home.

He walked back the way they had come and found that the queue had diminished considerably. Someone had been out, sifting and sorting through the refugees' papers and directing them to the appropriate authorities. He did not have to wait long before he saw Timothy striding down the line, notepad in hand and wearing his official smile.

'Timothy.'

'Richard, at last. I was wondering what had happened to you. You had me worried, old boy.'

'Just thought I'd get the family somewhere to stay for the night, first. I'm just on my way to the Governor's now.'

'Good thinking. You won't be going anywhere tonight, that's for sure. We've telegraphed London about the situation and they're sending out a ship straight away.'

'But that'll take days.   Aren't there any ships here that could take us?   There're plenty in the harbour; I've seen them.'

'They're needed here. With the current hostilities in Spain it would be suicide to reduce our fleet now by sending ships to England full of refugees. We have to wait. As I said, the Foreign and Commonwealth Office are well aware of the situation.'

'So what do we do now?'

'Well I need to get you on the manifesto, that's the first thing, then you wait until a ship arrives. Don't worry; I'm as anxious to get out of here as you are.'

'We're staying in a guest house just off Red Sands Road. Here I'll jot down the address for you.'

Timothy handed him the notepad and Richard wrote down the address of his temporary home.

'Any news of Elizabeth?'

'No, I thought you might have heard something.'

'We've got nobody in Málaga right now. They all came out on the same ship as you. If she makes it to Almería we might hear something. Still got a Consular chappie there, don't you know.'

'If you hear anything, anything at all, let me know Timothy. We are just so worried about her.'

'Of course old chap.'

He was back at the guest house in good time for lunch. He felt more relaxed than he had for some days; at last things seemed to be under control. He let himself in with the key that Mrs Underwood, the landlady, had given him and went straight to their room. Peter was stretched out on a truckle bed in the corner of the room, his cigarette cards strewn around him, fast asleep; his mouth hung open, redolent of the days when he was a baby, and his breath carried the sound of faint snores. Margaret had propped herself up on a pile of cushions, so that she could see better, and was carefully sketching her young son. When he saw her Richard felt as though a great weight had been lifted from his heart; if his wife had returned to her drawing, then she was feeling better. He flung a packet of cigarettes on the bed.

'Players. How wonderful.'

She put down her pad and pencil and picked up the packet.

'I haven't had an English cigarette in ages.'

She took one out and carefully placed it between her lips. Richard leant across and held out the lighter for her. She inhaled deeply, slowly, with a look of pure pleasure on her face.

'That's good. What about you? You're not having one?'

'Later. I had one while I was waiting in the queue.'

'How did you get on?'

'I saw Timothy.'

He saw a shadow pass across her face.

'Did he say if they had heard anything about Elizabeth?'

'No, he's heard nothing. But he did say there'd be a ship in a few days.'

'A few days?'

'We have to wait for one to come and get us.'

'From England? That'll take weeks.'

'No, from Malta. It should only take a day or so to get here and then we'll set off for home.'

He tried to sound as cheerful as he could but his wife was unconvinced. She returned to her sketching, the cigarette firmly clamped between her lips.

'Did you see the husband?'

'Mr Underwood? Yes. Pleasant enough chap, works for the Navy.'

There was the sound of a dinner gong being struck downstairs.

'Sounds as though lunch is ready.'

'Wake Peter up, will you, Darling, while I freshen up a bit,' Margaret said.

But Peter did not need waking; he was already stretching and looking around him in the dazed way that Richard recognised. He was still so young to be caught up in all this.

'Come on son, it's time for lunch.'

'Oh goody, time for grub,' the boy said, rolling off the bed and heading for the door.

'Hang on a minute, how about washing those hands first,' his mother told him.

Richard sat on the bed to wait for them.

'I saw Teddy in town.'

'Did you? Was he all right? How's Rosalind?'

'He was fine; moaning about the delay of course. Rosalind was at the hairdressers apparently.'

'At the hairdressers? I don't believe you.'

'It's true, she was. The manager of the hotel found one for her.'

'The town is full of refugees, all wondering where they will find something to eat and when they'll get home and Rosalind's at the hairdressers.'

'She said she couldn't go home looking like that, not in front of all those people.'

Margaret pulled a comb through her own tangled curls.

'Where are they staying?'

'The Rock Hotel.'

'Only the best for Rosalind.'

'He's invited us to dine with them tonight.'

'Oh God, I don't have anything to wear.'

'Of course you do. Wear your grey and white dress; you always look nice in that.'

She sighed.

'I only packed that at the last moment; Elizabeth said I would be all right with skirts and jumpers. She doesn't understand the etiquette of these dos.'

The memory of her daughter caused her to pause and look at her reflection in the mirror. She turned her head one way then the other.

'People say we're very alike,' she said. 'I can't see it myself.'

'Come on sweetheart, we don't want to keep Mrs Underwood waiting.'

Margaret had no alternative but to wear the grey and white dress; it was somewhat creased so she borrowed an iron from their landlady and pressed it as carefully as she could. The daughter-in-law brought them a jug of scalding water so that they could wash and by six o'clock they were all ready.

'Well don't we look smart,' Richard said, looking at their grouped reflection in the mirror.

'I can't see that we can do any better under the circumstances,' his wife added, looking not wholly convinced. 'At least it's not raining.'

The walk to the Rock Hotel took them almost twenty minutes. As soon as they arrived Richard went to the reception desk to ask for his friends.

'Mr Harcourt-Smith is waiting for you in the bar, Sir,' a liveried receptionist informed him. 'Just through there.'

Teddy and Rosalind were sitting at a glass table overlooking the Bay. Teddy wore his black evening suit and bow tie and Rosalind was wreathed in some concoction of pink tulle.

'Darlings, how lovely to see you.'

Richard tried not to look at his wife's face; he knew what she would be thinking.

'Rosalind, you're looking very smart,' he said, kissing her on the cheek. 'Teddy.'

'Hello old chap, glad you could make it. Margaret, my dear, how lovely you look. Come and sit here, next to me.'

'Teddy's booked our table for seven thirty. I thought you would probably not want to eat too late, what with all this bother going on. And the boy of course.'

She looked at Peter as if slightly astonished that they had brought him with them.

'Yes, I wasn't going to bother to dress for dinner tonight; just thought Rosie and I'd have something in our room but Rosie said no, we mustn't let standards slip, just because of a bit of fighting. Quite right ol' girl,' added Teddy.

He reached across and patted his wife's knee.

'So here we are. We were so lucky to get a room overlooking the harbour; the hotel's absolutely full. Well it's fairly new, you know and quite the place to stay. Of course Teddy had to speak to the manager but once he explained who we were, naturally there was no problem.'

'Drink?' Teddy asked.

'Gin and tonic please,' Richard replied.

'For me as well please, Teddy,' added Margaret.

'Three gin and tonics,' he told the waiter, who had been hovering for some time at Teddy's elbow. 'Rosalind?'

'Vermouth please, Darling.'

'And a sweet Vermouth.'

'Have you heard any news about the ship?' Richard asked.

'Probably the day after tomorrow. Coming up from Malta, according to Sir Reginald.'

'Teddy and I are going to just relax and enjoy ourselves until then,' Rosalind added. 'See a few old friends, do a bit of shopping, you know the sort of thing. The Carringtons have invited us over for lunch tomorrow. You remember them, don't you Margaret? William and Betty, they stayed with us last year. Well they have a wonderful place here. They wanted us to stay with them but I said no, much better to be in a hotel. We don't like to impose, you know.'

'If we're still here at the weekend, we'll all go to the Hounds. You'll enjoy that old boy, marvellous spectacle,' Teddy added.

'I do so hope we're not still here at the weekend,' Margaret said. 'I want to get my son back to England and safety as soon as I can.'

'Of course you do. Poor dear, and of course you must be so worried about your daughter. Have you had any news from her yet?' Rosalind asked.

Richard reached across and took Margaret's hand.

'No, nothing yet.'

'Oh my dear, children are such a responsibility. Some days I thank the Lord that Teddy and I never had any. I'm sure I don't know how I would have coped.'

'Well no need to worry about that now, ol' girl. Bit late for that sort of thing, eh, eh.'

'We're hoping that Timothy would have some news but he says there's nobody at the British Consulate now. They all left the same time as us,' Richard added.

'Of course they did. No option. They knew the city would be taken by the Nationalists sooner or later,' Teddy informed them. 'Latest news is that damned Civil Governor has run off and left everything. The whole city has been overrun.'

'Well maybe they'll impose some order on the place, now,' added Rosalind.

'Oh my God,' Margaret cried. 'What will happen to Elizabeth?'

'Don't worry Margaret, she'll be all right. She's very resourceful; I'm sure she'll be all right.'

Richard put his arm around his wife, who had started to weep large, silent tears. Teddy pulled out a large, freshly laundered handkerchief and began to mop his perspiring forehead.

'Look Marge ol' girl, I'm sorry. I wouldn't have said anything but I thought you knew the score. The city has been surrounded for days; bound to happen sometime.'

Rosalind sipped her Vermouth and waited for her friend to compose herself.

'They won't hurt Elizabeth; she's British,' she said.

'That's right; she'll be fine. She just needs to show her British passport and they'll treat her properly,' Teddy added.

'Would you like to order now, Sir?' the waiter asked.

Teddy looked at Richard and Margaret. Richard nodded.

'Yes, we'll go through now.'

Richard stood back to let Margaret and Peter follow the Harcourt-Smiths through to the dining room; he could not get Teddy's words out of his mind. If Málaga had fallen, where was his daughter now? Wherever she was, it could not be good. Was she one of those wretched refugees that they had seen trudging their way up from Estepona? He could not bear to think of it; he felt a wave of nausea sweep over him and for a moment was about to refuse his hosts' offer of dinner. Wherever she was, she was on the front line now; of that he was sure. He knew what that would be like and he also knew that a British passport meant very little in the heat of battle.

'Oh, Elizabeth,' he groaned, 'what have you done?'

CHAPTER 6

Elizabeth woke to the sound of church bells ringing. It was Sunday.

'Oh not again,' Ana complained, slamming down the coffee pot on the bar. 'Come on, let's go.'

Elizabeth felt Juan grab her arm and drag her towards the door.

'Come on, hurry. It's an air raid.'

'Where're we going?' she gasped, grabbing her coat and camera.

'Into the cellar, of course. Don't worry *cariño*, it'll soon be over.'

They followed the others down a flight of stone steps into a tiny room. It smelled cold and damp and she could see water dripping from the walls.

'I can't stay here. I have to get out,' she cried, pulling away from Juan.

For the first time she began to feel really frightened.

'No, you must stay Isabel. You can't go out there; it's too dangerous. You could get killed,' Juan said, trying to calm her.

'I can't breathe. I can't bear it. I'm sorry, I just have to get out. I can't breathe,' she repeated.

She was panicking now; the room was closing in on her and she felt as though a tight band was around her chest.

'Yes you can. Relax. Come on, take deep breaths, slowly now. That's it; breathe in slowly, through your mouth. Now let it out, slowly. Good girl, you can do it.'

He held her hands and pulled her close to him. She could feel the baby sandwiched between them. In the half-light she could see the people from the bar. The more experienced among them had brought their coffee with them and were sitting, drinking and chatting, unperturbed.

'What's happening?' she at last managed to ask.

She was beginning to feel embarrassed at causing so much fuss. Fine war correspondent she was, cowering in a cellar, whimpering about being claustrophobic.

'Don't worry, Isabel. We've had this every day now for weeks. They're German bombers.'

'Legion Condor,' a man next to them interrupted.

'They're trying to destroy our city,' a woman added.

'Yesterday fifty-two people were killed in a building off *Calle Nueva,* by one bomb. One bomb. Can you imagine that? It was over five hundred kilos. Dreadful,' an old man wedged up against Juan's back told her. 'Those poor souls never stood a chance. God help them.'

The enormity of the body count sent a chill down Elizabeth's spine.

'Do you think we're safe here? she whispered to Juan.

He shrugged.

'Who knows. We're safer here than in the street, that's for sure.'

They remained huddled together in the dark for almost an hour until at last they heard the church bells pealing the all-clear.

'Thank goodness.'

A sigh of relief rippled around the room and people began to relax; they chatted and even shared jokes as they climbed up the stone staircase; the danger had passed once again.

As soon as she was back in the bar, Elizabeth un-wrapped the baby and examined him. He was still alive but very quiet.

'It's not usual for a baby to be so quiet,' she told Juan. 'I must find him some food or he'll die.'

She pushed the bottle to his tiny lips, encouraging him to drink. The child took a few sucks then stopped, exhausted.

'He has no strength to suck, *el pobre pequeño,*' Ana said, looking over Elizabeth's shoulder. 'I don't think he is going to make it.'

'Oh Ana, don't you know anyone who would take him? Someone with a baby of their own for instance?'

The woman shook her head sadly.

'No, I'm sorry. Everyone is struggling to stay alive themselves. No-one wants to take on another mouth to feed, even a little one like that.'

'But he's so tiny and helpless.'

Elizabeth felt close to tears.

'Don't worry Isabel. I'll take you to the Caleta Palace. Maybe they will have something to spare.'

Elizabeth strapped the baby back to her chest and put on her coat.

'Ana, do you mind if I leave my suitcase here? I don't want to carry it around all day.'

'Of course. Here, put it behind the bar. No-one will take it from there.'

'Shall we go?' Elizabeth said, turning to Juan.

Outside nothing much had changed; the streets were quiet and a few people, like them, were emerging from cellars and shelters, blinking in the bright sunlight. However, as they walked northwards towards the Caleta Palace, they saw signs of more recent damage.

'This must have happened this morning,' Juan said. 'German bombs.'

A group of men were pulling at the rubble of an old house with their bare hands, looking for survivors.

'I don't think anyone could still be alive in there,' Juan said.

He tried to steer Elizabeth away from the ruin but, before he could do so, she saw a black-stockinged leg protruding from beneath a heavy, wooden door. Someone, probably an old woman, had not been able to get to the shelter in time.

'Wait. I want to photograph this,' she said.

As she focussed her camera on the rubble, she felt a wave of nausea hit her once again. The reality of what was happening was becoming clearer to her. It did not matter who was in the right, Nationalists or Republicans, innocent people were being killed here. She hugged the baby tighter to her body. If she could just save this one life it would be worth it.

As they continued up the street, Elizabeth could not get the image of the leg out of her mind. The stocking had been torn and the flesh below gleamed white and bloodless; the shoe was still in place, an old shoe, scuffed and worn down at the heel, moulded to the shape of an old woman's bunioned foot. It was an image detached from its owner, an image that she would show the world.

It was not far to the hotel, which stood in one corner of a large open square, untouched by the recent bombings.

Elizabeth pushed open the door and went straight into the restaurant.

'Do you have any milk for my baby?' she asked the first waiter she saw.

'I'm sorry *señora*. Are you a resident?'

'What's that to do with it? I need to buy some milk for this poor, starving child. Do you have any?'

She undid her coat and showed him the baby, who alerted by the angry sound of her voice, began to whimper.

'Well *señora*, it's just that we have very little of anything and I have been instructed to keep what we have for the guests.'

'In that case we'll take a room,' Juan said. 'I'll speak to reception; you sit here for a moment.'

He motioned her towards a table in the corner. Elizabeth sat down and un-strapped the baby from her chest. She wrapped him in her shawl and began to rock him gently but his cries did not stop. She started to cry, her tears dropping silently onto the child.

'*Señora*, would this do?'

The waiter had returned carrying a small jug. She looked inside it.

'It's goat's milk,' he explained.

Warm goat's milk, how wonderful.

'Thank you so much,' she said, pulling the glass bottle out of her pocket and filling it with the milk.

There was not much; in fact it did not quite fill the feeding bottle but it was enough. This time, when she pushed the teat into the baby's mouth, he began to suck strongly.

'Careful now, don't overdo it, you'll get wind,' she cautioned and wiped some dribbles of milk from his chin.

The child was still feeding happily when Juan returned.

'I've got a room,' he announced. 'And it has a bath. There is hot water once a day, first thing in the morning and we can have some breakfast.'

He looked very pleased with his news then he noticed the baby drinking and asked:

'Where did that come from?'

Elizabeth pointed to the waiter, who was now clearing away some plates from one of the tables.

'So shall I order some breakfast?' he asked her.

'What do you think.'

Juan spoke to the waiter and within minutes they had a pot of strong coffee, some rather solid-looking bread and a small flask of olive oil in front on them.

'What shall we do next?' Elizabeth asked a little shyly when they had finished eating.

'Would you like to see the room?' he asked. 'Then we can go back and pick up your suitcase.'

'Yes that would be a good idea. I need to clean the baby and it would be nice to put him down for a while.'

'There's just one thing,' he said, his voice dropping to a whisper. 'I told them we were married and that he was our baby. They would not let me go up to the room with you otherwise.'

She looked at him and smiled; the lie filled her with pleasure. Imagining him to be her husband seemed the most natural thing in the world.

The room was elaborately decorated with ornate brass ornaments and plush fabrics: two heavy oil lamps stood each side of a large, mahogany bed, which was draped with a thick, blue velvet bedspread the same colour as the curtains. The bath was simple: a white, enamelled, cast-iron tub with brass taps; it stood behind a Japanese screen at one end of the room.

'There's no toilet,' Elizabeth said.

'She said it's at the end of the passage,' he replied, walking over to the window and looking out.

They were on the fourth floor, overlooking the square. There were few people to be seen; everyone was avoiding the streets. He pulled the heavy curtains together, so that they almost closed but not quite; a single beam of light lit the room.

Elizabeth laid the baby on the bed and sat down beside him; his eyes were shut.

'Look why not leave him for now; it's a shame to wake him. You can clean him up later,' suggested Juan.

He pulled out a drawer from the chest of drawers.

'Let's make him a bed in here.'

Carefully Elizabeth moved the baby to the drawer. It was a relief to be free of him for a moment. She caught sight of her reflection in the mirror: her hair hung lankly onto her shoulders and her face looked strained.

'Oh God, what a mess. I'm going to have to have a wash, cold water or not.'

She felt Juan's hand on her shoulder, gently turning her to face him.

'You could never look a mess, Isabel,' he said. 'You are far too beautiful for that.'

'Juan,' she began.

He put his finger on her lips.

'Don't speak. Not yet.'

He leaned forward and kissed her on the mouth. She felt her lips part and kissed him back. The world seemed to shrink and concentrate on that small space between them.

The rest happened slowly, without haste. They were floating through a dream: they stood, not speaking, gently removing each other's clothes, piece by piece, savouring each moment, pausing to kiss each newly revealed secret. She ran her fingers down his chest, feeling the tautness of his muscles beneath the skin; she stroked his hair and let it slip through her fingers; she felt the firmness of his buttocks and a thrill ran down her spine; she closed her eyes in pleasure when his lips fastened on her breast. There was no hurry; they had so much to explore, so much to learn about each other. When at last they stood there naked, their clothes strewn at their feet, he lifted her in his arms and laid her on the bed. Elizabeth was not a virgin but neither was she very experienced in the art of lovemaking. She shivered, suddenly cold and nervous about what was about to happen but Juan was the perfect lover. He took his time; he wanted to please her, to explore her body in his own way, to teach her how to please him, to experience each sensation as if for the first time.

Later, when they lay side by side, soaked in each other's sweat, tired and happy, he turned to her and told her he loved her. She did not reply; she was too content to speak. As she lay there, tears filled her eyes and despite her happiness, she began to cry; his love had unlocked the fears and tensions of the previous few days and now they poured out of her, soaking her pillow.

'Are you all right?' he asked, tenderly stroking her hair.

'Wonderful,' she whispered. 'It's just that I'm so happy.'

He put his arm around her and hugged her to his chest. They lay there for a long time, not talking, dozing and waking and when they woke they turned to each other again, unable to satiate the longing they felt. At last, tired and sore, she sat up.

'We should go now. We can't stay here all day.'

'Why not?' he asked, pulling her down on top of him and kissing her breasts.

'Because ...' she said and rolled off him. 'We've got things to do.'

Juan's face became grave. She realised that for him too this had been an escape from reality. Now they had to face the rest of the day and the days to come. And what were they going to do with the baby?

'You're right. Come on let's see if there is any warm water left.'

He leapt out of bed and disappeared behind the screen.

By the time they arrived back at the Regina Hotel it was afternoon. Elizabeth had fed the baby the remainder of the milk and the child slept peacefully in its makeshift papoose. There were two foreigners at the bar, drinking coffee and sipping from large glasses of brandy.

'How did you get on?' Ana asked as soon as she saw them.

'Fine,' Elizabeth replied and told her about the goat's milk. 'I've got a room at the Caleta Palace for tonight,' she added.

'Good. I'm pleased.'

'Are you English?' one of the men at the bar asked.

'Yes. Are you?'

'Me? Hell no, I'm an American. Wilbur Ford at your service; Will to my friends.'

He made a mock bow.

Of course, how could she have thought for one minute that he was English, wearing those blue and white checked trousers. He was a stocky man in his early twenties, his hair

120

was neatly cut and, if it were not for being unshaven, he would have had the fresh, clean-cut appearance of the boy-next-door.

'Any relation to Henry Ford?' she asked with a smile.

'I wish. But no. However my friend here is from England, from Oxfordshire.'

He sounded the "d" in Oxfordshire. It made her want to laugh.

'How do you do?' his companion said.

He was a tall, lanky young man with blonde hair and deep blue eyes. He smiled pleasantly at her, revealing a row of uneven but very white teeth.

'Hello,' she replied, holding out her hand. 'My name is Elizabeth and this is my friend, Juan.'

'Pleased to meet you Elizabeth, and you too Juan. I'm Alex, Alex Reeves.'

He sounded slightly drunk. The men shook hands solemnly.

'So what are you doing here? I thought all the ex-pats had left,' Alex asked her.

Elizabeth gave them the shortened version of the last few days and then sat back to listen to their tale. It appeared that Wilbur was a journalist with the Washington Post; he had been in Valencia, where he had met Alex and they had travelled down by train together to see what was happening in Málaga.

'So what is happening?' Elizabeth asked.

'Well yesterday I drove along the coast road towards Marbella to visit the front line. Front line? It's a joke; there're no road blocks, just a wall of stones and a few militiamen with shovels. How do they hope to hold back the rebels with that? I asked their sergeant what they would do if the insurgents came and he just shrugged and said: "I'll take my men up into the Sierra."'

'So what defences do we have?' Juan asked, interested to have some first-hand news at last.

'Very little as far as I can see. They seem to consider it a sign of cowardice if they build any defences.'

'I met Colonel Villalba a few days ago; he's the new military commander of the militiamen. He's in charge of the entire southern sector,' offered the Englishman.

'What did he say?'

'He says he doesn't think the insurgents will attack Málaga. Despite the continuous bombing there's been no fighting at the front. He's convinced that they will just by-pass Málaga and head straight for Madrid.'

'Let's hope he's right,' Wilbur added. 'I could have died when he told you they have no ammo left. How can you fight a war with no ammo?'

'No ammo and no big guns. What with that and the rivalry between the Communists and the CNT, he hasn't got much chance of putting up any real defence.'

The men seemed tired; they were both in need of a bath and their eyes were bloodshot. They looked as though they had not slept in weeks.

'So are you a reporter too? Elizabeth asked Alex.

'Me? No, I'm not clever enough for that. I'm a mid-distance runner.'

'A runner? What do you mean, a runner?'

She was puzzled; running did not constitute a profession in her eyes.

'A runner, you know. I run races, the five thousand metres actually. Pretty good at it, too.'

'So why are you here?' Juan asked, also rather perplexed by this lanky young man.

'Good question. I've been asking myself the same thing. Well it's a long story but as I suppose you haven't got anywhere else to go this afternoon, I'll tell you it anyway.'

He took a drink of his brandy and began his tale:

'I belong to this athletics club, the Arlington Harriers, and last summer some members of our running team were selected to go to the Olympics in Berlin: a couple of hundred metre chaps, myself and a guy who runs a pretty fast marathon. But then, what with this Hitler chap and all those goings-on with the Nazis, our chairman decided we should boycott it; cancelled the whole show: plane tickets, hotel, everything. We were all pretty gutted, I can tell you. Months of training for nothing. Anyway, then I heard about the People's Olympics and I thought why not give it a try.'

He looked at them then, realising that they had no idea what he was talking about, explained:

'The People's Olympics was a protest version of the Olympic Games. I say "was" because that's been scuppered now as well. It was the new government in Spain, the Popular Front, that came up with the idea. They didn't like the thought of the Games being held in Berlin either, because of Hitler and all this fascist stuff, so they decided to host an alternative one in Barcelona. It was scheduled for July, just before the official Olympic Games. Well the idea really caught on and six thousand athletes entered, representatives of more than twenty countries; some were sponsored by left-wing groups, workers' associations and trade unions but some, like me, entered individually. It was going to be a terrific event: six days of sports, music, theatre, folk-dancing, a real international shin-dig. Then the Civil War broke out and it was cancelled. Some competitors never even made it to Barcelona because they shut the border immediately and most of those that had already arrived in Spain left in a hurry but there were a few of us, around two hundred idealistic souls, who decided to stay. We joined the International Brigade with the intention of fighting against the rebels.'

'You as well?'

'Yes, I stayed, obviously. I joined up with a group of militiamen in Barcelona but then we were transferred to Valencia to help there. It was such a bloody shambles; nobody knew what they were doing. There was no structure of command, no clear orders, no machine guns; the Navy seemed to be in the hands of the rebels and it was utter chaos. In the end I decided to leave. If I'd thought I'd have been of any use I would have stayed to help but I couldn't see the point of getting myself killed for nothing. It was ridiculous; we only had one rifle for every four men. There were no tanks and no aircraft. It was pointless to stay; I decided I'd be of more use reporting back to the British Government about what was actually happening here than dying anonymously in a ditch. So I headed for Gibraltar.'

Elizabeth was not sure she liked this man. Was he a coward or just being practical? He seemed to be trying to convince himself, as much as them, that his course of action had been the right one.

'So here we are,' Wilbur took up the story. 'I bumped into Alex on the train and we got talking.'

'What are your plans now?' Elizabeth asked, interested in his journalistic strategy.

'Well it's hard to tell. The place is falling apart. I can't get any copy out to my paper because all communication lines are down; I've been told I'm not welcome in the Nationalist zone because my paper is not right-wing enough. Then to cap it all my camera's been pinched. It's not easy to do my job right now.'

He lifted his glass and drank some more brandy.

'I've got a camera,' Elizabeth told him. 'In fact that's the real reason I'm still here; I want to make a photographic record of what I've seen.'

'Have you indeed.'

He pulled out his wallet and looked inside. It was full of American dollars.

'Would you like to sell it to me? I'll make it worth your while.'

She looked at him; his face was flushed from the brandy and he seemed unsteady on his feet.

'No, of course I wouldn't. I just told you why I'm here, to take photos. I can hardly do that without a camera, can I now?'

'Yes I know all that but this is more important than a few snaps of ruined buildings. I need a camera to chronicle the war. It's my job.'

'Well get one somewhere else. I need mine.'

She was incensed. Who was this arrogant man to belittle her attempts in this way? Did nobody take her seriously? She felt Juan's hand on her shoulder.

'*Cariño*. Don't let him bother you,' he whispered.

'All right, all right.'

The American held up his hands in mock surrender.

'Just an idea you know.'

'Well sorry but no,' she repeated.

'So is this little chap yours then?' Alex asked, changing the subject by pointing to the baby.

'No, I found him abandoned in the ruins. I wish I could find his mother; I'm getting really worried about him.'

'Not a good time for kids, that's for sure,' the American agreed.

'You know that all the consulates have shut up shop and sent their staff home?' Alex asked.

'I heard something to that effect. I know the British Consulate is empty because I came past it yesterday. Do you think we're the only Brits left?' she asked sadly.

Was it only yesterday she had arrived? It seemed a lifetime ago.

'No, there's that chap that lives on the Colmenar Road, Sir Philip somebody. I hear he's going to be appointed temporary Honorary Consul. He may be able to help you if you want to leave.'

'I'm not sure I'm ready to leave yet,' she replied, looking at Juan. 'I don't know what I'm going to do.'

'Well don't leave it too late.'

'I'm off tomorrow. I'm going to try to get through the Nationalist lines and get to Seville,' Wilbur said.

'Bit risky, isn't it?'

'Well I thought I'd say that I was a freelance journalist working for the Daily Mail in London. That should be right-wing enough for them, don't you think.'

He laughed and drank more brandy.

'But don't you need papers or something?' Elizabeth asked.

'I'll say they got stolen with my camera.'

They all laughed at his audacity and Alex ordered more brandies and coffee.

'One for you?' he asked Elizabeth.

'No thanks, we only came to collect my case. We're going back to the Caleta now.'

She saw them look at Juan, probably wondering what their relationship was but she did not enlighten them.

'What about you Alex? What will you do now?'

'I'm going to report to Colonel Villalba tomorrow and join his militiamen.'

'But I thought you said it was a useless fight? Weren't you on your way to Gibraltar?'

'Yes, I know but what else can I do? I'm here now. This lot are even more badly organised than that shower in Valencia but the thing is, here nobody seems to be worried. It's almost as if they expect to win just because they are in the right. They think because there are so many of them that that will be enough to overcome tanks, bombs and experienced African troops. They don't seem to realise that strength in numbers is not enough.'

'Well good luck to you,' she said, shaking his hand.

'And you. Good luck with those photos.'

'I'll send you a postcard from Seville,' Wilbur joked.

She smiled and turned to Juan.

'Shall we go?' she asked.

He nodded and picking up her case followed her out of the bar and into the street.

CHAPTER 7

For the next few days Juan and Elizabeth spent most of their time either sheltering from the air raids that seemed to be intensifying daily or lying together in the big, mahogany bed in the Caleta Palace Hotel. In the evenings they ventured out to a nearby bar, where Juan could talk to his friends and Elizabeth would sit, holding the baby and sipping sweet Málaga wine, while she watched and listened to her lover. When they were alone they talked of their past but neither spoke of the future.

'Tell me more about your family, Juan,' she asked him one afternoon, when they sat in the café bar of the hotel drinking coffee that tasted strongly of chicory.

'Well, my grandfather was a very wealthy landowner,' he began.

'Was?'

'Yes, he died last year. He was the "de la Luz de Montevideo" part of my name; it is a very old family that dates back to the *Conquistadores*. He owned a great deal of land, it stretched from Antequerra almost to Cordoba; he grew mostly cereals: wheat and corn but he also had acres of olive trees and a large olive oil factory in Estepa. At peak times he employed almost two hundred people.'

'So was he a good landowner?'

'He was just like the rest of them; his workers were not badly treated, not by local standards anyway but wages were low and they were only employed for two thirds of the year so the rest of the time they had to make do as well as they could, because there was no unemployment pay. There was a lot of resentment against the landowners because people worked hard but still could barely earn enough to survive, so a kind of rebellion started; it wasn't a movement against my grandfather alone, it was against all the big landowners. It was inevitable that it would happen sometime. Did you know that between them, one percent of the landowners owned over half of all the rural land in Spain, and what was left was only fit for grazing goats. There was too much wealth in too few hands. I'm not a Communist but even I could see the injustice of it.

I remember visiting my grandfather when I was a child; I would sometimes play with Natcho, the son of the man who looked after my grandfather's horses, and one day Natcho took me to his home. The workers' houses were all much the same. Natcho's house was a single room and in that room his whole family, his parents, his two brothers and his three sisters had to eat, sleep and live their lives. The floor was of dried clay and there were no windows or chimneys, only the one door for light and access. We went inside but the smoke from the fire made me cough and my eyes began to stream with tears. His mother had done what she could to keep it clean but nevertheless it stank of cooking oil and stale bodies. It could not have been more primitive.

Well as I said, the workers in the countryside were agitating for things to improve and at last the government decided to introduce a few reforms, nothing too drastic: they increased the weekly wage and they shortened the working day, then from sunrise to sunset, to a fixed eight hours for both men and women. But for some peasants it still wasn't enough; they wanted more, they wanted their own land, so the government began to introduce a programme of resettling peasants on land taken from the landowners. You can imagine how that went down. Some landowners, my grandfather included, refused to pay the increased wage and, instead of planting crops the next year, they turned their land over to pasture and got rid of their workers. My grandfather bought some sheep and instead of having to hire two hundred men, he hired just three shepherds. It was his way of saying that he was not going to be told what to do by the government.'

'What happened to the rest of his workers?'

'Well they were unemployed. Some men moved away looking for work and their families were left to fend for themselves; others tried to eke a living out of the poor soil and many just starved.'

'What about your father? Did he work on the farm too?' Elizabeth asked.

'No. My father has three brothers but it was the eldest who inherited the land when my grandfather died; I don't know what he intends to do with it. As you've probably gathered I don't have a lot to do with my family. My grandfather wanted my father to become a soldier but he was not interested; he became a solicitor. Another of his brothers bought some land in Seville and now breeds fighting bulls; the youngest brother is a doctor in Madrid.'

'Do they all support the rebels?' she asked.

'No, the youngest brother is a Republican too, like me. He's the only one I try to keep in touch with now.'

'So that's what this war is about, land disputes and agrarian reform?'

'Partly. There's been a lot of unrest for years now. Society in the countryside is still pretty feudal and people are tired of the fact that their lives and those of their families lie in the hands of the local landlord; things haven't changed for centuries. Sometimes it's hard to believe we are in the twentieth century.'

Elizabeth thought of the stability of her own home town in England. She had no idea what the local farm labourers were paid and had never been inside any of the neat little cottages that bordered the country lanes, although she had often admired their tiny gardens, where runner beans and potatoes grew alongside sweet peas and lupins. However they did not seem on the verge of revolution. Maybe the English were not revolutionary by nature; maybe their blood was too cold, she mused, or maybe it was just that they had passed that stage in their evolution.

She felt the baby stir and heard a faint cry.

'Juan I don't think the baby is very well. Come here a moment and listen to his chest.'

Juan bent over the tiny figure and placed his ear against the fragile body.

'He does sound a bit wheezy; there's a kind of whistle there. It's probably just a cold; keep him well wrapped up and we'll see how he is tomorrow.'

She held the baby against her; his head was hot and his breath was coming in short, sharp rasps. He finished off the milk she offered him and as she rocked him gently he fell asleep.

*

The next morning she was walking towards the harbour, intending to take some more photographs, when she saw Alex.

'Elizabeth. How are you?'

'I'm fine Alex. What about you? I thought you were going to join the Militia?' she asked, noticing that he still wore the dirty, white slacks and blue blazer that he had on when she first met him.

'I don't think that's going to happen. Things are deteriorating fast. I've just had a report that the rebels are about to attack from the north-west and,' he paused, 'and Quiepo de Llano is leading them.'

When she heard the general's name her heart seemed to stop.

'Well that's a name to make your blood run cold,' she said, trying to make light of her fears.

'Don't joke. You know as well as I do what that man is capable of doing. If they manage to break through they will be in the centre of the city in a couple of days. You should get out Elizabeth. Don't think that being English or being a woman will help you and that baby.'

'But where are the militia? she asked. 'Aren't they supposed to defend the city?'

'God knows. I've seen a few isolated groups of militiamen but no organised defence.'

Alex took hold of her arm.

'Think about it Elizabeth. I don't want to see you get hurt. Things are getting pretty serious now. Tell Juan what I've said.'

He smiled his strange, crooked smile, and walked away. She watched his retreating back for a few moments then decided to retrace her steps and wait for Juan in the hotel. Alex's words had unsettled her.

That night the baby's temperature rose; his body was hot and his breath came in even harsher rasps. By now Elizabeth was feeling very anxious; she sent Juan out into the deserted streets to look for a doctor. At around midnight he returned.

'I'm sorry Isabel. I can't find anyone to come out; they don't like to be on the streets at night. The best I could do was to get some sort of herbs from the old lady that's always sitting outside the Café Ingles, hoping for charity.'

Elizabeth knew whom he meant; she had seen the old beggar woman selling sprigs of rosemary and lavender each time she walked past the café.

Juan handed her a dirty screw of paper containing a few crushed plants; they smelled sweet and quite pleasant.

'What is it?'

'Some sort of arrowroot.'

'Are you sure it's all right for a baby?'

'She said it would be. We have to make a hot infusion using the whole plant and let it cool for a bit before we give it to him. She says it will bring down his temperature.'

'But she's just a dirty old beggar woman,' Elizabeth exclaimed. 'What does she know?'

'She's a gypsy,' Juan explained. 'The *gitanos* know more about herbs and plants than anyone. Anyway what else can we do for him? No doctor will come out tonight.'

She did as he instructed and once the infusion was cool she spooned some into the baby's mouth. He did not like it and pursed up his lips, refusing to drink, so she took a little of her precious sugar store and sweetened it. Only then would he accept some. Eventually, as the old gypsy had predicted,

133

his temperature began to come down but he continued to wheeze. He was very restless now and would not stop crying: a persistent wailing cry that tore at her heart. They took it turns to sleep while one of them paced the bedroom floor with the baby in their arms. At last the child fell into an exhausted sleep and Elizabeth was able to put him in his crib and climb in beside Juan.

The next morning the waiter told them that there was no food. He had managed to keep a little goat's milk for the baby but all he could offer them was coffee. They drank the weak coffee in silence then Elizabeth said she was going back to her room to feed the baby.

'Good. Stay there until I get back. I am going to see some friends; I need to know what's happening. Maybe I'll be able to find some food.'

'All right,' she replied.

Juan seemed very restless.

'But promise me you will stay here. Don't go out in the street.'

She nodded. He leaned across the table and kissed her.

'I love you, my little Isabela,' he said.

'I love you too Juan.'

Once he was out of the hotel, Juan slipped through the back streets and headed for the Colmenar Road; he kept close to the buildings, flitting like a shadow from doorway to doorway until he reached the city walls. He knew the house that Alex had mentioned, the one belonging to the old Englishman. It would take him at least half an hour to reach it.

'Hey you. What're you up to?'

A dark shape rose up before him, swaying wildly and blocking his path.

'Hey, Jaime, come and look at what we've got here. A bloody deserter, I reckon, off to join the fascists.'

He made to grab Juan by the collar but Juan was too quick for him and dodged down an alleyway. He knew there was no point trying to explain that they were probably both on the same side; there was no chance that they would believe him. Even though it was still early in the day, the man was obviously drunk and by the look of the heavy stick in his hand, dangerous as well.

'Come back here, you cowardly bastard. We'll show you what men are made of.'

The man was drunker than he looked if he thought Juan was going to respond to that invitation. Juan turned left at the end of the alley; he was not far from the Roman ruins, an area frequented by gypsies and vagabonds. He would have to go carefully. He ducked into a doorway and waited, listening for any sound of activity. The usual gypsy encampment was quiet and appeared to be deserted. Cautiously he made his way up the road towards the church; then he heard them. He turned back to the church and tried to open the door; it was locked. He crouched down in the corner of the porch, making himself as small as possible. There must have been about twenty youths, all armed in some way; one carried a rifle, another a pitchfork; most had thick staves of wood in their hands and one enterprising individual had made himself a lance out of sugarcane. The leader marched at the head of this band of vigilantes, a flaming torch held aloft. Juan held his breath, hoping that the church was not their target.

'We'll head for that old bastard Tomas's place first,' the leader said.

'Yes,' the others chorused.

Their feet tramped in unison, echoing through the deserted streets.

'I hope he's there,' one of the youths said. 'I want to see his miserable face when that precious bar of his goes up in flames.'

'Yeah. Thinks he can keep us out, does he,' said another. 'Fascist pig.'

Juan waited, motionless, pressed as deep into the shadows as he could manage but the gang were not interested in churches; they had a personal score to settle. They were so close he could see the recent scars on the leader's neck, barely disguised by his red kerchief but they did not look his way. He waited until they had turned the corner and were out of sight, then set off again, this time at a run.

He had soon left the city behind him and was striding along the now deserted Colmenar Road. From here on the journey was uphill, through dense woodland but although the morning was cold and damp, the climb invigorated him. He knew the house was not much further but he could see no sign of it. As he walked on his thoughts kept returning to Isabel; she would be worried why he was away so long. She might even think he had abandoned her. Well that was a small price to pay if he could get her out of here. At last he saw the big iron gates ahead of him; they were locked. He peered through the bars. The house looked empty, the doors closed and all the heavy, wooden shutters pulled down; a Union Jack fluttered from the flagpole in the garden. Juan grasped the iron bell and rang it as hard as he could. The sound rang out across the valley like an alarm.

'*Quien es?*' a harsh, country voice called.

'My name is Gomez. I've come to speak to Sir Philip about an English woman.'

There was a long pause then Juan saw the side door open and a man come out. He seemed very old and had a deformed leg, which he dragged, painfully, behind him as he walked towards the gate.

'You're to come in,' he said as he slid back the bolts and opened the gate. 'Follow me.'

Juan was led into a large, gloomy living room, where the imposing figure of the new Honorary Consul sat behind a mahogany desk. A rather faded photograph of King George V hung on the wall behind his head. Sir Philip Willington was a big man, with a florid complexion and a neatly trimmed moustache; he wore an immaculate white suit and a pink carnation in his buttonhole.

'Señor Gomez?'

'Sir Philip, please forgive this intrusion but I had to speak to you.'

He could not take his eyes off the pink carnation; how on earth had the man come by such a thing?

'Yes, well, what is it man?'

'My name is Don Juan Francisco Gomez de la Luz de Montevideo. I believe you know my father.'

The Honorary Consul peered at him intently.

'My God, so it is. You're Emilio's son; I can see the likeness now. Well I never. And how is your father?'

He got up and came round his desk to grasp Juan by the hand.

'My father is well, I think. He and my mother are in Seville. They went as soon as Seville fell to the *fascistas*.'

He saw the Honorary Consul frown at this reference to fascism.

137

'Ah. And you stayed here I take it?'

'Yes but that is not why I'm here. I don't want anything for myself. I need your help for a dear friend of mine, an Englishwoman.

'Come and sit down. I'll get Jesu to bring us some tea then you can tell me all about it. Jesu. Tea please.'

He turned to his guest.

'I have to apologise; I cannot offer you anything else but tea. There are only the two of us here now; I had to let the rest of the servants go. Well there's some gin if you care for it but maybe it's a bit early for that.'

'No, please, tea is fine. I have to hurry; the Englishwoman is waiting for me.'

'Very well then. How can I help?'

He explained as succinctly as he could how Elizabeth had come to be stranded in Málaga.

'There is talk of the city falling to the Nationalists any day; I don't think it will be safe for her here. I wanted to know if you could get her on a ship back to England.'

The man folded his hands carefully in front of him and did not speak for a minute or two.

'She's left it a bit late, old chap. There's no-one left here anymore. They've all gone. I sent my wife and family back to England as soon as I got wind of it. Safest place for them, you know. Look old chap, I'd like to help but I can't see how I can. The telephones are down; I can't even get through to Gib to see when there's another ship coming. I'm sorry, really I am.'

'But there must be something you could do for her. Her parents have already left; she's on her own.'

'Why didn't she go with them when she had the chance?'

'I don't know. I think they got separated,' he lied.

138

'Well I don't think she has any option but to stay put until it all quietens down, then we can see about getting her repatriated.'

'No, it's impossible for her to stay in Málaga; the city is in ruins. There's no food and hardly any water. It's dangerous enough now, what about when *El Tercio* arrives.'

'I'm sure the Legionnaires will know how to treat an Englishwoman. They are the most disciplined of troops and they have no quarrel with England, after all. Your friend will be perfectly safe. However if you are so worried, I suggest you bring her here and she can stay in this house until it all settles down.'

Juan drank the tea; it was hot but tasteless. He would have preferred a cup of strong, sweet coffee.

'Well thank you, Sir Philip. I have to go now.'

'What will you do? The Nationalist army will be here any day. They already have troops in Colmenar; that's barely half a day's march from here.'

'I don't know. I'll tell my friend what you said and maybe she'll take your advice and come and stay here.'

'Do that. Oh and give my best regards to your father. Fine chap, your father, one of the old school.'

'I will.'

Juan knew it was useless; Elizabeth would never agree to hide herself away in the Honorary Consul's house. He had to find out what was really happening; he would visit his friends and see if they had any more news.

It took him less than half and hour to get to the bombed building where he knew his friends were hiding. He checked that nobody was watching before he slipped under the wooden planks that supported the broken doorway and crawled into the building.

'Manolo,' he called. 'It's me, Juan.'

A figure emerged from the darkness.

'Come in. Pull the door shut before anyone sees you.'

His friend hugged him.

'Good to see you, Juan. Where have you been? We thought you'd gone with the others.

'How's the leg?' Juan asked.

His friend leaned heavily on a wooden stick, his right leg helpless.

'It's still here. Like me.'

'Have you heard what's happening? Is anyone coming to relieve the city?'

'Don't be mad. They're running like rats from a sinking ship. There's nobody left to defend the city. You should do the same. Head for Almería and join the Republican army while you still have time.'

'What about you? What are you going to do?' Juan asked.

'We'll do what we can. At least we'll die defending the city we love,' he said.

He had moved out of the gloom and now Juan could see the full extent of his injuries; the leg was completely smashed and a bone protruded from the flesh just below his knee. Someone had bandaged it after a fashion and put it in a rudimentary splint; the bandages were soaked with blood. He would never be able to walk to Almería on that leg; he probably couldn't walk more than a few steps.

'Where are Alvero and Felipe? Have they left you?'

'No, of course not. They've gone to see if they can find any food.'

Juan sat down next to his friend. The smell of rotting flesh was unbearable.

'Have you seen a doctor?' he asked, pointing to the leg.

140

'No. There's no point; it's past saving. Don't worry about me. You get away while you can. The army needs you.'

'I know but there's a complication.'

'How on earth can things get more complicated than they are?' his friend asked with a wry laugh.

'I've met a woman. I have her to think about her now and the baby.'

'Baby? That was quick work.'

Juan laughed.

'Not mine. A child that had been abandoned. Isabel is looking after it.'

'Isabel, nice name. Well, all the more reason for you to go as soon as possible. Get out of here and I mean soon. Nationalist troops are coming from the north-west and the north-east; your only escape is along the coast. That road is still clear and once you get to Almería you'll be all right.'

'Is there nothing I can do to help you, Manolo?'

He knew the answer but it pained him to leave his friend here facing certain death, if not from the fascists then from his poisoned wound.

'Nothing. Now go. Don't waste time on an old fool, like me.'

There was a noise at the entrance and instinctively they both moved back into the shadows; it was Felipe.

'Hello there, Juan. Come to join us?' he said, throwing a sack of potatoes on the table. 'That's all I could get.'

'Good work. At least we'll eat tonight.'

Nobody asked him where he had got them.

The man sat down beside them.

'Juan came to see if we had any news,' Manolo explained.

'An Italian convoy has been spotted in Colmenar,' Felipe told them. 'I wondered how long it would take them to get here; we've known that they were heading for Málaga for a some time.'

'So that's it then; the city is almost cut off. Your only way out is along the coast road. You need to go soon, Juan, you and your woman,' Manolo repeated.

'I know. Take care, Manolo.'

Juan bent down and hugged him then left. His words worried him; he had to get back to Isabel.

The child did not look at all well. Elizabeth had warmed the milk but he would not drink. She tried spooning some more of the infusion into his mouth but he was not interested. He was awake and for most of the time he lay there looking at her, the only sound that of his laboured breathing. Every so often he would screw up his little face and start to cry angrily. She was feeling desperate now; this was worse than the time Peter had the colic and she and her mother had been up all night with him. Now, like then, she had this terrible feeling of inadequacy; she did not know what to do to help him. She lay on the bed and tried to shut out the sound of his cries. There was a knock on the door.

'*Pase*,' she called, getting up and smoothing her skirt.

'*Señora, perdoname.*'

It was the waiter.

'It's about the baby. Is something the matter with him?' he asked.

'Yes, I think he's sick. Can you help? Do you know where I can find a doctor?' she said.

'I'm not sure *señora* but maybe I can help. I have lots of children of my own. Can I see him?'

She lifted the baby up and handed him to him.

'He's quiet now but sometimes he just screams and screams. I just don't know what to do.'

The waiter regarded the baby very solemnly.

'He is very sick *señora*. I think this baby has the bronchitis. I cannot help you with that. You must take him to a doctor. I am sorry.'

He handed the baby back to her.

'Can you find me a doctor? Is there one near here?'

'Yes, close by. I will go now to my cousin's house; their neighbour is a doctor. Maybe he will come if I ask him. It is not far. Do not worry *señora*, I will not be long.'

'Oh thank you so much.'

She wanted to hug him. At last someone was going to help her. She closed the door behind him and sat down on the bed, rocking the baby from side to side and singing softly to him.

The waiter was as good as his word and within half an hour there was another knock at the door.

'*Señora*, may I present Don Doctor Raphael Morales'

'Come in doctor. Thank goodness you're here.'

The doctor was a very serious man; he wore a dark suit and spectacles and carried a small, leather bag. He nodded at Elizabeth but did not smile. He took the baby from her arms and began to examine him. He took a stethoscope from his bag and listened to his chest; he opened the baby's mouth with a spatula and looked at his throat; he tucked a thermometer into the child's armpit and while he waited for it to register he asked Elizabeth whether the baby was eating all right. She waited patiently until he had completed his diagnosis.

'Well his temperature is fine but he is not a well baby,' the doctor said at last, rewrapping the child in his shawl and handing him back to Elizabeth.

He looked at her then asked:

'Are you English?'

'Yes.'

'And is this your baby?'

'No, he's not mine.'

She explained to the doctor how she had found him in a doorway.

'So you have no idea where he came from?'

'None.'

'And have you tried to find his parents?'

'Well not really. I have asked a few people but to be honest I didn't know how to go about it. Actually I have spent most of my time looking for food for him.'

'But what about the police' Why did you not go to the police?'

He was looking at her very suspiciously now. She did not reply; she did not know why she had not gone to the police straight away with the baby. At first everything had been so chaotic and then, later, she had not wanted to abandon him again. She felt her eyes pricking and struggled to keep back her tears; a wave of self pity stole over her. After all she had only been trying to help this child and now she was being accused of what? What was he insinuating, that she had stolen the child? She swallowed hard and said:

'Tell me about the baby. Is he going to be all right?'

'He has bronchitis; his lungs sound as though they contain a lot of fluid. It is a very dangerous condition for one so young and under-nourished.'

144

'Can you give me some medicine for him? I can pay you. I have money.'

'No, *señora*. I have no medicine. Just keep him warm, give him lots of fluids and pray to God.'

He picked up his bag then added:

'And when he is better take him to the police station and let the proper authorities take care of him.'

He gave her a curt nod and left. Almost immediately the door opened again. It was Juan. Thank God, she thought, throwing herself into her lover's arms and clinging to him. She felt his arms go round her, holding her to him, trying to calm her.

'It's all right, Isabel. It's all right,' he murmured, stroking her hair.

When she calmed down he sat her on the bed and said:

'Now tell me what has happened. Who was that who just left?'

'A doctor. The waiter went to get him.'

'So, what did he say?'

'Apart from telling me that I should have taken the baby to the police? He says he has bronchitis; he says to keep him warm and pray to God.'

She could not keep the bitterness from her voice.

'Oh my little Isabela, I am so sorry.'

Juan put his arm around her and pulled her to him. She began to cry again; she put her head on his shoulder and she cried. She cried for the child's innocence, for her own impotence and for the sheer injustice of it all.

'Maybe he'll pull through, *cariño*. He's a little fighter you know,' Juan said trying to comfort her but they both knew it was only words.

When she had calmed down and washed her face in cold water, Juan took her by the hand and said:

'Isabel, I have some bad news. My friends tell me that they have heard that a convoy of lorries is bringing Italian soldiers to the front. They are already in Colmenar. You cannot stay here now. You must leave right away.'

'How can I? The baby is too sick to move; I have to keep him warm,' she protested. 'And anyway, what about you? I'm not leaving without you.'

'Now Isabel, be reasonable. It's not safe for you here. There's no food. If you don't get shot, you will starve to death. You cannot stay.'

She could hear her father's voice agreeing with him. Everyone wanted her to leave.

'I could take you up to the Honorary Consul's house; he has said you could stay with him until things blow over. You'd be safe there.'

'You don't believe that, Juan. We're not safe anywhere in this city. No, I'm not going anywhere without you.'

'At least you and the baby would have something to eat.'

They argued for a while until, at last, Juan agreed that they would wait a few more days to see if the baby's condition improved and then they would leave together, no matter what. Hungry and tired, they curled up together on the bed and slept.

Elizabeth had been dreaming she was back in England, walking across a field with Willow; it was summer and the corn was ripe and ready for harvesting. She could hear the soaring song of skylarks and the sound of distant church bells.

'Isabel, wake up. It's an air-raid.'

146

Juan was shaking her and the sound of the church bells was now deafening. She grabbed up the baby and hurried down into the cellar below the hotel. Although this cellar was just as dark and damp as the one in the Regina, it was much larger, with high vaulted ceilings. She felt no untoward fear about joining the rest of the residents, huddled on the floor.

The bombing went on long into the night and when they were eventually able to return to their room it was almost morning. They freshened themselves a little with the cold water that was by now nothing more than a brown dribble from the bath tap and went in search of breakfast. Elizabeth's stomach ached from hunger and she could not get rid of the bitter taste of bile in her throat. Once again there was no food in the hotel, not even some milk for the baby. Elizabeth mixed the last of the sugar with some water and gave it to the baby to drink. He sucked at the teat then fell asleep again, too weak to even cry. She wrapped him in her shawl and tied him to her.

As they were about to leave the hotel the manager asked to speak to Juan. He led him into his office and closed the door. Elizabeth felt nervous; was this something to do with the baby? After a few minutes Juan returned. She looked at him expectantly.

'He wanted us to pay our bill now. He says everyone is leaving; I think he was frightened we would run off without paying.'

'I've got some money,' Elizabeth said, reaching into her coat pocket.

'No, there's no need. I've already paid. Anyway here in Spain a lady always allows the gentleman to pay for everything.'

She smiled; she did not feel like a lady.

'What about tonight?'

'I've paid for that as well, *cariño*.'

They walked out into the square. Most of the bombs seemed to have landed in the area nearest the port and the destruction was widespread. The air was filled with dust and the smell of cordite. They headed for the Café Ingles but it was closed and the windows boarded up.

'Let's try the Regina. Maybe Ana will have some fish,' Elizabeth suggested.

She was beginning to feel trapped in this city. It was all very well for everyone to tell her she must leave but where could she go? There were no boats going to Gibraltar now. Instinctively she grabbed Juan's hand. As though he could read her fears he said:

'Don't worry Isabel. Tomorrow we will head east. We'll try to get to Almería. My friends tell me that it's still in Republican hands; we'll be safe there. Then we can look for a boat to get you to England.'

She shook her head.

'I'm not leaving you Juan.'

'Fine. One step at a time. First we must get out of Málaga.'

'But Almería is miles away.'

'I know but we'll try to get a lift from someone, maybe in a lorry. Don't worry *cariño*, it will be all right.'

Elizabeth said nothing. She was worried; and it certainly did not feel as if everything would be all right.

When they arrived at the Regina, Alex was in the bar talking to a man they did not recognise. The man wore a ragged uniform and a black cap with the insignia of the Militia on it.

'Alex,' Juan said, grasping his hand. '*Buenos días*. How good to see you but what are you doing here?'

'I could ask you the same. I thought you'd both be gone by now. Didn't Elizabeth give you the news?'

They both looked at Elizabeth. She shrugged.

'I didn't want to worry you, Juan.'

'What news?'

'The rebels are attacking from the north-west.'

'I know that already and there are Italian troops on the road into the city. They'll be here any day,' replied Juan.

'That's not the worst of it,' the militiaman interrupted. 'All lines of communication are down, there's no electricity and the Civil Governor has abandoned the city. He flew to Valencia this morning, leaving the citizens of Málaga to their fate.'

'My God.'

Juan looked at Elizabeth.

'It is time to move. We can't delay any longer.'

'All right, we'll go tonight,' she whispered.

'I'm coming with you,' Alex said. 'There's safety in numbers.'

'All right, we'll come here as soon as it's dark. Bring as little as possible.'

He turned to the militiaman.

'What about you?' he asked.

'I don't know. I want to stay and fight but I haven't seen an officer in days. No-one in my platoon has the foggiest idea what to do.'

He coughed and turned away to spit on the floor.

'How's the baby?' Alex asked Elizabeth.

'Sleeping for the moment, thank goodness,' she replied, touching the bundle, protectively.

Ana appeared from behind the bar; she looked tired.

'*Hola, señorita. Cómo está usted*?' she asked, coming up to Elizabeth and kissing her on both cheeks.

'I'm fine Ana, and you?

The woman shrugged.

Elizabeth dropped her voice to a whisper:

'But the baby is not well; he has bronchitis.'

Ana let out a cry of anguish; to her bronchitis was a death sentence.

'Hush, don't wake him; he needs to sleep,' Elizabeth said.

'Oh, *el pobre niño, el pobre pequeño*,' Ana continued to cry. 'I will pray to God for him; I will say a dozen "Hail Marys" for him. Oh, *el pobre pequeño*.'

'Ana, is there anything to eat? Anything at all?' Juan asked.

'No, I'm sorry, there's nothing. We've had nothing since Thursday when Pablo brought us some more fish. Now we hear that his boat has been sunk.'

She shook her head.

'These are awful times, *señorita*.'

'What about something to drink?'

'Here have a glass of anise; it's full of sugar and it will warm you up.'

She poured out two glasses of the white, sticky liqueur and handed them to them. Elizabeth drank hers down in a single gulp, grateful to put something into her stomach. The taste reminded her of the aniseed balls she used to suck as a child, holding them in her mouth and rolling them around her tongue until the sugar coating had dissolved, leaving only the tiny seed of aniseed. The alcohol was quick to reach her brain and she giggled.

'I think this must be a bad dream and I am about to wake up any minute,' she said.

'It's no dream, Isabela but maybe it will soon be just a bad memory,' Juan said taking her hand in his. 'Come on, let's see if we can find some food elsewhere.'

He turned to the Englishman.

'Tonight then, Alex. We'll meet you here at about six o'clock.'

'All right, Juan. I'll be here.'

The two men clasped hands. Then Juan turned to the militiaman.

'Good luck and take care.'

He could see the soldier had no rifle.

Juan and Elizabeth tried a few more cafés but there was no food anywhere; everyone had the same tale: no supplies had been able to get into the city for days.

'Why don't we just go back to the hotel and rest?' suggested Elizabeth. 'We'll have a long way to go tonight.'

'You're right. We'll do that.'

At six o'clock they awoke; it was already beginning to get dark. The baby had not disturbed them once, so they both felt refreshed from their sleep. Elizabeth pulled her suitcase out from under the bed.

'I don't think it's a good idea to take your case,' Juan said. 'We're going to have to walk a long way; it will only weigh us down. Take what you need and leave the rest.'

Elizabeth looked at her meagre belongings with dismay; what to leave and what to take? She thought of her mother trying to decide what to leave behind. Unlike her she had no safe place to leave her things; she must take the essentials and throw the rest away. At last she settled on filling a shoulder bag with a few necessary items such as her toothbrush, her passport, some English money and some pesetas, a small square of soap and some spare knickers. She dressed carefully, putting on an extra layer of everything; at least she would be warm tonight. Reluctantly she pushed the rest of her belongings into the case and shut it. She would take her camera and the film but her notepad and diary she abandoned. Somehow she did not think she would have any difficulty in remembering the events of the last few days.

'That's done,' she said. 'Now I'll get the baby ready.'

She went to lift him from his makeshift crib; he seemed to be sleeping. She picked him up gently, trying not to wake him but his little body felt cold and rigid; her stomach turned over.

'Juan, something's wrong with the baby,' she cried in dismay.

She put her hand on his face; it was like ice. She shook him very gently, all the time talking to him in the soft, baby-talk she kept just for him but he did not open his eyes so she began to massage his little arms and legs. There was no response. A feeling of hopelessness overwhelmed her and she turned to Juan with tears running down her cheeks.

'Juan, Juan what is it?' she cried looking at him in desperation.

Juan took the child from her and placed his head against the baby's chest. He looked up at her and shook his head sadly.

'Isabela, I'm so sorry but the poor little boy has died. It's all been too much for him.'

A wail of anguish rose from her stomach. It was too much. This poor child had never had a chance. Elizabeth took the baby back and clasped him to her breast. She could not speak for the weight of the sorrow that pressed down on her; she felt an infinite sadness for this tiny life that had chosen such a bad time to make its entry into the world. He had been doomed from the start; in her heart she had always known that it had only been a matter of time but none of that eased the pain that she felt right then as she held his thin, dead body in her arms. Her tears ran down onto the child's face, bathing him in her love. Gently she wiped them away.

'What do we do now, Juan?' she managed to ask at last.

'We can't take him with us, Isabel. The best thing to do is to leave him here; someone in the hotel will find him and arrange for him to be buried.'

'But we can't do that. We can't just leave him.'

'Don't be silly, what else can we do? There's no way we can bury him here in the city. Do you want to end up having to dump him in the street?'

Elizabeth began to cry even more. It was not right to just leave him but what else could they do? She watched as Juan straightened the covers on their bed.

'Here lay him in the middle. Tomorrow the maid will find him and take care of it all. I promise you.'

She laid the baby down and straightened his dress, then she carefully wrapped him in her shawl before putting him on the bed.

'Won't you need that shawl?' Juan asked quietly.

'No, I want him to have it.'

She stroked the cold forehead, then leant down and kissed him.

'Goodbye little one.'

Tears still running down her face, she turned to Juan and said despairingly:

'I don't even know if he had a name.'

'Well you can give him a name now. Give him a Spanish name.'

'No, it's too late now. God has taken him, God can give him a name,' she said angrily.

It was so unfair that this innocent child should die with no-one to mourn him. She had tried to help him but in the end her efforts had been useless.

Juan took something from his pocket and placed it on top of the child; it was a silver crucifix.

'They'll think he's been baptised now,' he explained.

'I thought you didn't believe in the church anymore,' she said.

'I don't, not really. My sister gave me the cross when they left. She was very upset that I wasn't going with them; she and my mother cried and begged me to go but I was very stubborn. I wouldn't leave. My mother said I'd be killed if I stayed. I told her it was more likely I'd be shot if I went with them and then I'd be putting them in danger too. In the end my father dragged them away but not before Lucy ran back to me and gave me this cross. "It will protect you Juanito," she said. "God will look after you." So maybe now, God will look after this poor child instead.'

'Thank you Juan,' she said, kissing him.

'Isabel, it's time to go. Come on.'

'Yes Juan, I'm ready.'

She wiped her tears away with her handkerchief and took one last look at the dead child lying on the bed.

CHAPTER 8

The journey back to England was slow and uncomfortable. The ship from Malta had arrived on the Saturday morning, scuppering the Harcourt-Smith's plans to go to the Calpe Hounds. Richard had collected their boarding pass from Timothy and at six o'clock he, Margaret, Peter and Willow were standing on the crowded dock waiting to board.

'Do you think we'll get on? Doesn't look as though there's a lot of space for all these people,' Margaret said.

'It's not as big as the other one, Mum but this one's a cruiser. There'll be a lot more space inside. It looks a bit old though,' Peter told her.

'At least it's a ship and it's going to take us home. I don't care how old it is,' Richard replied.

Peter stretched himself to his full four feet nine inches in an effort to read the name on the side of the ship.

'What's it called Dad?'

'Arethusa, I think.'

'Oh yes, that's it. '

Peter rummaged in his haversack and pulled out his cigarette cards.

'Look, here, it is. *HMS Arethusa*, built in 1933. It's terrific.'

His parents were not listening to him. The gangplank was being lowered and the crowd surged forward in anticipation. They recognised many of the people that had been on *HMS Bulldog.*

'Put that away for now, Peter and give me your hand.'

'Don't let go of him Richard.'

'Keep close together now, we'll try and get through over there; there seems to be a gap.'

Margaret carried Willow under one arm and with her free hand grabbed hold of Richard's jacket; the three of them edged their way forward, through the throng of people that pushed and shoved their way towards the ship. Everyone was desperate to be the first aboard.

'Stand your ground,' Richard instructed his family, as one burly man attempted to shove Margaret to one side.

'I'm trying to.'

'Dad, I'm squashed. I can't see anything.'

'Hold on Peter; we'll be aboard any minute. I can see the gangplank; it's not far. Just keep tight hold of my hand, old chap.'

'You're hurting me.'

'Sorry son. Just hang on there.'

The noise was deafening; the evacuees shouted to their families, instructing them to keep together, children were crying, dogs barked, a seaman attempted to bellow instructions at them through a megaphone, and periodically, as though that was not enough, the ship's siren was sounded. Richard felt he was at the gateway to hell; he pushed himself forward, dragging his family behind him. At last they reached the gangplank and were permitted aboard. Two sailors directed them down a stairwell into an open area that was fast filling up with evacuees. It stank of cigarette smoke and body odour.

'Oh Good Lord, this is frightful. Richard, did you get us a cabin?'

'No, I'm afraid not. It was impossible. This isn't a cruise ship you know, Margaret. If we'd waited for a cruise ship we'd have had to wait until 3rd March. I didn't think you'd want to do that now. '

'No, I suppose not. It's just .....'

Her voice tailed off.

'We're jolly lucky that this ship was on its way back to England, otherwise we'd be stuck here even longer.'

Richard instantly regretted his sharp tone; his wife looked so despondent.

'Look Darling, it won't be for long. Let's just try and make the best of it. We'll get ourselves a comfortable spot to sit down.'

He looked around him; the room was almost full.

'Dad, there's some chairs over in that corner.'

'Well spotted young fellow. Right let's get ourselves over there.'

He followed his son to a stack of deckchairs and pulled out three, which he set up in a row against the wall.

'Perfect. We'll be as snug as bugs in a rug. Good lad.'

Peter settled himself down straight away and brought out his cigarette cards again.

'Want a game Dad?'

'Later Peter. There'll be plenty of time to play cards. I think I'll just see what's what first. We need to find out what to do with Willow.'

'Oh can't she stay with us? Please Dad. She's really quiet. I bet she's frightened.'

The dog was curled up on his lap, looking very subdued.

'I can't see how, old chap. What about when she wants to go to the toilet? No, I think she'll probably have to go below again.'

'Well you could always ask.'

'All right, I'll ask someone. I'll leave her here for now but keep a close eye on her, mind.'

He turned to his wife, who was leaning back in the deckchair, her eyes closed.

'Will you be all right here for now, Margaret?' he asked.

'Fine. See if you can get me some water will you. I seem to have developed a cold; I can't stop coughing.'

'I'll be back in a minute.'

The first person he met was Teddy Harcourt-Smith. He was standing on deck, smoking a cigarette and leaning on the rail that looked back towards land. The ship was slowly edging away from the harbour, swinging out of the Bay of Algeciras into the Straits and heading towards the Atlantic. The rock that was Gibraltar stood, isolated and proud, against a sky that was changing rapidly from shades of deep purple to a blushing pink. As the sun rose, the sky above them flooded with light.

'Red sky at night, shepherd's delight; red sky in the morning, sailor's warning,' Teddy said.

'Does that mean we're in for a bad crossing?'

'Could be. So you made it then old chap. Where's the family?'

'Down below. And Rosalind?'

'Oh she's in the cabin. Says she's not coming out until we reach Portsmouth.'

'A cabin? You've got a cabin? How on earth did you manage that?'

'No problem old boy.'

He tapped his nose and grinned.

'Turns out Rosalind's brother went to school with the captain. He was delighted to help out.'

A man whom Richard recognised from the International Club, came across to speak to them.

'It's a disgrace. I can't believe we're being treated like this. British citizens subjected to this.'

He waved his hand around vaguely.

'No better than refugees. I shall be writing to my MP when I get home, I can assure you of that. I'm surprised that you're putting up with it, Harcourt-Smith.'

'Calm down now, old chap. It's an emergency after all. What's a fellow to do; we've all got to make sacrifices at a time like this.'

The man turned to Richard.

'Cholmondley,' he said, holding out his hand. 'John Cholmondley, Diplomatic Service.'

'Richard Marshal.'

'Marshal? Any relation to the Marshals of Kings Abbot?'

'No, I don't think so.'

The man turned back to Teddy.

'And to cap it all, they cancelled the Hounds. Can you believe it.'

'Any news on Belgium?' Teddy asked.

'Looks like we may have persuaded that Hitler chap to guarantee their neutrality. We don't want a repeat of last time, now do we?'

'So Britain will back them?'

'Too soon to say but I expect so. Depends what France intend to do.'

'You can't trust that man,' interrupted Richard. 'We've seen what he is capable of in the Rhineland.'

'Only taking back what he believes is rightly theirs. Not our place to interfere. No need to rush into another bloody war; nobody wants that,' Teddy replied.

'Certainly not Herr Hitler,' added John Cholmondley.

'How can you be so sure?'

'Believe me when I tell you that the British government is well aware of Hitler's plans; they have been involved in talks with the Germans for some time.'

'Talking's no good; I get the distinct impression he's a man for whom actions speak louder than words,' added Richard.

'Winston would agree with you.'

'Whatever you may think of Herr Hitler, you have to admit that he is a bastion against Communism,' said Teddy.

'And why aren't the British doing anything to help the Spanish?'

'The conflict in Spain has nothing to do with us,' added Cholmondley. 'And we couldn't interfere, even if we wanted to; we are signatories of the non-intervention pact.'

'I know all about that; greatest cop-out going,' replied Richard. 'But what's actually happening? What have you heard? Does anyone know what's happening there?'

'His daughter's still there,' Teddy explained. 'In Málaga.'

'Oh, I am sorry old boy. Bit of a worry, what.'

'We just can't get any news. Nobody seems to know what's going on. My wife's going out of her mind with worry. Even the BBC aren't giving a clear picture.'

'Oh no point listening to the BBC; they pick up the Nationalist broadcasts from Seville and the Republican broadcasts from Madrid and make a dog's dinner of them, a sort of average news summary. Quite meaningless really, neither side are giving anything away.'

'God bless my soul, there's old Harry Wycliffe. Excuse me chaps, I must go and say hello to the old fellow,' said Teddy.

They watched Teddy lurch across the deck to speak to an elderly man in a black overcoat.

'Well, I'd better be getting back to my family. It's getting rather rough now,' Richard said, eyeing the rising swell. 'Nice to meet you.'

'Yes, delighted. Look if I hear anything I'll let you know. But don't get up your hopes; communication is pretty awful at the moment and what we do get is mostly propaganda.'

'I realise that but I'd appreciate anything, anything at all.'

'Maybe we'll meet up later.'

'Maybe.'

Margaret and Peter were still sitting where he had left them; Margaret had her sketching pad on her knee and was drawing the scenes around her. He threaded his way through the recumbent bodies.

'I told the servants they're to let no-one in the house and to keep it all locked up,' a man, who looked vaguely familiar, was saying to his companion.

'You'll be lucky old chap; they'll be in there like a shot and rob you blind. You see, by the time you get back there'll be not a stick left.'

'Communist bastards, if it weren't for my wife and children I'd stay and fight them off myself.'

'It's just such a bind. Mummy and Daddy were coming out to see us. It's Felicity's 21st this month, and we thought what fun, let's invite all the family and have a big party. Now

161

we shall have to have it in Winchester,' a middle aged woman was complaining.

'Winchester eh? Not quite the same as Marbella, old girl.'

'Well if it goes on until the summer we shall probably stay for Ascot,' said a smartly dressed woman, wearing a white cloche.

'Of course, why not, and Henley. We usually go home for Henley anyway.'

Richard was not an impassioned man, in fact, more reasoned and measured in his approach to life than most but now he felt a rage rise up within him at these people. Were they ignorant of the situation or merely vain and selfish? People were fleeing for their lives and some were dying. His daughter was there for God's sake and all they were concerned about was that this war should not inconvenience their own petty lives.

'Darling, what's the matter?' Margaret asked, putting her sketchpad to one side.

'Oh nothing. It's just that these people make me so mad.'

'Come and sit down with us.'

'Did you see the captain, Dad?'

'Oh God, no. Sorry old chap, I forgot. Tell you what, just keep Willow quiet and we'll say no more about it.'

Peter hugged his dog close, then carefully arranged his coat across the animal's back to disguise her.

'Did you find out any more news about Málaga?'

'No nothing. I think we're just going to have to wait until we get to England. I promise you I'll do everything I can to find Elizabeth once we're home.'

He put his arm around Margaret and squeezed her against him. Her body was limp in his arms; it was as though all the fight had gone out of her.

'Don't worry sweetheart, we'll find her; I promise,' he murmured, burying his face in her hair.

Margaret's brother was waiting for them in Portsmouth when they docked. He was an older, slightly heavier version of Margaret, with the same curly brown hair and pale blue eyes. He wore a tweed jacket and cord trousers and stood on the dock waving his cap wildly.

'There's Uncle Brian. Hello Uncle Brian', shouted Peter. 'Hello.'

'He can't hear you, Peter. Just wait, we'll be disembarking any time now.'

'He's seen us, Mummy. Look, he's waving.'

'All right young fellow, calm down now. We'll be off soon enough.'

Richard felt as much excitement as his son to be standing there looking at English soil again. The journey had seemed to endure forever. They had trouble getting enough water to drink and the food, although edible, was tasteless. When he drank the watery soup and ate the stale sandwiches, he had thought back, with a pleasure that he never expected to have, to the meal they had eaten with the Harcourt-Smiths. The delicate fillets of sole and the sirloin of beef had seemed a decade away.

From the moment they had left the shelter of the bay of Algeciras the weather had been dreadful, with gale force winds that buffeted the ship day and night, causing their belongings to career around the lounge and the decks to be awash with seawater. Crossing the Bay of Biscay had been a nightmare but even then, neither he nor Margaret had succumbed to sea sickness, and even Peter, although more subdued than usual, had kept his sea legs. Not so some of

163

their companions, who spent the entire voyage heaving and retching into paper bags or hanging over the deck rail. Their complaints about the political situation had given way to the groans and moans of the afflicted and the air around them stank of stale vomit and bad breath.

'Thank goodness that journey is over,' Margaret said.

She stood beside him, wearing her blue coat, her bags strung over her shoulders, holding Peter by one hand and Willow's lead in the other; her eyes were filled with tears.

'Are you all right?'

'Yes, I'm fine.'

'Come on then, let's get off this damned ship.'

Margaret's cough did not improve; she went to the doctor but all he said was that she had probably caught a chest infection from the sea crossing and prescribed cough syrup and a menthol vapour rub.

'You don't seem to be getting any better, Maggie,' her brother said. 'Why not try inhaling this.'

He held up a bottle of eucalyptus and menthol.

'Just put a spoonful in a bowl of hot water and inhale it. Here I'll do it for you.'

Moments later he came back into the room, carrying a bowl of hot water and a towel.

'Come on now, sit yourself down and put this towel over your head.'

'Oh Brian, don't make such a fuss; it's only a bit of a cough.'

'Maybe but try it anyway.'

She was sitting in her brother's lounge, with her head above the steaming bowl, when Richard returned.

'Hello, is that you in there?' he asked, pulling up the towel and peering at the damp face and streaming eyes of his wife. 'What are you doing?'

'It was Brian's idea; he's worried about me.'

Margaret bent her head over the bowl and replaced the towel. Richard put his hand on her back and stroked it gently. He, too, was worried about his wife; since Elizabeth had left she had changed. She had always been a quiet woman, happy with her own company, her garden and her painting but now she had become withdrawn; it was only Peter who could animate her these days and draw her out from the darkness that covered her soul. On top of that, the cough she had developed since they left Spain seemed to be getting worse; now he did not know if her unwonted lethargy stemmed from that or her worry over Elizabeth.

'I thought we might have a drive out and look for a cottage,' he suggested. 'Brian says we can take the car. He says there's an estate agent in the village. What do you say, old girl?'

'All right,' she mumbled. 'I suppose we can't impose on Brian and Susan forever.'

She lifted the towel again.

'Actually, I need to go into Wareham, anyway, to get Peter's new school tie. They said it would be in today.'

'Good. Right, well we'll do that then. Give me a shout when you're ready; I'll be in the garden.'

The estate agent was extremely helpful; he showed them the details of a number of small cottages in the area and even offered to take them there himself.

Richard knew it was the one for them the moment he saw the look on Margaret's face. The cottage was down a narrow, winding lane that was so overgrown with hedgerow that the estate agent had to abandon his car and lead the way on foot.

'I'm not sure if this is exactly what you want,' he said. 'It's bigger than your average cottage but it does have that country cottage feel about it.'

'Look at the garden,' Margaret whispered to her husband. 'It's just perfect.'

Richard knew exactly what she meant. The lawn was spattered with daffodils, and a tangle of wisteria and honeysuckle rambled its way up the side of the house and along the adjacent stone wall. Margaret took his hand and they walked together along a path built of crazy paving that wound its way through the empty flower beds and round to the back of the house. Here the garden opened out and seemed to merge with the fields at the bottom; there was a small, walled area, completely overgrown with weeds but suitable for growing vegetables and, under the apple trees, wood anemones and columbines grew.

The agent was busy extolling the benefits of country living but Margaret was not listening. She headed straight for a large out-building next to the back door.

'What's in here?' she asked.

'Ah.'

He looked at the house details.

'I think it's probably a storage shed, or maybe a potting shed.'

He took out a key.

'Let's have a look, shall we.'

He unlocked the door and stood back to let Margaret enter.

'Oh Richard, this is perfect.'

They stood in a wide room with a stone floor and a glass skylight.

'It would need some more light, of course and I'd have to have some shelves over there.'

She pointed to the east wall, then turned to face Richard, her face alight with excitement.

'We'd need to paint it white, to reflect the light better. And I could put my easel right there.'

'All right, Darling, let's look at the rest of the house before we decide,' he said. 'We don't even know how much they want for it.'

He instantly regretted his words because at once the light died from her eyes and she turned and walked away. For a brief moment he had had his old Margaret back and he had let her slip away again. He followed them outside and back around the house to the front door. It was all academic now; they would have the house no matter what.

CHAPTER 9

Alex was waiting for them outside the Regina Hotel as planned. Like Juan he carried no luggage.

'Where's the baby?' he asked almost at once.

Juan shook his head, sadly.

'Oh I am sorry Elizabeth. I know you were pretty fond of that little chap. Never mind he's probably better off.'

Elizabeth felt Juan squeeze her hand; she said nothing.

'Right, let's get going while it's quiet.' Juan said. 'We'll take the back streets until we are away from the port then we'll pick up the main road. What do you say?'

'Fine. You lead the way,' Alex replied.

It proved quite difficult walking through the narrow streets at night; there were no street lights and the moon's pale rays did not penetrate the dark alleyways but Juan knew the way. By the time they had passed the cathedral and reached the park their eyes had become accustomed to the night. Elizabeth felt nervous; the trees cast strange shadows and she could hear people moving about in the dark.

'Don't be frightened,' whispered Juan. 'They're only people like ourselves, resting here for the night.'

Nevertheless they kept close to the walls of the fortress, avoiding the camp fires; there seemed to be hundreds camped there, waiting for morning. Eventually they reached the bull ring and the Paseo Maritimo; at last they were on the road to Almería. They walked until dawn, stopping from time to time to rest by the roadside. At first they made good progress, arriving in the small fishing village of La Cala after only a couple of hours.

'Juan, I must sit down; my legs are killing me,' Elizabeth complained.

'Good idea. Why not stop here for a bit? Look, there're some benches outside this bar,' Alex suggested.

'I wish there was something to eat,' she moaned. 'I've never been so hungry before.'

'Here, have some water.'

Alex handed her a bottle of water and she took a sip. She would have loved to drink and drink from it until her thirst was sated but she knew it was all he had.

'Go on, have a little more,' he urged.

'No, better to save it for later,' Juan said, taking the bottle from her. 'Come on I think we should move on.'

Nobody argued; they knew he was right. Wearily they resumed their journey. The road ran by the beach and alongside an old railway track; the sea was calm and still, a glittering carpet beneath the moon.

Juan took her hand.

'Do you know, there's an old gypsy story about the moon,' he said.

'Yes, what is it?'

'Well, there once was a gypsy couple who were very sad because they had no children. So one night the wife sang to the moon asking her to give her a child. The moon took pity on the gypsy woman and granted her wish and very soon the woman became pregnant. But when the child was born his face was as round and as white as the moon. The gypsy husband, whose skin was the colour of olive wood, looked at the baby with his round, white face and flew into a rage. He thought that this baby, so pale and still, could not be his. Immediately he jumped to the conclusion that his wife had been unfaithful to him and he pulled out his knife and killed her. Then he took the baby to a hilltop, wrapped him in his mother's shawl and left him there under the moon. When the moon saw the abandoned child she took pity on him and took him to live up in the sky with her. So now, you see, when we look at the moon, if the child is happy, then the moon is full and, when the child is sleeping, the moon becomes a cradle to rock him.'

Elizabeth looked up at the full moon and smiled.

'So now the child is happy?' she said. 'That's lovely.'

'Actually it's an old song and the words are much more beautiful than my simple version. One day when this is all over I'll sing it to you.'

'So you sing?' she asked.

'A little.'

'And play?'

'Just the guitar. I've always loved music ever since I was a small boy. But not now; I left my guitar at my parents' house.'

'You should keep playing, Juan. Now is the time for music, more than ever. People need something to keep their spirits up.'

'Maybe later; maybe when this is all over I'll teach you some Spanish songs.'

'What about you Alex, do you sing?' she asked.

'Me? Not likely. No, my voice is as flat as a pancake. The only time I was asked to sing in the choir was when they wanted to bring the tone down a few octaves.'

'I'm sure you're not as bad as that.'

'Trust me; you don't want to hear me sing.'

'Well if you can't sing, what can you do? Tell me about yourself, Alex. Where did you live in England?' Elizabeth asked.

'Near Oxford. Do you know a small town called Wallingford? It's on the Thames.'

'No, not really. Is it pretty?'

'I suppose so; it's just your regular market town. It has a nice bridge over the river and there're some good pubs; it's not a bad place to row from. We've got quite a good rowing club there actually; done quite well at Henley in the past.'

'So do your parents still live there?'

'Yes. They've lived there for years; my sister and I were born there.'

'Your sister?'

'Yes, I have a sister called Angela. She's older than me. She's all right really but she used to boss me about a lot when I was a kid. She's married now and has twin boys, Alfred and Michael. Her husband's a nice chap; he's a rower.'

Twin boys, Elizabeth thought of the two boys with one pair of shoes. She wondered what had become of them.

'So you still live at home then? she asked.

'Yes. I've only just taken my finals,' he admitted.

So that was why he had given his occupation as a runner; he was still a student.

'So apart from running what do you think you'll do when you get back to England?' Juan asked.

171

'When, or if, I get back, I expect I shall go into some kind of business. I don't really know. I'm not ready to settle down yet; I still have a lot of travelling to do. All I do know is that I don't want a life like my parents.'

'Are they unhappy then?' asked Elizabeth.

'No, I don't think so but I'm sure they're bored. Their life is so grey and dull. My father is a don at the university; he spends most of his life with his nose in a book. When he's at home he just potters about in the garden or plays opera on his gramophone.'

'Well maybe that's what makes him happy,' said Elizabeth. 'My father is much the same and he always seems very content.'

She thought of her parents and their life together; they were always so affectionate towards each other. When her mother was painting her father would often bring his books and just sit beside her, not talking but happy to be near her.

'Yes but your father has not lived in the same village all his life, nor worked at the same job, with the same people. I couldn't stand it. There's so much more to see and do.'

'What about your mother?'

'Mother does what father wants. She doesn't complain but I often see her looking sad. She reads a lot; different books to my father, she likes romances and novels where the heroine runs away with a wild adventurer. She should have been a novelist or a playwright; when we were small she would tell us wonderful stories, full of mystery and magic.'

He laughed.

'That's probably where I get my wanderlust from: her tales of explorers and foreign lands.'

'What's that?' Elizabeth asked.

The sky behind them had been lit up by a series of flashes and they heard the sound of distant explosions.

'They must be bombing the port,' Juan said. 'Come on we must try to walk a bit faster.'

They continued in silence for a while, keeping the sea on their right and every so often passing through dark, damp tunnels, where Elizabeth had to hold tightly to Juan's hand and let him lead her, as she shuffled along, feeling her way carefully over the uneven ground. All the time they were aware of the flashes in the sky, like traces of distant fireworks and forgotten revelries. Elizabeth tried not to think of what was happening there, of the unsuspecting people by their camp fires, of Ana and the hotel, of Alberto, of Maria, and instead concentrated on making her tired legs take her further away from the danger. Despite Juan's exhortations their pace had slowed and by the time the sun was climbing out from the sea, they were only just approaching Torre del Mar.

As dawn broke Elizabeth looked around her in amazement; she had been aware for some time that they were not alone on this road but she had not realised that they were part of such an exodus. As far as she could see in both directions, there were people, hundreds of people walking in the same direction: wounded men, women, children, old people, goats, donkeys, even some chickens in a crate. The entire city seemed to be on the move. An immense silence hung over them, broken only by the plaintive cries of the children begging for food and the curses and moans of the elderly, who struggled to keep up. There was no need for them to speak; there was nothing to say. They all knew that they had to walk as fast as they could to avoid the danger. If they dawdled they would die; this was a race for their lives and even the

173

youngest among them seemed to know it. They urged their crying children on and when someone's grandmother gave up and sat by the roadside, too exhausted to continue, they walked on without her. They had to reach Almería and safety at all costs.

'*Que desbandá*,' Juan murmured, visibly moved to see so many homeless people.

Elizabeth wondered how far these people had come; some were wrapped in coats and blankets, others had nothing more than a single garment to wear; some were barefoot, their feet torn and bleeding. One old woman sat by the roadside, weeping, her legs swollen with ulcers, the blood running down into her sandals. There were so many children, dozens and dozens of children, most of them under ten years old. Some were lucky and sat in baskets astride rheumatic-looking donkeys, others rode on their fathers' backs or lay in their mothers' arms but many more ran behind, their tiny legs trying to keep up with their families, terrified they would get lost, and all of them crying for food.

'Exactly how far is it to Almería?' asked Elizabeth.

'Well it's a hundred miles from Málaga; so we're looking at another three days and three nights, if we can keep up the pace,' answered Alex.

Elizabeth groaned; she did not want to tell them but already she felt unable to walk any further. Her feet were sore and she was frightened to remove her shoes in case she could not put them on again; her back hurt and she was still desperately hungry.

'Keep an eye out for a lorry. Maybe we'll be lucky and be able to get a lift,' Juan said but with little conviction.

'What's this?' Alex asked. 'Maybe we'll be in luck.'

A huge cloud of white dust was being thrown up from the dirt road by a convoy of lorries that was heading towards them. The drivers drove fast, honking their horns continuously with the expectation that everyone would jump aside in deference. They cut a swathe through the exhausted pilgrims, who stumbled and fell to avoid being mown down. As the first lorry reached them Alex and Juan leapt to one side, pulling Elizabeth with them.

'The bastard,' swore Alex. 'Did you see who that was? It was that swine Colonel Villalba; so even the commander has left now. Well that means Málaga has had it; she's on her own now.'

'Looks as though he's taken most of his troops with him,' Juan added.

'Gutless bastard,' Alex repeated.

Elizabeth said nothing; she was thinking of Ana and Maria. Were they still there? What would happen to them? She turned to Alex who was trying to brush the dust from his already dirty trousers.

'Do you know what's happened to Maria?' she asked.

'No, the last I heard she'd joined up with a group of Communists.'

'Was she staying in Málaga?'

'She said she was but I really don't know. She was supposed to meet me at the Regina on Wednesday but she never turned up.'

'What will happen to her if the Nationalists catch her?'

'Nothing good, I can tell you,' Alex replied.

'They will either shoot her immediately or they will put her in prison and shoot her later. It will be better if they shoot her immediately,' said Juan.

'My God, that's terrible. Does she realise that?' Elizabeth asked.

'Oh yes, she realises it. That's why she'll fight them. I know she'd prefer to die fighting. I don't have to explain to you what will happen to her if the Nationalists capture her, do I?'

Elizabeth shivered; poor Maria, she was full of bravura and great ideals but how would she survive if they caught her. She was only a young woman, like her.

'What's that noise? It sounds like more guns.' Juan said.

The sound of heavy gunfire could be heard coming from somewhere behind them.

'I can't see anything,' Alex replied.

'Come on, let's try to move a little faster,' Juan urged.

He looked worried. Elizabeth sighed but let him take her hand and pull her on faster.

'Hang on chaps. Just a minute,' Alex said suddenly.

He disappeared through a wooden gate, then reappeared a minute later with his pockets full of oranges.

'I just spotted these in that garden back there. Here try one.'

Elizabeth ripped off the peel and put a segment in her mouth. It was very bitter but she swallowed it nevertheless. It wuld help quench her interminable thirst.

'Ugh. Seville oranges, no wonder nobody had picked them,' she said but ate it all anyway.

'Makes good marmalade,' Alex said, screwing up his face as he chewed. 'My mother makes pretty good marmalade; she usually sells it at the local fete to raise money for the repairs to the church tower. Want another?'

'No thanks. I'd prefer a slice of toast with some of your mother's marmalade and a nice pot of tea.'

The bitter juice of the orange was making her feel sick. She would have loved a long cool drink of water.

'I think it's made me thirstier than ever,' she complained.

She could hear the whinge in her voice and felt like a little child, tired and disappointed.

'Try to last out for another hour and then we will stop again and share some of Alex's water,' Juan suggested. 'We'll get through this, you'll see.'

They trudged on. It seemed to Elizabeth that they had been walking alongside the sea forever. The mountains once more came down to meet and run beside them; the road was now sandwiched between the steep granite face of the sierra and a narrow, rocky beach. They were so close to the sea that, as the waves broke on the rocks, sending up a fine salty spray, they could feel the cool droplets on their faces and hair. Seagulls swooped down on them, screeching, looking in vain for scraps. The travellers were closer together here, no longer strung out in small groups but moving in a continuous stream. Elizabeth looked at her immediate neighbours: a woman with two small children and her mother. The children were pulling at their mother's skirt.

'*Mama, tarda mucho? Mama? Tarda mucho?*' they repeated over and over again. Their mother did not reply; she could not answer her children. She did not know how much further it was; all she knew was that they must keep walking. The one question in everyone's mind was when would they arrive in Almería.

Alex walked ahead of her; she thought how young he looked. Even after walking all night, his long rangy legs were striding ahead and there was still a bounce in his step. Juan on the other hand seemed sad, even morose; he walked with his head down and his shoulders slumped in despair. Only

177

when Elizabeth spoke to him did he smile and the light return to his eyes.

They were so intent on covering as many kilometres as possible, so locked into their own small discomforts that they did not notice the ships creeping up on them. The first time they realised that something was wrong was when the people behind began to scream and run past them.

When the first shell hit, Elizabeth thought that the end of her world had come; the road in front of her burst open in an explosion of earth and sand, its entrails hurled high into the air. The noise of the explosion seemed to swallow her, obliterating all other sounds; she could hear nothing, just a ringing in her head and then silence. The blast hurled her forward in a cascade of falling debris; for a moment she lay there stunned. Then her deafness lifted and she could hear the screams. She tried to scramble to her feet, to get herself out of danger but she could not move her legs; something lay across them. More shells were exploding now, first one then another and another; the ground heaved and trembled beneath her as if it were an earthquake. She gave up her struggle and lay still, covering her head with her arms and waited, hoping she was not about to die. Her eyes and nose were full of grit and she could taste sand in her mouth. Her legs were pinned to the ground but otherwise she appeared to be unhurt, bruised and battered but uninjured; at least she could feel no pain. Was that a good or a bad thing, she wondered. She lay there, for what seemed a very long time, listening to the bombardment, hoping each explosion was the last. Her thoughts turned to her parents and her brother. Would she ever see them again? If she died who would tell them? They might spend years waiting for her to return, wondering what had happened to her, never knowing for certain that she was

178

dead. She realised how selfish she had been to slip away without telling them and tears of regret trickled down her nose and soaked into the earth. And all so she could take a few pictures. Her camera. Where was it? She became aware that she was lying on something hard; it was her camera. She lifted her body slightly and pulled it out. It was smashed beyond repair. So in the end this had all been for nothing. No, she reminded herself, it was not for nothing; she had met Juan. She had been witness to what was happening here. What did it matter if there were no photographs to tell the world? She would write about it, instead.

At last the shelling stopped; it was over. Now a silence hung over them, broken only by the moans and cries of the wounded. She twisted her head round to look for the ships. They were just off shore. She could see the sailors walking along the deck; if she stretched out her hand she could almost touch them. She had to get up; she had to find safety. She was still unable to move her legs. She twisted herself round to see what was pinning her down; it was Juan's body.

'Juan. My God, Juan, are you all right? Juan, speak to me.'

And Alex, where was he? Had they been killed? Was she alone?

'Alex, are you there? Alex?' she called frantically.

She struggled to get free, pulling at Juan's inert body as best she could; but she could not move him.

'Hang on; it's all right, I've got him. He's alive.'

It was Alex. He pulled Juan up and helped him to the roadside.

'Here, old chap, just sit there for a minute,' he said, gently propping him against a rock.

Juan's eyes were open but he did not seem to know where he was; he moaned quietly to himself.

'Elizabeth, are you all right?' Alex asked, helping her to her feet. 'Are you injured?'

'No, I don't think so. But what about Juan, is he all right?'

Straight away she could see he was injured; there was a large gash on his forehead that was bleeding profusely and his left arm hung awkwardly by his side. She stood looking down at him, unable to speak, the tears streaming down her face.

'Juan, Juan. Speak to me,' Alex said, holding him by the shoulder. 'You've been hurt but I don't think it's too bad old chap. Come on now, look at me.'

Juan lifted his head and smiled weakly.

'I'm all right, Alex. Really, I'm fine. Just give me a minute or two. Where's Isabel? Has she been hurt?'

'She's all right. She's here, right by your side.'

Juan tried to stand but a shaft of pain made him cry out and he collapsed back onto the ground.

'*Mierda*. I think I've broken something,' he said.

'I'm here, Juan. I'm here. Keep still my Darling, let me look,' Elizabeth said, kneeling beside him.

The panic that had been paralysing her disappeared when she saw that Juan needed her. She carefully removed his jacket and his shirt; both were torn and soaked in his blood. A bone had made a ragged cut through his flesh and now protruded from his shoulder at an unnatural angle; his chest was a mass of cuts and lesions, either from the mortar fire or the road, she could not be sure which. He was badly injured, she could see but it was hard to assess the true extent of the damage because of all the blood.

'I think your shoulder is broken,' she told him. 'We need to clean you up a bit. Alex, would you mind getting some water from the sea to wash him down. The salt will act as a good antiseptic.'

She looked around for a suitable container.

'Look there's an old pot over there. That would do.'

When Alex returned with the water they poured it on Juan's wounds and cleaned him as best they could. Now it was possible to see that most of the cuts were superficial but there was one, where a piece of shrapnel had penetrated his chest muscle, which was bleeding heavily.

'Sorry old chap, this is going to hurt a bit,' Alex said. 'I'm going to get this thing out of your chest and stop the bleeding then I'll try to make you a bit more comfortable. There's not a lot more we can do until we can get you to a doctor, I'm afraid.'

Juan tried to smile but he looked as though he was about to faint.

'Hang on in there, old boy,' Alex said.

He removed his own jacket and placed it on the ground then he took off his shirt and in a single pull ripped it in two. He folded one half of the shirt into a pad which he placed on top of his jacket.

'Elizabeth, I want you to hold Juan's good shoulder for a minute while I try to pull this metal out of his chest.'

He smiled at her encouragingly.

'I wish I'd brought some of Ana's anise with us,' he added.

She felt her legs go weak with fear but did as he said.

'Look, I'm sorry old chap. I'll try to do this as quickly as possible but if we don't get it out soon, you could bleed to death.'

Even before he had finished speaking Alex had taken a firm grip on the shrapnel and jerked it out of Juan's chest. He held it in the air in triumph. Juan let out a roar of pain and his head dropped back. Elizabeth thought he had fainted until she heard him swear:

'*Mierda*. That hurt.'

'Sorry, old boy. Here's a souvenir for you.'

Alex dropped the shrapnel into Juan's lap, then took up the pad he had made from his shirt and pressed it on the wound to staunch the blood.

'Elizabeth, hold this in place for a moment.'

He took the other half of his shirt and wound it around Juan's body as a bandage to hold the pad in place.

'How's that?' he asked Juan.

'Fine,' Juan replied faintly.

Next he removed his belt and lifting Juan's arm as gently as possible, tied it against his body. Elizabeth saw Juan grimace with pain; he looked very white and a nerve in his cheek was twitching badly.

'There that might help you a little, at least for now,' Alex said.

'Thanks Alex. That's great. Help me up now please; we can't stay here. The ships may return any minute.'

It was obvious that their progress would be slow from now on; although Juan could walk, he had lost a lot of blood and was very unsteady on his feet. Elizabeth took his good arm and let him lean his weight on her. The road was a battlefield; there were dead and wounded everywhere and the cries and moans were like a blanket of sound that threatened to smother them. Elizabeth could not take it all in; it was a nightmare from which she could not wake. They passed a man who had been blinded; blood ran down his face and he wandered from person to person calling pathetically for his wife. A woman sat by the roadside, her dead child in her lap and her living one crying beside her; her foot had been blown off. There was nothing they could do to help these people; 'It's too much' she wanted to scream. 'I don't know what to do'. What had these poor people done to deserve such barbaric treatment? Children wandered lost, crying for their mothers; mothers cried out in vain, calling for their children. She thought of the dead baby and realised that they had been right; there was nothing she could have done for him. She was a mere passenger in this life; God or Fate would decide where she ended up. She could still see the ships. They were sailing close to the coast, heading west, back towards Málaga; they continued to fire at hapless travellers on the road, the explosions becoming fainter and fainter.

'I think we should try to find somewhere to hide and rest up for the remainder of the day,' Alex suggested. 'Then we can continue tonight when it may be safer. The ships may not attack during the night and, if they do, they will have more difficulty seeing us.'

Elizabeth thought it would make little difference; the ships had come very close to shore. Even without binoculars she had been able to see the sailors running about the decks, so they in turn must have had an excellent view of their targets. Nevertheless she agreed with Alex; by now she was deathly tired and, besides which, she knew Juan needed to rest.

'But where?' she asked.

There seemed nowhere to hide; they were completely exposed along this stretch of the road. They walked on further until they came to a narrow gully in the rock where a stream ran down into the sea.

'Up here,' Alex said. 'There's some sugarcane ahead; we can hide in there. It has to be better than here; we'll be sitting ducks if the gunboats return.'

They turned off the road and headed up the stream. Elizabeth stopped and bent down to wash her face in the water; she cupped her hands and drank from the cool water. It had a muddy taste but otherwise was delicious, slipping down her parched throat like wine.

'Juan, wait a minute. Let me get you some water. Alex do you still have the bottle?'

She filled the bottle and held it to Juan's mouth for him to drink.

'Good.'

She gave some to Alex then refilled the bottle for later. They continued upstream, stumbling over small boulders and splashing through the water until Alex was satisfied that the sugarcane that grew along the banks was dense enough to hide them. He stopped and turned inland, pushing the canes aside carefully so that they would not break and would spring back into place after them.

'Here, this is perfect,' he said.

They stood in a small clearing, no wider than a couple of metres, where the cane looked as though it had been trampled down by some animal. Elizabeth took off her coat and laid it on the ground.

'Juan, sit here, Darling,' she said, helping him to lower his body to the ground.

He was still very white and the perspiration lay in tiny beads along his forehead. He was more beautiful than ever, she thought, her desire surfacing through her concern. She bent over him and kissed him tenderly on the cheek. He smiled at her but she knew that his eyes did not see her. He lay down on her coat and instantly closed his eyes. She stretched herself out to one side of him and Alex the other, both trying to warm his body with their own. They slept all afternoon, lulled by the sound of buzzing flies and the gently rustling of the cane in the breeze, and only woke when the sun went down and the damp air began to creep into their bones.

'I think we should move on now,' Alex said, standing up and stretching his long legs. 'Do you think you're up to it, Juan?'

'Yes of course, I'm fine,' he replied. 'I'm feeling much better now.'

He did not look better; his wound had been bleeding again and Alex's makeshift bandage was now soaked in blood. He tried to smile but the pain and exhaustion were too much for him. Elizabeth looked at Alex. He shook his head and whispered:

'We have no choice Elizabeth, we have to move on. We must get him to a doctor.'

It was dark in the shadow of the mountain and what little light there was from the stars did not penetrate the narrow valley, so walking on the uneven ground proved difficult. Juan stumbled once and Elizabeth heard him swear in Spanish again but when she tried to help him, he pushed her away.

'I'm all right. Do not worry so, *cariño,*' he told her. 'We'll be back on the road soon. We should be in Salobreña by morning.'

CHAPTER 10

Their progress was slow and painful. They walked in silence, every step seemed to exhaust Juan more and more; she could see he was trying to muster every last ounce of his strength in order to continue and it pained her to see him suffer so. The wound in his chest had stopped bleeding now but from time to time he complained of pains in his head and said he felt dizzy. They took it in turns to help him along but his body was becoming heavier and heavier; she wanted to stop and rest but he would not let them.

'Tomorrow we can rest,' he said. 'When we are safe.'

Even the main road was difficult to negotiate in the dark: in places the surface had collapsed leaving gaping craters; the bombardment had thrown up enormous boulders and created landslips from the mountain which blocked their way. There were dead bodies and the carcasses of animals to avoid, abandoned possessions and broken-down carts. They felt their way gingerly, testing the ground with their feet in case it should throw up a sudden surprise and trying to follow the people in front of them. At about three o'clock in the morning they heard the rumble of a lorry.

'Down onto the beach,' Alex ordered, dragging Juan off the road. 'We'll hide in the rocks until we see who it is.'

There was no sound of gunfire as the lorry approached; it seemed to be travelling at a normal speed and came to a halt a few metres ahead of them.

'It's the Red Cross,' Elizabeth shouted. 'Oh thank God.'

The lorry was in fact a large white Ford van, with a red cross painted on its side. Within seconds of stopping it was surrounded by a crowd of desperate people, all crying out at once:

'Take my child, please take my child.'

'My son is sick; please take him to the hospital.'

'Look at this child. He's badly wounded.'

'My wife has just given birth. Have you room for her and the baby?'

'Please take my little girl, she's dying.'

'Please help us. My child has dysentery; he's dying.'

The cries rang through the night, tearing at Elizabeth's heart. How could one small van take so many? Who would they choose to help and who would they leave to die? Elizabeth and Alex dragged Juan across to join the crowd. A tall, upright man with thick, white hair climbed out of the lorry; he wore a military uniform with the insignia of the International Red Cross on his breast pocket and a soldier's beret. He held up his hands and began to speak to the people in halting Spanish with, what Elizabeth thought, was an American accent; she was reminded of Wilbur.

'All right folks, calm down. My name is Norman; I'm with the International Red Cross and I'm here to help you get to safety.'

He paused unable to continue for the cries of the refugees all clamouring for his attention. When the crowd saw that he was not going to continue they gradually quietened down.

'That's better. Now we want to help as many of you as possible but as you can see our truck is not very big. We can manage almost forty of you on each trip and then we'll be back to get some more. I'm sorry we can't take all of you in one go but you'll just have to be patient and keep walking until we return.'

He turned to his assistant.

'We'll get the children and their mothers on first,' he whispered to her then addressed the crowd again:

'I know some of you have been injured but when you get to Almería there's a hospital with doctors and medicine; you'll be able to get food and fresh drinking water and somewhere to sleep. I'd love to take you all now but I'm going to have to start with the weakest, the children. They are our priority.'

The crowd opened up allowing the children to make their way to the front.

'All right son, up you go.'

He lifted a small boy into the back of the van; a woman carrying a baby climbed in behind him.

'Right, who's next?'

Elizabeth watched as he helped more people into the van; it was filling up rapidly. She pushed her way through the crowd until she stood beside him.

'Are you going to Almería? Can you take my husband? He's badly hurt; he needs a doctor soon or he'll die.'

The man turned towards the sound of her voice.

'Are you English?' he asked.

'Yes but my husband is Spanish. He needs your help.'

'I'm sorry, we're full already. You heard what I said, we can only take the most vulnerable: the young and the weak.'

'But have you no room for my husband? He'll die if you don't help him.'

'I'm sorry. We only have one truck, my dear. We're working alone but we will be back as soon as we can.'

'It will be too late by then.'

'Truly, I am sorry. Just try to look after him until we return.'

'But you're a doctor, won't you look at him at least?'

He paused, stroking his thick, white moustache.

'Where is he?' he asked at last.

Alex pushed Juan forward; he staggered into the light of the headlamps, blinking in bewilderment. The doctor looked at him. He was a sorry sight; he wore Elizabeth's coat which was two sizes too small for him and was stained with mud and blood; his trousers were ripped and his face was streaked with dirt. He seemed unaware of what was happening and stared about him wildly.

'What happened to him?' the doctor asked.

Alex explained as briefly as possible what had occurred.

'We're worried because he's lost a lot of blood and now he doesn't seem to know where he is. We think he may have concussion from the explosion.'

The doctor sighed.

'All right then, put him in the front with us but I can't take you two as well. Sorry.'

'No, that's fine. We'll walk. Just take him.'

'Listen, when you get to Almería, go to the International Red Cross Hospital; we'll leave him there. You'll have to look for him and it may not be easy; there're thousands of refugees in Almería and the hospital is full.'

'We'll find him. Thank you.'

Elizabeth was crying by now. She put her hands up to Juan's face and pulled it towards her, kissing him gently.

'We'll come for you Juan. We'll find you my Darling. We'll find you.'

Alex pulled her away and lifted Juan into the front seat. He was anxious to get him in the van before the doctor changed his mind.

'Isabela. Where is my Isabela?' Juan asked, looking about him and trying to get up.

'She'll be along soon, old chap. You just go with the doctor now, we're coming later. It's for the best; you were just holding us back you know. Don't worry; I'll look after her for you,' Alex said, pushing him back into the seat.

'Right we're off. Ready?' the doctor asked his assistant, a young nurse whose pretty face was marred from strain and lack of sleep.

She nodded and climbed into the front seat, sandwiching Juan between herself and the doctor. They closed the van doors and drove off into the night, leaving a crowd of distraught people behind them. Elizabeth and Alex watched the tail lights until they became tiny specks of light and eventually disappeared, then Alex put his arm around her.

'Come on Elizabeth. He'll be all right now. They'll look after him once he gets to the hospital. He'll be fine.'

She nodded, unable to speak for the tears that were choking her. Would she ever see him again?

'Come on, we've still got a long way to go,' Alex said, pulling her along.

She shivered; the wind from the sea was seeping into her bones making them ache.

'He wasn't American you know. Canadian more like,' Alex said after a while.

'Who?'

'The doctor chappie.'

'Why do you say that?'

'Well on the side of the van it said: "*Servicio Canadiense de Transfusiones de Sangre.*" '

'Blood transfusions?'

'Yes but it looks as though it's been stripped out and converted into an ambulance. He seems to be using it as a bus service right now.'

'Thank God he is. I wonder who he is?'

'Probably one of the International Brigade; I heard there were quite a few volunteers from Canada.'

'Well whoever he is, he's like an angel from heaven on this hellish road,' she said.

Together they continued walking. She was desperately tired and her feet were blistered and sore but she knew they had to keep going. Whenever she stumbled or faltered, and said she could go no further, Alex would take her arm and gently pull her forward. He never complained, although he must have been as tired and hungry as she was. She felt a sudden warmth towards him, glad that he had chosen to come with them; she would have been lost without him now that Juan had gone. He was so kind to her, almost like a big brother, concerned and caring, and he had saved Juan's life. It was unlikely that Juan would have made it so far without him. She thought back to the day she had first met Alex; she found it hard to believe that she had taken a dislike to him. She looked at him striding along beside her; he did not seem to be the same person anymore. They walked at a quicker pace now; Alex had been right when he told Juan that they would make better progress without him but now she had an ache in her heart instead.

By the time the sun had climbed over the horizon, exposing the straggling column of survivors to their enemies, they had reached Salobreña. The town appeared before them like a ghostly apparition, a white monolith that rose from the sea, incandescent in the faint light of the new day. At this point the road skirted the village, turning its back on the sea and heading through fields of almond trees. They could hear gunfire ahead and small clouds of black smoke floated up into a perfect sky.

'Hang on, Elizabeth; let's wait a minute. What do you think's happening?'

They were on the brow of a hill, overlooking the wide, flat plain where the Guadalfeo river ran into the sea; ahead of them was Motril and the winding road that climbed through the mountains to Granada. They could hear a deep throated rumble. As they waited the rumble grew louder and suddenly became a tremendous roar. Water was cascading down the valley. The mortars from the gun boats had breached the reservoir and now thousands of gallons of water were sweeping down through the steep valley to the plain below. They watched in horror as the green swathe of water poured down, washing away everything in its path, uprooting trees, smashing walls, bouncing rocks and boulders along like mere pebbles and burying everything, people, animals, houses, in mud and rubble.

'Oh my God. Will this never end?' Elizabeth cried.

She held her head in her hands and shook with terror. People all around her were screaming and crying in fear; nobody dared move forward; nobody wanted to descend into that hell.

'What are we going to do?' she cried.

192

Alex looked stunned; he took her hand and forced himself to speak calmly.

'We must wait, Elizabeth. It's impossible to get through that lot, not at the moment; we'd be swept away. Anyway we need to rest. Let's wait and hope that the bridge has held then we'll carry on tonight.'

'But we'll never get to Almería at this rate,' she wailed.

She wanted to howl with rage and frustration.

'I need to find Juan. I have to go on.'

'No. Now we rest; it's too dangerous to go on. Thank God we weren't down there with those poor devils.'

The water was spreading out over the flood plain and draining into the sea but it left in its wake a thick, black layer of silt and mud. From where they stood it looked as if the road had been washed away; there were no lorries, no people. And still the water came tumbling down the mountain, flooding the fields of sugar cane, tearing down the avocado trees and carrying all before it on its way to the sea.

'Look,' Alex said pointing out to the Mediterranean.

The ships were back; they could see them creeping along the coast, firing at isolated groups of refugees.

'It's all a game to them,' she said. 'Look they're targeting those people down there. They can see that they're women and children and they're still firing. I can't believe it. This is just one long nightmare; when will it end?'

She was screaming now and pulling at her hair. The road was flooded ahead of them and the gunboats were behind them. What were they to do?

'We can't go forward and we can't go back; we're trapped.'

'Now, Elizabeth, don't start panicking; that isn't going to help matters. Come here.'

Alex put his arms around her and held her against him until she quietened down.

'That's better. Now come on let's find a place to hide for a bit then, when it is quieter and the water has gone down, we'll go and take a closer look at the road. We've been lucky so far, maybe our luck will hold a bit longer.'

All around them people were running in panic. The ships had started firing on the town and the smoke from burning houses was darkening the sky. People were still climbing up the hill behind them, hoping to get out of range of the gunfire but when they saw the devastation ahead they too were at a loss what to do; some just sat by the roadside and waited.

Alex led her away from the road and into the almond grove; it was like entering another world. The trees were covered in delicate pink and white blossom that gave off a heady scent. She breathed deeply and for a moment her spirits lifted; the trees were so beautiful.

'There's not much cover here,' complained Alex. 'We'll have to climb a bit higher.'

They climbed to the top of the hill; the view across the glistening bay was spectacular. They could see for miles, back along the way they had come where the road was still full of refugees and ahead, as far as the fishing port of Motril; far behind them the white-capped peaks of the Sierra Nevada stretched up into a cloudless blue sky. Elizabeth breathed deeply, gulping in the sweet, clean air. She needed this moment of peace to drive out the demons of the night before. High above their heads eagles soared, and the air was filled with the trilling of skylarks. From up here even the gunboats that continued to fire unceasingly at the town below seemed so far away as to be of no threat, just distant, dull explosions. She was reminded of walking in the hills above Málaga, with

Willow by her side. What a long time ago that seemed and yet it was only a few days, not much more than a week. How her world had changed in such a short time. She thought of her parents and hoped they were somewhere safe.

'Look. I think the bridge is still standing,' Alex said, pointing towards the deluge and beyond.

'It's a long way off. Are you sure it's a bridge?'

'Pretty sure. Well we'll know soon enough when we get there.'

'Alex, I know you're right when you say we should rest but I don't want to walk through all that in the dark.'

She pointed down at the flooded plain.

'No, it would be too dangerous if we strayed off the road. We'll just wait a few hours then we'll go. We'll be away before nightfall. Don't worry.'

They walked a bit further through the scented trees until at last Alex said they could stop. It was not as secure as their previous resting place but they did not want to wander too far away from the road. Others had taken their lead and followed them into the almond grove; they spread out, searching for shade and somewhere to sleep.

'You rest first, Elizabeth. I'll just sit here for a bit and keep an eye on things,' he said, propping his back against the gnarled trunk of an old tree.

Elizabeth did not argue; she flung herself onto the ground and was soon asleep.

Alex pulled his old cricket cap down over his eyes; he felt tired, more tired than he could ever remember but he knew he must not sleep. He looked at the supine figure of Elizabeth. In sleep she was even more beautiful; the ravages of the journey seemed to be suspended as she slept. He longed to reach out and touch her, to feel her soft skin, to run his finger along the line of those lovely lips. But he knew it was impossible; she was in love with someone else. He could see that; you would have to be blind not to know that she and Juan were lovers. It pained him to think of them together but it did nothing to dilute his own passion; if anything it sharpened it, the same way squeezing lemon juice on fish brought out the intensity of the flavour. He sighed. Even at a time like this his thoughts turned to food. He felt his stomach gurgle, protesting at its deprivation. How long was it since he had eaten? If he did not count those awful oranges, it must be at least thirty-six hours. He wondered how long he could survive without food. Three days, four, five? Well at least they had some water. He picked up the bottle and took a small sip.

He should never have come to Málaga. He should have gone back to England with the others as soon as they knew the Games were off. He was no soldier. He had considered it once, just before he started at university. His uncle was a regular soldier, a colonel in the Grenadier Guards; he had tried to persuade Alex that it would be a good career for him. 'Got the height, old chap,' he had said. 'And you can ride. Go on, give it a go; make a man of you.' Luckily Alex's parents had disagreed. As far as his father was concerned, nothing could take the place of an university degree. Alex sighed; he wished he was back in Oxford right now.

'Oh to be in England...' he murmured.

'What?' Elizabeth muttered, turning restlessly in her sleep.

'It's nothing; go to sleep,' he said, stroking her hair gently.

It all seemed so unreal. He tried to imagine his parents. What would they be doing right now? It was probably too cold for his mother to be in the garden; she might be preparing lunch. His father would no doubt be in his study, smoking his pipe and reading something by Trollope. And Angela? He felt a wave of homesickness as he thought of his sister and her family; it would be the twins' second birthday soon, next week maybe. He realised he was not even sure which day it was; all the days seemed to run together here. Maybe he'd be home in time for it. Wouldn't that be great and he'd take Elizabeth with him. Elizabeth would like his family, he felt sure. He drifted into a daydream where he took Elizabeth home to meet his parents and soon was asleep.

She slept a dreamless sleep and, when she awoke, saw that Alex too was sleeping. He still leant against the tree but his head had fallen onto his chest and his arms hung limply at his side. The sun was directly overhead; she looked at her watch and saw that she had only slept for a couple of hours. It was too soon to move yet. She turned onto her side and within minutes was asleep again.

'Elizabeth, wake up. It's time we got back to the road.'

She was awake in an instant; Alex was standing over her, shaking her shoulder.

'Come on; we need to go,' he continued.

'Yes, all right. I'm awake.'

She sat up, stretching her stiff limbs like a cat.

'Gosh, that feels better. I'm sorry Alex. Was I supposed to stay awake while you slept?'

'Doesn't matter. I got some sleep anyway. I'm just pleased that you've had a good rest. We'll be able to get on much faster now.'

They walked back to the road and resumed their place in the endless procession.

'I think we must be able to get through; people seemed to be moving forward at last,' Alex said.

'Can you see anything?' she asked him.

'Not really. Maybe when we get round that bend we'll have a better idea of what's up ahead.'

The stream of refugees was moving slowly. Alex took Elizabeth's hand and pulled her through the crowd, urging her forward. The road was elevated at this point, riding on stilts that carried it across the flood plain. Water gushed and swirled beneath it but no real damage had been done to the road and ahead of them stood the bridge, still intact.

'Well, our luck is holding,' he said. 'Thank God.'

'But when we cross the bridge we will be out in the open again and the gunboats will be able to see us,' she said.

'Oh come on Elizabeth. You can't have everything. Drowning or shooting, which is it to be?'

She tried to laugh but the danger was too real and all she could manage was a watery smile.

'Come on old girl. We'll make it, you see. We'll soon be in Almería, drinking that foul coffee again with Juan.'

He was very sweet, she thought, to try and cheer her up but she could not respond. She was numb with fear. When she thought of Juan, and she thought of him all the time, her heart felt like lead; there was a pain in her chest that would not go away. In the end Alex left her to her thoughts and they walked in silence, their attention focused on picking their way through the rubbish and not losing their balance on the muddy surface. The smell was putrid; all kinds of debris had been swept down by the water from the reservoir. It was like a scene from a World War One battlefield: the legs of dead animals stuck up from the mud at unnatural angles, trees stripped of their foliage stood stark against the sky. She tried not to look but the horror of the scene kept drawing her eyes back.

'Pity about your camera,' Alex said at last. 'It would have been good to capture this. I'm sure no-one will believe us when we tell them what it was like.'

'Ironic isn't it. That's the reason I'm here and the damn camera is broken.'

'Could be worse. Better that the camera was blown up than you.'

'Hey, I know those people,' she said suddenly.

Ahead of them were the twin boys and their mother. The boys now had a pair of boots each, albeit one pair was not really a pair, consisting of one brown boot and one black. She called out to them:

'*Hola.* Do you remember me?'

'*Si señora,*' they chorused.

They lifted their hands to their faces and mimed taking a photograph, then pointed to themselves.

'No, sorry, my camera doesn't work anymore. It was broken in the explosions,' she explained.

The boys shrugged and continued walking. Nothing had improved for this small family except that they now had an extra pair of footwear but the knowledge that they were still alive and had managed to come so far had a profound effect on Elizabeth. Her own hardships seemed petty; she at least knew where she was going. It might not be easy to get there but she had a goal. She would find Juan and then they would go to England together, to her parents' house. This family had walked for days and days and had no idea when they would arrive. They had left their home and had no other home to go to; all they could hope for was a safe haven where they could find food and shelter. Then what? They could not walk back once the fighting was over. They would have to start a new life in a strange town away from all their friends and family. She wondered what had happened to the boys' father. Was he alive or dead? Once these boys had a family; they had a father; they had uncles and aunts, grandparents, great-uncles and great-aunts, maybe brothers and sisters, a whole network of relatives that supported and united them. That had all been torn from them and now these two identical boys walked behind their mother, clinging to her skirt and into a new world.

Eventually they crossed the estuary and were back on the coast road, leaving Motril behind them. They walked through the night; now Alex kept close by her side, sometimes taking her arm to help her and asking her from time to time if she was all right. He seemed to be taking his promise to Juan seriously.

'Tell me about you and Juan,' he said. 'Have you known each other long?'

All our lives, she thought, it seems like all our lives but instead she said:

'Not really. I met him at the Regina. He was with the brother-in-law of our gardener.'

She paused. It did not sound like the start of a passionate love affair.

'Then we just fell in love.'

Her words sounded pathetic, like a love-sick teenager. How could she convey to this man how much Juan meant to her when she could hardly explain it to herself. She expected Alex to make some flippant remark but instead he put his arm around her and gave her a squeeze.

'Don't worry Elizabeth. You'll soon be together again.'

She felt her eyes fill with tears.

'So what sort of work did he do?' Alex asked.

She began to tell him about Juan and his family.

'So you see I'm really worried now that someone will recognise him and think that he's a spy. He is not safe; he's divided by his blood and his beliefs and is not at home anywhere.'

'Yes but he's got a foot in both camps in a way. There must be lots of other people in the same situation. There's one thing certain about this war, it has split the country in two, with no concern for families or blood-lines. But don't worry; I would think from what that Canadian chap said there will be such chaos at the hospital that nobody will be checking his name and anyway I doubt that anybody will be looking for potential spies.'

'You're probably right.'

Speaking about Juan made her sad. She should never have left him; but there had been no alternative. What if she could not find him again? The thought made her cold.

'Juan is very upset about his father you know; he loves him but he cannot talk to him. His father believes that Juan's loyalty should be first and foremost to the family, that his personal beliefs should come second. He won't see any other point of view.'

'Well, family is important. It's only now that I'm so far away from mine that I realise this.'

'Yes but it's more than that. His father believes that this Republican government will destroy the traditional Spanish way of life unless they are stopped. He sees himself and other families like his own as defenders of the Church and the Monarchy; he believes that the fascists are their saviours.'

'And Juan disagrees?'

'Absolutely.   He told Juan that if he stayed in the Republican zone he would never speak to him again and that he would disinherit him.   Juan's mother and his sister were heartbroken.'

'I can understand that.'

'It's tragic; Juan hates being cut off from his family; he loves them, especially his sister and now he will probably never see them again.'

'That may depend on who wins this war and if we all survive to see it,' Alex replied.

CHAPTER 11

It took them all that night and a further day and night to reach Almería. Their journey continued in the same relentless way: they walked by night and they tried to take a few hours sleep by day. The gunboats still stalked them and, if they were lucky, they had time to hide in the sugar cane until they passed by. Sometimes German aeroplanes flew overhead and dropped bombs on the road. Inured to the death and destruction all around them now, they picked their way through the dead bodies and passed the wounded with averted eyes, intent only on keeping their own exhausted bodies moving. Three days of salt and sun had made Elizabeth's eyes swollen and puffy and turned her fine English skin brown and dry; her lips were cracked and hurt each time she tried to speak and her tongue felt too large for her mouth. Her hair hung lank and greasy on her shoulders and she itched; worse than the aching bones and her raw and bleeding feet was that incessant itching. A hot bath and a soft bed were illusionary items from another world, another life but they kept reappearing in her mind to taunt her. A few times they saw the Red Cross van on its errand of mercy, collecting the children and gathering up the wounded. Alex ran over once to ask if they knew anything about Juan but the answer was negative. They passed through small villages where the inhabitants came out to watch them go by. Some brought them water and sometimes a few dates or oranges but most had no more food than the poor travellers and could offer nothing. By the time they had reached the city their hunger was like a wild animal within their bellies, desperate to be sated.

'We've made it Elizabeth, we've made it,' Alex said, hugging her. 'Now everything will be all right. We'll find Juan and we'll get a boat out of here.'

Almería was a smaller city than Málaga but like its neighbour it was a busy port. It was on the southern extremity of the Republican area and here at least law and order prevailed. The garrison of the Civil Governor was operational and both troops and police were in full view. The *Comité Provincial para la Evacuación* had set up a centre for the refugees where they could get food. It meant queuing for hours to receive a glass of milk and some dry bread, the only food that many of them had received in days but it was gladly received. The town was crowded with refugees, wounded soldiers and injured civilians but as yet it did not seem to have suffered any severe bombing or mortar attacks.

'We must find Juan,' she said. 'It can't be far to the hospital. Let's ask someone.'

'Hang on; the first thing we must do is go to the British Consulate and let them know we're here. They'll help us find Juan and also will be able to tell us if there's a boat out of here.'

'But Alex...'

'No "buts", first the Consulate then the hospital. Juan won't be going anywhere. Another hour won't hurt.'

Elizabeth was too tired to argue. She let Alex make enquiries and followed him through the crowded streets in silence. After so many days and nights travelling she found it hard to believe that they had actually arrived. There were people everywhere they looked; they wandered aimlessly along the road; they stood in small groups on the pavement talking; they sat on the kerb amongst their meagre possessions; they stretched out on small patches of the civic gardens to sleep the sleep of the exhausted; they queued for food; they queued for medical help; they queued for clothes; their animals drank from the public fountains where their children splashed in unashamed delight. There was a sense of relief and possibly hope, in the air.

'Alex, do you know where you're going?' she asked.

'Yes, we're here now.'

He led her into a tall, stone building and up a flight of marble stairs. They stopped outside a door that said: 'British Consulate', knocked and went in. A uniformed man asked them their business.

'We would like to see the Consul,' Alex said, brusquely.

'Wait here and I'll see if he is available,' the man replied, eyeing them rather suspiciously.

Elizabeth sat down on a hard, wooden chair; she was so tired that if he had not come back almost immediately she would have fallen asleep.

'Come this way please,' he said, showing them into a spacious but sparsely furnished room.

A man in his mid-fifties, with an imposing moustache and little hair rose from behind a large, highly polished table.

'Good morning,' he said, extending his hand to Alex in greeting. 'How can I help you?'

The Right Honourable Quentin Brooke-Smith wore a rather shabby pin-stripe suit and a plain white shirt. His head was like polished glass and to improve its appearance he had dragged his few remaining strands of grey hair across the top of it and plastered them down with oil; a pair of horn-rimmed glasses gave his pleasant, somewhat boyish face a more serious demeanour. He motioned for them to sit down.

Alex began to relate their story while the Consul listened gravely, his elbows on the table and his chin resting on his hands, nodding at everything the young man had to say.

'Yes, I heard that things were not good in Málaga but I hadn't realised that they were quite that bad. So the Consul has gone, you say?'

'Yes, the Consulate is closed. There's an Honorary Vice-Consul, or at least there was when we left. Things were changing very fast and of course we haven't heard anything since.'

'No, of course. Well I've sent most of my staff home; it's becoming too dangerous here now. The Government are still in charge of course but the insurgents are moving closer all the time. I'm just waiting for instructions from Madrid before I too pack up and go.'

'That bad?'

'Afraid so. Anyway, what can I do for you?'

'Two things actually,' began Alex. 'First of all we have to find a friend of ours who was wounded on the way here. Some Canadian chap and his nurse picked him up just outside Motril and said they would bring him here. We need to find him.'

'Oh, that must have been Norman. He and his team have been doing a damned, fine job bringing those poor devils here; must have saved hundreds of lives. Clever chap, you know, came up with the idea of a mobile blood transfusion service; that's what he originally came down here to do. Well when he saw the extent of the problem he decided it made more sense to strip his van and pack it with people instead. The Spanish look upon the chap as a saint.'

'Well we were pretty pleased to see him, I can tell you.'

'Well now, about your friend, I'm sure you'll find him in the International Red Cross Hospital; I can tell you how to get there. I'll draw you a bit of a map.'

He pulled out a sheet of paper from a drawer in the table and began to draw.

'There, this is us here, where I've drawn the X, and this is the hospital.'

He handed Alex the map.

'Now what was the second thing you wanted?'

'We need to get out of Spain and take our friend with us.'

'You know of course that that will not be easy. The only realistic way out of here now is by sea. However you may be in luck; I think there will be a ship leaving for Gibraltar in a couple of days. We can probably manage to get you on it. I take it you have proof of your identities, British passports for example?'

Alex looked at Elizabeth. She nodded and took her passport out of her bag.

'Yes we have our passports.'

'Good. Well there is a British ship not far away; it's been observing the fighting along the coast for the past week.'

'What? There was a British ship out there and it did nothing to stop those ships firing on innocent women and children?' Elizabeth asked outraged. 'We were in the midst of that. Our friend was injured in the bombardment and we could have been killed.'

Alex put his hand on her arm but she shrugged it off.

'Why didn't they stop them?'

The Consul looked at her, his face impassive and explained as though to a rather recalcitrant child:

'It was not their place to intervene; they were there simply to observe. Great Britain is bound by the Non-Intervention agreement; it is not allowed to interfere in other people's wars. It is stated most clearly that Britain has no right to carry out police measures within the territorial waters of another country.'

'But this wasn't a war; it was a slaughter.'

The Consul was obviously not going to be drawn into an argument with Elizabeth over the moral rights and wrongs of the British ship's actions. He turned back to Alex and continued:

'So you would like three passages on this ship to Gibraltar?'

'Yes, please, as soon as possible.'

'Well the ship will probably be here in a couple of days; I'll make sure your names are on the passenger list. Right, let me take down the details.'

He carefully copied their names from the passports.

'And your friend? What is his name?'

Elizabeth hesitated; which name should she give him?

'Juan Francisco Gomez de la Luz de Montevideo Rodriguez.'

'Spanish?'

'Yes. Is that a problem?'

'It most certainly is. We are not permitted to take any Spanish nationals,' he said, putting the top on his gold fountain pen and laying it down on the table. 'I'm sorry, it is impossible. I will arrange transport for the two of you but your friend will have to make other arrangements.'

'I'm not going without him,' Elizabeth said, emphatically.

'Well that's up to you. I will arrange the passage for two and suggest you call here again in a couple of days and I will give you your passes and let you know when you sail. Then it is up to you whether you go or not. However I cannot emphasise more strongly that this may well be your last chance to get out of Spain alive. I recommend that you both leave on that ship.'

Elizabeth was about to object again but Alex took her arm and pulled her to her feet.

'Thank you for your help. We'll be back in a couple of days.'

The Consul leant across the table to shake his hand.

'By the way, do you have anywhere to stay?' he asked him.

'No, we've only just arrived. The first thing we did was to come here.'

'Well try this place. It's pretty basic but we use it a lot and they always keep a couple of rooms for us. Here, give them this card and I'm sure they will find you something.'

He removed his business card from the drawer and wrote the name of the hotel on the back.

'Thank you. We'll do that,' said Alex.

Elizabeth did not speak; she had a feeling that she was being betrayed.

The hotel looked quite dilapidated from outside, with peeling stucco and loose window frames but inside it was clean and tidy. A young Spanish woman was about to send them on their way until Alex produced the magic business card; this changed everything and miraculously a room with two beds and clean sheets was found. There was no hot water but there was a wash basin and a couple of threadbare towels; to Elizabeth this was luxury. She was so grateful that she paid her share to the woman and did not query the fact that she had to spend the next two nights sleeping in the same room as Alex. Somehow, after what they had been through, such niceties seemed irrelevant.

While they waited for the maid to put the clean sheets on the beds, they sat in the bar eating hard bread and olive oil and drinking sweet, black coffee.

'Now can we go and look for Juan?' she asked, wiping the crumbs from her chin.

'Wouldn't you like to rest first? You haven't slept for almost twenty-four hours,' Alex said. 'You look all in. Why don't you lie down for a short while and then we'll go to the hospital.'

She did not have the strength to argue with him. They went up to the bedroom and she lay down on the bed just as she was and slept. How long they slept she did not know but the sun was low in the sky when they woke and its rays barely made it through the shutters and onto the tiled floor.

'Alex, wake up. We should go; it's getting dark.'

She shook him gently. He rolled towards her and stretched his long arms above his head; he looked so young.

'Right oh. Gosh that was good.'

'Yes, it's heaven to sleep in a bed again, isn't it.'

He sat up, now wide awake.

'Where's that map?'

'Here. Do you think you can find the hospital?' she asked.

'Yes, it's a doddle. Come on let's go or you'll be nagging me all night long.'

It took them about ten minutes to walk to the hospital; it was a grey, forbidding looking building with the flag of the International Red Cross flying from it. As soon as they entered the big, glass doors they knew they would have problems. There were injured people everywhere; some were lucky and lay on stretchers or makeshift beds, others supported themselves by leaning on the walls, while others lay on the floor, too much in pain to care. The air was heavy with the odour of carbolic and ammonia but it could not extinguish completely the smell of blood and human suffering. They made their way down the grim, grey corridors, carefully stepping over the bodies, looking for someone in charge. At last they spotted a nurse.

'*Perdóneme,*' Alex said. 'We are looking for a friend; he came here a couple of days ago. His name is Juan Francisco Gomez.'

'Sorry, I don't recognise the name. See if one of the doctors has heard of him.'

She pointed along the corridor. They continued a bit further until they came to a dispensary, where another nurse was distributing medicines to a long line of walking wounded. Then they saw a doctor, his white coat stained with dirt and blood.

'Excuse me, Doctor,' Alex began again.

'Sorry, I'm too busy. Speak to one of the nurses,' he said, brushing past them.

'This is not going to be easy, Elizabeth,' Alex said.

They carried on through a labyrinth of corridors, turning identical corner after corner until they came to what they had to assume was the admissions desk; one harassed nurse stood behind a counter trying to take the details of the wounded. It

211

was a kind of clearing house; the patients stood, lay or sat, heads down, eyes closed, waiting for someone to collect them and take them to a doctor. Two nurses moved amongst them checking pulses and labelling them according to their survival chances; those on the point of death or already dead received a black tag, the urgent cases received a red one and the less urgent a white one. An orderly appeared pushing a stretcher-trolley; he stopped near them and inspected the tag of a man bleeding profusely from a wound in his leg then he lifted him onto the stretcher.

'*Perdóneme*,' Alex tried again. 'What happens to the wounded that are brought here by the Canadian?'

'Norman? He usually takes them straight down to Emergencies and gives a list of their names to her.'

He pointed to the admissions clerk. Alex groaned. It would take ages to get close enough to speak to her. He turned to Elizabeth:

'Look you stay here in this queue and try to speak to the admissions woman. I'll carry on looking for him. I'll meet you back here in half an hour. Is that all right?'

Elizabeth nodded. She slotted herself in behind a woman with her arm in a makeshift sling; she had a white tag on her sleeve.

Between them they scoured the entire hospital but there was no sign of Juan; the doctors who found the time to speak to them did not remember him and the admissions clerk had no record of his name, neither as Gomez nor Montevideo. The next day they returned to the hospital again to look for him but they still could not find him; they questioned all the nurses and many of the doctors but nobody could remember Juan.

212

'I'm sorry but you can see what it is like here. It is perfectly possible that he was here and has been discharged; it's also possible that he died from his wounds. Maybe you should check the morgue,' one tired doctor explained.

At this Elizabeth began to cry and could not stop despite all Alex's endeavours to cheer her up.

'I want to go to the morgue,' she insisted.

'Look Elizabeth, I don't think that's a good idea. It won't be pretty and anyway I'm sure Juan's not there. He's probably been discharged.'

'I want to be sure.'

'I tell you what, I'll go and look in the morgue.'

'No, I want to see for myself.'

They took the stone staircase down into the basement following the signs for *Cadáveres* until they came to the morgue. As they were about to push open the double doors a man in green overalls came running towards them.

'Stop. Where do you think you're going? No-one is allowed in there.'

'I'm sorry, we're looking for someone. My husband,' Elizabeth explained. 'He was brought to the hospital a few days ago but we can't find him. We thought he might be dead.'

'Well I'm sorry about that but you still can't go in there; it's restricted.'

'We just want to see if he's there.'

'*Señora,* I don't think you understand; we are dealing with at least a hundred dead bodies every day. If your husband died a few days ago he won't be here now; he's probably buried in an unmarked grave on the edge of the city.'

At this Elizabeth began to wail and berate Alex:

'I knew we shouldn't have waited. We should have come straight to the hospital the minute we got here. Now what do we do? How can we find him?'

The tears were running down her face in an uninterrupted stream. Alex put his arm around her and held her to him, letting her cry out her rage and frustration on his shoulder. When she had quietened a little he led her back up the stairs to the main hospital. Ahead of them was a familiar figure with a black beret.

'That's the Canadian,' Alex said. 'Hey, Norman.'

The doctor stopped and turned to see who was calling him; he frowned slightly, not recognising them.

'Thank goodness we've found you,' began Elizabeth. 'We can't find my husband; he doesn't seem to be anywhere in the hospital.'

'I'm sorry, do I know you?' he asked politely.

'Not really. We met you a few days ago outside Motril. You took our friend with you in your van; he was badly injured. Now we can't find him,' Alex explained.

'I'm sorry; we've brought so many people here over the last week that I have trouble remembering them all.'

'Yes, I understand. Look my husband is Spanish; his name is Juan Francisco. He had a broken collarbone and was wounded in the chest and in the head. We told you we thought he might have concussion.'

'Yes, wait a minute, I do remember him; he was wearing your coat.'

'Yes, that's him, in a blue checked coat.'

'Well he was not good as far as I can remember. By the time we got him here he was delirious. I dropped him off at the Emergency room and that was the last I saw of him. Don't they have a record of him? I always give them a list of

214

the names of the wounded; it's easier that way because some of them are barely conscious by the time we arrive.'

'No, no-one seems to have heard of him. Oh, I don't know what I'm going to do,' Elizabeth cried.

She struggled to fight back the tears.

'I'm sorry but maybe you have to face up to the fact that he has probably died of his wounds. So many people do; it's not always the gravity of the wound that kills them, it's because they are already very weak and unable to resist the infections that set in.'

He looked anxious to get away from them.

'I'm sorry I can't be more help. It's tough but my guess is that if you can't find him then he's dead.'

'Thank you, we'll keep looking,' said Alex, squeezing Elizabeth's hand.

He led her back to the hotel in a daze. She was not crying anymore; there were no more tears to cry. It was as though there was a heavy stone in her chest, just below her heart; it had been there since they had helped Juan into the ambulance and it would not go away. She looked at the lost children wandering through the streets, calling for their mothers and she felt nothing; she thought of the dead baby abandoned on their matrimonial bed and shed no tears. Juan was dead. Everything else faded into insignificance before this awful realisation. Now she would never be able to introduce him to her parents; she would never take him to England and show him her special childhood places: the stream in the woods near her grandparents' house where she used to sit and read, the beaches that they went to each summer holiday, the country lanes where she cycled. Now they would never marry and have a family of their own; they would not be able to watch their children grow up; they would never have grandchildren. All too soon he had left her to mourn him alone. And what of his family? Would they ever know what had happened to him? Would they have to spend year after year wondering if he were still alive? She had no way of contacting them and they did not know of her existence.

She left Alex talking to the hotel owner and went up to their room alone. She filled the wash-basin with cold water and placed it on the floor by the bed. Her blisters had burst and bled, sticking the skin to her shoes and as she carefully tried to remove them they started to bleed again. She placed her feet in the cold water and sat looking at them for a while. Her toes were black with bruises and it looked as though she would lose her toenails; the soles of her feet were hard and the skin was cracked leather but only her heels bled. She bent down rubbing the soap between her toes and round her ankles; it was agony to touch them but she rubbed harder and harder, rejoicing in the pain, until her feet were at last clean. She heard Alex come into the bedroom but she did not look up.

'There was a message from the Consul. The ship arrives in Almería tonight. He says we have to go to the Consulate first thing tomorrow morning to collect our boarding passes. Elizabeth, are you listening? We have to go tomorrow.'

'I'm not going,' she said. 'I'm not going without Juan.'

She lifted her feet out of the water and dried them carefully. Then she turned to Alex and said:

'I've told you Alex; I can't go without him. I have to find him.'

'Elizabeth, I really am sorry but we have to face facts. If Juan were alive we would have found him or he would have found us. He knew we would go to the Consulate for help;

216

I'm sure he would have got a message to us if he were still here. I know it's hard to accept but it's almost certain that he's dead.'

'I'm staying here until I find out what has happened to him,' she insisted.

'No Elizabeth, you're coming with me. I promised Juan I would take care of you and I mean to keep my promise. Be realistic for a moment; you've seen what it was like on the journey here and we can only imagine what atrocities are happening in Málaga right now. Do you really want me to abandon you here alone? The Republicans are in control at the moment but the Nationalists are not very far away; they could be here in a couple of days. What will happen to the city if they attack? What will happen to you? You have no money and no clothes and once that ship sails, you have no way of getting out. I'm not going to leave you here.'

'I need to know what has happened to him.'

'Look, do you think Juan would want you to risk your life looking for his dead body? You cannot help him now. Your place is with the living, not the dead.'

'It doesn't matter what happens to me now?'

'Of course it matters. Just because Juan is dead it doesn't mean that he is forgotten. As long as you and I are alive, he will live on in our memories and in our hearts. Don't sacrifice yourself for nothing Elizabeth. Juan would not have wanted it.'

She looked at him sadly; he was right. There was nothing more they could do. If Alex was leaving and the Consulate was closing she would have nobody to help her if she stayed; she knew she would never be able to manage alone. She would leave but she would not forget.

They stood on the deck of HMS Hood and looked back towards the land. It was barely daylight when the ship began to pull away from the shore. She could see a few lights in the town as people began to stir and the repeated flashing of the lighthouse, a warning to approaching ships. They headed south-west towards Gibraltar, leaving the barren coast and the cold sierras behind them. For a while they could see the road they had walked, the road where they had learnt about human suffering and endurance, where they had left some small part of themselves. It snaked along between the sierra and the sea, an insignificant highway for a battlefield. People were still fleeing from Málaga and the carnage continued; they could see the 'Baleares', 'El Almirante Cervera' and the German 'Graf Spey' cruising leisurely along the coast firing at the refugees. There was nothing they could do but watch in despair. Only a few days before they had been part of it; now they were on their way home.

CHAPTER 12

Juan stood on the hilltop overlooking the Gulf of Almería. He could see the destroyer pulling away from the shore and heading west and he knew she was aboard. There was a pain in his chest that had nothing to do with his wounds, an ache that he knew no doctor could cure.

The journey in the ambulance was no more than a hazy recollection of alternatively slipping into unconsciousness and being rudely awakened every time the truck hit a pot hole or a rock in the road, sending the pain shooting through his shoulder each time like a fresh wound. He remembered someone carrying him into the hospital and the glare of overhead lights but little else until he awoke to find himself in a hospital bed in a long narrow ward; all around him people were groaning in pain. He tried to sit up but his good arm failed him and he fell back on the bed with a bump that caused him to gasp. His chest and left shoulder were tightly bandaged and a further bandage seemed to be wound around his head. He touched it gingerly with his free hand. A doctor was moving along the ward, checking each patient. When he reached Juan, he stopped.

'Ah, you're awake,' he said. 'How do you feel?'

'All right, I think.'

The doctor bent over him and shone a light in his eyes.

'Good, no sign of concussion. You've been lucky,' he said. 'If someone hadn't removed that shrapnel from your chest, I doubt that you'd have made it.'

'Am I all right then?'

'You've lost a lot of blood but we gave you a blood transfusion as soon as you got here. You're still very weak but you'll live; just rest up for a few days and then you can be on your way.'

He checked that the bandages were still in place, then moved on to the next bed. Juan's neighbour did not seem to be so lucky; the doctor looked at his wounds and immediately called one of the nurses across to him.

'Take this man down to surgery, right away. That foot is going to have to come off or he'll lose his leg.'

The nurse removed the brake from the gurney and within minutes she and the man had disappeared. An orderly was moving from bed to bed giving the men water. He stopped by Juan's bed.

'Water?'

'Please,' he said, trying to lift himself on one elbow.

The man placed his hand under Juan's head and raised it so he could drink. The water was warm but he drank it gratefully.

'How long have I been here?' he asked.

The orderly looked at the tag at the end of the bed.

'Two days,' he replied. 'More water?'

Juan shook his head and the orderly moved on to the next bed.

Two days. Isabel and Alex would be arriving any time. What had Alex said? It would take at least three days to get here, and that was before the bombing started. He tried to remember exactly where they had been when Alex had made his prediction; somewhere near Torre del Mar he thought. So if he had been in the hospital for two days, then they should arrive in Almería tomorrow or, at the latest, the day after. They would come straight here to look for him, of that he was sure. He wondered if they were safe. Anything could have befallen them on that road. He should not have left her; he should have insisted that he stay. But even as he thought it, he knew it was foolish; he had been in no shape to walk for three more days. He put his hand on his chest; the wound was tender to the touch but it did not hurt when he breathed. He tried moving his left arm and immediately a sharp pain shot through his shoulder. He wriggled his way up into a sitting position, pausing from time to time to let the pain subside, until at last he could see what was around him. He leant back against the wall and looked at his fellow patients. At first glance all seemed well; most of the patients were shrouded in clean, white bandages and hooked up to some kind of transfusion. They lay on makeshift beds or hospital gurneys that were pushed against each other, leaving only a narrow passage for the nurses to walk through. Their eyes were closed, and they lay, lost in the oblivion of morphine, their moans floating in the air like some discordant music. Then he noticed the injuries: men without legs, children without arms, old women covered in cuts and bruises. The doctor was right; he had been lucky.

Two women were making their way along the ward with a food trolley; they were dishing out bowls of soup to those that were conscious enough to eat. The smell of the food made him realise how hungry he was; he could not remember the last time he had eaten anything, never mind anything hot. By the time they reached his bed he was salivating.

'Can you manage?' one of the women asked him.

'I think so.'

She propped the bowl on his knee and put a spoon in his free hand.

'Be careful now.'

The soup was made from potatoes and onions; it was thin but to Juan it tasted better than anything he had ever eaten. At first he tried to use the spoon but the gap between the bowl and his mouth was too great, so he abandoned it and picked up the bowl in his good hand. He drank it down greedily and instantly felt revived.

'Nurse,' he called.

A nurse, who was redressing the head wound of the man in the next bed, looked up.

'When can I get out of here?'

She moved to his bed and looked at his tag.

'It depends on what the doctor says but I would think in a couple of days.'

'I need to leave today. Can I speak to the doctor?'

'All the doctors are busy. You'll have to wait until tomorrow. Someone will come and look at you tomorrow.'

'But I feel fine now.'

She took no notice of him and carried on treating her patient. When she had finished she turned to Juan.

'I'm going to remove the bandage on your head. Just keep still for a minute.'

She leant across him to unwind the gauze; she smelled of carbolic soap and garlic. He looked at her; she was probably no more than twenty but the strain of these last few days was etched on her face. She looked exhausted. He continued to watch her face as she carefully removed the dressing from his forehead, then cleaned the area with iodine. The pungent smell of the liquid and its subsequent sting, as it made contact with his raw flesh, caused his eyes water.

'That's healing just fine,' she said. 'I don't think we need to put anything else on it.'

She gave it a final swab of iodine and then examined his other bandages.

'Any pain?'

He shook his head.

'These are fine for now. The doctor will probably want to them redressed before you leave.'

'When will that be?'

'You're a great hurry to get back out there,' she said. 'I told you, the doctor decides that sort of thing. Just get some rest now.'

He watched her pick up her things and move on to the next bed; her step was slow and her movements automatic.

Juan touched his head; there seemed to be a cut running from his left eyebrow up into his hairline. Nothing to worry about she had said. He lay there watching her as she moved along the line of beds, changing dressings and occasionally calling for assistance with some task that was outside her sphere. The orderly, who had been giving out the water, reappeared.

'Come quick; you're needed in Emergency,' he told the nurse. 'They've just brought in another batch of wounded.'

The nurse hastily finished dressing the man's wound, fixing the bandage into place with a large safety pin, and ran after the orderly.

Who were these injured people? Could Isabel or Alex be among them? They should not be here, he decided, their place was back in England, not caught up in a civil war in a strange country. If only he could convince Isabel to leave, he knew that Alex would take her back. But Isabela would not go without him; she would come looking for him and then she would stay. No, it was too dangerous. He could not allow her to put herself in such danger for him; it was romantic foolishness. There was only one thing he could do; he would disappear.

He looked along the ward; there were no medical staff to be seen. This was the moment to make his move. If he stayed and waited for Isabel he knew she would never go home. And what would she face if she remained in Spain, abandoned by her compatriots and caught between warring factions? If the Nationalists caught her they might throw her in prison; there was the threat of injury, rape, starvation, even death. He could not even guarantee her safety in the Republican zone; there was no safe place. No he could not risk her life in this way; he loved her too much for that.

The staff had had no time to remove his clothes and he still wore his trousers and shoes; Isabela's coat had probably been thrown away when he arrived. He stood up, testing his weight on his legs; they were fine, a bit wobbly but otherwise they seemed to work well. All his injuries seemed to be to the upper part of his body. He felt in his pockets; his papers and money were still there. He took one last look down the ward and when he was sure that there was nobody around he walked out. He headed for what he assumed was the exit, pushing past queues of desperate people, hopelessness written all over their faces. He passed doctors and nurses but no-one was interested in him; they were too occupied with the new arrivals, some of whom looked as though they would not last the night. All at once he was at the main door and out on the street. He stopped for a moment, leaning against the glass door, and breathed deeply, drinking in the cold, fresh air. Despite the persistent, nagging pain in his shoulder, he felt invigorated. Then he set off to look for the headquarters of the Military Governor.

They had been reluctant to take him at first but he convinced them that his injuries were superficial. They gave him a uniform and a gun, and told him to report to Army Headquarters in Valencia. Now, as he watched the British navy's HMS Hood take her away from him, he felt a sense of relief. She was safe. That was all that mattered. His Isabel was safe. When this war was over he would find her again; somehow he would find her. He turned from the sea and walked down to the railway station.

PART TWO

MAY 2007 ENGLAND

CHAPTER 13

Robert Percy of 'Percy, Percy and Rowland' was an elderly man; he had been Sir Alexander's solicitor for many years and before that his father, Rupert Percy, had held the post. He polished his rimless glasses with a spotless white handkerchief which he then replaced in the top pocket of an immaculate grey pin-stripe suit and, carefully placing the glasses on his nose, regarded the assembled group with that look of seriousness, mingled with sadness that he had cultivated over the years for just such occasions.

'As we are all now assembled, I will begin to read the will,' he announced.

He cleared his throat and began:

'I, Sir Alexander James Reeves, being of sound body and mind, do hereby....'

Kate tried to concentrate but the room was hot and stuffy and the solicitor's voice had already taken on a monotonous drone. She looked around the room; they were a small group: her great-aunt Angela, sitting in a velvet easy chair that dwarfed her tiny frame, her white hair carefully combed to disguise its sparseness and her blue eyes still twinkling despite the seriousness of the occasion, her uncle Jeremy, still a very fit man for sixty-five, dressed today in a dark serge suit and black tie and her cousins Ruth and Rachel, identical at birth and still identical forty-five years later in black georgette and three-inch heels.

'and in this, my last Will and Testament, I do give and bequeath my entire estate to be divided equally between my three surviving children and The Reeves Shelters Trust.'

He paused and looked at them over the top of his spectacles.

'Sadly, as you are all aware, two of Sir Alexander's children have passed away since this will was written. I did bring this to Sir Alexander's attention at the time but he said to let the will stand. That is why I have invited his grandchildren, Ms. Scott, Mrs Perry-Smith and Mrs. Pinkerton, as the surviving members of their respective lines, to attend today.'

He paused and looked at them, before continuing:

'Ms. Scott will inherit one quarter of Sir Alexander's estate through her mother Isabel Scott, née Reeves and Mrs. Perry-Smith and Mrs. Pinkerton will each inherit one eighth of the estate through their mother Rosemary Williams, née Reeves. Mr. Reeves as Sir Alexander's surviving son will inherit one quarter and the remaining quarter will go directly to the Reeves Shelters Trust.'

Nobody spoke, so he continued reading:

'I would also like to make a number of smaller bequests: the first is to my dear sister Angela, who I know has no need of more money and houses. I leave her my personal papers and collection of photographs. She has always been my dear friend and confidante and I know she will know what to do with them. She may also continue to live in my house as long as she wishes. The second bequest is to my secretary, Paul Ian Thomson...'

229

He continued reading for a few more minutes then placed the will on the table and looked at his audience.

'Do you have any questions?' he asked.

Kate's head was buzzing with questions but she said nothing. She was dazed by the news and incredulous that her grandfather had left her anything at all. She had been fond of him even though he could be a bit cantankerous at times but since she had grown up and moved to London she had hardly seen anything of him. She knew her cousins had made a regular point of visiting him and he was always invited to spend Christmas in one or other of their homes. She also knew that he never accepted these invitations, preferring to stay in his old manor house on the north Devon coast with his widowed sister and his housekeeper. As her grandfather had grown older he had become somewhat of a recluse, only leaving his home a few times a year to visit the children's shelters that he funded and review their progress. All other business he conducted from his house, summoning solicitors, accountants and investment consultants to him. His secretary, on whom he relied for all his correspondence with the Reeves Shelters, was a pleasant, reliable young man. Kate had met him in London on the odd occasion she had attended the opening of a new shelter.

'Yes. Exactly how much is my father's estate worth?' her uncle Jeremy asked.

She had noticed him staring at her during the reading of the will; he had looked displeased when he heard her name read out.

'Well,' began the solicitor, removing his spectacles and re-polishing them. 'I am not able to give you a definitive figure at this precise moment because we still have to receive the valuations of his various properties: the holiday cottage in

Dorset, the flat in Hampstead, the apartments in Nice and of course, the manor house. I am also waiting for the final calculations on his share holdings and other investments; there is not a great deal of cash, some hundred thousand or so.'

He paused and regarded them over the top of his glasses.

'I suppose you all know that over the years he has transferred a lot of his money to the Reeves Shelters Trust? During the last six months in particular he has made some very generous donations.'

'Well can't you give us some idea? A rough estimate would do for now,' her uncle insisted.

'Well I will do my best. Now remember that this is only a guess but I would estimate his entire estate to be worth something in the region of ten or twelve million pounds.'

Kate was astounded. She had known her grandfather was a rich man but not that he was quite so wealthy. She looked at the others; the twins seemed as surprised as she was but she could tell from his face that her uncle was disappointed. He would only be receiving a quarter of that: two and a half million. To her it was a fortune but maybe he had expected to receive his dead sisters' share as well. Kate was an only child, she would receive her mother's entire inheritance, Rachel and Ruth would share their mother's between them but her uncle Jeremy had three children to inherit his portion. She had always got on very well with her cousins; she hoped that this was not going to change things. She had read of perfectly happy families becoming estranged over the distribution of an inheritance; it did not seem to matter whether it were a few family heirlooms and grandmother's rocking chair or millions of pounds, it still unlocked the demons of greed and envy.

Her grandfather had been born into a donnish middle-class family, well provided for but not rich; he had started his working life as a reporter with a local newspaper then took up a career in publishing. When his parents died they left him and his sister a comfortable house and a few hundred pounds each. Her grandfather used his share to set up 'Apollo Books', a small company that published current literary works, re-prints of the classics and some poetry. It had been successful in a modest way but had never looked like making a millionaire of him, until that was, the day when the company was bought out by a much bigger and more aggressive rival. He then invested the proceeds of the sale in stocks and shares, at a time when the market was buoyant and found, to everyone's surprise, that he had a natural talent for making money. Although a generous man, he was never ostentatious and the first thing he did with his new-found wealth was to set up the Reeves Shelters' Trust. He and his wife had been joint presidents of the trust until her grandmother's death in 1964. Her death had affected him badly and he named the next shelter he opened 'The Elizabeth Reeves Shelter' in her memory.

'When do you think we'll know?' asked one of her cousins.

It was Rachel, or was it Ruth; it was very difficult to tell them apart. She waited for the solicitor to give her a clue.

'I would expect to have it all completed by the end of the month, Mrs. Pinkerton,' he replied.

So it was Ruth. Really it was a bit ridiculous to dress identically at their age; Kate was sure they did it just to have an advantage over people. Still she was quite fond of her cousins; when they were children they had spent many summer holidays together in North Devon at their

232

grandparents' house. The twins were much closer to her in age than Richard's children, so they had had a lot more in common. Nowadays she rarely saw any of them: the twins were married to men that worked in the City and lived within half a mile of each other; Edward was living in Australia, Sally was engaged to a teacher and Anne had become very religious and was living somewhere in India. Only the twins had any children; Ruth had a girl and Rachel a boy, born within days of each other. She wondered if they had planned it that way and what their husbands had to say about it.

'So what do we do now?' Jeremy Reeves asked.

'I'll be writing to you all individually to let you know the exact amount of your inheritance and, unless you advise me otherwise, I will transfer the money to your respective bank accounts as soon as it is released. I have all the details here.'

'Well hang on there; I might like to see some of the investments that my father had; they may very well be worth keeping.'

'By all means, we can make an appointment for next week and go over it all in detail if you wish.'

Kate saw the twins look at each other.

'Perhaps it would be a good idea if we came to see you too,' they chorused.

'Very well, I'll have my secretary come in as soon as we've finished.'

He looked down at his papers.

'Right, well, if there are no more questions then, I have nothing else to say, except that I will be in touch with you as soon as I have the final figures.'

When Kate Scott had entered Robert Percy's office that morning, she had never dreamed that she would leave it a

233

millionaire. The word made no sense to her; she had had to work for everything she owned up until then and now she had been handed an unbelievable fortune, on a plate. What on earth was she going to do with it? She closed her eyes and let the motion of the train rock her gently from side to side. The twenty-first century certainly held its share of surprises for her: first her parents, then Bill, now this. The train began to slow as it entered Twyford; she opened her eyes to check the station and caught a glimpse of her reflection in the carriage window. A serious face with dark, almond eyes looked back at her; she did not look like either of her parents, she thought. A cuckoo in the nest, that's what I am. Her mother had had the tall, willowy figure of a super-model and even when she was sixty she had looked stunning with her well cut, blonde hair and her enormous blue eyes. How on earth had she given birth to such a dark skinned, dumpy child as Kate? Her father had been a regular soldier and had had a soldier's military bearing; he had been over six-feet tall and in his youth, very blond. Once in school, when she was very young, the teacher told them about the Vikings and Kate had easily seen her father in the role of a Viking warrior; she liked the idea that he would always defend her and her mother from danger. If only the fantasies of children could sometimes come true; when the time came, her poor father had been unable to save either himself or his wife.

She had gone to her grandfather's funeral the week before. Although it was already the first week in May, the weather had been bleak and cold; a wet mist hung over the churchyard, coating the stone pathways with a slippery film and dripping from the gloomy yew trees that guarded it. The church too was cold, the heating having already been turned off for the summer but it was full of his friends, relations and

234

many of the children, some now adults, who had benefitted from her grandfather's kindness. She wondered how many thousands of children he had helped over the years and what had motivated him in the first place. He was certainly a well loved man and the vicar took his time reminding the congregation of this fact. For once the trite words that fell from his lips had a real ring of truth to them; this was a man who had selflessly given to the poor and needy for many, many years and at ninety-two years of age his Maker had at last called him to his side. If there was such a place as Heaven then she had no doubt that her grandfather would be there. As she listened to the eulogy she was surprised to realise that she had known very little about him. She had not known that he had fought in Spain during the Civil War, or that he had been part of the North African campaign during the Second World War. Nobody had talked to her about these things and her grandfather, although he had had time and money for children he did not know, had very little time for her. He had always treated her kindly but sometimes she had caught him looking at her in a strange way. Her mother said it was nothing; he was an old man she said, old men had funny ways. But Kate always felt that there was more to it than that; he seemed to keep an almost imperceptible distance between them.

She had been fine until they gathered by the graveside for the internment then, as she heard the vicar intone *'ashes to ashes, dust to dust'* she was again at the graveside of her beloved parents, crying for their unnecessary and untimely death and her tears flowed unchecked. She knew people were looking at her but she could not restrain herself. She cried and sobbed, oblivious to all around her; she cried for her grandfather, for her parents and for herself and her own wasted life. Afterwards, as she walked back to her car, she had felt drained, empty of all emotion and something of that numbness remained with her still.

She and Bill had been celebrating the arrival of the new millennium with some old friends when the news came. Bill had not wanted to go to Fred and Jenny's; he complained that he was not in the mood for an evening of inane chit-chat. He wanted to stay at home and ignore the whole, over-stated event but, for once, Kate had insisted and he reluctantly agreed. She was drinking her third glass of champagne, sitting on the sofa watching her husband drooling over Jenny's au-pair, when the telephone rang. It was her parents they said; there had been an accident. She was to go straight to the Royal Berks Hospital, to the A and E Department. They told her no more. She was sober in an instant. James, who was not drinking because he had to drive back to Henley that night, offered to take them. She sat rigidly in the back of his car, unable to say a word; her teeth were clamped tightly together and she could feel the tension in her jaw spread down her neck, into her shoulders and down her back. She did not move; she held herself in check, letting nothing slip away from her. If she did not move she would not have to think about what was waiting for her there in the hospital. Instead she tried to recall when she had last seen her mother but her memory would not function; try as she might, she could not remember if it had been the previous Sunday or the one before. She wanted desperately to conjure up her familiar face but could see nothing. Bill sat in the front next to James but neither man spoke; there was little they could say.

As soon as the car stopped, she leapt out and ran the short distance from the car park. Her heart was racing. She pushed open the doors to A and E. It was packed with people, some in varying states of drunkenness, others waiting patiently for injured relatives, a few hoping for some medical attention. She ignored them all and ran straight to the desk to give her name but, before she could even explain why she was there, a white-coated doctor was at her side, guiding her into an empty treatment room. She knew then, in that very moment, with a cold certainty that cut straight to her heart, that they were dead; she could read it in his face.

They had been on their way back from a New Year's Eve dinner at the home of their oldest and dearest friends when a car jumped the traffic lights in the centre of town and ploughed into the side of their Peugeot. Her father had died instantly but her mother survived until she arrived at the hospital, where she died twenty minutes later from internal injuries. The driver of the other car, who they later discovered to be five times over the legal limit, had escaped with a broken collar-bone and a few bruises. She listened to the policeman explain it all, patting her hand ineffectually as he spoke, while she stared at him uncomprehendingly.

'He'll be prosecuted for Drink Driving. I can promise you that,' he said.

What did it matter? Nothing would bring them back now, she thought. But, when he came up for trial, she went to Reading Crown Court to see him sentenced. He did not look like a double murderer; he was a young, callow youth, barely old enough to drive, never mind drink. He would serve his sentence and still have the rest of his life before him. She tried to feel anger towards him but he looked too pathetic, standing there in the dock in a blue suit that was slightly too big for him and wearing, probably for the first time in his life, a shirt and tie. He lost his licence and was sentenced to two years in prison; a year for each parent, she thought but still she could not get angry. She could hear her mother's voice:

'Forgiveness is stronger than anger Kate. Anger will consume you if you let it; it will gnaw and gnaw at your mind and eat away your heart but forgiveness will cleanse you,' she had said one day, when Kate came in from school filled with rage because her best friend had told tales about her to the teacher.

The train pulled into Reading station and came to a stop. Kate wiped a tiny tear from her eye, picked up her jacket and got off. She had told them at work that she needed the morning off to go to the doctor's; she thought they would ask too many questions if she said she was going to see a solicitor. However, now she did not feel like going back to work; there were too many extraneous thoughts going round in her head for her to concentrate. She pulled out her mobile and rang her boss's number.

'Geoffrey, it's Kate. Look I'm sorry but I still don't feel too well. I won't be in after all.'

'Did you go to the doctor?' he asked, solicitously.

'Yes, it's nothing serious. He just said to take it easy for a few days; he's given me a tonic.'

'Well don't worry about work; there's nothing pressing at the moment, nothing that can't wait a couple of days. See how you feel after the weekend.'

'Thanks, Geoff. I'm sure I'll be all right by then.'

She rang off, feeling like a naughty schoolgirl playing truant. She did not like deceiving Geoffrey; he was a good boss, even if he was a bit wimpish at times, and she felt guilty about taking advantage of him. Nevertheless, she collected her car from the car-park and set off for home.

Home was a tall, narrow, Victorian terraced house in Caversham, with recurring damp problems and an enormous mortgage. The gardens, front and back, were postage stamp size; the tiny square at the front she kept tidy and even managed to grow a few roses in it but the back one had been abandoned to take its chances with the weeds and brambles. She had lived there for almost six years and still had not managed to furnish all the rooms. For her it was a place to eat and sleep and nothing more. She had bought it with great illusions about how she would transform it into a delightful home, a bijoux town residence. She had plans for knocking down walls, installing modern bathrooms and a state-of-the-art kitchen; she even had a plan for the wilderness outside her back door but none of it had come to fruition. She lived in two rooms only, the kitchen, which doubled as a living area, and the bedroom. She had bought the house with the proceeds of her divorce, a bitter battle from which she had emerged scarred and much poorer than before. The small inheritance she had received from her parents had gone into the communal, matrimonial pot and disappeared in the final divorce settlement.

Since the divorce she had lived alone. There had been the occasional boy-friend and even lover but nothing had lasted. If challenged, she would be the first to acknowledge that it was probably her own fault; she still was not ready to trust anybody again.

She shut the door behind her and leaned against the stained-glass panelling. She closed her eyes; now she was a millionaire. A millionaire. She could leave this house, with its rising damp and its nocturnal neighbours who chose to run their washing machine at three in the morning. She could move to a district where she did not need to have both a car alarm and a steering-wheel lock on her car; where she did not have to pick empty beer bottles and fish and chip papers out of her garden every Sunday morning; where her neighbours all spoke the same language as herself. She sighed. It was a lovely idea but she was not sure she had the energy to do anything about it. Maybe she would feel differently when she saw the money in her bank account. Yes, she admitted to herself, it would be nice not to have to keep checking her bank statements every week to ensure there was enough money to pay the mortgage at the end of the month.

She went into her bedroom; the bedside clock said twelve thirty. She realised she was quite hungry. Well there was one thing she could find the energy to do; she would walk to the Caversham Arms and have some lunch. After all, money was no object now. She refreshed her make-up; struggled to tame her short, black curls into some semblance of a hairstyle; gave herself an extra generous squirt of perfume and went straight out again.

CHAPTER 14

When Kate went into work on Monday morning she had already decided not to tell anyone her good news. It was not that she was particularly secretive, or even worried, that she might be expected to share some of her good fortune with her colleagues, it was more a case of still not quite believing it had happened. She could not forget the odd look that her uncle Richard had given her when the will was being read and a faint voice seemed to be telling her that there was still time for things to go wrong. After all, there might have been some mistake, so she decided to keep her own counsel for the time being.

Kate was Geoffrey's personal assistant and Geoffrey was the Human Resources Director for an old established firm of biscuit makers in the centre of the town. She had been with the firm for more years than she cared to remember; in fact it was the only full-time job she had ever had. She had joined in 1979 straight from the local college of Higher Education. She had been a bright girl at school, studious but not particularly academic. When she left with three A-levels and a number of O-levels, her parents had apologised but told her quite firmly, that they could not afford to send her to university. In fact she had not been that bothered; she was

241

quite content to apply for a place at the nearest college instead and continue living at home. She worked hard, gained a Higher National Diploma and a number of certificates in typing, shorthand and secretarial skills; computer technology was new on the curriculum then, so she had developed her extensive computer skills piecemeal, over the years, by attending a series of short courses sponsored by the company.

She had never intended to remain with the same company all her life but somehow she never managed to leave. She began work in the secretarial pool and then, later, when the previous HR director retired and his PA left to have a baby, she was promoted to her current position. She had worked for Geoffrey for almost twenty years and had begun to believe she would still be there when he too retired. He was an easy man to work for, never demanding or bad-tempered; he remembered her birthday every year and was always solicitous if she needed time off but he was rather dull. Sometimes she would have preferred him to shout at her when she forgot some important papers for a meeting or misfiled the minutes; she would have felt he was more human if, occasionally, he came back from a business lunch smelling of wine or made a feeble excuse to leave early on a Friday. Instead he was a model of propriety. She often wondered what he was like at home but, apart from the fact that he had a wife and two children, she knew nothing about him. Nevertheless they rubbed along like two old shoes; she had worked for him for so long now that she could anticipate his needs and he, in return, gave her plenty of space to manoeuvre.

At first she had viewed her job as a mere stepping stone to better and more interesting work; she had toyed with the idea of taking a job in advertising and commuting to London each day but Bill had deterred her. What was the point of changing jobs when she would probably soon be leaving to start a family, he had said, and anyway, commuting was too expensive. Then, when she had suggested they have a baby, he had said that they needed to save first; he said they should wait until he was promoted to Senior Lecturer, then, when that goal was achieved, it was Principal Lecturer, then Head of Department. There was always a reason to delay it. Once his promotions had been achieved, he said they needed a larger house if they were to have children, better to wait until they had moved. So she waited and waited; in Bill's eyes the time never seemed to be right. Eventually, when she was thirty-five, she stopped taking the pill and did not tell him. It did not matter; by then their love-making had become perfunctory and she never did become pregnant. Either they had left it too late or it was just not meant to be. She became philosophical about it, or rather she had been philosophical about it, until the day she found out about Ursula.

'Ah, Kate. You're back. Are you feeling better?'

Her boss stood in the doorway, beaming at her.

'Yes thanks, Geoffrey. I'm fine. Shall I come in?'

'Give me five minutes while I make a quick phone call and then bring me the personnel files for tomorrow's promotion board. I'd like to go through them with you.'

'Right.'

She collected up the files, made coffee for the two of them and went into his office.

'Have a nice weekend?' he asked politely, as he did every Monday morning.

'Yes, quiet. I stayed in bed most of the time,' she replied.

She marvelled at how good she had become at lying; she had actually spent the weekend playing in a two-day golf

243

competition in Oxford. She and Bill had taken up golf shortly after they had got married. She remembered how he had come home one evening and announced that he and a colleague had decided to learn how to play. A flash of intuition told her that if she did not speak up at once she would be looking at years of weekends waiting at home alone for her husband to return from his regular golf game.

'I'd like to learn too,' she had said.

Bill had been too surprised to argue, so they began to take lessons. She never regretted it; Bill became hooked on the game and played every chance he could. Although she never became such an addict, at least she was part of this new obsession of his and included in his circle of golfing friends. In fact her golfing ability was probably the only thing about her that made Bill proud. He, who rarely bought her a birthday present and never bought her flowers, would happily put his hand in his pocket to buy her a new driver or a box of the latest golf balls.

'Right, let's see who we have here then,' Geoffrey said, arousing her from her daydream.

'Well the first candidate is a Mrs Rita Jones,' she began.

When they had finished reviewing the candidates, Kate went back to her desk. There was a post-it stuck on her screen; it said:

'Kate, a Mr. Percy telephoned. Give him a ring please. Jill.'

She picked it off and went in search of Jill. She was, as usual, at the coffee machine.

'Hi, Jill. Who's this Mr. Percy?' she asked, faking ignorance.

'Oh hello, Kate. Don't know. He wouldn't say what it was about, just that he needed to talk to you right away.'

'Did he leave a telephone number?'

'No but if you wait a minute, I'll get it off the machine.'

She finished pouring out a large cup of very black coffee which she topped with a squirt of whipped cream from the refrigerator and went back to her own desk.

'Here you are; this is it,' she said, handing another post-it to Kate.

Kate went into her office and closed the door. As she dialled his number she felt apprehensive. He had never telephoned her at work before.

'Mr. Percy, please,' she said.

'Who may I say is calling?'

'Kate Scott. I believe he wants to speak to me,' she replied.

'Oh yes, Ms. Scott. Just a moment and I'll put you through.'

Kate heard a few whirrs and clicks and then the nasal sound of Robert Percy's voice.

'Ms. Scott, thank you for calling back. I'll come straight to the point; we have a slight complication with your grandfather's will and I need to speak to you about it.'

'Yes? What sort of complication?' she asked.

She had known it was too good to be true; thank goodness she had not told anybody about it yet.

'As I say, it is rather complicated and I would prefer to talk to you about it in person. Can you come to my office one day this week?'

'Well Mr. Percy, that's a bit inconvenient to be quite honest. I had to take time off last week and I'm loathe to ask for another day so soon; we are very busy at the moment. Can't you tell me over the telephone?'

'No, I really would prefer to see you in person. I won't keep you long. Maybe you could come up early one evening if that would fit in better with your work schedule?'

'Well just hang on a minute while I check my diary.'

Kate opened her appointments diary. As luck would have it Geoffrey was away in Bristol for two days, Thursday and Friday. She could leave early on Thursday and he would be none the wiser.

'Would Thursday be convenient?' she asked. 'About six o'clock?'

'Yes, perfect. I'll see you then. Oh by the way, will you bring any personal documents that you have with you. You know: passport, birth certificate, anything like that.'

'Yes of course, if you think it's necessary.'

'Right, Ms. Scott, don't let me take up any more of your time. I'll see you on Thursday at six o'clock.'

She heard him put down the receiver. It was strange that he had not mentioned documentation at their original meeting. She wondered what he was being so mysterious about.

The next day they were so busy with the promotion board that she did not have time to think about Mr. Percy and his complications. They started with the first candidate at nine o'clock and finished just before one. The procedure was the same as always so the preparation had not been as onerous as it could have been. First the candidates were asked to complete a number of psychometric and aptitude tests to assess their potential; there were a number of vacancies within the company but Geoffrey was also looking for any

246

employees that warranted grooming or 'fast tracking', as he liked to call it. While the candidates ploughed their way through 'Belbin's Team Roles', a series of 'Myers-Briggs Personality Tests' and a couple of auto-perception tests, she split her time between checking that they were completing them correctly and escorting them one by one to their individual interviews with Geoffrey and one of his managers, Arthur Binns. While everyone else went into the Board Room for a lunch of sandwiches and coffee Kate set up the video equipment for the afternoon's task: a group discussion on a surprise topic, which Geoffrey led and Arthur filmed. She knew that Geoffrey would spend all the following day marking the tests and writing up individual reports on each candidate which he would then give to her to type, print and photocopy for him to discuss with the rest of the HR team on Monday. They never gave feedback to the candidates unless they particularly requested it. Once Geoffrey had finished his role in the process Kate had two days and the weekend to complete hers; there was plenty of time to slip in a visit to Percy, Percy and Rowland.

'Testing, testing,' she said in a rather self conscious voice, waving her hands in front of the video camera and twirling about.

She rewound it and played it back.

'Oh, very elegant,' a voice behind her said.

'Hi, Arthur, I thought you were having lunch.'

'I was but Geoffrey sent me up with a few sandwiches for you.'

He held out a paper plate with a couple of ham and cheese sandwiches.

'Thanks. That was nice of him.'

'Well he can be nice when he wants to, I suppose,' he said, a bit grudgingly she thought. 'So can I help you at all?'

'No thanks, it's all set up. It's up to you two now.'

'Listen Kate, I've been meaning to ask you something.'

He paused, fingering his collar nervously.

'Yes?'

'Well I wondered if you were planning on going to the staff picnic with anyone?'

'The staff picnic? That's in June isn't it?'

'Yes, I know it's a long way off but I thought if you had no other plans, you might like to go with me.'

'Well I don't usually bother, Arthur. Personally I'd sooner spend my weekends playing golf.'

'Oh,' he replied, looking crestfallen.

'It's just that I don't really know what I'll be doing in June; I don't want to promise you to go then let you down. Why don't you ask Beryl in typing? She goes every year.'

'Right, good idea,' he replied abruptly.

'Anyway, thanks for asking me, and thanks for the sandwiches.'

She began to re-adjust the position of the chairs and as soon as she heard the door close behind him she stopped, picked up her sandwiches and hurried back to her office.

She had been to the staff picnic once with Bill, the first year it had been held. In those days the company still owned a stretch of land alongside the river Thames, on the outskirts of the town, and everyone agreed that this was the best place to accommodate all the company's employees and their families in one go. Her department was responsible for arranging the event and she had to admit they were very successful at it. They set up marquees for the food and the bar and drew up a rota for manning the barbecues; they hired a live band and organised a range of activities: bowls, petanque, a Bouncy Castle for the children and fireworks in the evening. The festivities started at lunch time and went on until midnight. One year they hired a number of punts but due to the fact that too many people, having succumbed to the influence of the local Courage beer, fell into the river, they never repeated it. She had not bothered to attend for a number of years; she saw enough of her colleagues between Monday and Friday, she did not really want to spend her Saturdays with them as well.

Arthur was a pleasant enough man but he was in his late fifties, had never been married and as far as she could tell, had had little success with women. There were quite a few attractive men in the company but none of them had asked her out. She had begun to think that she had been more attractive to the opposite sex when she was married than she was now that she was both divorced and available. There had been a number of men who had liked to flirt with her and had made a point of dropping into her office for a chat during the day; mostly they had been married men and as she had been happily married at the time, or so she had thought, nothing had developed. Some of those men still worked for the company but they all seemed too busy nowadays to drop by.

Perhaps I've let myself go, she thought, regarding her face solemnly in the mirror by her door. True, there were a few more grey hairs now but she could soon see to those. The wrinkles around her eyes would be more difficult to disguise; laughter lines her mother had called them and, in her mother's case, it had been true because she was always laughing. When she received her inheritance she would treat herself to a new look, go up to Oxford Street with Maisie and buy some new clothes. She went in search of a coffee to wash down the sandwiches.

'Jill, late night shopping in the West End, is it Thursdays?' she asked, pouring herself a decaffeinated coffee.

'Yes, until eight or nine; I think some shops are open to nine.'

'I might leave a bit earlier on Thursday then and get the fast train up there.'

'Looking for something nice?'

'Oh, just something for a wedding that I'm going to.'

'Oh, lovely. Who's getting married?'

She knew she should not have said anything; what did her mother always tell her: 'A little lie will very soon lead to a bigger lie.'

'A cousin of mine, in Scotland,' she said, hoping that sounded vague enough to deter further questions.

'I have cousins in Scotland,' Jill began but Kate interrupted her:

'Sorry Jill, got to get back, Geoffrey is waiting for something.'

The trouble was that her standards were so high; she knew that. Bill had been the love of her life for twenty years. She met him at a student reunion in her old college; she had been chatting to her friends and getting slightly tipsy on cheap French wine when she saw him looking at her. He was so handsome in those days: tall and broad, with the physique of a rugby player, his fair hair a bit on the long side and those bright, blue eyes hidden behind a pair of dark rimmed spectacles. It was instant attraction on both parts. She discovered he was not an ex-student but a new lecturer in the Languages Department; he taught Russian and German to the HNC students and English as a Foreign Language to students from overseas and au-pairs. She would like to meet someone who looked like that now, she thought unrealistically, well maybe a bit more mature and definitely a more faithful. She finished off her sandwiches and coffee and began to open the post that Jill had dropped on her desk earlier. This was normally her first job each morning, to open the department's mail and distribute it then open her own and Geoffrey's emails and update the appointments book; because of the promotions board that had all had to wait until now. There was nothing of importance in the post but she did open a rather unusual email; it was from the Managing Director and was addressed to Geoffrey and marked "Confidential":

"Geoff, can I remind you that we need your report as soon as possible if we are to make an informed decision about the re-organisation of the Human Resources Department. It's time this company dragged itself into the twenty-first century. Henry."

Re-organisation? Geoffrey had not mentioned anything to her about a re-organisation. It was very strange; whenever there was a change in strategy or policy Geoffrey made a point of bouncing his ideas off her first. She could not believe something as major as this was happening without him saying a word. She read it again; the last sentence sounded ominous. Henry was obviously planning something drastic. She transferred the email to her boss's personal in-box and continued skimming the rest. He would know she had read it. Would he come and explain? Well she would know soon enough because it would be her job to type the report, whatever it was.

The rest of the day dragged slowly and she found her thoughts returning again and again to her grandfather and his will. She regretted having told Robert Percy that she could not see him until Thursday; she wanted to know now. She knew she could not induce him to confide in her over the telephone; she would either have to be patient or ring one of her cousins to see if they knew anything about it. She found Ruth's number first and dialled it quickly before she could change her mind.

'716 564 431,' a young female voice answered.

'Sarah? It's Kate. Is your mother in?'

'Hi Aunty Kate. No, she's at her bridge club. Can I help you?'

'I don't think so Sarah. What about your Dad, is he home?'

'No, he usually doesn't get in until after eight. Sorry. Are you sure I can't help?'

'Well, I don't know. Has your mother said anything about another meeting with the solicitor?'

'No. I know they were there yesterday and great-uncle Jeremy as well. Why, has the solicitor been in touch with you again?'

'Yes, he rang me this morning and said that there was some complication with the will but he wouldn't explain over the telephone. Did your mother say anything about that?'

Her niece did not reply.

'Sarah? Did Ruth say what the problem was?'

'Well, Aunty Kate, she did mention something but I'm sure it's nothing, probably just a mix-up with the paperwork.'

Sarah sounded a bit nervous; Kate could imagine her twirling a lock of her auburn hair round and round in agitation.

'So what is it Sarah? What's this mix-up?'

'I'm not sure if I should say anything. After all I might just upset you for nothing.'

'Sarah.'

'Oh all right Aunty Kate. Apparently great-uncle Jeremy has contested the will.'

'Contested the will? On what grounds? It seemed pretty straightforward to me.'

'Well. Oh, I don't know if I should tell you.'

'Come on Sarah, I shall know soon enough anyway.'

'He says you shouldn't have received anything in the will because your mother was not a Reeves. Don't tell my mum I've told you, please, Aunty Kate, she'll kill me.'

'Not a Reeves? What does that mean?'

'I don't know Aunty, that's just what I heard Mum saying to Dad. Please don't tell her I told you.'

'No, of course I won't Sarah. Thank you for telling me,' she said, her voice catching on the words. 'You're sure you don't know any more?'

'No, that's all I heard.'

As she replaced the receiver she noticed her hand was trembling. This was bewildering. So she was not the problem; it was her mother. Had her mother been adopted? Maybe she had been one of her grandparents' rescued children. Kate could not really remember her grandmother; she had only been four when she had died of breast cancer. Yet she had always thought how much her mother had resembled the photographs of her when she was young: tall and willowy and with the same blonde hair. It was Kate who was the odd one out. She remembered once asking her mother if she had been adopted and her mother had hugged her and said, no definitely not. Then she had gone to the box where they kept all their important papers and taken out Kate's birth certificate; she had read out Kate's name and showed her where it said the mother's name and where it said

253

the father's name. Then she had wiped her tears and told her not to be so silly, she was their own, dear, little daughter.

Kate switched off her computer and slid her files into her desk and locked it. She did not know what to make of this news. Perhaps Sarah had misheard her mother but it was unlikely.

That evening she went into her junk room to look for her mother's box; she found it under the spare bed. There was her birth certificate with her parents' names, Isabel and Brian Scott, clearly typed. She looked a bit further and found her parents' marriage certificate; her mother was described as the daughter of Elizabeth Margaret Reeves and Alexander James Reeves. Then she found it, her mother's birth certificate; it was the short version that many people elected to have because it was cheaper. It showed her mother's name and date of birth, and the area in which her birth had been registered, no mention of the parents. She rummaged a bit further and came up with her mother's old passport but that did not enlighten her any further, neither did her death certificate. She needed a copy of the full birth certificate. She could either phone the General Register Office or she could go on-line. Within minutes she had the web-site of BMD certificates on her screen. For sixty pounds they would post her a copy of the full birth certificate, guaranteed to arrive within twenty-four hours. She usually left home before the postman came, so when she completed the form she gave her address at work. She added her Visa details and sent it off. At the latest it would be there Thursday morning. She went back to the junk room and selected all the documents she thought she might need and put them in a plastic folder, ready to take with her to the solicitor.

254

The day had left her both physically tired and emotionally exhausted. She could not eat; her stomach was churning over and over. It was not so much about losing the inheritance; it was more about who she was. She did not know who she was anymore. She poured herself a generous glass of Chardonnay and switched on News 24. The announcer was explaining about Prince Charles and the size of the carbon footprint left by his personal household. Where did they come up with these names? Carbon footprint, she envisaged large sooty footprints all over the palace carpets. The wine was good; it was making her relax. She poured herself another glass. A bouncy presenter, with an enormous smile, was telling them that they were due for some very wet and windy weather. She leaned back and let the sound wash over her. Had her mother ever said anything about being adopted? She could not remember any such suggestion. Maybe her mother had not known. Maybe she had not been adopted. Maybe it was just maliciousness on the part of Kate's uncle. There were so many 'maybes'. If her mother really was Sir Alexander's daughter, why was Jeremy contesting the will? He was her brother, after all; surely he would know. She sighed. One thing was certain, she was not going to solve the puzzle until she spoke to Robert Percy.

She sipped some more of the wine; it was really very good. Where had it come from? Oddbins? Or had Maisie brought it round the other week? They had played in a friendly four-ball with Maisie's husband and his cousin and enjoyed themselves so much that she had invited them all back to her place for an impromptu supper. She knew Maisie had been trying to set her up with the cousin but he really was not her type, as she had explained to her the next day. Maisie was relentless; she was determined that Kate should meet a

255

man and settle back into the comfortable routine of being a two-some. There were times when Kate would have liked to be in relationship. It would have been nice to have someone to take her to the theatre or out to dinner; it would have been nice not to be the only single person in a crowd of married couples and she would have liked to have had someone to confide in when she had had a really bad day. She still felt lonely when she saw couples walking hand-in-hand on a summer's evening and then the yearning for the touch of a lover's hand became keener. In fact she found that the summer was the worst time to be alone; in the winter she could come straight home from work and shut herself in with the television and a glass of wine and trick herself into not feeling so alone but in the summer the evenings seemed to drag out relentlessly. She drank some more wine. Nevertheless, she told herself, despite everything, she was not ready for a new man in her life; her wounds had still not healed. She was not ready to give her trust to anyone else just yet.

It was the inefficiency of the Electricity Board that had alerted her. Kate dealt with all the paperwork in their home; in the marital division of labour, that allotted task had fallen to her. So when they sent her a bill for the purchase and installation of a new electric water heater, she telephoned to say there had been some mistake.

'I am very sorry Mrs. Horton, the accounts department have confused your two billing addresses. This should have gone to your house in Windsor. Please just ignore it and I'll arrange for a new bill to go to St. Leonard's Road,' the manager said apologetically.

'St. Leonard's Road?' she queried.

'Yes, number 134. That's correct isn't it?'

'Sorry, I'm getting a bit confused here. Our electricity contract is in the name of William Horton of 21, Waverley Court, Tilehurst.'

'Yes, that's right but the water heater was installed in Mr. Horton's Windsor residence, so the bill should have gone there. We have no excuse, I'm afraid. It says quite clearly on his records that all electricity supplies to the Windsor house should be billed separately. I do apologise.'

'Are you sure you have the name right? William Horton?'

'Quite sure.'

She could tell from his voice that it was beginning to dawn on him that there was something else going on besides a misdirected account.

'Don't worry about it Mrs. Horton. We will rectify the error from this end.'

'OK, well thank you for your help.'

She put down the telephone and leant against the wall. What did this mean? She could not ask Bill; he was not due home until late that night. He had told her he had a meeting about the coming school trip to Bremen.

She waited until seven o'clock then got into her car and drove to Windsor. She knew the town quite well; they had even considered buying a house there once. St. Leonard's Road was quite central, so she parked in a supermarket car park and walked down the main street until she came to number 134. It was a grey stone building set back from the main road. She climbed the steps and waited for a moment to allow the frantic beating of her heart to slow down before she knocked. She had brought the electricity bill with her and held it before her like a talisman.

Bill opened the door; he was holding a small child in his arms.

'It's OK. I've got it, Darling,' he called to someone in another room.

When he turned back to look at the caller he could not speak. He seemed to be struggling for air; this was the start of a nightmare he would want to end.

'This came for you,' she said, handing him the electricity bill.

Then she turned and left. There had been no need to ask him anything; his face told it all.

Later she learnt all the sordid details: her husband had been leading a double life for five years. His other wife, lover, girl-friend, mistress, paramour, whatever he liked to call her, had been one of his EFL students; she was a Czech immigrant who had come to England to learn English and find a husband. She had achieved both: she had learnt English and she had found Bill, Kate's husband. He was in love, he said; he had never been happier. They had two children, a two-year old and the baby she had seen in his arms.

She probably could have forgiven him his infidelity, after all she had often suspected that he had had brief affairs with his English students and she had attached no importance to them but she could not forgive this level of deceit. Envy and jealousy cut through her like a knife; it dominated her thoughts and poisoned her mind. He had made her wait so long for the right moment to bear his children that it never came and yet here was this woman, only twenty-six years old, half his age, and already with two children. No, that she would never forgive. She let the solicitor handle everything; it ate up all her savings, including the inheritance from her mother but she did not care. She could not speak to him. They split everything down the middle. Blame counted for nothing; fidelity and infidelity were weighed and found equal. In the court's eyes Bill had two children to support, whereas she was single and working. What price a broken heart? she asked. What price the wasted years of her youth? Nobody would give her an answer so the questions still plagued her.

CHAPTER 15

She worked through her lunch hour on Thursday so she could leave early with a clear conscience. BMD had been as good as their word and delivered her mother's birth certificate to her first thing that morning. Now she had everything she needed for the meeting.

At four o'clock she left her car in the company's car park and walked to the station; the train would get her into Paddington at ten minutes past five, which would leave her plenty of time to get to Percy, Percy & Rowland.

Robert Percy was waiting for her when she arrived; he was alone.

'Ms. Scott, do come in. Have a seat, please. Good journey?'

'Yes, fine.'

She sat down opposite and waited for him to begin; she was not going to tell him what Sarah had said. She watched him fussily arrange his papers, tapping them into a perfect block, then lean back in his leather chair and rub his hands together, slowly. He seemed to have difficulty in deciding how to start. At last he was ready to speak.

'Well, Ms. Scott, may I call you Kate?'

She nodded.

'Well, Kate. It seems that your uncle, Sir Alexander's son, does not agree with the terms of the will. In fact,' he paused. 'In fact he has told me he wishes to contest it.'

'Oh, on what grounds?' Kate asked, trying to show no emotion.

'Well, this is the difficult part' and again he paused. 'He maintains that your mother Isabel Reeves was not Sir Alexander's daughter and therefore her share of the estate should be divided between the two legitimate children of the marriage, himself and the heirs of his dead sister Rosemary.'

'And exactly what grounds does he have for this allegation?' Kate asked.

'He says that the family have always known that Isabel had a different father. It was never openly discussed but as usually happens with these things, everyone knew about it.'

'Well I didn't know about it and neither did my mother. If she had known she would have told me, I'm sure.'

'I don't know about that. I only met your mother once and as far as I was aware there were no irregularities about her situation vis-a-vis Sir Alexander. At any rate, your uncle has asked me to look into it for him.'

'Mr. Percy, I have here a copy of my mother's birth certificate. It states quite clearly that her father was Alexander James Reeves. What more proof do you need?'

'Actually, Kate we do not need any more proof. I am quite confident that Sir Alexander's will stands exactly as it was written but I am bound to investigate it a bit further.'

'What can you find out now? Grandfather is dead. My mother is dead. Who can enlighten you on what happened seventy years ago?'

'True. There is, of course, your great-aunt.'

'Angela? Yes, she might know more, I suppose. Has my uncle spoken to her then?'

'No, I don't think so. Your uncle bases his allegations on a mismatch of dates.'

'A mismatch of dates? What dates?'

'Your mother's date of birth was, I believe,' he paused, while he looked at the birth certificate. '3rd November 1937 and the date of your grandfather's marriage was 19th June 1937.'

'So? All that means is that my mother was conceived before they got married. Not the done thing in those days but hardly a hanging offence.'

'True. I'm just pointing out to you that this is probably the source of his suspicions.'

'So, what is going to happen now?'

'I just have to double-check that the will is valid, and then we will proceed. As I have already said, I cannot see this making any difference. It does not really matter who the actual father was, the important thing is that Sir Alexander registered the child as his own.'

'So that's it then? I don't need to do anything about this?' she asked.

'No, just leave it all to me. It means everything will be delayed a bit but I'll try not to keep you waiting too long for your settlement. As soon as I have any news I will let you know.'

Kate stood up.

'Right. Thank you for telling me. I'll just wait until I hear from you then,' she said, shaking his outstretched hand.

'Goodbye Kate.'

'Goodbye Mr. Percy.'

She stopped in the doorway and looked back at him.

'Even if what you find out has no effect on grandfather's will, I should like to know who my grandfather actually was, whether it was Sir Alexander or someone else. It is important to me, you know.'

'Of course, my dear, I will let you know all I can.'

As she toured the shops in Oxford Street, she could not stop her conversation with Robert Percy from going over and over again in her head. She was fairly confident that they would honour the will and pay her her mother's share but she was also fairly confident that there was some truth in Jeremy's accusation. There must have been something more than a bad alignment of dates to start a rumour which had persisted for seventy years. She knew she would not rest until she discovered what it was.

She pulled a navy Chanel suit from the rack and held it up against herself; it was very smart and would be so useful for work. But did she want smart? Did she want useful? If she wanted a new look she should buy something totally different to the rest of the clothes in her wardrobe, all those sensible, good quality outfits that identified her as a personal assistant from a hundred yards away. She needed something with a bit of panache, some colour, some style. She looked around her; this section of the store was aimed at smart, middle-aged business women. Well, that was what she was after all but was that what she wanted to remain? She put the suit back on the rack and moved on, looking for something younger and sexier. But what? A low-cut, white blouse caught her eye. That would be useful, she thought, pairing it up in her mind with various other items in her wardrobe. Useful, that word again. It was no use; she could not break out of the dressing habits of a life-time. If she wanted to look and feel different,

263

she needed someone to help her. She bought a pair of tights and some perfume and decided to call it a day and head for home.

She was lucky; a train was already standing in the station, about to leave. She settled herself into an empty carriage and began to think over her meeting. She was surprised that the news had affected her so strongly. It seemed to her that she had lived most of her life behind the secure walls of her family and now, one by one those walls were collapsing: first her parents had died, then her husband had betrayed her, now there were doubts about her grandfather. She felt exposed and alone; what did they say: 'we come into this world alone and we leave it alone.' Basically she was on her own and she had to face it.

As the train pulled into Reading station she decided to telephone her friend Maisie.

'Hi, Maisie. It's Kate.'

'Hi Kate.'

'Maisie are you busy? Can I come round for a chat?'

'Of course, is something wrong?'

'Not really, I just feel in need of a bit of a chat. It's not too late is it?'

'No, Bob is at a golf committee meeting; he won't be home for hours.'

'OK, see you in ten minutes then.'

Her friends Maisie and Bob lived in the centre of Reading in a big, Edwardian house near the hospital. Bob was an ENT consultant at the Royal Berks Hospital and Maisie was a physiotherapist. They had been friends for many years, long before Bill left. The men had met at the golf club and started to play golf together on a regular basis, then the wives met and, before long, they were going out as a foursome: dinners, concerts and even holidays together. Kate remembered how worried Bob had been when she had told them about the divorce; Maisie told her some time later that he had dreaded having to choose between them. But in the end Bill had made the decision for him; he never contacted his old friend again.

The walk from the station began to clear her head and the kaleidoscope of images that had been whirling around in her brain slowed to a halt. She began to feel more positive and allowed her thoughts to turn to the future.

Maisie looked concerned when she opened the door to let her friend enter.

'This is not like you,' she said. 'What's wrong?'

'Nothing's wrong, well not really. I just have some news I want to share with you,' Kate said, trying not to sound too mysterious.

'You've met a man,' Maisie said triumphantly.

Kate could not help laughing at this predictable response.

'No, of course not. Look, give me a drink and I'll tell you what it's all about.'

She sat in Maisie's kitchen, admiring the new oak-panelled cupboards and the granite work-surfaces and waited until her friend had poured out two glasses of white wine and sat down opposite her.

'I told you my grandfather died, didn't I?' she began.

'Yes, I'm sorry. He was quite old though, wasn't he?'

'Yes, ninety-two.'

'Well he'd had a good run for his money, then,' Maisie replied, drinking some of her wine.

'Yes, well he's left me some money in his will.'

'Great. Do you know how much yet?'

'Not exactly but it looks like two and a half million.'

She waited, enjoying the look of astonishment on Maisie's face.

'Two and a half million? You've got to be joking.'

'No, it's the truth. But there is a catch.'

'I knew it; there's always a catch.'

'He has not left it to me by name; he left it to his three children and as my mother is dead, I receive her portion.'

'So, what's the catch?'

'Well,' she found it harder to say than she had imagined. 'Well, there is some doubt about whether my mother was actually his daughter.'

She watched Maisie's eyes grow round with amazement as she related her conversations with Sarah and Robert Percy.

'So, you see, Maisie, I'd like to talk it through with you. I really don't know what to do.'

'You say the money is not the issue; you'll probably get that anyway.'

'Yes. It's whether I should do anything about finding out the truth or just leave things as they are.'

'Of course you know there is the possibility that you won't like what you find out. You may discover that you have a grandfather that you wished you hadn't. On the other hand, you may discover a whole clan of relatives that you didn't know about. If your mother had a different father, she may also have had other brothers and sisters. Do you really want to open such a Pandora's box?'

'I don't know, Maisie. Somehow I feel I owe it to my mother to find out who her real father was.'

'Blood isn't everything you know. From all that you've said, your grandfather loved your mother and treated her well. As far as he was concerned she was his daughter, and she

266

knew no other father. Do you think she would have rejected him if she'd known he wasn't her biological father?'

'No, my mother loved him. She often talked about her childhood and she was very happy.'

'So? Why put yourself through this turmoil? There could be nothing in it anyway. It could just be a straightforward case of greed on the part of your uncle. He's probably jealous that you are receiving something now and his own children have got to wait until he's dead.'

'You could be right. I'm sure he was upset at the size of the inheritance; I think he was expecting an awful lot more money.'

'Well ten million seems a lot to me.'

'Yes but I don't think he realised that his father had spent so much money on his children's homes. Apart from the houses, which have yet to be sold, there really isn't a lot of cash and I don't even think his investments have been that profitable lately.'

'Well maybe, if there had been more money in the pot, he wouldn't have begrudged you your share.'

'Who knows.'

'Some more wine?'

'Just a drop. I've still got to pick up my car from the car-park. I don't want to lose my licence.'

'What does it matter, you can afford to hire a chauffeur now.'

'It just doesn't seem real, you know, not the money nor this business about my grandfather. I keep thinking it's a dream and I shall wake up any minute and laugh about it.'

'So what do you want to do?'

'Well, despite the risks, I think I ought to at least make a few inquiries of my own. I'm beginning to realise that I

267

know very little about my grandfather and even less about my grandmother. My mother used to talk about them but I didn't really pay much attention. You know what it's like when you're a kid; all that seems like ancient history. I would like to know more, if only for my personal satisfaction.'

'So how will you begin?'

'I thought I might go and visit my great-aunt and see if she can tell me anything.'

'Great-aunt? Is she your grandfather's sister?'

'Yes, she's rather old but her mind seems to still be functioning pretty well. Also she has a couple of children of her own; sons who live in Oxford. They're older than my mother; they might know something.'

'Well, it's a start. How well do you know this great-aunt?'

'We're not really close but then I'm not really close to any of my family. She had been living with my grandfather for about twenty years, ever since her husband died, so I've seen her a few times.'

'Where does she live now?'

'Oh she's still in the house. Grandfather stipulated in his will that she could stay in the house as long as she wanted. I don't expect Jeremy was very happy about that either because now we can't sell it until she either dies or leaves.'

'Didn't your grandfather leave her any money?'

'No. I suppose he thought it wasn't worth it; she's ninety-four you know. I don't expect she'll live many more years. Anyway I think she has a good pension.'

'What about her sons?'

'Alfred and Michael? They've never married so there are no grandchildren. I've met them a few times over the years and got on quite well with them.'

Maisie poured them another glass of wine.

'No, not for me,' Kate protested.   'I've got to work tomorrow.'

'For God's sake, Kate, you're a millionaire.   Why the hell are you worried about work?'

'Because,' she said.

'That's it, "because", because you're stuck in a rut.   This is your chance to break free.   Take it.'

'Well you're probably right but I'm not breaking free tonight.   I'll wait until I actually have the money in the bank before I hand in my notice.'

They heard the sound of a car in the drive.

'Sounds like Bob is back,' she said.   'Look I'd better be going.   You tell him my news; I'm too tired to go through it all again.'

'All right, he'll be flabbergasted when he hears.'

'Thanks, Maisie, for everything, for the wine, for being such a good listener, everything.'

'Don't be daft, that's what friends are for.'

'Bye.'

Kate kissed her friend on the cheek.   She was feeling a bit tipsy but she knew the walk back to the car-park would sober her up.

'Bye Kate.   Let me know what you find out.'

She slipped out the front door as she heard Bob enter by the back, and headed towards the factory.   Despite the wine and the jokes, talking about it with Maisie had helped her form a plan of action.   Tomorrow she would telephone her great-aunt and arrange to see her.   It would be nice to go down to Devon for the weekend; she might even put her golf clubs in the car.

They used to go to the manor house every summer holiday when she was a child. It was a big, rambling building and all the grandchildren loved it; they would roam the corridors, tapping on the panelled walls, convinced that there were secret passageways behind them and any locked room that they came across was the cause of hours of speculation; they played hide and seek in the cupboards and pantries, under the stairs, in the endless nooks and crannies that the old house offered them; they slept together in huge double beds with four posters and canopies; they let the servants frighten them with tales of ghosts and smugglers and they believed it all. Those were holidays of magic and adventure, where the grounds were distant lands, the woods were enchanted and the beach was a treasure island. All too soon Kate had grown too old for their games and persuaded her parents to take her to Ibiza instead.

When her mother talked of her own childhood, it was not of the manor house; her grandfather had bought the house in the nineteen-sixties, when he first became rich. Her mother spent her childhood holidays in a cottage that had belonged to her maternal grandparents; it lay tucked in the folds and pleats of the Dorset countryside, within sight of Corfe Castle. It had lain empty for the last few years but Kate remembered visiting it many times with her mother. It too now came within the scope of Sir Alexander's estate; she wondered if it were possible to have it as part of her settlement.

She looked at her watch; it was only eight-thirty, too early to telephone her great-aunt and much too early to telephone Percy, Percy and Rowland. She opened up her computer and spent the next hour and a half typing up Geoffrey's reports.

She had tried to get him to put them directly onto the word processor but he refused.

'I can't think clearly like that,' he had said. 'I have to write it in long-hand first, so that I don't miss anything out.'

In the end she had given up and instead struggled with his scribble, crossings-out, balloons and arrows until she made sense of it all. She knew that most of the other managers worked directly on the computer and their secretaries only had to edit the appearance of the document but not Geoffrey.

She dialled Robert Percy's telephone number thinking that he would think it strange her telephoning again so soon.

'Percy, Percy and Rowland,' answered a voice.

'Robert Percy, please,' she said. 'It's Kate Scott.'

There was a pause, then she heard his familiar voice.

'Kate, there's no news yet I'm afraid. I haven't even had time to speak to your uncle.'

'No, I realise that Mr. Percy. This is about another matter.'

'Yes?'

'I believe you said that the cottage in Dorset was part of my grandfather's assets?'

'That's right.'

'Do you know how much it is worth?'

'Well, we only have an approximate valuation from the estate agent; it's been a bit neglected over recent years so I don't think we will get its true value.'

'Well roughly?'

'Roughly? I should say about four hundred and fifty thousand, if we are lucky. Why the interest?'

'I would like to buy it or have it instead of the equivalent amount of money. Let's say the cottage and only two million pounds.'

She smiled to hear herself say the words. It still seemed ludicrous that she, who normally had problems paying her mortgage, was bargaining with her solicitor in millions.

'You see that cottage originally belonged to my grandmother's side of the family and I know my mother was very fond of it so I would like to have it to live in,' she added.

'Well in principle I don't see a problem but I would have to put it to the other beneficiaries. Maybe it would be best to leave that until we have resolved the first issue.'

'Of course, I agree entirely but I just wanted you to know that I would like to have that particular house.'

'It is duly noted. It would be one less property to put through the hands of an estate agent, and less expense,' he conceded.

'Good. That's all I wanted to say. Goodbye for now.'

'Goodbye Kate. I will be in touch as soon as I have something to report,' he said.

CHAPTER 16

It took her almost three hours to reach Barnstable and then another half hour along the twisty, winding lanes before she arrived in Croyde, a picturesque Devonshire village where tourists gathered to look at thatched roofs and eat clotted cream. Her grandfather's old house was outside the village, down a series of even narrower lanes whose high, hawthorn hedges obliterated all from view. Apart from a brief visit to attend her grandfather's funeral, she had not been to the house since she was a child. She parked her car on the gravel drive and walked up to an imposing, oak door. The place seemed deserted but nevertheless she rang the bell and waited. After a few minutes the door was opened by a middle-aged woman, wearing a housekeeper's uniform.

'Hello Agnes. Do you remember me? It's Kate, Isabel's daughter.'

'Of course I remember you. How are you Miss Kate?'

'I'm very well thanks, Agnes. So you're still here then.'

'Yes, where else would I be? I'm staying on to look after Miss Angela.'

Kate thought it strange that Agnes always referred to everyone as Miss So-and-so or Master Something. It was as though she had watched a surfeit of old movies and thought of herself on the set of 'Upstairs Downstairs'. She seemed to be from a different era.

'I believe my great-aunt is expecting me,' Kate said.

'Yes. She told me to make up the guest room just this morning.'

Agnes had a distinctive West Country brogue; she had been born and bred in Barnstable and came to work for Sir Alexander when she was only eighteen. She led Kate into the living room where her great-aunt was sitting in a wicker chair by the window.

'Shall I take your bag up to your room, Miss Kate?' she asked.

'Please, if you don't mind,' Kate replied.

She approached the window. Her great-aunt seemed to be sleeping. Her eyes were closed and her thin chest rose and fell in a regular rhythm. Her head rested on a blue, tapestry cushion and every so often her mouth opened to expel a tiny spurt of air. You could not call it snoring; it was more like a cat purring. She looked even frailer than she had at the reading of the will; her bones were clearly visible through the blue transparency of her skin and there seemed to be not an ounce of flesh on her. A blue chiffon scarf was tied around her throat and fastened with an enormous lapis lazuli brooch. Kate did not want to wake her so sat down in a chair alongside. After a few minutes her great-aunt seemed to sense her presence; she opened her eyes and looked at her great-niece. At first Kate thought she did not recognise her but then she said:

'So you've arrived, have you?'

'Yes Aunt Angela, I've just got here.'

'Good, is Agnes looking after you?'

'Yes, thank you.'

Her aunt pulled herself upright in the chair and studied her carefully.

'Well my dear, it's just as I thought the other day, you don't look at bit like your mother, or your grandmother for that matter. You're quite the ugly duckling, aren't you.'

Kate choked back the urge to cry; this was not what she had hoped to hear.

'Never mind my dear; they took a lot of living up to, beautiful women the both of them.'

She closed her eyes again and Kate thought she had gone back to sleep but after a few seconds she spoke:

'Ring Agnes, would you, and ask her to bring us some tea. Oh and some scones as well. I know she made some this morning, especially for you.'

Kate got up to leave the room.

'No, ring the bell. It's just there on the wall.'

She saw an electric switch on the wall by the curtains and pressed it. A few moments later Agnes appeared.

'Agnes would you bring us some tea please, and some scones,' Kate said, beginning to feel like the lady of the manor.

Agnes nodded and left.

'So my dear, what was it you wanted to talk to me about?' her great-aunt asked.

'It's about the will,' she began.

'I thought as much,' chuckled her great-aunt. 'There's nothing like an inheritance to bring everyone out of the woodwork.'

Kate began to feel uncomfortable but she reminded herself that Angela was a very old woman; it was amazing she was so lucid at her age. She should forgive her the occasional sharpness of tongue.

'Well Aunt, it's not so much about the inheritance, it's more to do with what my uncle Jeremy has been saying.'

'Jeremy? That greedy worm. I saw his face when old Percy said I was to stay in this house for the rest of my life; he was furious. Ridiculous really, it's not as though he's got that long to wait for me to die, is it?'

Kate said nothing.

'So, what's he been saying?'

'He wants to contest the will because he says that my mother was not grandfather's real daughter.'

'Oh, does he? So what do you expect me to do?'

'Nothing really, I just want some information. You're probably the only person still alive who was there when my mother was born.'

'There are others,' she said, wagging her head, knowingly. 'What does the birth certificate say?'

'It says that Alexander Reeves was her father.'

'Well there you are.'

'Yes but is it true? Why would my uncle say that if it wasn't true?'

'Who knows the ways of men?' her great-aunt replied enigmatically. 'Ah, Agnes, that was quick. Lovely, I'm just ready for a cup of tea.'

She turned to Kate.

'Darjeeling. Do you like Darjeeling?'

Kate, who never drank tea, did not know one blend from the other but she nodded vigorously.

'But Aunt Angela, can't you tell me anything?'

'Drink your tea first and then I'll see what I can remember; it's a long time ago you know.'

The tea was refreshing and surprisingly good; she drank two cups and ate one of the scones. Her great-aunt barely touched anything but looked on encouragingly. Once Agnes had cleared away the tea tray, she began to tell Kate what she could remember. She spoke in a soft, sing-song voice and at times Kate had to strain to hear her.

'Your grandfather met Elizabeth when he was in Spain during the Civil War; he told me he felt responsible for her and, as soon as they arrived back in England, he took her to her parents' house, somewhere in Dorset. He was only a very young man in those days, easy going and carefree, with nothing on his mind except sport and girls but when he came back from Spain he was a completely changed person; it was as though he had grown up in a matter of months. I was older than him but not by much and we'd always been very close, so he would come and talk to me about what he'd seen over there. It was terrible; there were many things he could not bring himself to utter. We spent hours and hours just walking around Oxford, I lived in Oxford then you know, sometimes never saying a word. It seemed to help him to be somewhere familiar and solid. He told me once that it was the suffering of all those children that affected him most; he had been unable to help any of them and this weighed very heavily on his conscience.'

'Is that why he started the Reeves Shelters?' Kate asked.

'I suppose it was, although he never said so.'

'So how did he meet my grandmother?'

'He met her in Málaga in 1937, the same year your mother was born. I think she had been living there with her parents and when the war broke out they came back to England.'

'And my grandmother?'

'She stayed for a bit longer, I can't remember now why that was but anyway, that was when she met Alex.'

'So they fell in love?' Kate asked.

277

'I don't think so, not at first. He loved her, I know. I remember him telling me, the first day he got back, that he had met the most beautiful woman in the world and one day he was going to marry her. He was always a bit spontaneous like that. But I think Elizabeth loved someone else but she never told me who it was. She never complained about Alex but I knew he was not the one for her.'

'But they got married, didn't they?'

'Oh yes, Alex always got what he wanted; he always had, even when he was a child. He wanted Elizabeth so he married her.'

'So you don't think they were lovers before they came back to England?'

'No, I'm sure they weren't. Elizabeth, as I said, lived with her parents in Dorset and Alex went down to visit her every weekend. Then one day, before any of the family had even met her, he announced that they were getting married in June. We were astounded; we knew nothing about her. My father was particularly angry. He had plans for Alex to continue with his studies; he did not want him getting married so young. But Alex would listen to no-one. We didn't even get to meet her until the wedding day and then of course we understood; by then it was obvious that she was pregnant. The baby, your mother, was born in the November.'

At this point her great-aunt stopped.

'I'm sorry, my dear, I find this all rather tiring. Perhaps we could continue later on, after lunch. I think I need a bit of a nap now. Perhaps Agnes will take you up to your room.'

She lay back on the cushion and closed her eyes. Kate bit back her disappointment and went in search of the housekeeper.

Her great-aunt had instructed Agnes to prepare a light lunch in the conservatory, overlooking the ha-ha and the meadows beyond. An enormous cedar tree dominated the view. Kate had forgotten about that tree; now she remembered how she and her cousins used to scramble up the lower branches, playing some game of which she could no longer recall the rules.

'What a lovely view,' she said.

'Yes, it's my favourite. I like to sit here in the summer and watch the birds come down onto the lawn. It's not warm enough in the winter but it's nice now,' she answered.

She pointed to a wooden box, bound with brass straps and a large brass lock.

'I asked Agnes to bring this down for you to see. It was your grandfather's. You remember he left me all his papers and photographs; nothing important you realise, just family mementos.'

Kate stretched out her hand and touched it. Did the answer to her quest lie within this box?

'Let's eat lunch first and then you can have a look through them,' she continued.

As though on cue, Agnes came in carrying a dish of poached salmon and a green salad.

'I can't eat anything too heavy,' her great-aunt explained. 'I hardly ever eat meat any more, just some fish and vegetables. I hope this is all right for you?'

'Yes, it looks lovely,' Kate replied.

'There's a rhubarb tart for dessert and clotted cream,' she added.

'Sounds wonderful.'

Her aunt ate very little; she drank half a glass of white Burgundy and a little water but did not touch the rhubarb tart.

Kate ate everything; she found the salmon delicious, the wine irresistible and thoroughly enjoyed the tart.

'Well that was lovely,' she said, wiping her mouth with the damask linen napkin that her aunt had handed her.

'You've got a good appetite, I see,' her great-aunt commented.

'Well I enjoy good food and wine, and anyway I was hungry.'

'Your mother had a good appetite too,' she said. 'But she never put on any weight.'

Kate was sure she looked at her waist-line as she spoke.

'Can I have a look in the box now?' she asked.

'Yes, let's get Agnes to clear away and then you can lift it up onto the table.'

The suspense was making her nervous; or maybe it was the wine. She found it difficult to stop herself from hurrying her great-aunt. When, at last, she opened the lid, it was actually a little disappointing; the box contained bundles of old letters, some torn and dog-eared photographs and an assortment of oddments including a silver cigarette case, an old fashioned fountain pen, a broken camera and a baby's shoe.

'Where do we start?' she asked.

'Well, here's as good as anywhere,' her great-aunt replied, picking up the old Kodak camera. 'This belonged to your grandmother. I remember now, that was why she didn't leave with her parents; she had some high-falutin ideas about being a reporter and wanted to take photographs of the Civil War.'

'Did she take any?' Kate asked.

'Yes, I think there are a few here of Málaga.'

She handed her a battered album. Kate started to look through it; it was interesting but it was not what she was looking for. There were a number of faded black and white photographs of a bombed city and lots of ragged, miserable looking people.

'Who are they?' she asked, pointing to a group of young men, standing in a shop doorway, smiling at the camera.

'I don't remember. I think your grandfather knew who they were.'

She pushed her glasses higher up her nose and looked closer.

'I think one is an American but the others look like Spaniards to me.'

'Is my grandfather one of them?'

'Alex? No, Alex is not there. But there is one of Alex, somewhere, with his arm around a Spanish man. Ah, here it is.'

She handed a loose photograph to Kate. The men were not smiling in this one. She turned it over; someone had written: Alex and Juan, February 1937.

'Can I keep this one?' she asked.

'Why not, they'll probably all get thrown out when I die. I don't know why Alex left them to me. I'm not sure what he expected me to do with them. The young people today aren't interested in the past; nobody wants to know what we did when we were young.'

'Can you tell me anything about my grandmother's parents?' Kate asked.

She could see that Angela was losing interest and would soon be suggesting that they leave it until later but she did not want to stop now.

'Elizabeth's parents?'

'Yes, did they ever go back to Spain?'

'No, I don't think they did. Her mother died pretty soon after they got back to England, if I remember rightly. She picked up TB on the boat home and never recovered; she died in 1939.'

'But she went to Elizabeth's wedding and she was alive when my mother was born?'

'No she wasn't allowed to go to the wedding; as soon as they found out she had TB they put her in a quarantine hospital in Poole. Only her husband was allowed contact with her. Of course nobody wanted her to infect Elizabeth or the baby.'

'Oh, how sad, the poor woman must have been distraught.'

'I never met her but I remember that Elizabeth was broken-hearted when she died.'

'What happened to her father?'

'I can't remember; he was an old man by the time he died. I met him when he came to the wedding; he gave Elizabeth away. I remember he was a well-read man; Father and he got on very well. I think he was probably the main reason that Father eventually accepted Elizabeth into the family.'

'Did they say anything about Elizabeth being pregnant?'

'No, of course not. We all tried to hush it up. Anyway everyone thought it was Alex's child, even her father.'

'Did Alex say anything?'

'He never denied it was his. In fact he was very happy to have Elizabeth as his bride and a child as well. In the end I'm sure he thought of your mother as his own daughter. Maybe she was but I have my doubts.'

Kate picked up the cigarette case; it was silver and had an inscription engraved on the inside: "Alex all my love Elizabeth. April 1940".

'That was Alex's. She gave it to him for his birthday. He used to smoke in those days, everyone did. We didn't know that it gave you lung cancer and heart disease then.'

Her great-aunt paused then said:

'Look my dear I'm feeling a bit tired. Why don't you take that box up to your room and have a look through it. We can talk some more later.'

'Of course Aunt, how selfish of me to keep firing all these questions at you. I'll have a look through these things then I might drive up to the golf course and see if I can get a game tomorrow.'

Her aunt had stopped listening and was drifting off into a world of her own, so Kate picked up the box and left.

Her room was at the end of the passage and overlooked the tennis courts; she stood for a few moments looking out. A squirrel was sitting on the fence, nibbling at a nut.   She put the box on the bed and tipped it out. The baby shoe had originally been pink but time had faded it to a grubby grey; it had a pink label tied to it which read: 'Isabel Reeves 6lb 12oz'. She put it to one side and began to look through the photographs; there were more of the bombed city and some of dead bodies and people with tremendous injuries. Had her grandmother actually taken these? It hardly fitted with the image she had of this glamorous woman. She picked up one of a stone house on a hillside; maybe this was where she had lived. She turned it over; someone had written: *'Finca del Niño'* 1937. She put it to one side and continued sorting through the album; most of the photographs were views of the countryside or a record of the devastation that her grandmother had witnessed but some were of people that she must have known because she had noted their names on the reverse side of the photographs.   Then she turned to the

283

letters; they were mostly written from Elizabeth to Alex during the Second World War, telling him about the children and how they were coping; by then they not only had Isabel but Rosemary and Jeremy as well. They were affectionate, loving letters, full of concern for his well-being and safety but they gave Kate no clue to the real relationship between her grandfather and Isabel. She found a bundle tied with red ribbon; these were from Alex to Elizabeth and told her, as much as the censor would allow, about his time in North Africa. He had missed her and he had missed his children. It seemed he was a captain; she found his cap badge in the box. It was all so strange, reading the words of these young people and trying to equate them with her grandparents, who to her had always been old. Her head was beginning to ache from reading the closely written script; she decided to leave it for a while and have a break.

The golf course car park was full and she had to park her car on the side of a grassy bank by the entrance. She walked down towards the club house to look for the Secretary. He was standing by the eighteenth green collecting the score cards as the players finished; there was a competition and he looked busy. She decided it would be better to wait until he had finished and went into the bar to buy herself a drink.

'An orange juice, please,' she said to the barman.

While he prepared it she looked around her; she was in a large open room, with picture windows that afforded a view of the eighteenth green, the first hole and an undulating landscape of sand dunes covered by thick, coarse, grey grass that glinted with a silver light in the afternoon sun. It was a moonscape broken only by verdant putting greens, closely mown and watered; there was not a tree to be seen. The golf course looked long and challenging, and with the stiff breeze that was blowing directly from the sea she knew it would be difficult to play.

'I see there's a competition today,' she said to the barman when he handed her the drink.

'Ar, it be the Fleming Cup,' he replied.

'What about tomorrow? Any competitions tomorrow?'

'No, not tomorrow.'

He was obviously a man of few words, so she took her orange juice and sat at a table outside where she had a clearer view of her surroundings. The more she looked at the course, the keener she was to play it. She knew her great-aunt would not mind if she disappeared for a few hours to play golf; she would probably be glad to be free of her and her endless questions for a while. She noticed that the club secretary seemed to have finished collecting the cards and was now heading for his office. She hastily swallowed the last of her drink and set off after him.

'Excuse me,' she called.

He stopped and looked at her; he was a young man with a pleasant expression.

'Can I help you?' he asked.

'Yes. I'm just down here for a couple of days and wondered if it were possible to play golf tomorrow?' she asked, smiling at him encouragingly.

'Do you have a handicap?'

'Fourteen,' she replied. 'I'm a member at Reading Golf Club.'

'Well I can't see any problem. Are you on your own?'

'Yes.'

'Ah, well, I'll have to pair you up with someone I'm afraid.   We don't allow singles on the course at the weekends.'

'That's all right.   I would prefer to play with someone anyway.'

'Which course do you want to play, the East or the West?'

'That one,' she said, pointing back to the course she had been looking at.

'The East.   OK, come with me and I'll put your name down on the list.'

She followed him into his office and waited while he spoke to his assistant and passed over the score cards for her to process.   Then he picked up the starting sheet for Sunday.

'What about nine o'clock?' he asked her.

'Perfect, that way I'll be back in time for lunch.'

'Your name?'

'Kate Scott.'

'Right that's done.   You just have to pay your green fee in the pro's shop before you play.   Your partners are a Margery Green, Hugh Barnes and Fred Potts; they're all members here.   You'll get on fine with them.'

'Thank you very much.   Nine o'clock then.'

Her great-aunt was in the lounge watching the television when she returned.   She collected a few photographs from her room then went in to join her.

'Ah, there you are?   Did you have a nice game?' she asked.

'Oh I didn't play Aunt; I just went to book a game for tomorrow.   You don't mind do you?'

Her great-aunt shook her head.

'I used to play you know. Haven't played for a long time now, though.'

Kate was surprised at this news; something else she had not known.

'What about grandfather? Did he play?'

'Oh yes, when he was a boy. He was very good. You'll see his name on the trophy boards; he was always winning things. He wanted to be a professional you know but Father wouldn't hear of it.'

'So where was that then?' Kate asked.

'In Wallingford, before he went to Spain. He was good at all sports: running, football, hockey, rowing. He was always winning things,' she repeated.

Her aunt drifted off, lost in her memories for a moment.

'Aunt Angela, I found some photos. Can you tell me anything about them?'

She placed the photographs in her great-aunt's withered hand. Angela opened her eyes and looked at her; it took her a moment to recognise Kate again, then she continued as if nothing had happened.

'Yes, I remember he wanted to go to the Olympics but I don't think he went in the end.'

She put on her reading glasses and looked at the photographs.

'No, I don't know who these people are. This one might be the man Elizabeth was in love with,' she said, pointing to the man identified as Juan, 'because I do remember that Alex told me that they were together, when he met her.'

'What else did he tell you, Aunt?'

'Well, when he first came back, he told me he didn't know what to do; he was very unhappy he said, because he was in love with a woman who loved someone else. I remember I told him not to waste his time; I said if she didn't return his affections, he should look elsewhere. There were lots of other girls about and he was quite a good catch. Then he told me that the man she loved had died so he was sure that in time he would have a chance with her. That was Elizabeth I suppose because he went down to visit her every week, you know. In the end he must have persuaded her to marry him.'

'Well I expect the baby was an important factor,' Kate added.

'Oh yes, women of our class did not have illegitimate babies in those days. It would have ruined her and broken her parents' hearts. Alex saved her from all that.'

'Did he ever go back to Spain?'

'No, never. By the time the war had finished in Spain, he had joined up and was at officer training school.'

'What about after the war?'

'No, I don't think so; he never spoke about it. I think Spain had burnt a hole in his heart; he never wanted to go back again. When he was demobbed he went back to his old job as a journalist with the Oxford Globe. Elizabeth and the children moved back from Dorset where they'd been living with her father throughout the war and they all moved in with my parents.'

'Did my grandfather get on well with Elizabeth's father?'

'Yes, I think so. I never heard him speak badly of him. I remember he was quite fond of Elizabeth's brother. What was his name? Philip? No, Peter. He was called Peter. He was just a teenager when they married, a few years younger than Elizabeth. He used to visit them quite regularly in the first years of their marriage but then he moved away to the north of England, or it may have been Scotland. I'm not sure. It was a long time ago,' she repeated.

'Can I keep some of these photos, Aunt?'

'You can keep whatever you want. Take the whole box if you like. It will only go to my sons when I die and I'm sure they won't want it.'

'Thank you, I will. I'd like to read their letters more carefully. There may be something there that I've missed.'

'Very well my dear. Now would you like a small sherry? I usually have one about this time of the evening.'

By ten to nine the next morning she had paid her green fee and was standing by the first tee waiting for her companions to arrive. A small, bubbly woman, with a woollen hat covering her grey hair, was the first to arrive.

'Good morning, you must be Kate,' she said. 'I'm Margery and this is Fred,' she added, pointing to a rangy youth who was climbing the path towards them, his bag of clubs slung over his shoulder. 'We just need Hugh then we can get off.'

'Is that him?' Kate asked.

A man in a blue windcheater was hurrying towards them.

'Yes, that's Hugh. He always leaves it to the last minute. Come on Hugh, we were due off five minutes ago,' she shouted down to him.

'Sorry,' he gasped as he arrived, puffing slightly from the exertion. 'Hugh Barnes,' he said, holding out his hand to Kate.

'Kate Scott.'

She took his hand; it was warm and his grip was firm and confident. He had a nice smile she thought and looked pretty fit; she wondered what his golf handicap was.

'OK, what are we playing?' he asked, immediately taking charge.

'Better ball?' suggested Margery.

'Good idea. You and Fred against Kate and me. OK?'

'Fine.'

They discussed handicaps and shots and eventually were ready to start. Fred, now that she could see him more clearly, was a pleasant teenager who looked as though his growing spurt had not yet come to an end; he seemed to protrude from his clothes in every direction, his bony wrists extending from the sleeves of his sweater and his trousers hanging at half mast. However if his first shot was anything to go by he was a competent golfer. Hugh teed off next, hitting a long ball straight down the middle of the fairway. Then it was the turn of the ladies; Margery's ball was off line but somehow managed to bounce back into the fairway. Now it was Kate's turn; she set herself up carefully, concentrating on the shot. She did not want to make a mess of her shot in front of people whom she had only just met. Her backswing was slow and smooth and she made firm contact with the ball, sending it bounding along the fairway for almost two hundred yards.

'Great shot, partner,' Hugh said, smiling at her.

The morning was warm and sunny but, as Kate had already guessed, the prevailing wind on this course was from the sea and it exerted an enormous influence on the flight of the ball. For the first time in ages she began to enjoy herself; she forgot about Bill; she forgot about Jeremy and his accusations; she forgot about the money and her grandmother and she thought only about the game. The two teams were equally matched and there was never more than a hole up or down in the entire game. They arrived on the eighteenth tee all square.

'Right Kate, we can get them here. I'm sure Margery will never get up in two but you may be able to.'

'Hey, no pressure please. This is supposed to be fun,' she protested, unable to repress a laugh.

He was right; they managed to win the last hole but not through any skill on Kate's part. After two magnificent shots, Fred's ball lay twenty feet from the hole. Hugh's ball lay in a hollow short of the green, also after two shots. Margery had lost her ball and was out of it and Kate's ball was in the bunker. Hugh played his ball first; it was a delicate shot that flew through the air, landed just on the edge of the green and ran across until it reached the hole where it hesitated for the briefest of moments before dropping in to the accompaniment of cheers from a group of members enjoying a drink on the clubhouse terrace and whoops of joy from Kate.

'Well that was very enjoyable,' Hugh said as they all shook hands afterwards. 'Maybe you'd like to play with us another day?'

'I'd love to but I'm going back to Reading this evening,' Kate replied.

'Well stay for a drink at least,' he said.

Margery picked up her golf bag and slung it over her shoulder.

'I can't stay, sorry. Jimmy's expecting his lunch at two,' she said. 'Nice to meet you Kate; it was a pleasure to play with you.'

'I haven't time for a drink either,' said Fred. 'I'm playing again in twenty minutes.'

'Looks as though I'll have to drink alone then,' Hugh said.

'I've got time for a quick one,' said Kate. 'My great-aunt said lunch wouldn't be until about two-thirty.'

'Great, what will you have?'

'A glass of white wine would be nice. Shall we stay out here? It's such a lovely day it would be a shame to sit inside.'

'Fine, I'll bring it out.'

She sat down on a wooden bench and waited for him to come back. He was a very amusing man; she had not laughed so much in a long time.

'Here we are,' he said, putting the glasses on the table in front of her and pulling up a chair.

Now that the others had gone, Kate felt slightly awkward and waited for him to speak first.

'So you live in Reading?'

'Yes, live there, work there and play golf there, pretty boring really.'

'Reading Golf Club?'

'Yes.'

'I know it; I played some inter-club match there once. It's a bit short but it's got some interesting holes, if I remember correctly.'

They talked for a while about the changes that had been made to the course since he had last played there, then Kate asked him if he lived in the Barnstable area.

'No, I live in Bristol but I have country membership here; since my divorce I come down here most weekends to play.'

'It's quite a way. Don't you belong to a golf club in Bristol?'

'Yes, I've been a member at Bristol and Clifton for years but my ex-wife still plays there. I can't stand bumping into her all the time, especially when she's with that new boyfriend of hers. He's a right prat. I'd sooner drive down here and play in peace.'

'So what kind of work do you do?' she asked wanting to steer the conversation away from divorced wives.

'I'm an architect.'

He started to tell her about his work. As she listened she could not stop herself assessing him; he was quite good-looking, nothing striking but his features were regular and pleasant. He was well-built, not fat but a little on the stocky side; his hair was a good feature, thick and wavy, with not too much grey and she loved the sound of his voice, with just the hint of a Bristol accent.   Yes, he was actually very presentable.

'Sorry?'

He had been asking her something.

'I said what do you do for a living?'

'Oh, nothing very exciting, I'm the PA to the Human Resources Director of a small company,' she replied.

'Do you enjoy it?'

Nobody had asked her that for a long time; she hesitated before answering.

'I can't say I really enjoy it but I'm not unhappy working there.   I've got into a routine I suppose, after twenty-odd years.'

'Is that shorthand for 'in a rut'? he asked.

This was the second time this week that someone had suggested she was in a rut.

'Maybe.'

'You're staying with an aunt then?' he asked, changing the subject.

'My great-aunt,' she replied.   'She's my grandfather's sister. I'm just down for the weekend.'

'Do you often visit your great-aunt?'

'No, this is the first time actually.'

'So, you're not likely to be coming back?'

'I don't have any plans to come back.'

'Pity, it would be nice to play golf again.'

293

'Well why don't you come and play at Reading?' she suggested, the words leaving her mouth before she could stop them.

'That would be nice, what about next weekend?'

'Oh I can't say just like that; I'd have to check my diary. Why don't I give you a ring when I get back?'

'OK. Here's my card.'

He handed her a buff coloured business card. She read: Hugh Barnes RIBA. Underneath was printed an address, a telephone number, a cell phone number and an email address.

'Plenty of ways to get in touch with you here,' she said, smiling. 'I'm sorry I don't have a card but you can have my telephone number if you wish.'

She waited for him to get a pencil out of his pocket then dictated the number which he wrote down on an old score card. She looked at her watch.

'Look I'm sorry; I have to go. My great-aunt is rather old; she doesn't like her meals to be late,' she explained.

'Fine, I understand. Have a safe journey back to Reading.'

'Thanks. Well, goodbye then.'

Again the awkwardness had returned.

'Goodbye.'

He leaned towards her and kissed her quickly on the lips. Kate was too surprised to speak; she turned and walked back to her car. What an interesting man, maybe she would telephone him after all.

When she arrived home the light was flashing on her answer machine. She dropped her bag in the hall and pressed the button to see who had called.

'Hello Kate, it's Bill. I just thought I'd give you a call to see how you were getting along. It's been a long time since we've seen each other; I thought maybe we could meet up for a drink one evening. I'm still on the same number, 8778778. Give me a ring.'

'What a cheek. Who the hell do you think you are, ringing me for a drink as though nothing's happened?' she shouted at the machine.

She could not believe the temerity of the man; they had not spoken since the day she had found out about him and Ursula and here he was ringing her as though she were an old friend. She sat down on the sofa, shaking with rage. This could only mean one thing; he wanted something. Maybe he had heard about her inheritance but if so, how? He did not know her relatives very well. She had told nobody at work. The solicitor would not have said anything to him and the only person she had confided in was Maisie. Well, whatever it was about, she was not going to speak to him; if it was anything important he could contact her solicitor. She deleted the message from the answer machine and took the receiver off the hook. As she poured herself a glass of wine from the open bottle in the refrigerator, she congratulated herself on the fact that she had refused to let him have her cell phone number. He was not going to ruin her evening she decided, putting a CD of Mark Koefler in the machine and selecting a bundle of letters from her grandfather's box.

CHAPTER 17

A couple of weeks later she was just about to go for lunch when Jill shouted through to her:

'Hang on minute, Kate, there's a call coming through for you.'

She picked up the receiver as soon as it began to ring.

'Is that Kate Scott?' a man's voice asked, rather hesitantly.

For a moment she thought it was Bill and was about to hang up then she realised that the voice, although familiar, was nothing like his.

'Yes, can I help you?'

There was a pause, an almost embarrassed silence as though the caller expected to be recognised.

'Hugh, is that you?'

'Yes. I could never get through on the number you gave me so I thought I'd try to track you down at work. I hope you don't mind?'

'No, of course not. I'm sorry I've been having some problems with my telephone,' she lied.

Bill had continued in his efforts to contact her, on each occasion leaving a message on her answer-phone, so she in the end she had disconnected the machine and each evening, when she arrived home from work, she took the telephone off the hook. She had forgotten she had given Hugh her home number.

'I wondered why I hadn't heard from you,' she added.

'Well actually you were going to telephone me as I remember it.'

'So I was, about golf. Look I'm really sorry. It's just that I've been so busy lately that I haven't had time to arrange anything yet.'

'No, don't apologise. It doesn't matter. I was just wondering how you were.'

'Fine, I'm fine,' she said, thinking how much better she felt for hearing his voice.

'I have to come up to Reading next week on business and I wondered if you fancied meeting for a drink or perhaps going out for a bite to eat?'

'That sounds rather nice. Which day are you coming up?'

'Well I can arrange it according to when you're free,' he said.

'Doesn't sound very important business,' she said, laughing. 'How about Wednesday?'

'Wednesday's great. Where shall I meet you?'

'Do you know Reading?'

'Sort of.'

'Well there's a very nice French bistro near the Hexagon centre, it's called 'L'Escargot'. Shall we say about eight-thirty?'

'That sounds good. Do I need to book a table?'

'I can do that if you like; it's not far from where I work.'

'OK. Eight-thirty on Wednesday it is then.'

'By the way, how did you get my number?'

'Well you said you worked for a biscuit company and this was the only one I could find in the directory.'

'Quite the little sleuth, eh.'

'Well you know what they say: "where there's a will there's a way." Actually it wasn't very difficult.'

'Look I've got to go. I'll see you next week then.'

'Wednesday,' he repeated.

She received two important telephone calls that day; the second one was from Robert Percy to say that there was no problem about her having the cottage as part of her inheritance. Her uncle Jeremy had been unable to substantiate his claim that the will was null and void and nobody else cared whether she had the broken-down cottage or not.

'I would suggest you have a good look at it first; you may change your mind when you see the state it's been left in,' he advised.

'Can you post me the keys then?' she said.

'I can but it would probably make more sense if you collected them from the estate agent. Sanders and Sanders have been looking after the property, and I use that term loosely, since your parents died. They were the only ones who ever went down there as far as I know.'

'Do you have a phone number for them?'

'Yes. They are in the same village so there should be no problem about arranging to pick up the keys.'

He dictated the telephone number and name of the person to contact.

'I still haven't got the final figures on the inheritance,' he apologised. 'This business with your uncle has delayed things somewhat. I shall be in touch as soon as I can.'

'That's OK. There's just one question, Mr. Percy. Have you or anyone in your office been in touch with my ex-husband?'

'Your ex-husband? No, most certainly not. We have no reason to be in touch with him and we would certainly not have informed him about your inheritance.'

'It's just I have a feeling he knows and I was wondering how he could have found out.'

'He may have seen Sir Alexander's obituary in the Times. Perhaps he is just guessing that you were named in the will. Is he bothering you? Do you want me to do anything about it?'

'No, there's no problem really. It was just a suspicion I had.'

'Well if that's all Kate, I'll say goodbye.'

'Goodbye Mr Percy. Thanks for the good news.'

There was nothing planned for the weekend, so she decided to go and have a look at the cottage right away. She picked up the telephone again.

'Maisie? It's Kate.'

'Hi, Kate, aren't you at work?'

'Yes and I'm rather busy, so I'll make this quick. How do you fancy a weekend in the country?'

She did not want to get into a long gossipy conversation with her friend.

'Sounds good. Where and when?'

'Dorset, this weekend.'

'Is it a golf competition?'

'No, it's nothing like that. I'm going down on Saturday to look at an old cottage I have inherited. I thought you might like to come with me.'

She could hear Maisie tossing the idea around in her mind.

'Why not, it would make a change. I'll have to speak to Bob first though but I don't think there'll be any problem because I'm pretty sure he's got a knock-out competition this weekend and I wouldn't see much of him anyway.'

'Great. Give me a ring when you know.'

'When were you planning on coming back?'

'Sunday afternoon I expect. I think I'll book a room in a hotel for Saturday night; I'm not too confident about what we'll find when we get to the cottage. It'll be my treat by the way.'

'Even better, don't fancy sleeping with lots of spiders and mice.'

Kate arranged with Mr. Nesbit of Sanders and Sanders that they would meet him at the cottage on Saturday morning at eleven o'clock. At five to eleven she drove up to the entrance and parked next to a shiny, new Volvo; the driver was standing next to his car, smoking a cigarette and obviously admiring his recent purchase.

'Mr Nesbit?' she asked as she closed the door of her rather battered Punto.

'Yes. You must be Mrs Scott,' he replied.

'Ms. Scott,' she corrected him automatically.

'Sorry. Anyway Ms. Scott, here are the keys.'

He looked enquiringly at Maisie as he held out an assortment of keys attached to a large plastic disc with "Sanders and Sanders" embossed on it.

'My friend, Maisie Brownlow.'

'Do you want me to show you both around or wait for you or something?'

'No. I know the house already; I just want to have a look around before I decide what to do with it,' Kate said, taking the keys. 'But you can give me some information.'

'Yes, of course.'

'How long has it been let?'

'Well your mother put it with us about twelve or fifteen years ago; I'd have to look in the files to be accurate. She said no-one in the family wanted to use it anymore and it was better to let it out during the holidays. But the problem has been that it is not exactly your ideal holiday let. The house is a long way from the main road and there are no local shops. What's more it's not near any of the more popular beaches and, apart from the odd pub or two, there is very little to do around here. Also, and I did point this out, it has never really been furnished for holiday makers.'

'So it's furnished then?'

'Yes but with the original furniture. If you like musty old antiques, it's probably fine but most people these days want a television and a washing machine; some people even ask for a dishwasher. They bring their portable computers with them and want to have access to the internet but there's not even a telephone line here either. As I said, I did point all this out to your mother and father a couple of times but they said they didn't want to change anything.'

'So it's not been let very often then?'

'Sometimes we have a group of young teachers who rent it for the Easter holidays; they're walkers and spend most of their time out of doors. Then occasionally in the summer we get people who can't find anywhere else available but no, the truth is, we don't let it very often. I suggested that we get rid of the furniture and let it unfurnished but your mother was not happy about that either, so basically we have just been keeping an eye on the property to make sure there were no squatters or vandals hanging about.'

Kate wondered how much they were paying Sanders and Sanders for this service but she said nothing.

'Fine, well I'll have a look around and bring back the keys this afternoon.'

'No need. You can keep them; we have a second set in the office. However, if you don't mind, I would like you to sign for them,' he said, producing a receipt book.

Kate duly signed her name, shook his rather flaccid hand and waited until he had driven away before turning to Maisie and asking:

'So, what do you think of it?'

'Well it's a lot bigger than I imagined but I can see what you mean about being run-down.'

The house, because it was better described as a house than a cottage, was built of Portland stone and had a gabled roof. A very old wisteria wound and twisted its way up drainpipes and along guttering and draped long bunches of delicate, purple flowers along the walls. Huge lavender bushes lined the pathway to the house and the air was filled with the sleepy buzzing of bumble bees.

'Come on, let's have a look inside.'

Kate felt a twinge of excitement as she fitted the key in the lock. Robert Percy had not been exaggerating when he said it needed some repairs; she could have written a list of them from where they were standing in the doorway, in a pool of sunlight that lit up the rather gloomy hall and highlighted the broken banister, the stained carpet and a cupboard door that swung from its single remaining hinge.

'It's very dark,' commented Maisie. 'Why don't we let in some light?'

So they walked from room to room, pulling back the curtains and opening the windows to let the light breeze, with its heavy scent of May blossom, flow through the house.

'That's better; now we can see what we're doing. Let's check out the kitchen first.'

One look at the kitchen told Kate that everything would have to be replaced; she could not even bring herself to open the grimy cupboard doors nor look in the refrigerator for fear of what might have been left inside and the stone flagged floor was covered with the dirtiest carpet she had ever seen.

'My God, don't they send anyone in to clean?' asked Maisie.

'From the look of this room, I would guess not.'

They moved on into the lounge.

'This isn't too bad. Apart from replacing these rotten window frames and repainting these ghastly, yellow walls, it's perfectly liveable. I think your grandparents must have been smokers; this room looks and smells like an old pub.'

Kate could see that Mr Nesbit's description of the furniture had been fairly accurate; it was ancient. She was no expert on antiques so would never be able to decide which items were worth keeping and which were destined for the rubbish heap. She banged the back of an easy chair, waited for the dust to settle then sat down to contemplate her new acquisition.

'So?' she asked her friend.

'So? So, it's lovely, or rather it will be lovely once you get the workmen in and clean it up a bit. I think you'll have to have a surveyor look at it, Kate. You never know what problems there could be with a house this age. Dry rot, wet rot, rising damp, falling damp, it could have it all.'

Kate laughed at her friend. She was glad she had invited her to come; it made it all much more fun and stopped her from slipping into morbid thoughts about the past.

'Yes, you could be right. I think it's going to cost a pretty penny to do it up. No wonder none of the others were bothered when I said that I wanted it.'

'But what will you do? Do it up and sell it?'

'I don't know yet, Maisie. I might just keep it as a weekend retreat.'

'Are there any golf courses nearby?'

'I'm not sure. There's one near Poole and there's the Isle of Purbeck Golf Course but I don't know if there's anything closer.'

'An important consideration for a weekend cottage, is easy access to a golf course.'

She laughed again.

'Come on let's look upstairs.'

They explored the bedrooms and bathrooms, opening cupboards and looking under beds. It was as if someone had walked out forty years before and left everything as it was; apart from a general air of mustiness and thick layers of dust covering every available surface, nothing had really been touched. The holidaymakers must have come with their swimming trunks, fishing rods and walking boots, then left again leaving no trace behind them. It remained her great-grandparents' home. There were sepia coloured photographs of people she did not recognise on the dressing-tables and watercolour paintings of local views on the walls; one room was lined with books, their spines cracked and the paper yellow with age. Bouquets of dried flowers were arranged in delicate china bowls, their blooms covered in dust.

'Your mother obviously never changed anything here,' said Maisie.

'No, I don't think she did.'

'What about your grandmother?'

'I don't think she ever lived here. She came to visit her father and when her children were small they used to come here for the summer. I remember my mother often talked about the house.'

'Didn't she bring you here?'

'Yes, sometimes but we usually went to my grandfather's house in North Devon with my cousins.'

'So how long has this house been in your family?'

'According to my mother, her grandparents bought it just before the War, when they returned from Spain. They rented it at first because they never intended to stay; they were going back to Spain once the war was over but then my great-grandmother died, so my great-grandfather stayed on here with his son.'

'So they were living in this house when your mother was born?'

'Yes, I would think so. Why?'

'Look around you, nothing's really been touched since then. Maybe, if we have a good search, we might find something that will tell us who your grandfather really was.'

'Well it's possible. Where shall we start?'

'How about in that library room?'

'OK.'

They systematically opened every drawer and cupboard in the room but could find nothing; they removed books and looked on the shelves. They even removed the paintings from the wall and looked to see if anything was taped behind them although Kate thought that Maisie was being a bit over-dramatic suggesting it.

'You've been watching too many detective programmes,' she said.

'You're right. There's nothing here. Why don't we take a break?'

'That sounds like a good idea. I think we passed a pub on the way here; shall we see if we can get some lunch?'

They closed the downstairs windows, locked the front door and set off to the pub. Kate had persuaded Maisie that it was not far so, instead of taking the car, they walked. It was a warm day and, by the time they arrived at the Dog and Badger, they were hot and thirsty.

'Two halves of bitter,' Kate ordered.

'Do you still have any food?' Maisie asked, eyeing the blackboard menu.

Kate realised that, for the first time in weeks, she was very hungry. They ordered a couple of rounds of sandwiches and a salad, then asked for two more beers. They chose a table in the garden and sat down in the shade.

'Where shall we look next?' Maisie asked.

'Well let's approach this a bit more scientifically. What sort of information are we looking for?'

'Well letters I suppose, or a diary.'

'A diary, that's a good idea. Lots of ladies kept diaries in those days; I wonder if my great-grandmother kept one.'

'Or your great-grandfather; didn't you say he was a writer or something?'

'Yes, of course. He may very well have kept a diary although I don't remember my mother saying anything about one.'

'Well diaries are supposed to be secret; you don't tell the whole world that you're writing one, do you.'

'I think you're right Maisie. If there is anything to be found, it will be in a diary. Time we got back,' she added, looking at her watch.

It was almost three o'clock by the time they arrived back at Badger's Cottage, which, they had discovered from the barman, was the name of her new house. They wasted no time in going straight back to the library and resuming their search, this time with more focused eyes. Maisie concentrated on the desk while Kate continued along the bookshelves.

'Kate, I think I've found a secret compartment. I knew there should be one in this desk; the Georgians loved their secret drawers. Hang on, yes I've got it.'

She pressed something at the back of the drawer and a tiny compartment shot forward.

'There's something in it,' she said, her voice rising with excitement. 'Look.'

She gave Kate a folded piece of paper. Kate's hands were trembling as she took it from her.

'It's probably nothing,' she said, trying to remain calm as she smoothed the paper open and began to read it.

'It's from my grandmother,' she explained.

'Well read it out then. I can't stand the suspense.'

Kate cleared her throat and began:

'February 1937, The Rock Hotel, Gibraltar.

My dear Father,

I am writing to ask you to forgive me for leaving the way I did. I know it must have caused you and Mother a great deal of worry but believe me I had no option. I was not strong enough to wait and listen to more of your very sensible arguments. I know that if I had not left when I did, I would never have left and then I would have spent all my life wondering what I had missed. Now I know and I am still too dazed to really understand what I have experienced. I have met some wonderful, brave people and seen some dreadful suffering; I have fallen in love and had my heart broken all within a few days. One day I hope I will be able to put into words what happened during those briefest of days but for now, all I can say is that I am no longer the same Elizabeth that sneaked out of the International Club looking for fame and adventure. That girl is gone forever; she is buried under the rocks and rubble on the road to Almería; she was consumed in the fires of Málaga. I only hope that you will love and cherish the new Elizabeth as you did the old.

As you can see from the notepaper I am in Gibraltar, waiting for a ship to take me home to England. As soon as I arrive I will write to you and tell you where I am staying. I will probably go straight to London but I will come and see you all as soon as I am settled.

Please give my love to Mother and tell her I am missing her very much and to Peter of course. I hope they are both well and that Mother is not too unhappy at being away from her beloved Spain.

Your loving daughter
Elizabeth.'

'I wonder why he kept it hidden in the drawer. There doesn't seem to be anything very important in it; it's just a letter from a daughter to her father,' Maisie said.

'True but it does say she fell in love.'

'Maybe she fell in love with your grandfather?'

'My great-aunt doesn't think so. She thinks there was someone else.'

'Well anyway we've found something. Perhaps there's more. How far have you got along those books?'

'I've done half this side. Why don't you start over there.'

They continued in silence for a while, then Kate found them. At first she could not speak; she stood there, turning one of the books over in her hands, frightened to open it.

'What's that?' asked Maisie.

'It says: *"My Journal 1936, Margaret Marshall"*.'

'1936? Are there others?'

'Yes, there seem to be quite a few: 1934, 1935, 1931.'

'Which year is it you want?' Maisie interrupted.

'1937. Here it is. It's here. My God, it's here, 1937.'

'Hand them down and mind how you get down yourself. I don't want you breaking your leg in this out-of-the-way place.'

Kate handed the journals to her friend and climbed down from the library steps. They placed them on the desk and stood looking at them reverently.

'I can't believe it.'

'Well don't get too excited, we don't know what's in them yet.'

Kate opened the first one and began to read:

'January 3rd 1937

New Year's Eve was very quiet this year. Nobody was in the mood to celebrate. The H-S's wanted us to go to their party and stay the night but R said no. He is very worried about the situation and sits by the radio for hours hoping to hear some news about what is going on. The servants are all nervous and every day we have some new face sitting in our kitchen. We are fast becoming the village meeting point.

Went up onto the ridge and painted the view of the village; quite pleased with it but need to work on the sky a bit more.

The light here is so clear that I don't find it easy to get the translucency of the sky quite right. R says it's lovely; but then he always says that.

Conception has a new recipe for patatas pobres; R loved it and even E ate some:

1 kilo potatoes
100 ml. oil
10 peppercorns
2 cloves garlic
¼ teaspoon cumin
½ teaspoon paprika
50 ml. water
1 teaspoon salt
1 teaspoon vinegar

Slice and fry the potatoes, mash the spices together and dissolve in water, add to the potatoes with the salt and vinegar. Cook until ready. Very simple and delicious.'

'Look there's a sketch of the village.'

She showed Maisie a pencilled sketch on the next page.

'Why don't we take the diaries back to the hotel and then we can read them in comfort,' suggested Maisie. 'There seems to be a lot of interesting stuff in them.'

'Yes, good idea. Let's see if there are any more, first.'

'Well what have we got? 1931, '34 -'35 and '37.'

'Here are some more: '32 -'33 and 1936, oh and 1930.'

'Maybe she didn't start writing them until 1930.'

'Well that'll do for now anyway. We'll come back tomorrow and see what else there is.'

'Yes and we'll have a look at the garden; I know it's overgrown but there are some interesting plants in there.'

The hotel was small and cosy, what the brochures now referred to as 'a boutique hotel'. Kate had booked two adjoining rooms with en-suite bathrooms and a shared sitting room.

'This is pretty swish,' said Maisie, once the porter had deposited her bag and left. 'Glad you're paying the bill.'

'Yes it's OK, isn't it. I especially asked for rooms with a view.'

She moved to the window and looked out; beyond the rolling, green hills she could see the sun glinting on the sea. The sky was cloudless and there was no wind; it promised to be a perfect evening.

'We'll be able to sit here with our gins and tonics and watch the sunset,' Maisie said, settling herself in a chair by the window.

'Have you forgotten this is a working trip?'

'Ah yes, "The case of the missing grandfather", I'd forgotten. OK back to work, Sherlock.'

They placed the books on the coffee table.

'Let's leave the earlier ones for now,' suggested Kate. 'I'll take 1937 and you take 1936. If there is another man in my grandmother's life, I don't think it was much before 1937 because she was in England most of the time.'

'But not all of the time; didn't you say her parents had lived there for some years? She probably visited them in the holidays.'

'Yes but these aren't her diaries; they're her mother's. Anyway let's start with the later ones then we can go back to the others.'

'OK, boss.'

They settled down to read. Kate was fascinated by her great-grandmother's entries; anything and everything seemed

311

to warrant a mention: there were recipes, household tips, gardening notes, pen pictures of their friends, pressed flowers, sketches, news from abroad, news from the village. On 5th January she noted that the first lavender was coming out and on the 6th that her neighbour's donkey had died. A week later she recorded that Peter had slipped off the bank behind their house and hurt his leg and that she had made a poultice of wild herbs to put on it.

'January 15th 1937.

E is still with us. I had expected her to return to England after the holiday but she says she is going to stay here for a bit. I'm worried about her. Why doesn't she want to find a job? Still it's nice to have her here a bit longer. R still worried about the war. Rebels in Seville, not that far away. Hopes they'll go straight to Madrid and leave Málaga alone.

Had to let Adela go; she has to look after her mother. Not sure how C will manage. Maybe E will give her a hand but I doubt it somehow.'

Kate lifted the book to her nose; it still smelled of lavender.

'January 19th 1937.

Bad news from the village, a dozen of the men have left to join the Militia in Málaga, leaving their wives and families to fend for themselves. I don't know how they will cope.

Remedios came to the house asking for work but I had to say no. C doesn't like her, said she would prefer to do it all herself rather than have to be behind Remedios all day long. Can't say she is my favourite person either; she is thin faced, with a sharp nose and an even sharper tongue. I think if she came here it would disrupt the harmony of our happy household.

R is complaining that he is not progressing very well with his book; says he can't concentrate on the past when history is being made all around him. I suggested he write a short piece about the current situation for The Times.

E spends most of her time walking in the hills with Willow. She has lost weight since Christmas. I hope she's not unhappy. She has taken some nice photographs of Peter and a lovely one of C.'

'27th January 1937.

R says Timothy has told him we must leave. Spent all night crying. Don't know where to go and don't want to leave my home. What will become of Conception and Juan? I dread to think what will happen to my garden without regular watering. R tells me not to be silly. Promises that we will come back as soon as it is all over. I don't think we will. I have a bad feeling about all this.

Pepe says he has had some dreadful news from his wife's pueblo; his father-in-law and two of his brothers-in-law have been shot. He is very upset. Everyone you speak to has some terrible tale to recount; this war is affecting us all.

Hadn't the heart to paint today, so just did a few sketches of the house. If we do leave I want something to remember it by.

Peter threw a tantrum, very unusual for him, he is always so placid. He insists he won't leave his model ships behind. I told him if we do leave we will take as many as we can but he was still upset.'

Kate turned the page and looked at the two sketches of the house; they were done in pen and ink and showed the house from two different angles. She wondered if her great-grandmother had ever painted them.

'How are you doing?' she asked Maisie.

'Nothing yet. It's all very interesting but not what you're looking for. How about you?'

'Not so far. The entries seem to have stopped for a while; the next one is in February.'

She continued to read:

'4th February 1937. Gibraltar

Our ship leaves tomorrow for England; R wants us to go without him. He is so upset about E. I can't understand what got into her to run off like that. God knows where she is now; I can't sleep at night for worrying about her. We have asked Timothy to find out what he can but he says it is impossible, everything is cut off. There is no way of contacting her even if we were sure she was still in Málaga. I keep telling R not to worry; if there's one thing I know about my daughter, it's that she is very resourceful. If she can get in touch with us, she will. Peter hasn't said anything but I know by his very silence that he is very upset about her. The only time he speaks is to moan about his models. I know he was unhappy at leaving so many of them behind but what else could we do.

We have had to stay in a small hotel near the border, because everything else is full but I don't mind, it means we don't have to listen to all those people complaining about the Spanish and their "bloody war". I can't stand it; they seem to have no idea of the suffering that's going on. I keep thinking about my poor C and how she will be faring without us. I hope we see her again one day but as every day passes I doubt it more and more.'

There was a sketch of the Rock of Gibraltar and another of a small boy cuddling a dog. Then the next entry was not until March.

She read further:

'1st March 1937. England

314

Back home in England at last. The ship was very crowded and we were all huddled into the public areas. Of course the H-S's managed to get a cabin but we had to sleep on the chairs in the lounge. Peter was OK but R has a stiff back and his neck is troubling him. The crossing was dreadful, high seas and strong winds; luckily none of us get seasick but there were lots that did. I spent as much time as I could on deck just to get away from the smell. Impossible to write in my journal but I did manage a sketch or two.

Weather's been awful since we got back; typical March, cold and windy. Good to see Brian and Susan, they have made us very welcome. R still has not got over E leaving us like that. He thinks I don't know but I have seen him sitting over his books, looking like a little lost boy; he can't work and he can't sleep. I feel the same. Can't settle to anything until I know what has happened to her. Thank goodness we have Peter; have been very busy trying to sort out his new school, so that has kept me from going completely mad. He's such a good-natured boy; I don't know what I'd do without him.'

'There are some sketches from the boat.'

She handed the journal to Maisie. There were a series of small drawings depicting her travelling companions.

'She's pretty good. But what a motley crowd. Look at the expressions on the faces of those two women; they'd turn milk sour.'

She handed the journal back to Kate.

'3rd March 1937.

R says it's about time we started looking for a house of our own; something small to rent until we can go back. It will have to be somewhere close by because I don't want to change Peter's school again and I enjoy Susan's company. Going to see the estate agent in Wareham, sometime next week. Hope we can find something with a garden; feel so sad every time I think of my poor garden in Spain.'

'5ᵗʰ March 1937.

'R thinks he's found the ideal cottage for us near Wareham. Tomorrow we are going to look at it.

Went into Bournemouth this morning with Susan, so took the opportunity to buy some paints. Will try and start some new watercolours next week when Peter has gone off to school.'

'6ᵗʰ March 1937.

Found our ideal house; not too big but big enough for the four of us. R has to negotiate the rent but as it's unoccupied I hope we can move in right away.'

'Look she's drawn a picture of the cottage, and isn't that a dried wisteria leaf?'

'9ᵗʰ March 1937.

Received a letter from E yesterday. Thank God she is safe; we both just sat and cried and cried. Still haven't seen her but hope she will be in touch soon.'

She turned over the page:

'15ᵗʰ March 1937.

E is home again. She looks dreadful; I have never seen her so thin and tired and she has a dreadful, haunted look in her eyes. She looks as though she needs to sleep for a week. A nice young man she met in Spain came with her; he seems very attentive but E has not said if there is anything going on between them. He lives in Oxford, so he only stayed the one night then he left.

Taught Susan how to make tortilla de patata but not sure that she and Brian really enjoyed it. He said he prefers his eggs scrambled and his potatoes separate, preferably mashed.

Now E is home R is much more his old self.'

'Ah, here's something,' she said. 'Listen to this Maisie.'

'25th March 1937.

I'm sure something is wrong with E. She spends all day in her room and often looks as though she has been crying. I asked her if it was something to do with Alex but she said no. He's been coming down each weekend to visit her and they go for long walks on the beach with Willow. I wonder if they are sweethearts or, as she keeps telling me, just friends.

Peter will be home for Easter, so that might cheer her up.'

'Well you're getting somewhere now.'

'2nd April 1937.

E decided to choose April Fool's day to tell us that she was pregnant; R thought it was a joke at first but when she started to cry we realised that she was serious. We didn't know what to say. R is heartbroken; he had such high hopes for E, now he thinks her life is ruined. I told him a new life is a wonderful thing, no matter which side of the bedclothes it is born. But he is still very upset.

At first E would not say who the father was, so we thought it must be Alex but then she told me that the father was dead and that was why she could not marry him. I don't know whether to believe her or not. She asked me not to tell R.

She seems to be having a bad time with morning sickness. Susan has given us a local recipe which is supposed to help. I called the midwife today and she said to take E to the doctor.'

'Here's another one.'

'20th April 1937.

Alex has asked R if he can have E's hand in marriage. He told him she was pregnant and they wanted to get married as quickly as possible to stop any tongues wagging. Seems his father is very proper and would not approve. Of course what else could R say but yes. But then he went and talked to E; he

317

told her she didn't have to get married just because she was pregnant, that we would look after her and the baby if she wanted. E said she loved Alex and wanted to marry him but I don't believe her; I don't think she does love him.'

'1*st* May 1937.

The wedding is fixed for 19*th* June and will be in All Saints' Church in Oxford. R, Peter and I are going up for the weekend. R wants to go to the Bodleian Library while we are there. Susan and Brian have been invited but haven't decided if they can go yet.

E's health is a lot better and she has put on some weight thank goodness; luckily she is so tall that she is still able to disguise her pregnancy quite well. Susan is going to make her wedding dress for her, so E and I went into Dorchester last weekend to buy the material. It's a beautiful white satin with a tulle veil. I know she will look wonderful.

My cough is getting worse. R says I must see the doctor but I can't see the point; he'll only give me some more cough mixture.'

'Look there's a sketch of the wedding dress.'

'And isn't that Corfe Castle?'

'Yes, I think it is. Listen to this entry; it sounds as though Elizabeth was having some doubts about the wedding, despite her mother's support. I wonder why she went through with it.'

'6*th* May 1937.

It's such fun to have a wedding to prepare for but I seem to be enjoying it more than E. She said she would help me make the cake but then she didn't feel very well, so Susan helped me. I am very pleased with it; it has three tiers, which should be enough. When I told her she must keep the top tier for the christening, she burst into tears and ran up to her

*room. I told R and he said he would speak to her again.
Even if it means humiliating ourselves we would sooner she
called off the wedding than married a man she did not love.'*

'15th May 1937.

*I am making some lavender sachets to go on the table as
small gifts for all the ladies. I hope E will like them.*

*Had a very bad night last night, could not sleep for
coughing. Have agreed to go to the doctor in Wareham
tomorrow. Very tired today so spent most of the day in bed.'*

'16th May 1937,

*Didn't feel well enough to go to the doctor today so he
came to visit me instead. I told R not to bother him but he
would not rest until he came. Says I'm not well and I have to
go into the hospital in Southampton for some tests. I said I
don't have time for that; we have a wedding to organise. At
last R said he would take me tomorrow morning and promised
to bring me back the same day.*

Must try to finish the lavender sachets.'

'Listen to this Maisie.'

'20th May 1937.

*I have been too upset to write anything in my journal for a
few days. They were very kind to me at the hospital; first of
all the doctor examined me then sent me to have an X-ray.
They put me in a separate room to wait for the results but
wouldn't let R stay with me. When they eventually came to
see me it was to say that I have TB. They won't let me go
home again. I must go to a sanatorium near Poole, where
they can treat me in quarantine and I won't be able to infect
anyone else. They say I will have to stay there for at least six
months until they are sure I am clear. I wasn't frightened
when they told me but when I saw the poster on the hospital
wall, with a picture of a little baby and the words "Protect*

319

him from TB" I began to cry. I know I won't be able to see my grandchild now.

All the family have been tested; everyone is fine and so now they have all been given a BCG vaccination to prevent them from catching it as well. Peter was taken out of school and tested but he is all right too. He and all the boys in his class have been vaccinated. If they are still all right in a few weeks R can come to visit me. They won't let me see Peter because he's a child and they won't let me see E because she's pregnant; it's too dangerous to vaccinate her while she is pregnant.'

'Oh the poor woman, locked away from everyone for six months.'

'28th May 1937.

Since I arrived I have just been lying in bed, feeling ill and very alone but the treatment they are giving me is helping my cough and I am feeling a little stronger already. Today for the first time I have done a few sketches. There is one nurse who has been particularly nice to me and so I drew her portrait and gave it to her. Don't feel up to asking for my paints yet as I still get easily tired.'

'Are there any sketches this time?'

'Just one, it must be the nurse she mentioned. There doesn't seem to be many more entries. The next one is June 15th.'

'15th June 1937.

Received a lovely, long letter from E today. She is almost as unhappy as I am that I cannot go to the wedding. She wanted to postpone it but R and Alex persuaded her not to because of the baby. None of us want the poor little mite to be born illegitimate.

320

I've read the letter three times now and still it makes me cry; what my poor daughter has suffered. My heart bleeds for her. But out of all that suffering has come some good; she will have a lovely child, a new life for her to cherish and love. And she has found a good man to marry her and look after them both. I told her in my reply, things could have been much worse. She wanted to know if she should register the child as Alex's or put the father's name. I did not hesitate to tell her to let the child be Alex's. Why complicate an innocent child's life for something that is no fault of theirs.

Doing some painting now but my heart is not really in it. E has promised to send me lots of photographs of the wedding. I write to Peter every day and receive a few lines from him each week but I suppose I can't really expect any more. He is after all only a child. Susan has been a good friend and is always writing and sending me things to keep me occupied. Strangely enough I am not as restless as I thought I would be. I sleep a lot; not sure if it is the illness or the cure.'

'So there should be some more correspondence somewhere,' said Maisie, when Kate had finished.

'Yes, I imagine that's why she is writing less in her journal, because she's busy writing to her family.'

'Well anyone who keeps a diary would also keep any letters they receive. Don't you agree?'

'True. Tomorrow we'll have another look for the letters. In the meantime let's continue with these. There's not much more here.'

They read on in silence for a while longer then Kate said:

'There's nothing else here. She even seems to have stopped doing her sketches now.'

'Well her condition was probably getting worse.'

'Or maybe she just had nothing to record in her diary anymore; her life must have been a lot more restricted. Did you find anything?'

'Apart from how to make *gazpacho* and the best time to sow green beans, you mean? No, nothing. I think we must look for the letters. But at least you now know for certain that Alex was not your grandfather.'

'Yes but who was?'

The next morning after a leisurely breakfast Kate and Maisie set off for Badger Cottage. The clouds had drifted in during the night and promised them a grey, gloomy Sunday.

'Look I'm pretty sure we're not going to find anything else in the library. Let's think about this. She spent the last year of her life in a sanatorium; she never came back here to live.'

'Yes, so when she died, her husband would have brought all her things back to the house. Now where would he have put them?'

'In her bedroom?'

'Possibly. Was there another room she used, perhaps to paint?'

'Of course, she must have painted somewhere and she would have needed somewhere to store her paints and easel.'

They walked around the house looking for a likely place until they arrived at the back door.

'What about this door? Where does it lead?'

At right angles to the back door was a door with a rusty padlock on it.

'Could be a coal shed or a potting shed maybe,' suggested Maisie. 'Why don't you open it up.'

Kate fumbled with the bunch of keys until she found what looked like a padlock key.

'This could be it.'

She put the key in the lock and turned it; the hinge of the padlock swung open straight away.   She removed it and pulled the door open; inside was a large, square room with a stone floor and glass window panes let into the ceiling.

'It's a studio.'

'Or a potting shed.'

The room was lined with wooden benches where once someone had grown seedlings and cuttings; empty flower pots, scattered soil, fertiliser bags and decaying leaves said that here, once upon a time, plants had grown and flourished, nurtured with love, basking in the clear, pure light that now had to fight its way through the dirty glass.

'Well we know she loved her garden.   What else did she do here?'

'Paint?'

A wooden easel was propped against the wall and a table at one end of the room was covered with old tubes of paint, twisted and hardened through lack of use; a battered tin can held an assortment of brushes and a dusty pallet struggled to reveal the colours of its previous life.

'Looks like it. So this is where she painted.'

'Ideal really, lots of light, close to the kitchen. Perfect.'

'Yes but not the place to store things, certainly not letters.'

Slightly disappointed they relocked the studio and went back into the house.

'Well what else did she do?'

'Cook?   Sew?   Write her journal.   The usual things I suppose.'

'Well there's no other writing area except the desk in the library and we know there's nothing in there.'

'She could have just sat at the kitchen table and written,' suggested Maisie.

'Yes.'

They pulled open all the drawers and cupboards in the kitchen but found nothing except a band of cockroaches under the sink.

'God, they'll have to go,' said Kate, unable to hide her disgust.

'They're the oldest creatures on the planet,' said Maisie.

'I don't care; they're revolting,' replied Kate, slamming the door shut. 'Well there's nothing here, and, if there ever was, it's long gone.'

'Let's try the sitting room.'

They abandoned the kitchen and turned their attention to the lounge.

'What's this? It looks like an old sewing cabinet.'

Kate pointed to a mahogany box with a hinged lid and a small drawer underneath; it was supported on four cabriolet legs.

'It's pretty little thing, isn't it.'

They opened the lid and sure enough it was full of reels of cottons and silks, scraps of material, old buttons and press studs, hooks and eyes, in short everything one needed to sew.

'What about the drawer?'

And there it was: a bundle of letters, written in an elegant script on faded blue velum and tied with a blue ribbon. As she picked them up something fell out.

'What's that?' Maisie asked.

Kate picked it up and held it to her nose.

'Lavender, I think.'

'Well at last we're getting somewhere,' exclaimed Maisie. 'Here give some to me and you read the rest.'

Rather reluctantly Kate handed a few letters to her friend; she really wanted them all to herself but could not disappoint Maisie at this late stage. They settled down on the sofa and began to read; they all seemed to be from Elizabeth to her mother. After a while, Maisie looked up and said:

'This is really sad. She knows her mother is dying but nobody wants to admit it.'

'I think I've got the one we read about. Was the date June 15th?'

'Yes, I think so.'

'Oh this is awful. What she went through.'

Kate fell silent and carried on reading. At last she looked up; there were tears in her eyes.

'I have his name.'

'You do? What is it?'

'Juan Francisco Gomez de la Luz de Montevideo Rodriguez.'

'Bit of a mouthful. What does she say?'

'A lot of it is general stuff about what she is doing and asking after her mother's health then she gets down to it.'

She started to read aloud:

'I'm so sorry Mother if I have disappointed you; I know you brought me up to respect myself and not get into situations that would get out of hand but I really could do nothing to prevent what happened. As soon as I met Juan I knew he was the man for me; I had never been in love before and I did not know how to control my feelings for him. To say I was swept away by it all sounds rather dramatic but the truth is that everything was different there. When people are dying in the streets, one's norms change. Maybe it's a basic

325

instinct of survival. We were alone, frightened and in love; we clung to each other. It did not matter to me what people thought; I just wanted to be with Juan. He made me so very happy, and even though it was for such a short time I don't regret a moment of it. I would have liked to spend the rest of my life with him but it was not to be. Now he is dead I feel as though my heart has been frozen inside my body; I am empty of all love and emotion. I hope that will change and I will be able to love his baby and in time I hope I can grow to love Alex who saved me from myself. Without him I would still be in Spain, alive and starving or maybe dead. I am not so lost that I cannot see what a service he has done me. I was going to spare you the details of my shame, as I'm sure you must view it, but in the end I felt I had to tell you all about your son-in-law that never was.

He was a wonderful man, kind, generous and thoughtful. He was born into a noble family: the "de la Luz de Montevideo" family, who have owned land in Andalusia for centuries. Although Juan was the grandson of an important landowner, he disagreed with the way that they continued to treat their workers like serfs and he quarrelled with his father and his grandfather about it. In the war he found himself on the opposite side to the rest of his family but he loved them still and always spoke warmly of them. He had a younger sister whom he loved very much and it grieved him to be parted from her and his mother. He often spoke of how much he missed them. His father was a lawyer and Juan too was a lawyer but he believed in justice for everyone, rich and poor. He believed in a better Spain and wanted to help bring that about but unfortunately he died too soon. When we were fleeing from Málaga he was wounded in a mortar attack and we believe he died later of his wounds. I say "believed"

326

because we became separated and then we could not find him. That was the hardest thing of all for me: not knowing if he was alive or dead. In the end Alex, with all his English logic, convinced me that he must be dead. Maybe I should have stayed and looked for him; every night I ask myself this same question but what does it matter now. It is too late, too late for me and too late for him. But I will never forget him and now at least I will have his child to love instead.

I hope you can bring yourself to forgive me Mother; you know I would never want to hurt you and Father."

Then she goes on about the wedding plans and things.'

'Well now you have what you wanted.'

'Yes.'

'So what next?'

'Now we can go and have a nice lunch and then I'll drive you home.'

'Sounds good to me.'

CHAPTER 18

Kate dropped Maisie off at her house and went straight home; the house seemed empty and drab after the boutique hotel. She felt a bit deflated; it had been an emotional weekend for her, delving into her family's past and now she did not know what to do with herself. She placed the letters and journals on the coffee table, poured herself a large glass of Chablis and settled down to look through them but after a few minutes she found her eyes closing. It had been a long day. She had discovered what she had been seeking but how did she feel about it? The truth was that she still did not know who she was; all she knew was who she was not. She was not the grand-daughter of Sir Alexander Reeves, a man known and respected by all his peers. She was the grand-daughter of a man called Juan de la Luz de Montevideo, of whom she knew nothing except the brief description that she had read in her grandmother's letter. She tried to examine her feelings dispassionately. Did it matter? Was she really bothered by this news? Did she really need to know who her grandfather was? She could not answer; she was too tired and too confused. She would do what her mother always advised her to do; she would sleep on it.

The next morning she telephoned Robert Percy to tell him she had seen the cottage and wanted to keep it, so he was to go ahead with transferring the deeds into her name.

'I've got good news,' he told her. 'The money has been finally confirmed and I am transferring two million, three hundred and seventy-two pounds into your bank account today. That is the amount that is due to you after I have deducted the value of the house in Dorset and your share of our legal fees. I have also kept back a sum to pay the inheritance tax. I will of course be sending you a letter with everything itemised but in the meantime I suggest you get in touch with your bank manager as soon as you can.'

She thanked him and immediately rang her bank and made an appointment to see the manager.

'Jill, I've got some rather important personal business to attend to today. Do you mind fielding my telephone calls while I'm out. I won't be gone more than a couple of hours.'

'No problem. Have you told Geoff?'

'No, I'll do that now.'

She could see her boss was at his desk, looking through some reports, so went straight in.

'Good morning Geoffrey,' she said, handing him his mail.

'Morning Kate,' he said without looking up.

'Geoffrey, I need a couple of hours off this morning, I hope that's all right.'

'This morning? But I need you to double check this report for me.'

'When do you need it by?'

'Thursday, in time for the Board meeting.'

'Well it's only Monday today. I'll have plenty of time to look at it when I get back. I'll only be gone a couple of hours. Put it on my desk when you've finished with it.'

He looked rather crestfallen but just as she knew he would, he allowed her the time off.

'What time will you be back?' he asked.

She had arranged to see the bank manager at eleven and made a quick calculation in her head:

'About one, one thirty, I should think.'

'OK.'

She had never met Mr Potts, her bank manager, before; her account had so little money in it that she never needed to speak to anyone except the cashier when she needed a new cheque book or bank card. She felt inexplicably nervous.

'Mrs. Scott,' he said, standing up behind his wide, mahogany desk and indicating that she should take a seat.

'Ms. Scott,' she corrected him.

'Ah, just so,' he said, looking at her file.

'What can I do for you?'

'I'm expecting a deposit in my account today and I wanted to talk to you about it.'

'Yes, and how much do you think this deposit will be?' he asked, scribbling something on a piece of paper.

'It's an inheritance from my grandfather; he died a few weeks ago.'

She no longer felt nervous; she felt irritated with this man. He had already pigeon-holed her as one of his smaller accounts and was probably wondering why his assistant manager was not dealing with her. He did not seem particularly interested in what she was saying, so she took great delight in telling him the exact amount:

'Two million, three hundred and seventy-two pounds, less transfer charges.'

He looked up instantly, unsure if he had heard correctly.

'An inheritance you say?'

'Yes, from my grandfather, Sir Alexander Reeves.'

The bank manager stood up and came round from the safety of his desk to stand before her.

'So you're Sir Alexander's granddaughter, are you? Well, I didn't realise that.'

'No, I bet you didn't,' Kate thought but did not reply; instead she nodded.

'Quite a tidy sum to leave you. What did you say, two million, three hundred and seventy-two pounds?'

'Yes, I would like some advice on how to invest it. I'll need a few thousand for immediate expenses, say twenty, then I want to invest the rest.'

He wrote down what she said then asked:

'Do you have any idea what sort of investments you want to make? Low risk? High risk? Short-term, long-term? Do you want to receive the interest in the form of an income?'

'I think you'll have to explain the options to me, Mr. Potts, I'm not very knowledgeable about this sort of thing. I would like a regular income, enough to live on; I've also inherited an old house and I will need money to renovate it but besides that, I think I will just invest the rest.'

'Fine, I think we will find you a mix of high and low risk; the former will offer you the promise of a high return but with greater risk and the latter will give you a more modest but more secure return on your investment. Perhaps we should look at some short term investments as well, in case you decide to buy yourself a flat in Spain for example.'

They talked for a while about the various options that were open to her and arranged to meet the following week to finalise the arrangements. Now that Mr. Potts knew she was an heiress, he could not have been more charming. She wondered if she was going to find that this happened a lot now.

'Thank you, Mr. Potts. I'll see you next week then.'

'Yes, thank you Ms. Scott. As soon as the money arrives in your account I will telephone you to let you know and I will put it straight into a twenty-four hour call account so that you don't lose any interest.'

As she walked back to work she at last began to realise what was happening to her; this money could change her life. Her talk with Mr. Potts had made it clear that, if she did not squander her inheritance, she would have more than enough money to live on for the rest of her life, and that was just from the interest. She no longer had to work. She could travel; she could do whatever she wanted. Her route took her past a number of estate agents' offices, so she decided to stop at the first one and put her house on the market.

Her life was going to change and already she had taken the first step. The second one was to tell Geoffrey she was leaving; that would be more difficult. She was not sure how to go about it.

He was not in his office when she arrived back at work but he had left the report on her desk for her to type. She picked it up and was going to put it in her in-tray when the words 'Human Resources Department Re-organisation' caught her attention. She started to read it. It was the report that the Managing Director had been hassling him about. It looked as though she did not need to hand in her notice after all; they were about to make her redundant. No wonder Geoffrey had said nothing to her. The report opened with a summary that stated that the Board wanted all managers and directors, and that included the Human Resources Department as well, to do their own typing, keep their own records and files and make their own appointments. It argued that modern technology made it easy for managers to do all these tasks themselves and removed the need for the additional expense of secretaries, typists and most of all personal assistants. They were to move towards a paperless office system. Then followed a number of pages of calculations showing the savings that would be made if the following people were made redundant: there were eight names on the list. She ran her finger down them; there was Jill's name, Heather's, the training manager's secretary's and then she spotted her own. Well she knew it made sense; the company was years behind other companies in their office management practice and HR was the worst of them all. All the senior managers had expensive, state-of-the-art computers and used less than half of the capabilities open to them. The truth was they all liked the status that went with having their own secretary and a personal assistant was even better but it was not cost efficient and she would be the first to admit it.

She wondered when her boss would tell her what was planned. She decided to use the report as an introduction to the topic and see what he had to say but she would not tell him about her own plans just yet.

Kate was halfway through the report when he arrived back from lunch.

'Hi, Kate. You're back I see. Everything go all right?'

'Fine thanks Geoffrey. All right if I come in and see you for a moment?'

'Yes, fine.'

She picked up the half-finished report and went into his office.

'OK, fire away. What's on your mind?' he asked.

'It's this report. I wondered when you were going to tell me about the redundancies?'

'Oh that. Well Kate it's not easy. You know I don't agree with any of this; the office is running very smoothly as it is; we all do our jobs well, you especially. I don't know why Henry wants to rock the boat.'

'I expect it's the money.'

'Yes, that's what he says but it's not as though we can be sure that the quality of the work won't go down. If managers are going to have to do all their own secretarial tasks, their other work will suffer. It won't work. I know it won't.'

'Well I expect they will have to keep on some of the services: photocopying, printing, reception.'

'Yes, of course. In fact Kate, I'm glad you brought that up because I was thinking of recommending you for the post.'

'Post? What post? Photocopying? Reception? Me? Are you joking Geoffrey? I'm not going to go back to doing that work; I've been here for twenty-odd years. That's the sort of work I did when I first started.'

'Oh, it wouldn't be like that; you'd be head of Office Services and receive the same salary you do now. You would be working for all the departments, not just me; it's a very responsible job. '

'I'm sure it is. Thank you for thinking of me Geoffrey but I really don't want to start working for the entire management team after years of being your personal assistant. It's not for me. I'd sooner take the redundancy package.'

As soon as she left the building she saw him; he was standing on the corner opposite, waiting for her. She turned right and walked away quickly, pretending she had not seen him.

'Kate, hi, I thought it was you,' he gasped, running along beside her. 'I've been trying to contact you, you know but your telephone is always engaged. Is there something wrong with it? You really should get it looked at.'

She did not reply and tried to increase her pace but he only did the same. She was not going to outrun him so she would have to try to outwit him.

'I'm sorry Bill, I'm in a hurry. You know what it's like in the lunch hour, so many things to fit in.'

She tried to make her voice sound pleasant.

'No problem, I'll just walk along with you and keep you company.'

She did not reply but continued walking.

'How are you keeping? I must say you're looking well. Is that a new haircut? Very chic.'

What the hell does he want, she thought. Her hairstyle had not changed in ten years at least and she knew that today if she looked anything, it was hassled and tired.

'No, same old style,' she replied.

'Well it really suits you?'

That's it, same old style, she thought, he gets to call the tune and I have to dance. Am I mad or something, running away, leaving my telephone off the hook, pretending I'm not at home? Why am I frightened of this pathetic man? She stopped suddenly and turned to face him.

'Look Bill, what is it you want? I've told you I'm busy. I have no time and no inclination to talk to you; just leave me alone.'

'I only wanted to see how you were. I miss you Kate. You can't wipe out twenty years of marriage just like that.'

'Oh I think you know very well that you can; it's quite easy really. You've proved it.'

'Oh Kate, don't be bitter. I just want us to remain friends.'

'What, pick up where we left off? What about your new family? What do they say about it?'

She knew it was about the money; she could see the greed glinting in his eyes. How had she ever loved this man? They say love is blind but she had not realised it for herself until now.

'Ursula is always so busy with the children she doesn't have much time for me these days. I sometimes think she just wanted to marry me so that she could have a family and stay in England.'

She stifled a laugh; did he really believe that she was such an idiot? So now the blame was being passed on to the dim au-pair. What a bastard he was.

'Well you'll have to sort that out with her; it's none of my business. Now please excuse me. I have to get on.'

She did not know what put the idea into her head but she hesitated and then said:

'By the way how's Bob? Haven't seen him for ages.'

'Oh he's fine. His handicap's down to six now.'

So it was Bob who had told him about the money. All these years he had been pretending that he was no longer Bill's friend and he had been seeing him all the time. She wondered if Maisie knew.

'Look Bill, let me try to make it perfectly clear to you. Don't phone me. Don't write and don't try to see me. It's over. You made your choice in 2001, now you can live with it. If you bother me again I will go to my solicitor and take out a restraining order against you.'

He looked at her horrified.

'But I haven't done anything Kate, only tried to speak to you.'

'I've told you I don't want to speak to you. Leave me alone or I'll make you leave me alone.'

Was it her newfound wealth that gave her the power to speak to him like this? She could snap her fingers and a solicitor would take care of it all for her and she did not need to worry about how to pay his bill; yet another difference that her grandfather's money had made to her life.

He said no more, turned on his heel and made off the way he had come. She waited until he was out of sight, then retraced her steps and continued with her plans for lunch. It was as though a heavy weight had been lifted from her shoulders; she was taking control of her life at last.

She almost forgot about her dinner date with Hugh because Geoffrey kept her so busy on Wednesday. He seemed to be going through every outstanding item he had in his work agenda in an effort to clear the back-log while he still had the exclusive use of her services.

'Hello Kate. It's Hugh, I just wanted to check you're still OK for this evening?'

'Hi, Hugh. Yes, I hadn't forgotten. I'm rather busy today but I'll be there; I've booked the table for eight-thirty.'

'Fine, see you then.'

He hung up. Had she been a bit too abrupt with him? She hoped not. The encounter with Bill had left her feeling edgy and sharp-tongued. She had not intended to let it spill over into other relationships. She picked up the telephone and rang him back.

'Hugh?'

'Yes?'

'It's Kate. I just wanted to be sure you knew the name of the restaurant?'

'L'Escargot.'

'Yes that's it. Well, see you tonight then.'

She made an effort to make her voice sound as warm as possible.

'Looking forward to it,' he replied.

Her telephone rang again. This time it was Robert Percy.

'Kate, I've got some news on that other matter you asked me to look into,' he told her.

'Good.'

'Your great-uncle Peter is still alive. We've tracked him down to a nursing home in Whitby. I don't know if you will be able to get a lot out of him though; he's rather old and according to the matron his memory is not as good as it used to be.'

'Tell me about it. But does that mean he's not really compos mentis?'

'No, it just means he has good days and bad days. On the good days he can hold a perfectly lucid conversation.'

'Do you have an address for this nursing home?'

'Yes, have you got a pencil? Right.'

He dictated the address then added:

'He has some family. The wife is dead but there are two sons. One lives nearby, so I can give you his telephone number, if you like.'

'Please. I'll ring him before I go to visit his father.'

'Well is there anything else you'd like me to do?'

'No thank you Mr Percy, you've been most helpful. I'll take it from here.'

She folded the piece of paper and placed it safely in her handbag.

She did not get home until almost eight o'clock; Geoffrey had kept her talking over various points in his report that he was still unsure about. The monthly Board meetings always made him nervous and he liked to use Kate as a sounding block for his ideas before he presented them to the Board. If she stuck to her original plan of walking along the river bank and cutting up into the town to reach the restaurant she was going to be late, so she abandoned it and ordered a taxi. She had still not made up her mind what to wear; she wanted to look good, smart but not too glamorous and perhaps a little bit sexy. There was nothing new in her wardrobe; she pulled out her usual standby: a fitted, black dress with a short skirt. At least she still had good legs, she thought, as she pulled on a pair of fine, black tights and slipped her size five feet into some black court shoes with rather high heels. She decorated her ensemble with a chunky necklace of bright stones and a pair of simple gold earrings. She applied her make-up deftly and quickly and, was just squirting herself with Chanel Number Five, when the doorbell rang to say that the taxi had arrived.

Hugh was already sitting at the table, drinking a glass of wine, when she arrived. Kate looked at her watch; no she was not late. He must have been early. Now he rose to greet her.

'Hello,' he said, shyly kissing her on the cheek.

'Hello, Hugh. Sorry, am I late?'

'No, I was a bit early so decided to wait at the table for you. Sorry, I've already started,' he said, indicating his drink. 'May I order something for you?'

'The same would be fine.'

She felt awkward; she was not used to dating. It was a habit you soon became unaccustomed to once you passed a certain age. They made some small talk for a while, discussing the weather, his journey up from Bristol, her day at work, until the waiter delivered them from the banalities of polite conversation by producing the menu. Once the food was decided upon and ordered and a suitable bottle of wine selected, they both seemed to relax.

'So have you put us down for the competition yet?' he asked.

'No, I'll telephone and do it tomorrow. It's the Sunday after next. Is that all right for you?'

He pulled out a slim, leather diary and consulted it.

'Yes, that's fine. I'll make a note of it.'

'I'll request a tee time about eleven. Will that give you enough time to get here?'

'Oh, I'll probably come up on the Saturday and stay overnight. I've got a room at the Royal for tonight. It seems a nice enough hotel; I'll stay there again.'

'It's pretty central.'

'Maybe I could buy you dinner that evening?'

'Perhaps you should wait and see how much you enjoy this evening, first,' she joked. 'You may change your mind.'

'I doubt it.'

His words, confident and challenging, hung in the air between them while he tasted the wine that the waiter was offering him. Once approved and poured, he continued:

'What are you doing this weekend?'

'I'm thinking of going to Whitby to see some relatives,' she replied, making her decision to visit Peter in that very moment.

'Oh, are you from Yorkshire?' he asked.

'No, I'm not.   I'm from round here, Berkshire, Oxfordshire.   My parents lived in Henley, my grandparents were in Oxford and I've lived in Reading most of my adult life. Pretty boring really.'

'Not at all, I think the countryside around here is spectacular, the Berkshire Downs and the Thames valley. It's very beautiful.'

'My great-uncle Peter is in a home; he's eighty-one.   I thought I would visit him before he dies.'

'Sounds a bit morbid. Is he ill or something?'

'No, I don't think so. I don't really know; I've never met him before.'

'Forgive me for saying so, Kate but this all sounds a bit strange.'

She realise she would have to explain, so she told him about the cottage in Dorset and trying to trace her biological grandfather.   She omitted to mention that she had inherited over two million pounds.   She did not want to deceive him nor had she thought about how it would affect their budding relationship; she just did not tell him.

'Are you going alone?' he asked.

'Yes. I might go by train. I think it's probably quite direct from Reading.'

'I'm not so sure. I expect you'll either have to change in London or in Birmingham, then again in Leeds or maybe Middlesbrough.'

'Oh, I can't be bothered with that, I'll drive,' she said.

'Would you like me to go with you?' he asked quietly.

She looked at him; she would like his company but something said she should slow down a bit.   There were so many changes in her life right now she did not want a

341

romantic commitment as well. Dinner was fine but a weekend away together? Maybe later.

'That's very kind of you,' she replied. 'But I'm going to meet his son's family first. I think it would be better if I went alone.'

'Of course. Just trying to help.'

To cover his embarrassment he poured her another glass of wine and took a generous mouthful of his own.

'Tell me more about this old cottage you've inherited,' he said.

So she told him all about her weekend in Dorset with Maisie and described the cottage and its grounds.

'It sounds as though you've got a lot of work on your hands.'

'Yes, it needs quite a lot doing to it. I'm not sure where to start.'

'Would you like me to have a look at it for you? I could perhaps give you some ideas.'

Of course, she had forgotten he was an architect; he would be able to see it through more professional eyes.

'That would be wonderful if you have the time. I'm sure it has endless possibilities; it's just that I can't imagine them.'

'It's not far from Corfe Castle, you say?' he said.

'About ten miles as the crow flies but more like eighteen through all those twisty lanes.'

'My parents are from Swanage,' he said. 'So I know that part of Dorset very well. I used to spend most of my summers scuba-diving off the shore there. The sea is wonderfully calm and clear in some of those coves.'

'Do you still dive?' Kate asked.

'No, not really, I've only got time for one hobby and nowadays that's golf. I still have a go when I'm on holiday though. Last summer I went to the Costa del Sol for a couple of weeks and did a bit of diving with some friends, three chaps from the golf club; we split our time between playing golf and diving. Boy was I fit when we got home.'

'So you still enjoy it?'

'Yes but not as much as golf. You meet a nicer class of person on the golf course,' he said, his eyes twinkling at her. 'What about you?'

'Oh I'm no swimmer. I can thrash my way across a heated pool but that's about it.'

'No plans to swim the Channel then?'

'Not in your wildest dreams.'

The evening was a success: the food was delicious, the wine smelt of crushed blackberries and the conversation did not flag. Kate felt very much at ease in Hugh's company and told him so.

'I've enjoyed the evening too, Kate. It's a pity that it's over so soon. Would you like to have a coffee at the Royal?'

'I would but tomorrow I have to be at work early. Sorry. I'll telephone you when I have our starting time for Sunday.'

'And dinner? Do you think you could stand another dinner with me?'

'I think so; I'll force myself.'

'Shall we come here again?'

'Why not. Would you like me to book it again?'

'No need, I've already reserved a table.'

She did not know whether to be impressed or annoyed by the man's confidence; in the end she laughed. She let him kiss her goodnight but refused his offer to accompany her home, instead she had asked the waiter to call her a taxi. As they waited outside the restaurant he put his arm around her and said:

'Kate, this has been a wonderful evening; I've really enjoyed myself.'

'So have I, Hugh.'

He pulled her closer and squeezed her body against his, then kissed her again, more passionately this time. Gently she pulled herself free from his embrace; she was too old to be 'snogging' in the middle of Reading's shopping precinct, she told herself.

'See you next week, Hugh,' she said, heading for her taxi.

As she leant back in her seat she thought back over the evening. It was true; it had been a wonderful evening. So why had she brought it so abruptly to an end? She had not wanted to go to the Royal but she could have taken him back to her house to spend the night with her. What had held her back? 'Apart from the fact that you've only known him five minutes?' she heard her mother's voice ask her. Some things were so engrained that they could not change; she had to be able to tell herself that she loved someone before she could go to bed with them. Sometimes in the past she knew that she had been deceiving herself with this lie but it had sufficed at the time. This time it was different; she felt Hugh was a man she could fall in love with and she didn't want to rush it.

As she picked up the M42 and headed in the direction of the M1 she calculated that it would take her at least another three hours to get to Whitby and that was without any hold-ups. She hoped it was going to be worth it. She had re-read her great-grandmother's journals and her grandmother's letters and was not sure that Peter, even if he could remember those days, would be able to add anything to them but she felt obliged to explore every avenue. It was like compiling a mosaic; every little piece would add to the whole picture.

Her great-uncle's son, Tom, had sounded very pleasant on the telephone. Although they had never met he knew about her and her side of the family; he offered his condolences for her parents' death and apologised for not getting in touch with her. His father had moved to Yorkshire when he was still a young man, he said, then he had married a girl from the Dales and remained in the area ever since. Tom and his brother, Martin had been born and brought up there, so after a while the two sides of the family just lost touch. It was really only because they read of Sir Alexander from time to time in the national press that they knew about him at all.

Tom lived in Robin Hood's Bay, a picturesque fishing cove a few miles from Whitby. He had given her excellent directions and, at just before two o'clock, she pulled up outside a white-painted, terraced house, set into the limestone cliffs and overlooking the tiny bay. It was chocolate box charm itself, everything clean and neat and nothing out of place. Only the rough, stormy sea that lashed against the rocks and the cold east wind told you that this had been a place of fishermen, smugglers and shipwrecks: chocolates with hard centres. He was already waiting for her and after offering her some refreshments they set off for Whitby.

'Better if we go in my car,' he said. 'Reckon you've done 'nough driving for one day.'

'That's very kind of you. You're right; it is nice to sit back and look at the view for a bit. Tell me about your dad. What's wrong with him? Alzheimer's?'

'No, think it's just old age; 'e's been getting worse last few years, ever since Mam died. Sad; 'e's just given up.'

'What happened to your mother?'

345

'She 'ad cancer of stomach. None of us knew, not even 'er. She went in for tests, 'ad an 'eart attack and died. T'was then they discovered the cancer.'

'Well at least she didn't suffer.'

'No, tha's true but t'was a shock for us.'

'I'm sure it was. I'm very sorry.'

'Well, Dad 'as never been same since.'

'How is his memory? Do you think he can remember much about his sister?'

'Don't know. It's possible. 'E used to talk about 'er all time; very fond of 'Lizabeth, 'e was.'

They were driving along the coast road, with the sea on their right. Kate opened the car window so she could breathe in its salty, fresh smell. The roaring of the sea never left them; it was always there, underlying their conversation, tucking itself into her memory and invading her senses. It spoke to her of its power. It told her that it knew all the undiscovered secrets that she was seeking; it had been there when Peter was a boy and it would be there when he was gone.

'Sorry, I didn't catch that,' she said, winding up the window again.

'Got somewhere t' stay?'

'Yes thanks, I've booked a room in a hotel in Scarborough.'

'You're welcome t' stay wi' me and the missus. We've got a spare room now that the kids 'ave gone.'

'That's very kind but I've booked it now.'

'Well 'nother time.'

'Thank you,' she repeated.

She wondered how old Tom was; he was probably only about fifty but looked older. His skin was tanned and

346

weather-beaten, his face a maze of fine lines and day-old stubble and his eyes were a bright blue. Everyone in this family has blue eyes except me, she thought, irritably.

'Are you a fisherman?' she asked him.

'A fisherman? No, I'm a painter. There 'ent no fishermen in Robin Hood's Bay n' more, we're all artists.'

He seemed delighted with the idea that she had thought him a fisherman and chuckled to himself.

'Dad'll laugh when I tell 'im that,' he said. 'There's no-one 'ates the boats more than me.'

'But you live right by the sea,' she said.

'That's reet but not on it. I just paint it.'

'What about your father? Did he paint?'

'Aye, whole family are artists of one sort or t'other. My brother's a potter wi' a studio up near Whitley Bay. Think we must 'ave inherited the gene from our grandmother.'

'Margaret?'

He nodded.

'Almost there,' he said.

The outline of Whitby Abbey appeared on the horizon, stark and powerful against the darkening sky.

'How beautiful,' she murmured.

'Aye,' he agreed. 'Looks like rain.'

They wound their way through the narrow streets and parked by the harbour wall.

'T' is easier to walk from 'ere,' he said.

The nursing home was a converted house, overlooking the harbour. She imagined that it had once been a boarding house; it still had the smell of stale food and cheap floor cleaner that she remembered from seaside holidays.

'Mr. Marshall, have you come to see your father?'

347

A uniformed nurse, with a wide and ample bosom beneath the starched bib of her white apron, opened the door to them.

'Aye, Sister and I've brought cousin t' visit as well.'

'Come in. You're in luck, he's having one of his good days today. He ate all his lunch and now he's in the television room. If you like to go along to his room I'll bring him up.'

'Thank you.'

Tom led them along the passage and up some narrow stairs. Peter's room was not very large but it was comfortably furnished with a wide bed, a table for writing and two easy chairs; a door in the wall led to a built-in wardrobe and another opened into a small bathroom.

'This is nice,' she said.

'Aye, t'is not very large but t'is comfortable enough and clean. Staff are nice; treat the residents reet well; show respect for the old folk.'

He looked at Kate to see if she understood. It obviously pained him to have had to put his father in a home.

'Couldn't manage 'im at home. Weren't fair on missus. You know 'e's, well, not able to do things for 'imself anymore.'

Kate nodded; he did not need to spell it out.

'I'm sure he's very well looked after in here.'

'Aye and I come up and see 'im every other day. Used to come every day but got too much,' he explained.

The door swung open and there was Peter and the nurse. He had obviously once been a tall, handsome man, now bent with age and infirmity. Kate immediately recognised the family likeness.

''Ello Dad. Brought you a visitor.'

Peter turned to his son with a look of bewilderment.

348

'It's me Dad, Tom and this is Kate. You remember I told you she was coming up to see you. Come all the way from London she 'as Dad. Wants to talk to you about your Lizzie.'

The nurse helped the old man into the chair by the window and then left.

'Hello Peter,' Kate said, bending over and kissing him on the cheek.

The physical contact galvanised him.

'You don't look anything like your mother,' he said. 'Nor your grandmother.'

She smiled.

'So they are always telling me. However I can see that you are my grandmother's brother; you are very like her.'

'Like who?'

'Like Lizzie, Dad. Says you look like your Lizzie.'

'Poor Lizzie; she's dead you know.'

Kate nodded.

'Died of a broken heart.'

'Why was that Dad?'

'What?'

The old man looked at his son.

'Why'd you say she died of a broken heart?'

'Well why else would she die so young?'

'Peter.'

Kate took his gnarled hand in her own and stroked it gently.

'Peter can you tell me anything about the man that Lizzie loved? Did you ever meet him?'

All at once Peter became lucid; he looked straight at Kate and said:

'How could I have met him? I was only a small boy at the time. I knew nothing about it. It was only years later that

349

Lizzie told me that Alex was not the father of her first child; it was a man she had met in Spain, that time when she ran off and left us. She often talked about going back to look for him or his family; he had a younger sister you know. But she never did; she was always too busy with her children. She told me that if she went she'd look for my ships but I expect they're long gone by now. Some little Spanish boy will be playing with them.'

A tear ran down his cheek.

'Nobody knew about him you know, well apart from the family and Alex of course,' he continued. 'I liked Alex. I would have liked him to have seen my ships.'

He turned to his son:

'Why doesn't Alex come to see me anymore?'

''E's dead now, Dad. 'E died last month. Remember, showed you the obituary in the paper?'

'Dead? They're all dead now.'

He sighed and said in a whisper: 'Only me to go.'

He looked at Kate again.

'Who did you say you were? Are you Tom's wife?'

'No, I'm Kate, one of Lizzie's grand-daughters.'

'Lizzie's dead, you know. Died of a broken heart,' he repeated.

His eyes started to close and his head kept jerking forward onto his chest.

'That's all you'll get out of 'm this afternoon. Could come back t'morrow, if you think 'e could 'elp you any more.'

'No, that's all right. I don't want to bother him.'

'Won't bother 'm. T'morrow 'e won't even remember you were 'ere.'

He arranged his father in a more comfortable position so that he could sleep in peace and stood up to leave. Kate bent down and kissed the old man on the forehead.

'Goodbye Peter,' she said.

 As they walked back to the car, Tom asked her:

'That any use to you? 'E didn't 'ave much to say, did 'e.'

'Well I suppose it was. I'm glad I've met him; it makes it easier to picture my grandmother when I know the people that she loved. Also it was interesting to know that she was still talking about looking for her lover years later. She obviously never stopped loving him.'

'Glad it was useful, then.'

'Thank you very much for coming with me, Tom. That was very kind of you.'

'T'was nowt,' he grunted.

CHAPTER 19

She felt the bump as the wheels dropped and locked into place and there was that usual sinking feeling in her stomach as the aeroplane started to descend. She popped a piece of chewing gum into her mouth and began to chew it, trying to reduce the pressure that was building up in her ears. The over-talkative young woman sitting beside her was quiet at last; before they took off she confessed to Kate that she was terrified of flying and was now bent double, her head in her hands, moaning quietly to herself. Kate felt she ought to try to comfort her but thought better of it. Instead she picked up her novel and tried to continue reading. The aeroplane was lower now and she could see the baked, red earth of the mountains quite clearly before they continued out over the sea. The aircraft banked and turned so that it could approach the runway into the wind and below them a strip of golden beach curved its way along the edge of the sparkling blue Mediterranean. She felt excited about the trip; it was her first visit to mainland Spain and she had spent the previous week reading every guide book that she could find.

Geoffrey had been shocked when she had handed in her notice and immediately began to promise her all manner of unlikely inducements to change her mind. In the end she had felt it only fair to tell him the real reason for her departure, which was quite simply that she no longer needed to work. To give him credit he had been delighted to hear of her good fortune and wished her well; he even organised a farewell dinner for her and invited everyone in the department. She still felt a little tearful when she thought about it; she would miss him.

Her house was as yet unsold; there was a couple who had shown some interest in buying it but they were having trouble selling their own one bedroom flat. Maisie had promised to keep an eye it until she returned, so Kate left one set of keys with her and another with the estate agent, who promised to keep her informed of any developments. She had given no-one a date for her return but had promised to fly back if she was needed. Her plans were quite clear; she was going to try to trace the Luz de Montevideo family and she was going to learn a little about the country that had seduced both her great-grandparents and her grandmother. She purchased a one-way ticket, packed her golf clubs and booked herself a room in the Parador de Golf, over which they seemed to be flying at that very moment. She craned her neck to get a better view; it was a golf course in miniature. Then, before she could register any of the details, they had flown over it and were hurtling above the runway, about to land. There was a dull thud as the wheels touched down and Kate felt herself propelled forward; the aeroplane slowed and taxied into its disembarking slot. She was in Spain.

She collected her hire car with no problems and was soon slipping into the nose-to-tail queue of traffic leaving the airport compound. It was not far to the Parador and within ten minutes she had pulled up outside the door of the hotel; a porter came out to greet her and helped her unload her luggage. She liked the look of the place as soon as she saw it; the hotel was low and wide and of a distinctive Andalusian design that enclosed both gardens and a swimming pool. Her own bedroom led out onto a small open patio, which in turn stepped down onto the lawn that surrounded the swimming pool. It had all been designed for peace and relaxation. She was charmed by the simplicity of it; her bedroom was light and airy, with traditionally glazed tiles skirting a floor paved in warm terracotta blocks. The furniture was of heavy, dark wood that contrasted well with the plain white walls and a few minimalistic paintings gave an additional touch of colour to the room.

Kate decided to leave her unpacking until later and take a stroll by the sea. The beach was crowded with sun worshippers stretched beneath large, multicoloured beach umbrellas; others were swimming in the turquoise water. The hot sand burned the soles of her feet and as she hurried down to the water's edge to cool off, a gentle breeze from the sea caressed her skin; now her holiday was really beginning. She felt her cares slipping away from her. Today she would relax and explore the facilities; tomorrow would be soon enough to begin her investigation.

The next morning she rose early and headed for the first tee. She had arranged to play nine holes each day before breakfast, before the sun rose too high in the sky and began to scorch the land. There was nobody about except a few green staff and the occasional hotel guest wandering through the gardens. She was refreshed after her night's sleep and as she strode down the first fairway she felt very positive about what lay ahead. Now that she was here, in the city where her grandparents had met, she would surely find all the answers to her questions. She lined herself up and swung smoothly, hitting the ball firmly and sending it bounding along the fairway, scattering a group of young parakeets on its way. The birds rose into the air, squawking in protest, then resettled a few yards further away to resume their hunt for breakfast.

After her morning's exercise and a leisurely breakfast she drove down the dual carriageway into Málaga and pulled into a large underground car park next to the city's only department store, the Corte Inglés. A friendly taxi driver pointed her in the right direction and after a ten minute walk along a wide boulevard, lined with palm trees and Japanese maples, she came to the new headquarters of the British Consulate.

She surrendered up her handbag and mobile phone to the security man who, having checked that they were bomb-free and person-friendly, let her into the reception area. She took a number from the dispenser and waited her turn.

'Good morning, how can I help you?' a woman with an immaculate British accent asked her.

'I'd like to see the Consul please.'

'The Consul? Do you have an appointment?'

'No but I would really like to see him if that is possible.'

'May I ask what it is about?'

'I'm trying to trace someone, someone who lived in Málaga a long time ago.'

'Oh I can help you with that. Just a moment.'

She walked to the side door and pressed a security buzzer.

'Come through. It's easier than talking through that grill and you don't look like a terrorist to me.'

The young woman led Kate into an interview room. She sat down in front of a computer and motioned for Kate to sit opposite her.

'Right. Now who was it you wanted to find?'

'Well,' Kate hesitated. 'I'm not sure exactly; I want to speak to someone who was living here during the Civil War.'

'Goodness, the Civil War you say? That was, let me think 1935?'

'1936. 1936 until 1939.'

'Right, well most of the ex-pats who were living here then are now in the English Cemetery but let me search anyway.'

She typed something into the computer and waited a moment.

'Yes, just as I thought, most of them are now dead. There is one octogenarian, actually he's almost a nonagenarian, Walter Bristow. Well he's half American really; his father was Sir Alfred Bristow and his mother was the daughter of an American oil tycoon. Don't know if you've heard of them?'

Kate shook her head.

'Well according to our records he's still alive but I can't guarantee he's compos mentis, you know. Anyway he lives in a home, *La Residencia Blanca Paloma,* here in Málaga. Would you like the address?'

'Please.'

Kate could not believe her luck. Maybe this old man knew her grandmother or would be able to tell her something about her grandfather and his family. The woman copied the name and address carefully onto a piece of paper and handed it to her.

'Of course please bear in mind that our records are not one hundred percent full-proof. It could be that he has already died and nobody has thought to inform us.'

'So if that is the case, how do I find someone else who was here then, a Spanish person for example?'

'I would think that would be easier. Just go to the *Ayuntamiento* and ask for the department of *Padronamiento*. They have the records of all the inhabitants of Málaga.'

Kate stood up.

'Thank you so much. You have been very helpful.'

'If you're researching a book or something we have lots of photographs and records going back to the beginning of the nineteenth century,' she added.

'No it's nothing like that. It's a personal matter; but thank you anyway.'

She had no idea how to find the *Residencia Paloma Blanca*, so she decided to leave her car in the car park and go by taxi. It was a wise decision because as the taxi driver double-parked in order to let her alight, she could barely hear what he said for the blare of car horns from frustrated motorists; she could see that both parking and finding her way through the narrow streets was not for the faint-hearted.

The residential home was a tall, narrow building with no garden but splendid views of the port and the bull ring. She pushed open the door and went straight in.

'*La puedo ayudar en algo?*' the receptionist asked.

'Yes, I wondered if I might speak to Walter Bristow?'

'Are you a relative?'

'No.'

'Friend?'

'No, I'm afraid Mr Bristow doesn't know me. I just wanted to ask him a few questions.'

'Well I'm very sorry but that won't be possible; Mr. Bristow died yesterday.'

357

'Oh, my goodness, I am sorry.'

'Yes, well it was not exactly unexpected. He was very old you know, and he had not been well for some time,' the receptionist explained.

'Yes, I realise that. Well thank you anyway.'

'That's his son, leaving now,' she added. 'He's been clearing out his room. Maybe he can help you.'

She pointed to a tall, well-built man in his forties who was struggling to hold the door open with his foot while he manoeuvred a large cardboard box through the opening.

'Let me help,' she offered, grabbing hold of the door for him.

'Thanks,' he replied.

She detected a Texas drawl.

'I'm sorry to intrude but I understand your father has just died. I'm very sorry,' she said.

'Yes, well we've been expecting it for weeks now. But it still hits you pretty hard.'

'I had come here to see if I could speak to him,' she explained.

He propped the box on top of a low wall and looked at her closely for the first time.

'Did he know you?' he asked.

'No. A woman at the British Consulate gave me his name; I thought he could help me with a few enquiries I'm making.'

'What sort of enquiries?' he asked, frowning slightly.

'I'm trying to trace my grandfather's family. My grandmother and my grandfather met in Málaga during the Civil War and I wanted to trace some of his family.'

He raised an eyebrow.

'And you thought Pa could help?'

'Well as your father lived here such a long time, I thought, maybe, he would have recognised their names,' she explained.

'Well you're just a few days too late I'm afraid.'

'Yes, I realise that now. I'm sorry.'

'Look maybe I can help. I'm a historian and I'm actually in the middle of putting together an oral history of Spain.'

'Really?'

'Look if you can wait until I take Pa's things to my car, we could go and have a coffee and you can tell me exactly who it is you're looking for. You never know, it may be a name I've come across in my research.'

'That's very kind of you.'

'Just wait here; I'll be back in a tick.'

Kate sat down on the wall to wait. What did they say: when one door closes another door opens; maybe this man would be able to help her find her relatives. She wondered what he meant by an 'oral history'.

'Sorry to keep you waiting. My name is Larry by the way, Larry Bristow.'

He rubbed his hand on his jeans and held it out her. He had the broad shoulders and powerful arms of a sportsman, and brown, curly hair that had been cut very short. His face was square, very smooth and tanned and there was a deep cleft in his chin; he reminded her of some actor she had once seen. She took his hand and said:

'Kate Scott.'

'Well Kate, let's find ourselves a coffee.'

The way he drew out the syllables of the word 'coffee' made her smile.

'There's a neat bar near here that I go to a lot, or rather I should say used to go to because I doubt if I'll be coming back here much now that Pa's dead.'

He took her arm and steered her across the street towards a small bar, where the tables and chairs were set out on the pavement and protected from the summer sunshine by gaily coloured umbrellas.

'Outside or in?'

'Outside. I can't get enough of the sun at the moment.'

'Just arrived?'

'Yesterday. I'm staying at the Parador.'

'Nice.'

'What about you? Do you live here?'

'Yes, for now. I'm staying in Pa's old house. When he went into the home, almost a year ago now, we decided to keep it.'

'We?'

'My brother and I. He lives in the States, in Ohio. I don't know what we'll do now, probably sell it. We only ever came to Málaga to visit Pa.'

A long-legged waitress in a short denim skirt came out to take their order.

'What would you like?' Larry asked.

'Just a *café solo*.'

'*Café solo y café con leche*,' he ordered, then turning back to Kate, asked:

'So who is it you're looking for, your grandfather did you say?'

'Well, not exactly, he's dead. I want to find out if any of his family are still alive. According to some letters I've found, his family was pretty important in Málaga at the time.'

'Of course that could have changed; lots of things changed after the war. What was the family name?'

'Well my grandfather's full name was Juan Francisco Gomez de la Luz de Montevideo Rodriguez.   Bit of a mouthful, eh.'

'Not really. That's pretty typical; all Spaniards take both parents' surnames, first the father's then the mother's. Your great-grandmother would have been a Rodriguez and your great-grandfather would have been a Gomez. But when you get a family with a really old name, usually someone from the aristocracy, they like to pass it on from generation to generation, so the name gets longer and longer. It's quite likely that your grandfather's name was even longer than that. Anyway, you'll be pleased to know that I've come across that name before.'

'What "de la Luz de Montevideo"?'

'Yes, so it's possible that we'll strike lucky and find out something about them.'

'That would be great.'

She beamed at him.

'So, what sort of book are you writing?'

'It's a history book, as you'd imagine, contemporary stuff, interviews, memories of living people; what we call an oral history,' he explained.   'I've spent almost two years now recording conversations with people from all over Spain. It's been great fun and very rewarding. You know people love to talk about their past, their childhood, the people they loved, the places they lived. I can tell you it's really fascinating.'

He paused for a moment to light a cigarette and waited until the waitress had delivered their coffee before continuing:

'I've been all over the country; I started in Asturias and moved along the north coast, then worked my way down to Madrid and now I'm in Andalusia.'

'How do you find people to interview?'

'Well, it's a lot easier than you might imagine; I started with a number of friends and then they suggested friends of theirs, who in turn introduced me to others; it's become quite a chain. The British Council has been very helpful as well and of course I contacted the universities; their local history departments usually have names of people worth interviewing. You'll soon realise that the Spanish are a very open people; they love to talk, so, as I say, it's been quite easy. And of course they are very proud of their country so take any opportunity to spout off about it.'

'Sounds fascinating. You must speak excellent Spanish.'

'History and Spanish were my majors in college,' he explained.

'I wonder if you can find any mention of my great-grandfather's family in your research.'

'It's possible. At any rate it's well worth a try, especially if we can actually trace some of your relatives and interview them for my book.'

He drank some of his coffee and lit another cigarette.

'So, Kate, tell me a bit about yourself.'

'What would you like to know?'

'Well for a start, how long are you here for?' he asked.

'It's open-ended,' she replied. 'I've booked my hotel room for a month but I plan to stay here until I have found out something about my ancestors; I'm not going home empty handed.'

'What about work? Don't you have to go back to work?'

She shook her head.

'Wow that must be a great job. What do you do, write hotel guides for the Paradors?'

'No, nothing like that. Actually at the moment I'm not working.   I've just given up my job; early retirement I suppose you'd call it. So, you see I have no commitments.'

'Great, free as a bird. Right then, what can you tell me about your family? What have you found out so far?'

He pulled out a rather battered notebook and a pencil and listened intently while Kate recounted her discoveries, including the part where she had recently discovered that her mother was illegitimate. She handed him the photograph of Alex and Juan.

'I have some diaries and letters in the hotel and a few photographs too. This one is the most important I think; it shows my legal grandfather and his friend Juan and it was taken here in Málaga. I think this Juan is my biological grandfather but I'm not sure.'

'That sounds useful. If we do find any of his family and they still have any photographs of him, we'll be able to compare them. What about the diaries and letters?'

'I don't think the diaries are of much use because they were my great-grandmother's but the letters may contain something.'

'Well, why don't I see what I can find out at home; I'll look through my files and tapes and see if these names crop up at all. Then we can meet up again and you bring the letters with you. What do you think?'

'Yes that sounds fine. When?'

'Tomorrow OK?'

'Fine. Shall we meet here?'

'No let's meet in the centre. I don't suppose you've had time to look around Málaga yet?'

'No, only what I've seen from the inside of a taxi,' she replied.

'OK. Tell you what. Tomorrow I'll show you around the city. Get the cab to drop you off at McDonald's and I'll be waiting for you.'

'Great, I look forward to that. Maybe I can buy you lunch?'

'We can certainly have lunch but you can't buy it. You have to start getting used to the Spanish ways; here ladies don't pay the bill.'

'Whatever you say.'

She was beginning to like this energetic man, even though his chain-smoking was making her cough. She drank the rest of her coffee and said:

'Well I suppose I'd better let you get back to clearing out your father's room.'

'I've almost finished but I've still got to go to the funeral parlour and collect his ashes. I'm taking them back to the States at the end of the month and we're having a memorial service for him.'

'That's nice.'

'Well it's all a bit rushed here; the cremation was the day after he died. All the family are in the States and there was no time for anyone to come over and attend the funeral, so I decided I'd take him to them.'

He smiled, sadly.

'Pa had lots of friends back home, even though he'd lived here for most of his life. Of course most of them are dead now but there're still a few old codgers left. My brother's going to organise things that end. I just have to take Pa back.'

Kate stood up.

'Well Larry, I'm very pleased to have met you. It's extremely kind of you to offer to help me.'

'No strife Kate, glad to be of assistance. See you tomorrow then.'

'Yes, what time?'

'Eleven o'clock?'

'Perfect,' she said, explaining about her new morning routine.

'Yes, well you wouldn't want to break it on the second day. That would be like me, every January 2nd, when I break my annual resolution about giving up smoking.'

Kate smiled and shook his hand; it was warm and dry, and his grip was firm. It could have been her imagination but, it seemed as though he held on to it just a fraction longer than necessary.

It was very hot by now and there was no breeze at all, so she decided to walk back to the city centre through the park. By the time she entered the cool avenues of overhanging trees and tropical plants, she was sweating profusely and one of her new sandals was rubbing her heel. She sat down for a moment by an ornamental duck pond to rest and think over the morning's events. Her conversation with Larry had certainly sounded promising but she did not want to raise her hopes too quickly. She found Larry rather attractive; there was something particularly seductive about his confident manner and his powerful body. Without intending to, she found herself comparing him to Hugh; he was much better looking and probably younger but he didn't make her heart skip in the same way that Hugh did.

She smiled when she thought of her lover; he had looked rather disappointed when she told him she was leaving but he had said nothing. He had driven her to the airport and he had telephoned her last night. In fact, just recently, he had taken to telephoning her every day, visiting her every weekend and occasionally taking her to a mid-week dinner as well. After the third date, she had invited him to stay overnight at her house and, one night after an evening at the Welsh National Opera in Bristol, she had stayed in his small flat. Gradually they had drifted into a warm, loving relationship but with no specific ties. He was an interesting and lively companion, an ardent lover and a good friend but he had not declared his love for her. He had seemed upset that she had planned a trip to Spain without him but he did not deter her from going, even though she admitted that she had no idea when she would return. Would it have made any difference to her plans if he had behaved differently? She could not answer that. She wondered what he was doing now.

She became aware that someone was standing in front of her; it was a woman, a tall, stout gypsy wearing a fringed shawl and a dirndl skirt. Her skin was the colour of walnuts and her black eyes stared at Kate without the least sign of warmth. She had an ample bosom, encased in a tight, red blouse and her arms were strong and powerful; she extended her hand towards Kate, the palm open in supplication. Kate could not understand the words she spoke but she knew she was asking for money. Her voice managed to be both menacing and wheedling at the same time and her gaze was fixed on Kate's handbag. As Kate stood up, clutching the bag to her chest, a second woman, younger and slimmer than her companion but dressed in a similar manner and with the same threatening attitude, moved in to stand next to her. She, too, held out her hand in a supplicant manner and began to chant in a monotonous, nasal voice:

'*Por favour, algo por el niño. Tenemos hambre.*'

Kate was now aware of a skinny child hanging onto the gypsy's skirt; he looked at her with large, brown eyes that told her nothing.

'*No comprendo,*' Kate said, firmly and tried to push past them.

'*Señora, algo para comer. Por favour, señora,*' the younger woman continued, still blocking her path.

She stepped closer and her voice took on a more threatening tone. There was a strong smell of garlic and sour body odour and Kate began to feel slightly dizzy.

'*No, no comprendo,*' Kate repeated.

She was nervous now because she was surrounded; the bench prevented her from retreating and the two women prevented her from moving forward.

'Go away,' she shouted at last. 'Get away. Leave me alone.'

The women ignored her and moved even closer; Kate felt the younger woman pluck at her sleeve. Panic was beginning to set in.

'Leave me alone,' she repeated, her voice rising alongside her fear.

The women moved closer and the child continued to watch her from the cover of his mother's skirt, his brown eyes, unwavering.

'*Que pasa aqui?*' a deep voice asked. '*Fuera. Dejá está mujer en paz. Fuera de aquí.*'

An old man had come to her aid; he waved his walking stick at the gypsies and shouted at them in Spanish. The two women turned away from Kate and looked at him with distain; they muttered something incomprehensible and grudgingly stepped aside to let Kate escape. They stood watching as Kate and the man walked out of the park and along the pavement.

'You must take more care, young lady,' he admonished, speaking to her gently in English. 'It is not a good idea to sit in the park on your own.'

'But what did they want?' she asked, trying to steady her voice and stop herself trembling.

'Begging,' he replied. 'They wanted money for food and when they saw you were alone, they tried to frighten you into giving them some. They would not have hurt you, stolen your handbag yes but not hurt you.'

'It didn't feel like that. I was quite frightened,' she admitted.

'Well please take more care next time. Are you new to Málaga?' he asked.

'Yes, I just arrived yesterday.'

'Ah well, the gypsies are very clever; they know how to identify the innocents abroad,' he said. 'You will find that Málaga is a lovely city; it is not a dangerous place but, like everywhere in the world, there are always those who are opportunists. Take care of your handbag and don't wander into lonely places on your own and you'll be all right; I promise you.'

'Thank you very much for your help. May I buy you a coffee? I think I need to sit down for a minute.'

He looked at his watch.

'It's rather late for a coffee but I normally have a *fino* and a *tapas* at this hour. Would you like to join me?'

He led her to a crowded bar in a busy shopping street.

'This is *Calle Larios*; where all the women in Málaga come to spend their husbands' money in these rather, expensive shops,' he said, waving his stick in the general direction of the rows of elegant shops and smiling as he did so.

He was a short man who, despite his age, carried himself very upright; he had a shock of thick, white hair and his moustache was neatly trimmed into a fine line; he was immaculately dressed in light trousers and a tweed jacket underneath which he wore a carefully buttoned, green waistcoat, with a gold watch chain, drooping from one pocket. His ensemble was completed with a perfectly knotted, yellow, bow tie. As he walked beside her, he rapped his silver tipped walking stick, the same one he had brandished at the gypsies, on the pavement in time to his steps.

'They serve the best *tapas* in Málaga here,' he told her, as they took their seats at the bar.

She could believe him; a medley of refrigerated dishes covered the length of the bar: deep-fried crab claws, tiny fish pickled in oil and vinegar, snails in a garlic sauce, bite-sized pieces of roast pork, tiny broad beans mixed with chopped cured ham, chunks of pork in a tomato sauce, prawns, steamed mussels, deep-fried artichokes.

'What would you like?' he asked her.

She chose a *tapas* of the broad beans and a glass of dry sherry; he had the roast pork and another sherry.

'Are you here on holiday?' he asked.

'Sort of, I'm trying to trace a relative,' she said.

'A Spanish relative?'

'Yes.'

'What's the name of your relative?'

'I don't know exactly; the surname is Gomez de la Luz de Montevideo Rodriguez.'

'Well there are thousands of Gomez and almost as many Rodriguez but la Luz de Montevideo, that's a name that stands out. That's the name of our mayor.'

Kate put down her glass and looked at him in disbelief.

'The mayor?'

'Yes, Vincente Herrera Gomez de la Luz de Montevideo Garcia. He kept his grandmother's name; they all did. It is a name that goes back generations. Now why would a young Englishwoman like yourself want to find someone with that name?'

She hesitated, feeling awkward about explaining her search to someone she barely knew but after all, he had come to her rescue and, for that alone, she felt she owed him an explanation. Briefly she told him about how her grandparents had met during the Civil War.

'So you're looking for your grandfather?'

'Well his descendants, or maybe someone who knew him.'

'It was all a long time ago; not many people want to talk about those times now. Most people want to forget that the Civil War ever happened. But you may be lucky; maybe Señor Herrera will be able to tell you something.'

'How can I contact him?'

'I suggest you go to the *Ayuntamiento* and ask for an appointment.'

It all sounded so easy. When she met Larry the next day, she would ask him to go with her to the town hall. She ordered another round of *finos* and a further *tapas* for herself; her companion declined, saying he did not want to spoil his appetite.

'My wife will have my lunch ready at two o'clock exactly and if I don't eat it all, I will be in trouble,' he confided, with a smile.

They sat at the bar chatting like two old friends, watching people come and go. Alfredo, for that was his name, seemed to know everyone in Málaga and their conversation was constantly punctuated with pauses while he greeted newcomers, asking after their families or exchanging opinions on the latest *corrida*.

'You know a lot of people,' she commented.

'Well, I have come here for my glass of *fino* and *tapas*, at this time of day, now for fifteen years,' he said. 'Ever since I retired, and sometimes even before that. I used to work in that bank over there.'

'Would you like another sherry?' she asked.

She was feeling very mellow and in no hurry to end their conversation.

'No, I'm sorry, *señora*, I must go home for my lunch now.'

He stood up and bowing very slightly, took her hand, which he raised to within an inch of his lips.

'*Encantada*. It has been a pleasure to meet you. Enjoy the rest of your holiday and good luck with your search,' he said.

'Thank you,' she replied. 'I've enjoyed our conversation.'

'Don't forget what I said about taking care.'

In the convivial atmosphere of the bar she had almost forgotten the experience with the gypsies.

'Of course, and thank you so much for rescuing me,' she added.

As she already knew he would, he refused to let her pay and settled the bill before he left. She remained at the bar for a few more moments, watching him thread his way through the tables, pausing every so often to shake hands with someone or have a few words with another.

She thought Hugh had decided not to telephone and went in to dinner with a vague feeling of disappointment but at midnight her telephone rang.

'Kate?'

'Hi sweetheart.'

She was feeling slightly tipsy and wished he was there beside her.

'I hope it's not too late; I've been having dinner with some friends tonight and only just got home.'

'No, it's not too late.'

She struggled to keep her voice from trembling. After all why shouldn't he have dinner with friends? She could not expect him to live the life of a hermit just because she had come to Spain.

'Do I know them?' she asked, trying, without success, to make her voice sound normal.

'You know her, Margery and her husband Guy.'

'Oh yes, how is she?'

Margery was the woman from their very first meeting on the golf course in Devon. She felt the relief sweep over her like a warm blanket. What was happening to her? Why did she care so much about whom Hugh saw when she was away? They were supposed to have a modern relationship: no ties.

'She's fine. Her husband's a funny old stick though, a lot older than her. He looks a bit like a meerkat, tall and skinny, with horn rimmed glasses.'

'I didn't know meerkats wore glasses.'

'You know what I mean. Anyway, he hardly said a word all night. No wonder Margery's out on the golf course so much.'

'What does he do?'

'Nothing now, he's retired but I think he was something to do with insurance.'

'Does he play golf?'

'No, hates it; I could tell by the way he kept getting up to change the music every time Margery started talking to me about the golf club. He's a cyclist. Goes out every morning and cycles twenty miles, rain or shine.'

'Doesn't sound as though it was a fun evening.'

'It was OK. There were a couple of their neighbours there as well, Tim and Roger. They've got a holiday home in Spain, somewhere near Málaga. I told them you were out there at the moment and they said they're going there at the end of the month, so they'll probably get in touch. I gave them your number.'

'Oh Hugh, why did you do that? You know I'm here to do a specific job; I don't want to waste my time socialising with people I don't know.'

She tried to keep the irritation from her voice.

'Just thought you'd like some company.'

'I don't need any company.'

'So how's it going anyway?'

She struggled to push her annoyance to one side; she did not want to quarrel with him over the telephone.

'I think I'm making some progress. I've met this guy whose father's just died and he says he might be able to help me. He's writing a history of the area, or something like that; anyway he's done a lot of research and seems very happy to talk to me about it.'

'Sounds a start. Who is he? Spanish?'

'No, he's a Yank. His father lived here for years.'

She could tell he wanted her to explain more about this man she had just met but instead she said.

'Yes, I've made two new friends today,' and began to tell him about Alfredo.

They chatted on for a while, relating the trivia of their day, happy to hear the sound of each other's voices. She told him how she was playing golf every day. He relayed a joke he had heard and described a problem he was having with the construction of a new building, then they both admitted they were tired and said goodnight.

CHAPTER 20

By eleven o'clock the next morning she was standing outside MacDonalds waiting for Larry. He had suggested MacDonalds as a meeting point, he later admitted, because it was central and easy to spot, not because he was a hamburger addict.

'Hi there,' he called, striding up the ramp from the underground car-park.

She waved.

'Hi, Larry.'

'Gee, you're very punctual. Can tell you're English,' he said, bending over and giving her a quick kiss on the cheek.

'I was keen to get started,' she said. 'It's such a lovely day.'

He looked about him as though he had only just become aware of the weather.

'Yeah, I suppose it is. Still a bit early for me, though.'

He lit a cigarette and blew the smoke slowly into the air, obviously enjoying the sensation.

'Coffee?'

'Good idea.'

'Follow me. I know a great place to have breakfast.'

'I've already eaten,' she admitted.

'OK, brunch then.'

The café he took her to was all cream and gilt rococo with elaborately carved stucco on the ceiling and big glass lamps. The chairs were painted in gold and upholstered in pink damask, and smiling cherubs hung above them, bunches of plaster grapes in their tiny hands. It was like stepping back in time; she was undecided whether she liked it or found it simply gross.

'They do real good coffee here,' he said.

'The pastries don't look too bad either,' she commented, examining the display counter where tiny, bite-sized pasteries topped with strawberries rubbed shoulders with brilliant white meringues stuffed with fresh cream; where Florentine biscuits, their fruits like sparkling jewels, sat beside almond tarts, slices of chocolate mousse and fruit pies. It was the most delicious array of cakes and tarts that she had seen outside of France. But, better than that, were the chocolates: row upon row of handmade chocolates. Their strong, sweet smell permeated the air.

'Or the chocolates.'

'Yeah, they're quite good. Not my thing really but I knew you'd like them.'

He smiled and gave her a wink.

They chose a table outside so that Larry could continue smoking while he ate his breakfast and, as soon as they had placed their order, she asked:

'Well, have you found out anything?'

'Yeah, I think I have. You were right; there was a sister. Juan Antonio Gomez de la Luz de Montevideo had two children: Juan Francisco and Eloisa Maria. I've discovered quite a few references to her. She was quite a socialite after the war; her name appears in all the society columns. It seems she married a wealthy banker, Jorge Herrera Banderos and went to live in Madrid. They moved in very elevated society, mixing with politicians and minor aristocracy. They had five children, two of whom died very young but the other three are possibly still alive. One of them is....'

'The mayor of Málaga,' she interrupted.

Larry looked at her in surprise.

'Not quite. I was going to say, the father of the mayor of Málaga. He's her grandson. But how did you know that?'

She told him about her encounter with the gypsies and the intervention of Alfredo.

'You were lucky that guy was around. You could have gotten hurt, you know.'

'Well it's funny, I've always thought I could look after myself but now I'm not so sure. It's those moments of indecision at the beginning that make you vulnerable, while you're trying to work out if there really is a threat or if it's just an over-reaction on your own part.'

'Yes, I'm sure they're well aware of that. That's why they start out softly, appearing quite normal, and hoping to get your sympathy. They're just waiting for you to drop your guard.'

'Well enough of that. Let's get back to the sister.'

She felt both embarrassed and uncomfortable at the memory. She knew she should have been more alert and was not in the mood to be reminded of it.

'Well I don't have a lot more on her; it seems that her husband died in,' he paused and looked at his notes. 'Died in 1993 but I can't find anything else about her. She seemed to disappear from the society pages after that.'

'So they all lived in Madrid?'

'Yes.'

377

'Where are they now?'

'As far as I can tell, one son lives in London and an unmarried daughter still lives in Madrid but the eldest son came back to Málaga. He must be the father of your mayor. He married a local girl and has lived here ever since and, as you have already discovered, his son is also here. It sounds as though you've gotten yourself some pretty useful connections Kate.'

'So do you have an address for any of them?'

'Not yet, sorry.'

'So where do we go from here?'

'I suppose contacting the mayor is the most obvious approach.'

'Will you come with me to get an appointment?' she asked.

'OK. Eat up that sickly looking squodgy thing and we'll go there now. The town hall is quite close to here; it's in the park, probably not far from where you were almost mugged.'

She put the last of her pastry in her mouth and washed it down with the coffee, while Larry lit another cigarette.

'OK, ready? Let's go.'

As they walked to the top of *Calle Larios* and turned left into the *Avenida del Parque,* Larry gave her a potted history of the park.

'This was all reclaimed land,' he explained. 'Over a hundred years ago the sea came right up here, almost to the walls of the Arab fortress.'

He pointed up at a massive red fortress that sat above them, clinging to the steep rock face.

'At the end of the nineteenth century the city was doing so well that they decided to expand the port area and built three new quays. That's when they drained the land and laid out the park.'

They were walking down a wide avenue, beneath the shade of monumental rubber trees, avocados and jacarandas.

'Even as far back as the Roman period people brought new plants back here. Did you know that fruits such as the orange and lemon originally came from China?'

She shook her head.

'So when they decided to lay out a park along the lines of English and French parks they imported more exotic varieties. Apparently Málaga has a micro-climate that verges on the tropical, so whatever they planted flourished, no matter where it came from.' he continued.

Kate looked around her at the lush verdure on either side, then stopped beneath a large shrub with trumpet shaped flowers, and examined the plaque below it.

'I can see what you mean. Look at this one, it's from Peru: "White Angel's Trumpet" it says.'

'Well like I said, it's always been a busy, commercial port, all sorts of plants were brought back from overseas voyages. Most of them liked the climate and flourished; so now the city thinks of them as its own.'

They approached a classical building with marble columns flanking its main door. A wedding group were standing on the steps, posing for a photographer.

'Come on; this is it. Let's see if the mayor is at home.'

'You seem to know a lot about Málaga,' she said, ducking behind the wedding couple and following him up the marble steps into the town hall.

'Not really; it's all in the guide book,' he said, waving a yellow, pocket guide under her nose and giving her a wide grin.

After a number of wrong turns and redirections, they arrived at the mayor's office. A smartly dressed woman, sitting in front of a computer screen, asked them what they wanted.

'I'd like an appointment to see the mayor, please,' Kate explained.

His secretary checked her employer's diary and informed them that the earliest appointment she could give them was in September.

'September?' But we're only in July,' Kate complained.

'I'm very sorry but the mayor's diary is fully booked for the rest of the month and in August he's away on holiday.'

'But I won't be here in September; I'm leaving in a couple of weeks,' she protested, a whine slipping into her voice.

'Well I'm sorry; there is nothing I can do. Can anyone else help you? Another department for example?'

'No, it's a personal matter. I need to speak to him myself. I wouldn't take up much of his time, I assure you.'

'No, I'm sorry. It's impossible.'

Kate was about to protest again when a man in a grey suit opened the door behind the secretary and said something that Kate could not understand.

'I'm sorry Señor Herrera, this woman wants to speak to you on a personal matter,' she explained. 'I've told her it is impossible for you to see her before September but she won't go away.'

He looked at his watch.

'What time is Señor Alvarez due?'

'In fifteen minutes.'

'Well, OK, send her in now. Let's see what this personal matter is all about.'

The secretary looked coldly at Kate but nevertheless got up and showed her and Larry into the mayor's office.

Larry spoke first, explaining that he was there as an interpreter and friend of Kate.

'We do not need an interpreter; I speak perfect English,' the mayor told them.

He was a rather corpulent man in his early forties; his dark hair was oiled and combed flat to his head and his face had a hawkish look, emphasised by black, piercing eyes and a large hooked nose. His suit and shirt were immaculately pressed and looked expensive. He sat down behind a massive rosewood desk, inviting them to sit opposite him.

'As my secretary has already explained, I have an appointment in a few minutes, so, if you don't mind, can we get straight to the point.'

His manner was rather brusque but Kate was not bothered; she was eager to begin.

'Thank you for seeing us; I'll try not to take up too much of your time, Señor Herrera. My name is Kate Scott, and well, the reason I'm here is that I'm trying to trace some members of my family. My grandmother was English but I believe my grandfather was Spanish; his name was Juan Francisco Gomez de la Luz de Montevideo Rodriguez.'

The man stared at her.

'What do you mean you believe he was Spanish? Don't you know?'

He had picked up a gold fountain pen and was twirling it between his second and third fingers.

'Not for sure. You see, my grandparents met in Málaga during the Civil War and, when the city fell to the Nationalists, they had to leave in a hurry. It was during their flight to Almería that they became separated. My grandmother managed to get on a boat back to England but I think my grandfather was killed. Sometime later my grandmother married an Englishman and nobody ever spoke about my Spanish grandfather again. In fact, it was only very recently that I learnt of his existence. Anyway, I have come to Málaga to see what I can find out about him. My friend, who's been helping me look through some old records, told me that your name was similar to my grandfather's and, as it is quite an unusual name, I thought you might be able to help me.'

'Well I was not born until 1965 so I know very little about the war except what I have learnt at school but I should tell you that if your grandfather was a Republican I very much doubt that he was a member of our family. As far as I remember all our family fought on the side of the Nationalists; he would have had no need to leave Málaga at that time, with or without an Englishwoman.'

He put down his pen and seemed about to dismiss them.

'But surely there can't be many people with that particular name?' she insisted.

He hesitated for a moment then continued:

'No, that's true, our name is very distinctive; I personally know of no other family called Luz de Montevideo in Spain and I have information on all our relations. If you are right that this man, who you claim was your grandfather, had the name you say he had then it is most surprising. My aunt has constructed a family tree that goes back to the eighteenth century, when our ancestor returned from Montevideo in Uruguay. If this man is a relative of ours, his name will be on it.'

Kate's heart gave a skip; this could be the information she needed.

382

'Is it possible to meet your aunt?'

'It would be a little difficult; she lives in Madrid. She is rather elderly now and rarely leaves home but I suppose I can telephone her for you.'

'Thank you that would be a great help. Maybe she could fax the relevant part of the family tree.'

'I doubt if she knows about such things as fax machines but it may be possible. Is there anything else?'

Once again he looked at his watch but did not show any particular interest in getting rid of them. In fact he now seemed intrigued by her story.

'Well I wondered if your father was still alive and if we could speak to him? He might remember something from those days.'

'He is very much alive but I doubt if he can help you any more than I can. He was not born until the end of the war.'

'Still I'd very much like to meet him.'

'He doesn't live in Málaga anymore; he moved out to Antequera when he retired. He has poor health and the doctor recommended that he live in the mountains.'

'I'm sorry to hear that but maybe if we could get in touch with him,' she persisted. 'It would mean so much to me. I'd be happy to drive out to meet him.'

He looked at her.

'What exactly is it you want from our family, Señora Scott?'

'Like I said, I just want to trace my grandfather.'

'And then what?'

'And then nothing. I'm not after your money if that's what you're thinking.'

'Money is what motivates most people, Señora Scott. May I not be forgiven for thinking that it too motivates you?'

'Well you're wrong.'

She sat in silence for a moment then continued:

'I just need to find out who I am. Until just a few months ago, I thought I knew who my parents and grandparents were; now I'm not sure. I don't need your family's money, Señor Herrera; I don't even need to be recognised as part of your family but I do need to know who my mother's father was and why his identity was kept a secret for so many years.'

When he did not reply she continued:

'Even my mother never spoke about him; I don't know if she even knew of his existence. It's as though all memory of him has vanished with my grandmother's death and I find that rather sad. Please Señor Herrera, I just need to know who he was.'

He tapped his desk with his pen and looked at her for a moment.

'Well I can telephone my father and see what he says. I can't guarantee that he'll agree to see you; he's a very stubborn man and, as I said, he's not well. However, I have to admit, you do have some of the family likeness about you; I'd never have taken you for an Englishwoman. Maybe there is something in your story, after all.'

'Thank you.'

'I can't promise anything. Leave me your address and I'll be in touch. If he refuses to meet you, you will have to find some other way to prove your theory.'

'That would be wonderful. Here let me give you my telephone number. I'm staying at the Parador del Golf,' she added.

She scribbled both her mobile number and the telephone number of her hotel room on the back of an address card and handed it to him.

'Señora Scott, I will do what I can. But now please forgive me but I have an important visitor in two minutes.'

He stood up and shook hands with them both.

They stood watching the wedding party that still posed before the photographer on the Town Hall steps, while Larry lit a cigarette. The bride and groom looked unbelievably happy, holding hands and smiling into each other's eyes. Were we ever like that, Kate wondered, thinking back to her own, fated marriage? The photographer was rounding up the wedding guests now, a look of impatience on his face; two of the small bridesmaids had slipped away into the park and pretended not to hear their mother calling them.

'Waste of money,' Larry said. 'Better off, just living together.'

'Some people like the stability of marriage,' Kate replied.

'You ever been married?'

'Divorced.'

'So much for stability.'

'What about you? Are you married?'

'Of course not.'

'Girlfriend?'

'Not at the moment, no.'

He inhaled deeply then let the smoke out very slowly, making perfect rings that floated up into the air and evaporated.

'God, I was dying for that. Damned "no smoking" ban. It'll be the death of me.'

A young boy from the wedding watched in wonder as he made smoke ring after smoke ring.

'You're pretty good at that.'

'Years of practice.'

'What did you think of the mayor?' Kate asked.

'Typical politician, doesn't give anything away.'

'You're right. I couldn't decide if he was interested in my story or annoyed that I was making enquiries.'

'He's probably waiting until he knows exactly who you are and if you're worth cultivating or not.'

'What now?'

'Well I think we've done enough detective work for one day; let me take you to the Picasso museum instead.'

He blew another smoke ring. She smiled at him; he really was such good company.

'OK, then lunch afterwards. Culture always gives me an appetite.'

CHAPTER 21

They did not hear from the mayor for three days, so while they waited Larry showed her the sights. They visited botanical gardens, churches, an Arab castle, a flamenco museum, walked up to the fortress and admired the view, explored the narrow, winding streets of the old town, wandered around the cathedral, watched archaeologists excavating the Roman theatre; by the end she felt that she knew the city as well as Larry. They ate *tapas* in crowded street bars and fish in *chiringitas* on the beach; they drank *fino* at lunch time and strong red wine in the evening; at night they walked through the park arm-in-arm, listening to outdoor concerts and laughing at the street entertainers. Never once did he suggest he take her back to her hotel; he simply called a taxi for her, kissed her chastely on the cheek and wished her goodnight.

Then on the fourth morning, as she was going into breakfast, the receptionist called her:

'Señora Scott. There is an envelope for you.'

It had an official looking logo on it that read: '*Ayuntamiento de Málaga.*'; she took it from him and opened it carefully. It was from the Señor Herrera.

'*Dear Señora Scott,*

I have spoken to my father and he knows nothing of your grandfather. However he is intrigued by your story and would like to meet you. He usually comes into Málaga once a month on business matters and suggests that you meet him in the Málaga Palacio for lunch. He will be in Málaga on the 21ˢᵗ. My secretary will book a table for two o'clock. I hope that this meets with your approval.

I have also asked my aunt to post you a copy of the part of our family tree that relates to the twentieth century; maybe you will find what you are looking for there.

I am afraid we will probably not have the chance to meet again as I am going to the north with my family for the summer.

Yours sincerely,

Vincente Herrera Gomez de la Luz de Montevideo Garcia Alcalde de Málaga'

She folded the letter carefully and put it in her pocket; she would telephone Larry as soon as she had finished breakfast. It was starting to come together at last. She reviewed the situation, scribbling a summary of the events on the back of the envelope:

1 Alex Reeves was not her grandfather

2 Her grandfather was Spanish and had died in the Civil War

3 She had found people with the same name as him

4 There was a family tree (copy in the post)

5 She was to have lunch with a man who could be his nephew

Yes, she was making progress but she still did not know anything more about her grandfather, other than his name.

She had arranged to meet Larry outside the *Ayuntamiento* at eleven. He was standing on the steps, smoking one of his interminable Marlboroughs, when her taxi pulled up. She felt herself start to smile when she saw him; he was beginning to become a familiar presence in her life. She realised she would miss him when he left.

'Hi, there. Right on time again. I don't know how you manage to get these Spanish taxis to be so punctual.'

'Just comes naturally.'

He kissed her on both cheeks, took a final drag of his cigarette and threw it down on the pavement.

'Right, let's see what we can find out today.'

'Where are we going?'

'To the records office to see if your grandfather's death was registered.'

'Do you think that's likely? I mean, we don't know where he died, do we.'

'No but we do know where he was born. We have to start somewhere.'

A helpful security guard pointed out the way to the *Departamento de Empadronamiento.* After the usual number of wrong turns they arrived at a hatchway in the wall and took their turn in the queue. When their turn arrived, Larry explained to the young man sitting behind a glass panel what they were looking for.

'I don't think we can help you with that; our records don't go back that far. You probably need the *Registro Civil*; they have all the information of births and deaths. Was it someone from Málaga?'

'Yes but we are unsure of where he died.'

'And this was in the 1930s?'

'Yes, probably 1937.'

'Well I doubt if they would be able to help you either. That was during the Civil War wasn't it?'

Larry nodded.

'I don't think they have any records from that time; almost everything got lost. You could try the *Registro Civil Central*; they may be able to help.'

'Where are they then?'

'In Madrid but you can telephone them, or check it out on the internet.'

He scribbled a web page address and a telephone number on a piece of paper and pushed it under the glass.

'Thanks, we'll do that.'

'Or church records, they didn't suffer so much damage. He could be listed there.'

Once again they found themselves standing on the steps of the *Ayuntamiento*.

'Not a lot of help there then.'

'When I get home I'll check out this website and see if it's any use then tomorrow, before we meet, I'll ring the place in Madrid.'

'OK.'

She felt deflated; another day to wait. They were making progress but slowly.

'Couldn't we telephone them now?'

He looked at his watch; it was almost twelve o'clock.

'Or this afternoon?'

'No, they won't be open this afternoon. Remember we're talking about a government office here; civil servants don't work after lunch. But we could try now; we might be lucky.'

'Here, use my mobile.'

He took her mobile telephone and sat down on the steps to dial the number. She sat next to him. She could hear him being put through to various departments, each change punctuated by bursts of classical music.

'This is taking forever,' he said, pulling out a packet of cigarettes and trying to extract one.

'Here, let me.'

She took out a cigarette, placed it between her lips and lit it, then gave it to him. She felt like a movie star in a forties film, Lauren Bacall or Olivia de Havilland.

'Thanks.'

He took it gratefully.

'Yes, I'm still here. OK, I'll hang on.'

At last he seemed to be through to the right person and she heard him give her grandfather's name. He reached in his pocket and pulled out his notepad, balanced it on his knee and wrote something down.

'Yes, yes, I've got that. Yes, I understand. Thank you for your help.'

He rang off.

'So?'

'We have to ring back later and they will tell us what they've found out. She gave me a reference number; they'll look into it and have something for us by tomorrow or the next day. Hey, don't look so glum; every step is a step in the right direction.'

'You don't know that; we could be hanging about for them and then in the end they can't tell us anything.'

'Well she did say not to get our hopes up. It seems that hundreds of people are trying to trace relatives lost during the war. It isn't easy, you know. Those records that do exist are incomplete and they don't necessarily contain the names of everyone who was shot, especially where there was no trial. If he was in prison then there may be some record of him, or,

391

if he was enlisted in the Republican army but if he just died, like so many thousands, a casualty of war, then we probably won't find anything.'

'So we just wait?'

'Yes, I'm afraid so. There were thousands of people killed in the war, many buried in communal graves. Some regions are trying to make restitution, digging up the bodies so that they can be identified and letting the relatives give them a decent burial. But there will be others that will never be found and their relatives will never know for sure what happened to them. You must face the fact that your grandfather could be one of them.'

'I know.'

'Cheer up; you're having lunch with the mayor's father in a couple of days. Maybe he'll have something to tell you.'

'I doubt it.'

'How about I buy you a glass of cold, white wine?'

'And some *boquerones*?'

'You're on.'

CHAPTER 22

As it was high season, the Málaga Palacio Hotel was packed with tourists. She pushed her way through the crowded lobby and made for the restaurant.

'Can I help you, *señora*?' the maitre d' asked.

'I am meeting Señor Herrera,' she replied.

'Of course, follow me.'

He led her to a table by the window, where an elderly man was already sipping a glass of sherry and contemplating the view.

'Your guest, Señor Herrera.'

'Thank you Jaime.'

He stood up and took her hand.

'*Encantada señora*. Please sit down.'

She sat in the seat opposite him, with her back to the window.

'No, please sit here, beside me, then you too can enjoy this stupendous view of our lovely city.'

She moved to the next seat.

'What would you like to drink?'

'A *fino* would be lovely, thank you.'

'An excellent choice. I can see you have already adopted our ways, *señora* ...'

He hesitated.

'Kate, Kate Scott.'

'Señora Kate, or should I call you Señora Caterina?'

She smiled. His English was excellent but his accent was typically Spanish. She thought of Manuel in 'Fawlty Towers'.

'Kate's fine.'

'So, have you been in Málaga very long?' he asked.

'A couple of weeks, that's all.'

'And do you intend to stay a long time?'

'That depends.'

'On what, my dear?'

'On whether I have any luck tracing my grandfather.'

'Ah yes, your grandfather. I'm sorry my dear, I don't think I'll be able to help you there.'

She was about to ask him why he seemed so sure, when the waiter arrived with the menus.

'Good, I am quite hungry. I left home rather early this morning and didn't have time for much breakfast.'

His eyes skimmed the list of dishes on offer then he snapped the menu shut.

'I can recommend the turbot,' he said, 'and the red mullet is very good.'

'I think I'll just have a salad,' she replied, 'and perhaps some *gambas*.'

'The usual for me, Tomas,' the mayor's father said.

He was an older, more rotund version of his son; his hair was so black that she thought it must be dyed and it was plastered against his head with a sweet smelling oil. He had obviously been a handsome man in his youth but now age had loosened the skin around his neck and it hung in folds on to his collar; there were few lines on his face but the skin was no longer taut and sagged around the jowls. His hands, carefully

394

manicured, were those of an old man.   However he was obviously a man for whom appearances mattered and she was glad that she had fitted in a trip to the hairdressers the day before and put on one of her more elegant dresses.

'So you don't remember my grandfather, Señor Herrera?'

'Please call me Vicente.'

'Isn't that your son's name?'

'Yes, my oldest son, my first-born but we always call him Tito at home.'

He poured some oil on his salad, then generously sprinkled it with salt.

'So you are here to find out about your grandfather, are you Kate?'

She nodded.

'And how old do you think he would be if he were still alive?

'At least in his nineties, I would say.   But I'm pretty sure he died in the war.'

'What makes you so certain?'

'Nothing specific, just circumstantial evidence I suppose.'

She began to relate how her search had began and, without giving him too much detail, explained about the letters and the diaries.

He poured them both some wine and sat back to listen while they waited for their fish to come. He was an attentive listener and she had the feeling that he was weighing up everything she said, very carefully.

'Oh and by the way, your sister sent me this copy of your family tree.'

She opened the document and laid it out on the table, as best she could.

'Look this is you, and your brothers and sisters. Here are your parents. Now this is interesting; this is your mother and here, next to her, it says in brackets "*hermano?*". Now why the question mark? Did your mother have a brother or didn't she? And if she did, where is his name? I find it very strange.'

'Let me see that,' Vicente said, taking out his spectacles.

'Well I don't remember anyone speaking about Mama's brother. As far as we were concerned she was an only child. Maybe he died.'

'But if he had died then it would say so. Look at this entry for a Ricardo Gomez, it says "died in infancy." I don't understand it. Do you think your sister would be able to explain it to me?'

'She might; she drew it up, after all. Took her years to do.'

'It's very beautiful.'

Even though all she had was a photocopy of the original, she could see the penmanship that had gone into drawing it. The names were written in a delicate copperplate hand and beside many of the names were small sketches of children, animals, cherubs, ships and even angels.

'Yes, she has tried to capture something of the person or their time in these tiny drawings. Look here, this person died very young, so she has placed a cherub next to his name; this one was a ship's captain, hence the sailing ship and here are the hunting dogs for my great-grandfather.'

'It's exquisite. I suppose this man was a farmer because there are bales of corn, and this one here must be your grandfather. What's she drawn for him?'

'He was a judge; those are the scales of justice.'

396

'Very beautiful and very intriguing. I must write to your aunt and thank her and ask her about that strange entry next to your mother's name.'

'Good idea. Ah, here is our main course. *Buen provecho.*'

He poured her some more wine.

'From Galicia,' he explained. 'Pure *Albarino* grape.'

'It's delicious.'

'Of course you know, you could always ask my mother; if anyone knows whether she had a brother or not, she will.'

'Your mother?'

'Yes, I don't know why you didn't think of it.'

'I just assumed your mother was dead.'

'No, not at all. She is very old now but she still lives an independent life.'

'In Madrid?'

'No, here in Málaga.'

Kate could not believe what she was hearing; Juan's sister was still alive. She was in Málaga. For the first time she felt that she was going to solve this mystery.

'Do you think I could, could I meet her?' she asked, her excitement making her falter.

'I don't see why not.'

'You realise that if this is the same Eloisa Gomez de la Luz de Montevideo that lived in Málaga at the outbreak of the Civil War...'

Kate paused, making some calculations in her head.

'If she is my grandfather's sister that would make her my great-aunt and that would mean my mother was your cousin.'

She stopped in triumph. Vicente was staring at her.

'You do have the Montevideo nose. The nose of a *conquistador*, we've always said.'

Kate lifted her hand to her face, self-consciously.

'It's quite possible; that is, if she is his sister,' he continued. 'As I said, all the Luz de Montevideo family are related in some way. But you'd have to ask her.'

'When can I see her?'

'Well, she is very old. I would not want her to be upset. I will have to think about it; after all, if she had a brother, there must be a reason that she has not mentioned him to her family,' he added.

'I understand your concern but I assure you I wouldn't do anything to distress your mother. I just need to confirm that Juan was my grandfather and to try to understand why this information has remained hidden all these years.'

'I have to admit that you've aroused my curiosity now. I will speak to her and let you know what she says.'

'Thank you so much.'

'But let me say this; if she doesn't want to see you then that's the end of it. All right?'

'Yes, of course.'

'Now eat your *gambas*; they are much nicer while they are still warm.'

By the time Kate telephoned Larry to give him her news, he was already on his way over to meet her.

'I've just rung the registry in Madrid. They've gotten some news for us.'

'What do they say?'

'Well they have no record of his death but they do have a record of his birth; born in Málaga on 21st March 1917. And it seems that someone of that name, possibly him, was a prisoner in one of the *checas* in Cuenca.'

'So, if he was a prisoner, don't they have a record of his release, or his execution?'

'Apparently not. The only entry with his name is the date of his arrest, 12th August 1937. After that nothing.'

'Did you ask about his name appearing in any records after the war, maybe in the register of marriages?'

'Yes but there was nothing. Sorry, not a lot of good, really.'

'Well, maybe we'll do better with his sister.'

'If she'll talk to us, that is.'

Two days later Kate received a rather formal letter in a large, white envelope with the crest of the Montevideo family on it.

'Dear Señora Scott,

My mother, Doña Eloisa Gomez de la Luz de Montevideo Rodriguez, has graciously agreed to meet you tomorrow at eleven o'clock. Her address is "Los Altos del Puerto, 4, 3b, Paseo de la Farola." Please remember what we discussed; she is an old lady and I do not want her upset.

I hope you find what you are looking for. If you decide to stay in Málaga, I would be pleased to see you again,

Kind regards

Vincente Herrera Gomez de la Luz de Montevideo"

Eloisa Gomez de la Luz de Montevideo Rodriguez was a very frail, eighty-four year old but what she lacked in physical strength, she made up for with the sharpness of her mind. She sat in high-backed chair, her hands resting in her lap, looking at them through tinted glasses that hid her eyes from scrutiny. She probably weighed no more than forty-five kilos; her skin hung in folds from her arms and neck and her cheeks were hollow. Her face, despite being a network of tiny lines, still had the form of its youth and she had applied her make-up discreetly and expertly. Her clothes were neat and spoke of good taste and money; she wore a dove grey silk dress and, despite the heat, matching stockings and black court shoes. Around her neck she had placed a triple string of pearls, a single pearl earring in each ear and an enormous ruby on one of her rather skeletal fingers. Kate was immediately in awe of her.

'*Buenos días señora*,' Larry began.

He had come with Kate so that he could translate for her and had even brought a small voice recorder with him. Eloisa made no objection to either; Kate could see that she was eager to learn who she was. She motioned for them to sit down and rang a small bell on the table beside her. A young Rumanian woman came in.

'Lourdes, please bring us some iced tea,' she said.

Her voice was soft and well modulated; it did not sound like the voice of an old lady. While they waited for the maid to return with the tea Larry explained briefly why they were there. Kate looked around the room; they were in a very fashionable apartment overlooking the port. She could see the lighthouse quite clearly and the ships moored in the harbour.

'You have a beautiful view,' she said to Eloisa.

'Yes, I like it very much; there is always so much to see and of course I don't go out a lot now, just to the hairdressers and occasionally to the shops, so I spend a lot of my time just sitting here by the window.'

She pointed to a pair of ancient binoculars by the window.

'There's plenty to see: cruise liners, cargo ships, fishing boats and birds. I like to watch the birds, the seagulls especially.'

She continued to talk about her apartment until Lourdes came in carrying a tray with three porcelain cups and saucers, a pot of tea, a jug of ice and a bowl of sugar. Kate watched as the maid put the tray on the small table in front of them; she was desperate to begin questioning Eloisa but could see that nothing would be said until all the preliminary niceties had been fulfilled.

At last Eloisa turned to her and asked:

'So how can I help you, my dear?'

Kate took a deep breath and began:

'Doña Eloisa, as my friend has just explained, I am looking for members of the Luz de la Montevideo family in order to find out more about my grandfather.'

She paused but the old woman made no response.

'My grandfather's name was Juan Francisco Gomez de la Luz de Montevideo Rodriguez. I wondered if there was anyone in your family with that name?'

The old woman leaned forward, peering at her.

'Juanito? He was my brother. My son said you were looking for him.'

'Is this him?' Kate asked, passing her the photograph of Alex and Juan.

The old lady took the photograph and held it close to her eyes for a moment then she said:

'Yes, that's him. That's Juanito. Just a minute, my dear.'

She picked up the bell and rang it again.

'Lourdes, go to my bedroom and in the dressing table you will find a blue, leather box. Please bring it to me.'

She looked at Kate again.

'Come closer please, into the light,' she said to Kate.

She took her hand and held it tightly.

'You look very like my brother, softer, more feminine but the nose is the same and the deep, brown eyes. He was very handsome you know.'

She looked at her again and shook her head.

'The truth is you don't look very English. You could pass for a Spaniard very easily. So you think my brother might be your grandfather?'

She did not seem surprised by Kate's question; in fact she almost seemed to welcome it. She sat back in her chair and continued:

'Juan wrote to me about a woman; perhaps she was your grandmother. I've still got the letter, somewhere. I know he loved her but I did not know that they had been lovers; he never said. I'm sure he never knew there was a baby.'

'No, he couldn't have known; I don't think my grandmother knew she was pregnant until she arrived back in England,' said Kate.

'Ah, here it is.'

Lourdes had returned, carrying the leather box; she handed it to her mistress and left.

'In here somewhere, I am sure I have that letter. I kept all his letters, you know. He wrote to me whenever he could; we were very close.'

She rummaged in the box and eventually produced a folded piece of paper, which she handed to Kate.

'The woman was called Elizabeth. Was that your grandmother?'

'Yes, her name was Elizabeth Marshall in those days.'

'He called her Isabela,'

Kate unfolded the letter; the writing was very faint but she could just make out the signature. It was from Juan.

'Would you mind?' she said, passing it to Larry.

402

He read it aloud, translating fluently from the Spanish:

Madrid, March 1937

My dearest Lucy

I hope you and our parents are safe and well.   I am writing to you now because tomorrow they are sending me to Guadalajaro, to the front line; there is going to be a great battle but I am confident we will win against the Italians. After all we are fighting for our country, not just to earn a few lira.

You are all I have left little sister and before I die, because I am sure many of us will die tomorrow, I want to write my farewell to someone I love.

When you left me in Málaga I saw such misery and suffering that I cannot begin to describe it.   I wandered around the city for a few weeks, sickened to my heart by what was happening.   Then I met my Isabela.   Isabela, her real name is Elizabeth, is a beautiful, brave English girl and I am very much in love with her.   I wish you could meet her Lucy; her hair is the colour of the corn in August and her eyes are blue, like lavender.   But more than that, it is her soul that I love, her brave, honest soul that is forever seeking the truth.

We spent but a few happy hours together then we had to flee the city to escape from the rebel troops and the Italian invaders.   We travelled on foot to Almería with a friend, an Englishman.   It was a hard journey, with no food and no rest but Isabela did not complain.   Then, before we were even half-way there, we were attacked by mortar fire from the ships; I was injured but the others were unharmed.   I remember the Englishman helping me but then I don't know what happened.   We became separated and the next thing I remembered was waking up in a hospital in Almería and a doctor sewing up a wound in my chest.   He explained that I

403

had been brought in the night before in an ambulance of the International Brigade. Thanks to my friends I was not going to die. I lay in that bed all night thinking about them; they still had at least another day's walking ahead of them. All around me people were dying; some were calling for their mothers and others were just crying in pain. It was awful to see such suffering and yet all I could think about was Isabela.

That was when I made up my mind. I knew what I had to do. I did not want her to suffer any more; I wanted her to go back to England to safety. I knew if I stayed there in the hospital she would find me and having found me she would want to stay with me. Was this what I wanted for my beautiful Isabel? No, I didn't want her to give up her strength, her beauty, maybe even her life for our war. I could not let her do that.

So when the doctor had gone and the ward was quiet, I left. I made straight for the Military Governor's headquarters and asked to enlist. At first they were doubtful; they said I was wounded and to come back when I had recovered but I insisted. I told them I wanted to go to Valencia to fight so at last they agreed and gave me papers and a rail pass; I left Almería the next day.

I don't know what happened to my darling Isabela. I hope she is safe and well and I hope she is happy. I will never forget her and tomorrow when I go into battle I will be thinking of her and of you, my dear sister.

May God unite us once again, your loving brother
Juan.

'So he didn't die in Almería?' Kate asked.

'No, whatever gave you that idea?'

404

'Well my grandmother and her friend searched for him at the hospital and when they couldn't find him they were convinced that he was dead.'

'No, he just left to save Isabel; he wanted her to go home to safety. Did she go?'

'Yes, she and their friend managed to get on a British boat in Almería that took them to Gibraltar.'

'Good, that's what Juan wanted her to do.'

'But he never contacted her again.'

'Well it was impossible while the war was on; there was no way of contacting anyone. You couldn't just get on a flight to England like you can today; anyway he didn't have a passport and they would never have given him one.'

'So what happened to him?'

'Well like he said in his letter, he went to Valencia to enlist; they sent him to Madrid and he fought in the battle of Guadalajara. He wrote to tell me of their victory against the Italians; he was very proud. But then in April he was sent to Brunete; the fighting there was even worse and it continued until July. They were heavily outnumbered by the Nationalist troops and Juan was wounded again and later captured. He was kept in prison for almost a year and it was only thanks to the efforts of our father that he survived. I'm not sure if you've read of the infamous "*paseos*", where each night they would select a dozen or so prisoners from the "death list" and take them out and shoot them?'

Kate nodded. She had read of them but never thought that they had anything to do with her or her family.

'Well my father managed to keep Juan's name off the "death list" for almost a year. He knew the warden of the prison; they had been at university together. He wrote and told him that Juan was his son and asked him to do what he could for him.'

'So what happened? How did he get out? Did he escape?'

'No, nobody escaped from those prisons. For a start they were all starving; they had no strength to escape. I remember he wrote to me once that all he had eaten for two days was dried orange peel. No, it was my father again; he had many friends in the government. From the minute Juan was arrested my father petitioned them for his release. Our family name goes back many generations; my father had a lot of powerful connections. At that time there were at least one minister and several important generals who were related to us by marriage, and a second cousin who was Bishop of Toledo.'

She opened the box again and took out another letter.

'He managed to smuggle this letter out of the prison. They were allowed to write home but everything was heavily censored. He bribed one of the guards with some cigarettes that my father sent him to take this into the town and post it.'

She handed it to Larry to read:

Cuenca, November 1937

My dear Lucy

I hope this letter reaches you. I have given ten of my precious cigarettes to one of the guards so that he will post it in the village and avoid the censor.

I will begin at the beginning just like you always used to ask me to when I read you a bedtime story back in our dim and distant past, although I can barely remember those days now; they are almost expunged from my memory by the horror of this war. Well after the battle at Brunete, I tried to make my way back to the Republican zone but I could hardly walk; I had been shot in the leg. It was not serious but it slowed me down and I became separated from the rest of my battalion.   I was hiding in a barn one night when some Nationalists found me and took me prisoner. I was lucky that it was them and not the Legionnaires; they didn't take prisoners. They took me straight to a prison somewhere near Cuenca. So far I have not had a trial but they say I will be tried soon, although the truth is, I am in no hurry because I know the only verdict they will give will be death.

They have put me in solitary confinement; I don't know why. You cannot imagine what it feels like the moment they slam that prison door behind you and you are left totally alone in your new home, a tiny, concrete cell, no more than two metres wide. There is an iron bedstead but some of the springs are broken and the wire mattress cuts into my back. They have given me a blanket and I have a washbasin and a toilet but most of the time there is no water. The door of my cell is made of concrete reinforced with steel and has no handle; the guard opens it with a key and slams it hard to shut it. I think the sound of that door slamming will remain with me all my life; there is such a finality to it. I have a window but it is too high to look out and has iron bars and no glass, so the wind and the rain come in. I have learnt how to pull myself up by holding onto the bars and pressing my legs against one of the walls but I can't hold this position for long because my leg has not healed properly yet and is still very weak. However it does mean I can get an occasional glimpse of the sky and look at other prisoners exercising in the yard outside my room. I am allowed to join some of the prisoners for one hour each morning and walk around the yard. We are not supposed to speak to each other but we manage to exchange a few words and I learn about who has been shot *and who has just arrived. This is the only time I get to speak to anyone other than the guards but I don't really mind about that because as soon as I get to know someone they disappear and a new prisoner takes their place.*

It is difficult to sleep at night, not just because of the awful bed but because night-time is when they come for you, to take you on a "paseo"; everyone lies awake wondering if this will be their last night.   You hear the guards' footsteps approaching and when they pass your door you cry with relief; you ignore the moans and screams of those chosen and only then can you let yourself drift off into a thankful sleep. Sometimes a group of prisoners are taken out during the day to be tried at the court but we never hear of anyone being released; when the guards return they delight in letting us know that they have all been shot.

At first I had nothing at all but since your money and cigarettes have been arriving life has got a little better; I have been able to barter for paper and a pencil, and I even have a razor and a bit of broken comb. My worldly possessions are as you see very simple. I use most of what you send me to barter for food because there is very little to eat and what there is, is dreadful.. There have been days when we have had nothing and had to rely on the kindness of the local villagers who sneak up to the perimeter at night and throw black bread and potatoes over the wall. Normally we have one meal a day, usually a thin soup or some kind of gruel, never any meat nor fruit. How I would love a dish of olives or some delicious dried ham.   So many awful things are happening in the world and I lie here and dream about food.

I hope you and our parents are well my little sister. I think of you all every day. One day I will be out of here and I will

go to England to find my Isabela, then we will come to see
you.

Dear sister, take care of yourself,
Your loving brother Juan

'But he never came?'

'No he never came.'

'I thought Juan and his father did not get on,' said Kate.

'They disagreed about politics but they were still father and son; my father loved him.'

'So what did he do when he left prison?'

'I don't remember exactly. He wanted to go to look for Isabel but by then, although the war was over in Spain, a new war was raging in Europe and it was impossible to get to England. He wrote to me from Madrid, from Barcelona, from Alicante; he seemed to be moving around a lot but I don't know what he was doing. Even though the war was over it was still very dangerous for anyone who had supported the Republicans; there were mock trials and mass executions weekly. Most we did not hear about, so I was constantly worried about Juan and whether he'd been arrested again.'

'He didn't come back to Málaga?'

'No. My father wanted him to come home; he even wrote to him when he was about to be released, after the war was over but he refused.'

She picked up Kate's photograph of Juan and Alex.

'I thought he might come back to see his friend but no.'

'Does she mean "go to England" to see his friend?' Kate asked Larry.

He repeated her question to Eloisa.

'No, come back to Málaga,' she repeated. 'His friend had come from England to see how he was but by the time we had written to Juan's old address to tell him, he had already moved on. It took three months for the letter to catch up with him.'

'But Alex never came back to Spain,' Kate insisted. 'He thought Juan was dead.'

'Is this Alex?' she asked.

'Yes. He married my grandmother, the woman you call Isabel.'

'Well that's the same man that came here in 1940. He wore a soldier's uniform and he was a bit fatter than he is in the photo but I can assure you it was him. He was on compassionate leave, on his way back from North Africa and he broke his journey to come here and look for Juan. I thought it a bit strange but assumed he must have been a very close friend of Juan's. He told me they had met in Málaga in 1937.'

She turned the photograph over.

'Yes, look here; it says Málaga 1937. He was your grandfather you say?'

Eloisa looked confused, so Kate asked Larry to explain how they believed that while Elizabeth had been in love with Juan, Alex had been in love with Elizabeth and had married her. Later, when she had Juan's baby, Alex never said anything, just allowed everyone to think it was his child. While he spoke to her Kate picked up her cup and drank some of the tea; she did not know how to respond to this new revelation. Her head was spinning with questions. Why had her grandfather come to look for Juan? Why had he kept the news that Juan was alive from Elizabeth? Was it because that he wanted Elizabeth for himself, child or no child?

'Why would he do that?' the old woman asked.

'I expect he loved her and didn't want anyone else to marry her,' Kate replied, lamely.

'But Juan loved her too. The last letter I have from him is dated November 1945; he was on his way to the French border. He said he planned to travel through France and get someone to smuggle him into England where he would ask for political asylum. He was so sure he would find Isabel.'

She stopped talking and drank some tea, then blew her nose and continued:

'He would have been so happy to know that he had a child. It's very sad to think that he died not knowing that he was a father. If only that friend of his had confided in me, I could have written to him and told him; but we didn't know.'

'How did Juan die?'

'He was shot trying to cross the border into France. He was with three other men; they waited for a night with no moon and made their way to a small village in the Pyrenees. Some villagers hid them in a goat shed until nightfall and then they tried to cross over. They almost made it; they were on French soil, running down the hill towards freedom when the Guardia Civil ambushed them. They shot three of them, including Juan but the fourth escaped. It was he who wrote to me later to tell me what had happened.'

She blew her nose again.

'I'm sorry, please excuse me, it makes me cry to think about him. I was very fond of my brother you see. The worst thing is to think of his body lying there on the mountainside for the vultures to pick at. My father wrote to the regional governor as soon as he heard but we never received Juan's body. I expect his bones are still there, bleaching in the sun.'

Kate looked across at Larry; she did not know what to say. After a few moments Eloisa seemed to recover her composure and said:

'So tell me about your mother. What was her name?'

411

'Isabel,' Kate replied, realising for the first time the significance of her mother's name.

'Do you look like her?'

Kate laughed.

'No, not at all; she was very like her mother, Elizabeth, tall and blonde. I don't even look like my father; he was very blond and English looking too. I think I must be a throwback.'

'Well my dear, look at this photograph of my brother when he was a boy. Do you see the family likeness?'

'Yes, my goodness, you're right. I look a lot like him.'

'Keep it. In fact keep the letter where he first mentioned Elizabeth as well. I'd like to be generous and say have all his letters but the truth is I just can't part with them. They are all I have of him now.'

Kate put the photograph and the letter in her handbag.

'I wonder if you could explain something to me?'

'Yes, my dear.'

'Your daughter sent us a copy of your family tree; there was no record of Juan's name. I can see that you were very fond of your brother, so it seems a little strange that nobody ever spoke of him.'

'Yes, it probably is strange by your standards, my dear but you have to realise that here in Spain, even after the Civil War ended, people were frightened. Nobody wanted to own up to being a Republican or having a Republican in the family. My father was frightened for me and my mother; he forbade us to speak about Juan. Then when I got married, he told me to say nothing to my husband. He said it was better to pretend that Juan had never existed than to try to explain what had happened to him. So that is what we did. In the end, even when it did not matter anymore, when Franco was dead, I

412

didn't talk about him. How could I? How could I admit to my husband and my children that I had lied to them all those years? No, it was better to keep quiet. Until now, when you turned up, my dear.'

She reached across and clasped Kate's hands.

They sat in silence for a moment then Eloisa spoke again:

'So his friend married his woman and brought up his child. How extraordinary.'

'Why extraordinary?'

'Well he never once mentioned it to me; Alex never said anything about Isabel or a child, not in 1940 nor some years later when he came again. He never even told me he was married.'

'He came to see you again?'

'Yes in 1943, and again after the war, in 1946; that was when I told him Juan was dead.'

'Did you hear from him after that?'

'No, never. Mind you, by then I was married and living in Madrid, so maybe he tried and couldn't locate me.'

'You know I always thought he was my real grandfather,' Kate admitted. 'Nobody knew about Juan, even my mother did not know about him; they kept it all very secret.'

'How sad: a father who never knew his daughter and a daughter who never knew her father.'

The door to the living room opened and Lourdes appeared; she had come to remove the tea tray.

'Well my dear, it's time for my rest. I have enjoyed meeting you, even though it has brought back some very sad memories. Do come and see me again. After all you are family now.'

413

She held out her hand; it was soft and warm. Kate took it in her own and bending down, kissed the old lady on both cheeks.

'Thank you Eloisa. Thank you so much. I will come again.'

'Call me Lucy my dear, he always did.'

When they stepped outside, the heat hit them straight away; it was over forty degrees according to the neon sign that flashed above the chemist shop.

'Let's find a bar,' suggested Larry. 'I'm parched.'

'Yes, I think I need a stiff drink after that,' she said.

They walked past the lighthouse and down to the promenade where they strolled leisurely along looking for a bar with tables outside.

'Larry, which way is Almería?'

He stopped and pointed ahead of them.

'Just follow the road by the sea and eventually you will come to Almería.'

'So this is the road they took?'

'Juan and Elizabeth? When they were leaving Málaga do you mean?'

'Yes. This is where they walked, along here beside the beach?'

'Yes but it was a bit different then of course, not so many blocks of flats and fewer shops and restaurants. But yes, this is the old road to Almería. Nowadays you would use the motorway but at that time this was the only road.'

She walked in silence, thinking about what she had learnt from Juan's sister. It was hard to imagine thousands of frightened, hungry people fleeing from the city along this palm tree lined avenue that bordered a beach dotted with

414

brightly coloured beach umbrellas. Today people were swimming, sunbathing, seeking shady spots to cool down, sipping long drinks in the beach bars, studying the menu; the only fear in their minds was not being able to wrest every single moment of pleasure from the day. She closed her eyes and tried to imagine what it must have been like to walk two hundred and fifty kilometres with no food and hardly any water, to be terrified that at any moment you would be shot or captured, to hear your child crying for food and be unable to give him any. Despite the heat a shiver ran down her back and for a moment she thought she could hear the cries and moans of the ghosts of the past but it was only the wind in a palm tree.

'Are you all right?'

She opened her eyes; Larry was looking at her anxiously.

'Yes, I'm fine. Let's go and have that drink now.'

Eloisa picked up her mobile phone and dialled her grandson's number. She waited while it rang a few times, then a sleepy voice answered:

'*Digame.*'

'Vicente, is that you?'

'*Si, abuela.* I was having a *siesta.*'

She looked at her watch.

'A *siesta* at this time? You are turning into an old man before your time, Vicente.'

'I am on holiday, *abuela.*'

'So?'

'What do you want anyway?'

She could hear the strained note of patience in his voice.

'It's about this girl, my brother's granddaughter.'

'What about her?'

'I think we should organise a family party so that everyone can meet her.'

'Is that wise?'

'Why not? She is family after all.'

'So she says. What exactly does she want, this girl?'

'Want? I don't think she wants anything, other than the truth.'

'I can't see the point in raking up the past like this. You have to remember, *abuela,* that no-one in the family knew about your brother until the other day. People are going to ask questions; they are going to wonder why you lied about him.'

'I didn't lie about him; I just never mentioned him. And anyway, don't lecture me, young man; if I kept quiet about him, it was to protect you and your father. Even you must remember what it was like before Franco died.'

There was silence at the other end then her grandson spoke:

'So what do you want me to do?'

'Get in touch with all the family and invite them down here for a family reunion. We can hold it at your place in the country; that's a big old place that hasn't seen much life lately.'

'But Antonia hates that sort of thing.'

'Well she'll have to put up with it for once; she's your wife, you sort it out. We'll make it for 12th October, that'll give everyone time to get themselves organised.'

'That's a public holiday, the feast of St Pilar.'

'I know, the patron saint of the Guardia Civil. A little ironic, don't you think? They managed to squash my brother but they couldn't squash his genes; he will live on through his granddaughter.'

416

'*Abuela*, I think you're getting a bit fanciful now.'

She began to protest but he carried on:

'OK, I'll do it. I'll ring them all this weekend but I do think you're going to regret it.'

'Maybe but I can't explain to you how much it means to me to know that my poor brother, who would never have hurt anybody and who was murdered for his beliefs, had a child of his own. I'm an old woman now, Vicente. Before I die I want to see this girl welcomed into our family. She deserves it; after all she is a Luz de Montevideo.'

'All right *abuela*, leave it with me.'

'Thank you Vicente; you're a good boy really.'

The mayor of Málaga laughed. His grandmother still spoke to him as if he were a small boy.

'Oh Vicente, tell your aunt that she can stay here, with me, in the flat; but not to bring that mangy cat of hers.'

'OK *abuela*.'

Eloisa switched off her mobile and called for her maidservant. She felt elated at the thought of a party and seeing all her grandchildren and great-grandchildren again.

'Bring me some writing paper and a pen, please, Lourdes.'

She would write straight away to Kate and invite her to meet her new family.

By the time Kate got back to her hotel she was feeling calmer; a large gin and tonic had settled her fractured nerves. She stood on the cold floor and stripped off her clothes, then slipped into her bathing costume; moments later she was floating in the pool, letting the cool water caress her skin. She had the swimming pool to herself; everyone else was sleeping the Spanish *siesta*. She struggled across to the other side, glad that there was no-one to see her infantile attempts at the breast stroke, and hung there, letting her legs drift to and fro.

She had wanted to find out about her grandfather and his family and now she had discovered more than she could ever have hoped for. She had warmed to Eloisa straight away; she was old but her mind was as sharp as ever and she had clung to the memory of her brother through all these years despite everything. Kate remembered how the old lady had pressed her hand and asked her to visit her again. She resolved that, before she left Málaga, she would go back to see her. It gave her a strange feeling to realise that she had relatives who, until a few months ago, she never realised existed.

But it was not her Spanish grandfather that occupied her thoughts, rather it was her English one. She had talked for hours about these new revelations with Larry but still could not come to terms with them. From where she stood, it looked as though Alex had deliberately kept Elizabeth and Juan apart; if he had told his wife that Juan was alive there was no evidence to support it. From what she had read, she was convinced that Elizabeth truly believed that Juan died in the hospital in Almería. Was that why her grandfather had put so much energy and money into his children's homes? He had kept another man's child from him. Did homing abandoned children help to ease his conscience? She could not answer.

She thought back to the day she had attended the official opening of one of his homes, Whiteleaf House; she had only gone because it was in Reading, right on her doorstep. Her grandfather had noticed her as soon as she entered the room, his eyes lighting up with recognition; she had gone straight across to him and kissed him on the cheek, the skin like dry parchment beneath her lips. He had smiled and greeted her

418

warmly, then he had resumed his conversation with the local Member of Parliament. It fell to his secretary, Paul Thomson, to show her around. She had to admit she had been impressed; the Trust had bought a large Georgian house on the edge of the town and completely renovated it. The building stood in half an acre of garden bordered by hawthorn hedges and she remembered that there was a large hornbeam that spread its branches in symmetrical unity across the tiny lawn. The house had ten bedrooms, all designed for single occupancy, a communal kitchen, a dining room and a study area, a games room, accommodation for the staff, administration offices and a TV lounge. Whiteleaf House catered for children between the ages of ten and sixteen; they were encouraged to live together as a family and help and support each other whenever possible. She knew the Trust had a number of homes: some for younger children and at least one for children with learning disabilities but all were designed around family units and the staff had been chosen with great care. She met some of the children that day and when they were alone Paul explained the reasons they were there. Most came from families broken by drug abuse and violence but one poor boy had lost both his parents in a fire that had destroyed his home and left him an orphan. He had been there almost two months and still had not spoken to anyone other than a twelve year-old girl who had taken him under her wing.

She pulled herself up out of the pool, wrapped her towel around her and walked back into her room, leaving a trail of glistening, wet footprints on the tiles behind her.

Without bothering to check the number she picked up the telephone and dialled; she knew it by heart. As she waited, listening impatiently to the ringing tone, she could sense the water dripping off her costume and onto the floor.

'Yes?'

'Hugh? It's Kate.'

'Hi, Kate. This is a surprise; I was going to phone you later. Is everything all right?'

'Fine. Look Hugh, can you get some time off work?'

'I suppose so. When?'

'Now, tomorrow, as soon as you can. I've got this beautiful room with a big, wide bed and I miss you. It's all booked and paid for until the end of the month. Why don't you come and join me?'

'Well Kate,' he hesitated.

She waited, holding her breath.

'I'd love to. Look I'll ring you back as soon as I've got it all fixed.'

'Great. Oh and by the way, bring your golf clubs.'

She replaced the telephone and slipping out of her wet bathing costume lay down on the bed. It would be good to see him again; it was true what she had said; she had missed his company.

When Robert Percy had telephoned her before she left and asked her if she would represent the family on the Board of the Reeves Shelters Trust she had hesitated. Why her? It was simple he explained: Jeremy did not want to do it and she was next in line, the eldest grandchild. He was very persuasive:

'This was your grandfather's life's work; he wanted someone from the family to carry it on. You are the obvious choice.'

She had not been convinced that it was that obvious at the time but now she saw the inevitability of it. Who else could it be to take up his torch and run with it?   She more than anyone else shared his past; he might not be her biological grandfather but the ties of love were there. Two men, Alex and Juan had loved the same woman and each in his way had deceived her. She had tracked down Juan for the sake of her mother and grandmother; now for Alex's sake she would represent the family on the Board of the Reeves Trust. Alex had loved his wife and he had loved his children. Who was she to judge him after all these years?

Now she, who had been deprived of children of her own, would be able to bring some happiness to children abandoned by others.   She thought again of the boy whose parents had died in the fire; when she had looked in his eyes she had seen the emptiness of her own life. She did not know what the future held in store for her but one thing she knew: it no longer needed to be empty.

The sound of the telephone ringing broke through her thoughts and a smile came unbidden to her lips; it would be Hugh ringing back.

AUTHOR'S NOTE

Although the characters in this novel are ficticious, the historical details are based on actual events that took place during the Spanish Civil War in February 1937, in the city of Málaga.

Like many people I had never heard about the massacre on the Málaga - Almería road. I knew of the bombing of Guernica, immortalised by Picasso; I had heard of the siege of Madrid and the battle of the Ebro, but nowhere had I read anything about innocent women and children being shelled by German and Spanish gunboats as they tried to flee to safety. It was while I was writing an oral history on women in contemporary Spain that one of my interviewees started to tell me about what had happened; her own father had been caught up in the events of those terrible days. I was so intrigued by what she had to tell me that I immediately began to write this novel.

I am indebted to the people to whom I spoke about the Civil War and to a number of excellent books on the subject, including:

'Málaga Burning' by Gamel Woolsey

'Spanish Testament' by Arthur Koestler

'Blood of Spain' by Ronald Fraser

'The Spanish Labyrinth' by Gerald Brenan

'Spain Under Franco' by Max Gallo

CPSIA information can be obtained at www.ICGtesting.com
Printed in the USA
LVOW12s2134190114

370100LV00016B/878/P

9 780957 689107